D0035492

SIGNET ONYX

WOMEN OF PASSION AND AMBITION

☐ **WORLD TO WIN, HEART TO LOSE by Netta Martin.** Alexandra Meldrum stormed the male bastions of oil and property, using anything—and anyone—to win back her family's honor. Now she has it all. There's only one thing more she desires. Revenge. Revenge on the one man who is her match in business and master in bed. (176863—$4.99)

☐ **INTERIOR DESIGNS by Margaret Burman.** The steamy marriage and partnership of Dell Shay and Danny Dannenberg and their hot new interior design firm for rich and famous clients willing to pay any price to make their most lavish fantasies come true. But soon the picture-perfect marriage and business partnership betrayed a shocking masquerade.
(178068—$4.99)

☐ **BLOOD SISTERS by Judith Henry Wall.** The best of friends—one had brains, one had beauty, one had talent, one had a deadly secret. From the day they pricked their fingers they swore they would always be friends through thick and thin. And they were. All except one who made them question their friendship—and their husbands. The one who disappeared with a deadly secret . . . (404149—$4.99)

☐ **BY HER OWN DESIGN by June Triglia.** A woman of passion, a man of revenge—in the high stakes world of fashion where the design of a dress is but a small part of the cutthroat competition. (404246—$5.99)

☐ **FOREVER by Judith Gould.** Sweeping from the penthouse suites of Manhattan to the luxurious world of Brazil's fashionable elite, this dazzling novel captures the excitement and glamour of life and love at the peak of wealth, passion, and danger. "Deliciously dishy."—**Rex Reed**
(404009—$5.99)

*Prices slightly higher in Canada

Buy them at your local bookstore or use this convenient coupon for ordering.

PENGUIN USA
P.O. Box 999 — Dept. #17109
Bergenfield, New Jersey 07621

Please send me the books I have checked above.
I am enclosing $_____ (please add $2.00 to cover postage and handling). Send check or money order (no cash or C.O.D.'s) or charge by Mastercard or VISA (with a $15.00 minimum). Prices and numbers are subject to change without notice.

Card #_____ Exp. Date _____
Signature_____
Name_____
Address_____
City _____ State _____ Zip Code _____

For faster service when ordering by credit card call **1-800-253-6476**

Allow a minimum of 4-6 weeks for delivery. This offer is subject to change without notice.

THE
COLOR
OF
LOVE

by

Sandra Kitt

A SIGNET BOOK

SIGNET
Published by the Penguin Group
Penguin Books USA Inc., 375 Hudson Street,
New York, New York 10014, U.S.A.
Penguin Books Ltd, 27 Wrights Lane,
London W8 5TZ, England
Penguin Books Australia Ltd, Ringwood,
Victoria, Australia
Penguin Books Canada Ltd, 10 Alcorn Avenue,
Toronto, Ontario, Canada M4V 3B2
Penguin Books (N.Z.) Ltd, 182–190 Wairau Road,
Auckland 10, New Zealand

Penguin Books Ltd, Registered Offices:
Harmondsworth, Middlesex, England

First published by Signet, an imprint of Dutton Signet,
a division of Penguin Books USA Inc.

First Printing, March, 1995
10 9 8 7 6 5 4 3 2 1

REGISTERED TRADEMARK—MARCA REGISTRADA

Printed in the United States of America

PUBLISHER'S NOTE
This is a work of fiction. Names, characters, places, and incidents either are
the product of the author's imagination or are used fictitiously, and any resemblance to actual persons, living or dead, events, or locales is entirely
coincidental.

To my parents,
Ann and Archie,
who gave me pride
and taught me to
have a fair heart.

ACKNOWLEDGMENTS

I would like to also thank Police Officers Kevin O'Connor of the Midtown North Precinct in Manhattan, and William Gamble of the Police Benevolent Association.

A special thank-you to Police Officer Ronald Singer of the 70th Precinct in Brooklyn, New York, for answering hundreds of questions, and for being patient.

Finally, I'm grateful for the medical information given by Dr. Anthony Mustalish, former Chief of Emergency Medicine at Lenox Hill Hospital in New York City, and for his wonderful sense of humor.

Prologue

Leah Downey walked gracefully down the oak staircase while sipping from a half finished cup of coffee. She was alone in the house and, for this morning at least, was grateful for the solitude. The silence was like a vacuum, safe and hermetic, buffering her against a night spent with bad dreams. She'd just finished her morning shower and had donned underwear on skin that was still damp. Properly awake now, her mind was preoccupied with the presentation she had to make that morning. That and the fact that her sister, Gail, had not come home the night before nor had Leah heard from her. It was not an unusual occurrence but sometimes a disturbing one.

Leah walked into the den, located beyond the back of the stairwell and just before the kitchen, where all her work of the previous night still lay spread out over desk, chairs, floor, and propped against the walls. She stood thoughtfully as her gaze scanned the pads of paper with their rough thumbnail sketches and layouts, hastily colored in with markers. She was totally focused on the dozen or so ideas while mentally organizing the commentary she would use to accompany each one. Seeing the artwork fresh after several hours of sleep and rest, Leah could instantly tell which ones would be part of the presentation and which she would save to rework for future projects. Her concentration was a good counterpoint to any temptation to review the dissatisfaction of the previous night. With efficient quick movements she separated out the good stuff that she would finish at her drafting table after she got to work.

Heading to the kitchen for another cup of coffee Leah pulled free the towel which she'd turban wrapped around her head during her shower. As she absently finger tussled her hair to loosen the thick strands, she heard a key turn in the front door of the three-story brownstone. Her sister's voice could be heard down the narrow hall.

"Leah?"

"I'm in the kitchen," she called out, refilling her coffee cup.

The early morning quiet of the large house was shattered with Gail Downey's arrival, with her clanging arm bracelets and tapping heels. Leah turned to face her sister as Gail appeared in the kitchen doorway looking every bit as fresh and pulled together as when she'd left for work twenty-four hours earlier.

"Who's that man in front of the house?"

"What?"

"There's some white man sitting on the steps to the basement. Who is he?"

Leah Downey looked at her sister in confusion. "I have no idea. Why didn't you ask him?"

Gail looked impatient. "Because he didn't look as if he'd understand a rational question."

"You mean you were afraid," Leah teased.

Gail sucked through her teeth. "Not of some white man. Unless he's crazy."

Leah headed toward the living room, opposite the staircase at the front of the house, with Gail right behind her. Standing close together, they looked through the curtains out the window to the street below. There, sitting on the steps, was a man. He was seated almost in profile to their point of view. He sat with his body hunched forward as he stared at the ground. He wasn't a derelict. He was dressed in clean jeans and sneakers, and a casual white shirt was visible under a dark blue windbreaker. He had about two or three days' worth of beard on his face. His hair, although a bit long, was slightly rumpled and out of place.

Leah noticed all of this in a few seconds and knew there was no danger. She remembered him. The man now seated in front had been standing in the middle of the street as she and Allen had arrived at her house the night before. Allen had collided into him.

Leah turned to her sister. "You'd better go shower quickly if you don't want to be late for work."

"And what about him?" Gail asked, pointing toward the silent figure. "We should call the police."

Leah thought for a moment as she peered at the preoccupied man again. "What for? He's not bothering anyone. Just go get ready."

"Is the Suit still here?" Gail asked sarcastically, turning away from the window, already losing interest in the stranger.

"You know Allen never stays the night. He's either allergic to the sheets, or to me. Anyway, I sent him home. I had work to do."

"What on?" Gail asked, hanging up a jacket in the hall closet.

"Editorial presentation. Cover art for next month's list. I'm designing the lead five book jackets."

"Up again all night?" Gail asked.

"Just a little after two. I got a few hours' sleep."

Gail made an impatient sound. "They're not paying you enough for this."

"You're right," Leah readily agreed, drinking from

her coffee. "But I don't get the praise or the raise until I do the work."

Gail picked up her heavy tote from where she'd dropped it next to the base of the stairs. She stepped out of her shoes and bent to pick them up. She eyed her sister's coffee cup. "I hope there's more of that. Did you make breakfast?"

Leah smiled as Gail began to climb the stairs. "I'm not having any, and you don't have time."

"Oh yes I do . . ."

Gail slammed a door upstairs, and the sound resonated for a second down the stairwell. Slowly Leah turned around and made her way back to the window. She hugged herself and imagined that the early hour and Gail's unceremonious arrival would have stirred the man by now and he'd be gone. Bending forward, she lifted the sheer curtain panel and looked out. He was still seated on the steps. Leah turned sideways and leaned her shoulder against the window frame, and watched him.

She had no idea why she did. There was something about the slope of his broad shoulders, lowered head that began to make her curious about him, and concerned. She'd experienced somewhat the same thing the night before when Allen had bumped into him, but there had been no reason to think more about him. But right now he seemed so thoroughly alone, so out of place on her doorstep, that it seemed unkind to make him move.

Leah finally let the curtain drop into place and turned toward the kitchen. For whatever reason the man on her stoop brought to mind the man in a recurrent dream. Except that her dream was always one of terror and the man in it was always trying to reach her, to hurt her. Her dream was a nightmare that was too close to the real thing and a stark reminder, in the dead of night, of being mugged at knife point two years earlier. Leah had never been able to figure out the pattern, to pinpoint the word or action, the person that set into motion the terrifying adventures of her sleep state. But the dream happened often and always left her feeling defenseless . . . and angry.

"Leah?"

She jumped at the interruption on her thoughts. Her sister's unexpected loud command only added to her general edginess. She'd had the dream again last night. She turned her head and called back. "Yeah?"

"Can I borrow your black and white short dress? You know, the one with the square neckline?" Gail yelled from the floor above.

Leah frowned, puzzled. "You're going to wear that to work?"

"Of course not to work. I think I might need it for the weekend."

The weekend? Leah didn't ask. She shrugged. "Sure, go ahead. It's almost seven-thirty."

"I'm almost ready."

The door slammed again.

The sound was a reminder to Leah that she herself was still in a robe. She set a mug and napkin on the small kitchen table and the one remaining English muffin for Gail to find. Then Leah left to go dress for work. She'd planned on leaving early, knowing that if she could get to her office an hour before anyone else, she'd have more than enough time to finish her boards for the eleven o'clock meeting. And she didn't want to give Mike Berger, the other art director in the department, a chance to claim any of her ideas.

As she approached the stairwell, she remembered the man in front of the house. For a second she checked her motion, tempted to have another look at him. But as she climbed the stairs to her bedroom, all the details of having seen the stranger for the first time the night before came back to her anyway.

Allen had come home with her after work, and they were going to have dinner together. He'd bought a bottle of wine at the corner liquor store. The late September evening had been mild, and children were still playing street games in the twilight. Teens hung around stoop fronts playing boom boxes and talking. Allen had been telling her in boastful details about his new promotion when he'd collided with the stranger now sitting on her front steps. The wine bottle dropped and smashed on the sidewalk, spraying Allen. He had cursed and blamed the man.

"You dumb ass," Allen had exploded. "Look what you made me do!"

But the man was not paying attention. He lifted his left hand, maybe in apology, and mumbled something incoherent. He was wavering somewhat unsteadily on his feet, his attention on the kids playing in the street.

Leah had grabbed Allen's arm, afraid that, in his anger, he might retaliate against the man. "Allen, forget it. He's probably drunk," she'd said as she pulled him away.

But Leah had stopped momentarily and looked back at the man in the street. He'd moved awkwardly, reached out, and grabbed hold of the lamp post; he'd held on as if it was the only thing in the world he had to sustain himself. He'd given no indication, as a matter of fact, that he was aware of what had happened around him. Perhaps he wasn't. He had sad gray eyes. Hurt eyes.

Leah came back downstairs dressed in a calf-length off-white knit skirt, worn with a long tunic sweater in the same color and fabric and belted at the waist. Gail had designed the outfit. Leah had combed out her hair so that her thin face with its high cheekbones and pointed chin was framed. Mascara, blusher, and lipstick were all the makeup she ever used. She'd accessorized with one wooden bracelet, unlike her sister's half-dozen silver ones, and low-heeled boots.

"Put orange juice and cereal on the grocery list," Gail said from the kitchen.

Leah shook her head, mildly annoyed. "You put them on the list. I don't eat cold cereal."

In the den she piled all the artwork together under her arm and, on her way to the kitchen, carefully placed all the work in her black portfolio. Gail, now in a fresh outfit, sat finishing the English muffin. Leah put her empty cup in the dishwasher and began wiping the table.

Gail glanced at her quizzically. "What's the rush? I'm not finished yet."

"I am," Leah announced.

Gail merely shrugged. "I suppose that's a subtle hint that it's time to leave for work."

"*I* have to leave soon. You're on your own. You never tell me your schedule or what your plans are anyway." Leah began wiping off the table with a damp sponge, making wide, energetic strokes and forcing Gail to sit back out of the way.

Gail frowned at her. "Boy, are you in a mood. What did Allen do to you last night? Or didn't he?"

"I told you I was up late working."

Gail chuckled. "Before or after he left?"

Leah signed and tossed the sponge into the sink. She turned to lean back against the edge and crossed her arms over her chest. Hoping to distract her older sister, she asked, "And where were you last night?"

Gail made an indifferent gesture with her shoulders and stood up. She smiled at her sister, but Leah could see that the smile held neither coyness, humor, nor teasing.

"Out. You don't need to know about last night. And I won't be here for the weekend."

"Oh," Leah responded blankly. Allen was going to be away, too, visiting his folks in Philadelphia. She was suddenly aware that neither her sister nor Allen had asked her to accompany them. Already Leah was feeling a bit lonely and excluded.

"I told you when I came in this morning," Gail said defensively.

Leah slowly shook her head. "No, you didn't. You said, could you borrow my dress for the weekend."

Gail nodded her head and gathered her things. "Same thing," she said.

At the door, Gail looked through the cut-glass windowpane and turned back to Leah. "He's still sitting there. I should tell him this is not a shelter for the homeless."

"He's not homeless," Leah responded automatically.

"I wish you'd stop talking as if you know him," Gail said impatiently.

Leah merely opened the door and ushered her sister through it. "I'll take care of it. I'll see you Saturday night. Or Sunday afternoon."

"If he's here when you come home tonight, call the police," Gail advised. She hurried down the stairs, shoulder bag and tote distorting her gait. She cast a disgusted look at the man. "Shoo! Go away!" she advised him from a safe distance. The stranger ignored her, never even indicated by any movement that he was aware of her presence. Gail gave up in irritation and, waving briefly to her sister, headed for the corner.

Leah waited until Gail was out of sight before she turned her attention again to the man. Suddenly he raised his head and turned to look directly at her. For a shocked moment their eyes met, and she felt a tumult, a frisson of some unnamed sensation that squirmed through her stomach. It wasn't fear, but it made Leah take full notice of him. And it made her feel strangely surprised. She nervously looked at her watch, and then stepped back inside the door to get her things.

Leah was finally ready to leave. She opened the door again and unconsciously sucked in the cool morning air, hoping it would clear her senses like some mentholated medicine. And then, with one hand on the doorknob, Leah had a sudden thought. She quickly retraced her steps back to the kitchen. There she found an old, chipped coffee mug and filled it with what remained of the coffee. She took it with her as she finally left the house.

He was still there.

Leah came slowly down the stairs. She approached the man where he sat on the top step leading to the cellar. He made no notice of her presence. Nor did he notice the offered coffee. Leah moved cautiously forward and placed the cup on the cement ledge next to his right hand. She didn't ask him to leave, nor did she ask if he needed help. She watched him for a moment longer, and when he still didn't acknowledge her, she turned away and crossed the street toward the subway.

Leah turned back once. He was no longer the only one on the street. The neighborhood was in motion as residents began their day. The Asian kids from next door were still struggling into the straps of their knapsacks as they ran up the street on their way to school. Beth Rosen, Biddy to her friends, waddled toward her car, which would take her to a job at a Brooklyn junior high school. A delivery truck rattled heavily over the uneven roadway. One teen yelled out to another, "Yo, man . . . wait up."

And then Leah saw the man pick up the mug. He stared at it for a long time before bringing it to his lips. He turned his body cater-corner and leaned his shoulders against the cement wall that supported the handrail for the steps. From where Leah stood, she could make out some sort of writing on the back of the windbreaker he wore. It was an oddly positioned name, something that read: Jay Eagle.

PART ONE

Chapter One

When it started raining later in the afternoon, the first thought that came to Leah's mind was whether or not she could use it as an excuse to beg off attending her sister's fashion event that evening. She looked out the window behind her at the gray November afternoon made even grayer by the concrete skyscrapers and canyons of Manhattan, and by the dullness of the East River. On the other hand, Leah reasoned, she was grateful that the weather wasn't going to precipitate into the season's first snowfall.

She heard the snapping sound of two fingers and turned to face Jill, the hyper-kinetic senior art director.

"Hello. Earth to Leah. Come in, Leah Downey . . ."

Leah couldn't help chuckling sheepishly, since she'd been caught in the act. She swiveled on her stool to face her drafting table and her department supervisor. "Sorry. You wanted something?"

Jill sat comfortably on the edge of the low supply cabinet placed adjacent to the drafting table. She tilted her head as she regarded her co-worker. "Boy, you were really out in deep space. What's going on?"

Leah shrugged. "Not much. Just trying to decide between three concepts for that text on money management."

"Oh, you mean *The Money Tree*." Jill leaned forward and took a quick glance at the sketches on Leah's table. "Go with green or gold, dollar signs or a money bag . . ."

"Or a tree," Leah finished helpfully. "Why didn't I think of that?" she asked dryly.

"Because you were busy daydreaming. I envy you," Jill said suddenly. She gently shook her head so that her straight blond hair danced and then settled in an attractive pageboy that curved along her blunt jawline.

Leah raised her brows. "You're envious because I daydream?"

"Because you obviously have such a rich fantasy life. Your imagination must work overtime. That's probably why your designs are so good."

"My designs have nothing to do with my daydreams."

"With your sex life, then?" Leah laughed. "Well, it must come from somewhere. You're really good, and you know you're really good."

Leah ignored the compliment. "I don't think you want to discuss my imagination or my sex life, Jill. What's up?"

Jill crossed her legs and then uncrossed them. She tossed her head again, examined her nails, which were chewed, short, and ugly. "It's not about work. I was just wondering if you'd like to go out for drinks or dinner after work. We haven't done that in a long time."

"I know," Leah said with some hesitation. "But I seem to recall that you never had time for that once you met Larry."

Jill crossed her arms over her chest. Then she uncrossed them, playing with the sleeves of her sweater. "Well, that's all over."

"Oh, I didn't know."

"I knew it wouldn't last," she announced.

However, Leah guessed by her colleague's expression

and her suddenly pink cheeks that it had been a painful ending.

"He made up with his wife. Now she's pregnant."

"That didn't take long."

Jill sighed. "It only takes one time. Anyway, the next time I'll look for someone like Allen."

Leah looked confused. "Allen?"

"You guys have been together forever. I never hear you complain, and you never seem to have fights. Perfect. Any day I expect you to announce your engagement."

Leah shifted nervously, recalling the phone argument she and Allen had had two nights ago. She felt uncomfortable being the subject of Jill's speculations. Of talk about marriage . . . and a lifetime. "We haven't talked about it yet."

"Wouldn't it be romantic if he gave you a ring for Christmas?" Jill suggested with excitement. "God, I *love* stuff like that. I want to get a ring inside a cake, or a bottle of champagne . . ."

Leah grimaced. "Messy."

"So, how about tonight?"

"I can't."

"Oh." Jill's smile quickly disappeared.

Leah was surprised by her obvious disappointment. It wasn't as if they were good friends. In the past their after-work dinners had been fun but mostly extensions of work and office gossip. She and Allen had double-dated with Jill and a previous boyfriend several times more than a year ago, but double-dating was not Allen's thing. Although she and Jill had once or twice exchanged party invitations, Leah still never considered that that made them close friends. But she could sense that her co-worker needed to talk. Maybe about Larry and their breakup.

"I'm sorry. Gail's fashion show is tonight and . . ."

"Oh," Jill repeated.

"There's a reception and I really have to be there. I'm leaving a little early this afternoon to get ready. Maybe I can ask Gail if you can—"

"Oh, no. Don't bother." Jill laughed awkwardly. "We'll do it some other time." She got up to leave.

"Jill?" Leah detained her a moment longer. "How about next week?"

"How about next week for what?" someone asked from the doorway.

Leah sighed patiently and rolled her eyes heavenward. It was Jill who responded to Mike Berger, the assistant art director, as he approached Leah's worktable. He looped an arm around Jill's shoulder with familiarity. He didn't wait for an answer to his first question.

"What are you working on?" he asked Leah.

She placed her arms flat on the drafting table, effectively covering the designs she'd created that morning. "*Illusions,* that beauty book by the former Ford model."

Mike chortled. "Jill probably gave it to you 'cause the model was black."

"How about because you know nothing about makeup?" Jill countered. She slipped from under his arm. "Come on. You want to fight, fight with me . . ."

Leah watched as Jill deftly led Mike away, telling him that she had another, more important project for him to work on. Leah disliked that Jill found it necessary to stroke his ego, but she disliked and distrusted Mike Berger even more.

Mike Berger was, as one of the editors had once phrased it, a poor excuse for a modern man. He was white, male, and not without talent. He was also sexist, spoiled, exuded a sense of entitlement and privilege, and was laughably unenlightened. Leah had learned to work around him with the same kind of equanimity with which she managed most situations she had little control over: by not taking it seriously.

Leah liked her position at a small publishing house in Midtown, near the United Nations. She was an assistant art director, a position equal to Mike's, but she was also considered the senior designer. She no longer considered that she might have gotten the job by virtue of being black and female in the right place at the right time. The bottom line was, she was talented and had proven her capabilities. She had been told many times by other artists, even in off-the-record remarks by editors, that it was she who was really the creative motivation behind the output of book designs and promotion. Jill was the real art director with a management style considered warm and fuzzy. Probably a smart tactic, Leah had always reasoned, given everyone else's propensity for climbing over other people's backs to advance their careers.

Leah knew that she could do the senior position job and do it well, but as far as she knew, no one had as yet suggested or supported that idea to management. It didn't matter to her. Justice was relative. She was happy not attending management meetings and dealing with the promotion department. And Mike was more than enough interference.

As her mind segued from one thought to the next, an idea insinuated itself into the free-flow. Leah quickly pulled forth a blank sheet of paper and began to quickly sketch in the basics for the cover of the *Illusions* beauty book. All because she'd been rehashing her history with Mike Berger. But she certainly wasn't going to thank him for the memories.

When Leah had first met him, Mike had been spending a lot of time pursuing anyone with breasts, although it took him a little longer to turn his pursuit to her. Leah suspected that Mike had decided she was too dangerous. But perhaps for want of any other opportunity, he did eventually make her a target. The thought spurred her idea as the sketch took shape. She could have written the scenario; the chase was steamed with jungle fever, as it were. She was black, still sweetly forbidden, taboo, and that must have made the pursuit all the more exciting to Mike. But Leah had no intention of being an experiment for anyone's ego or gratification.

Leah could recall in minute detail that afternoon, nearly three years ago, when he'd cornered her in a supply room between shelves of Strathmore paper and bristol board. Under the pretext of needing her help, Mike had followed her inside the narrow room and closed the door. Leah turned around to protest, but had found herself engulfed in an embrace and his mouth fastened to hers. She could have screamed, but she'd known that the implications would have worked more against her than Mike. She'd let her body stiffen and kept her mouth tightly closed against his attempt to force it open. His hands had quickly pressed over her with a boldness that made her breath draw in.

He finally pulled back impatiently.

"Come on," Mike breathed heavily. "What's the big deal? You know you've been wondering what would hap—"

Leah hauled back and belted him. She couldn't believe she was actually doing it, but nonetheless the punch landed on Mike's cheek, catching him completely off guard.

"Oowww!" He cringed in genuine surprise.

Leah pushed her way around him and got the door open. "You try that again and you're going to wish you never heard the words Black Power."

"I can get you fired," he said, but more hurt than angry.

"Before or after you explain why I hit you?"

Leah had hurried away to the ladies' room, where she'd locked herself in a stall and stood shaking for several minutes.

Mike had given up trying to maneuver her against a wall, but there remained a tension between them that was still sexual for him, suspicion for her. But she knew he'd never try anything with her again. And she felt sorry for his wife.

When the telephone rang, interrupting her concentration, most of the rough sketch was complete, and it was good. Still, when Leah answered she was distracted.

"Hello, Art Department."

"I don't believe it's raining," Gail said in annoyance.

"Could be worse."

"That doesn't make me feel better. People might not come tonight if the weather is bad. This could ruin my event. This is a pain in the ass."

"Calm down and stop exaggerating. People will come and it will be a huge success."

Finally, Gail chuckled. "You promise?"

"For whatever it's worth, sure."

"And Allen better not show up in a suit or I won't let him in."

"He hates the western look."

"I don't care. This is *my* event."

Leah rubbed her temple. "God, I hate it when the two of you go on this way. Why are you always at each other's throats?" She had expected another barbed answer from Gail, but she was surprised at the momentary silence.

"Ask Allen," Gail responded. "I have to go. There's still a lot to set up. Is Allen coming back to the house with you afterward?" she asked suddenly.

Leah felt an odd heaviness in her chest. "Probably. Why?"

"I don't want him to mess up my plans. I'll see you later. Bye." She hung up.

Leah sat holding the receiver a moment longer, completely confused by her sister's last remark. Did that mean Gail was going to be with someone else? She had lost count of her sister's short-term affairs and, given Gail's attention span for most things, wondered what exactly it was her sister was looking for. And did it really take so many men to find out?

She stared at the new sketch, put it away in a folder of ideas, and tried to turn her attention to the half-finished jacket of the money book. It was taped to the board, and she eyed it with disinterest. She felt distracted. Edgy. She wasn't looking forward to the show. She wasn't particularly looking forward to being with Allen. He was either going to complain about the people in his office, how he was not appreciated enough, or trash Gail's efforts. And Leah wondered who her sister was going to spend the night with this time.

Leah got up from her drafting table and left the studio to go to the small staff lounge. There she made herself a cup of hot tea, just needing the movement and activity to curtail her moodiness. No, it wasn't moodiness, she corrected herself as she returned to her drafting table. But rather than sit to work once more, she stared out of the window overlooking the river. She frowned at the way the rain continued to pelt the city, and for no real reason a hunched figure came to mind, the man she and Gail had found outside their home back in September. Leah suddenly wondered what had happened to him. Was he at this very moment getting soaked to the skin? He might get sick. Catch pneumonia. What if he fell down unconscious in the street somewhere? Would anyone notice him? Or had he disappeared back into his own life?

Leah tried to put her finger on the problem of her restlessness, but could only come up with dissatisfaction. But she also wished she hadn't relived the incident with Mike, the argument with Allen, or the total stranger who had haunted her dreams. She looked out over the city and felt a sudden need for something more. Something different.

There were so many things that she loved about New York. There were many more things that she disliked and found confusing. There was a lack of beauty and gentleness that Leah felt the city needed to soften the harder, unavoidable edges of day-to-day life, which was sometimes scary. Leah imagined that there were people who lived in the city who didn't know anything beyond their streets or neighborhoods. There were whole generations of city-locked kids who didn't know that the night sky was black and studded with a million brilliant specks of light called stars. In the polluted skies overhead they saw nothing, and they never looked up. People were living cheek by jowl without taking the time to know anything about the person right next to them. How could they do that? Where was the curiosity?

But there was danger as well. The man in her dreams: the one who'd mugged her. It had all come back again in September and in nights since then. She sometimes felt so fragile, but she didn't want to be helpless. She didn't want to be a prisoner, either, to an event that hadn't been her fault but which, nonetheless, sometimes threatened to engulf her. That in one moment on a summer's night her very soul and existence would have ended at a meager value of nine dollars . . . and the whim of a man.

The dream was always the same.

The crazy flight down the tunnel along hallways and

corridors continued with almost predictable regularity. Finally Leah would float, lift upward out of sleep into welcome daylight. She'd catch her breath and will her pounding heart to slow down. Then she'd curl up in the bed sheets, feeling small and needy like a child. Sometimes she was aware of the sound of her own voice, the low moans and whines of exhaustion and fear.

Suddenly out of blackness came the danger. The ominous man with the knife, not caring who she was but pursuing her relentlessly until she was worn out and unable to escape the presence gaining on her.

In the low tunnel light in her mind, the face was clear. It was the grinning black face of the man who'd attacked her. Once, in the dream, it had been the face of someone she didn't know at all, and once it had even been the face of Allen. Not chasing her, but laughing at her.

The attack had taken place on the nearly deserted Pratt campus where she'd taken an evening art class. At first to Leah it had seemed that it would be a mugging. That is, until the very quiet and opportunity of the moment became clear to Leah and to the man confronting her with a knife. She'd seen the change in his eyes, when he stopped being concerned about escape and a few dollars, and had lingered over the possibilities that had come almost simultaneously to both their minds. Instant panic and dread filled her. His response had been one of glee. He'd smelled sweaty and nervous, and he had not cared about her shaking hands and tremulous voice.

Leah's imagination had jumped to fast forward, to *afterward*, when she'd have to pull together her shattered wits and her used body; when she'd have to go for help and tell someone. She became paralyzed with fear when she further considered the other violent choices available to the attacker.

If she didn't show fear, she had tried to reason to herself, if she didn't demonstrate vulnerability, maybe he wouldn't think to hurt her. But it had been so quiet in the stairwell.

He'd started to laugh at her quick understanding of the situation. Leah's first thought had been that he was going to kill her when he was done. She thought about Gail having to call their father to tell him.

Leah had only put up a token attempt at resistance. She had been afraid of an outright struggle because of the knife. What if she made him mad and he just stabbed her . . . over and over again?

She could still feel weak with nausea when she thought of that knife held against her face.

He'd hit her with his fist, and when her head had resounded with a painful thud off the wall, she'd slid to the floor dazed. She'd been wearing a khaki jumpsuit. Fashionable and blessedly difficult. In his anger and frustration at the obstacle of the clothing, the black man had pulled and slashed at the fabric, cutting Leah's fingers and thigh, although superficially, when they got in the way. Her screams had been feeble, the mere utterances of defeat and helplessness. He'd hit her again.

And then, two floors above them, a stairwell door had opened and the voices and laughter of two female students echoed and multiplied the sound as they'd begun to descend. They must have heard her crying first and then, hurrying down the two flights, had found her alone, bloodied, among the ruin of her clothes and her class work. They, and the jumpsuit, had saved her. She had *not* been raped. She had *not* died a vile death. Only her spirit had been tortured and terrorized.

*   *   *

It was almost five o'clock before Leah arrived back in Brooklyn to get ready for Gail's fashion event. The moment she began to ascend from the Seventh Avenue station she knew she'd made a mistake. She should not have exited the station from this end. It was true that the stairwell would leave her two blocks closer to her home, but this end of the station was also mostly deserted, with too many deep shadows and dank corners, with sounds that echoed and which couldn't be identified.

It was only as Leah approached the stairwell leading to the street that she hesitated. She felt her heart lurch suddenly. Adrenaline pumped through her body as she had a flashback of another stairwell that had been equally deserted. Or so she'd thought. Leah braced herself, the sudden heat of panic making her skin break out in a sweat. She tried to rush up the stairs. Her purse strap slipped from her shoulder, and the heavy pouch thudded against her portfolio. The book she'd been reading slid against the newspaper, and the manila envelope, and the other sheets of paper that had kept her occupied on the hour long ride from Manhattan. Leah hastily juggled them back into position and finished the climb into the November night.

It had stopped raining, but car tires swished along streets that were still wet, and lamplight reflected off the shiny black surface. It was unusually quiet. Leah took a deep breath and started down the street in the direction of her home, planning to stop at a local market on the way.

She walked briskly to make up the time with a determination not to let her imagination take her hostage. But Leah heard footsteps behind her. Her heart pumped faster.

" 'Cuse me . . ."

It was a male voice. Firm and deep. The burden in Leah's arms shifted again, threatening to drop.

"Hey, miss. Hey, you!"

Leah never responded to hey, you.

"I think this is yours."

Was he kidding? Did he think she was stupid? Leah moved closer to the curb away from the buildings with their entrances and alleyways and opportunities for an innocent passerby to be dragged into. She drew in a breath. Should she start to run? He tapped her on the shoulder.

"Hey . . . is this yours?"

The voice was impatient now. Leah stopped and turned around. The man was older than she'd thought he would be. A little overweight. He carried a plastic bag of groceries in one hand. Several yards behind him stood a woman, waiting in front of a building Leah had already passed. The woman also held packages from the market. Leah looked at the man's outstretched hand. He held an envelope that was slightly soiled. It was a letter she'd received just that afternoon. It was about a piece of her freelance work that was being accepted for magazine publication. There had also been a check. She reached for the envelope, a smile defrosting her facial features.

"Yes, that's mine. Thank you."

"Didn't you hear me calling?" the man asked.

"Yes, but . . . I thought . . ."

"Uh-huh . . ." he murmured before Leah could finish.

The older man looked her over carefully. He pulled his shoulders back and glared at her, as if Leah had somehow offended him. She had, and she knew it.

He finally turned away, back to the waiting woman.

It seemed foolish to shout out thank you when she probably owed him an apology for her suspicion. But defensively Leah reasoned that he should have understood. It was late. She was alone. How could she have known his intentions were good? Hadn't he ever been a victim?

Some young men were hanging around the store as usual when Leah stopped for milk. The entrance had become some sort of staked-out territory for a group of local teens through which everyone else had to pass. Leah knew that she would have to endure their comments. She would have to rebuff come-on attempts. It was like running a gauntlet with no particular prize for having succeeded. Leah ignored the swaggering young men except to murmur, "Excuse me," as she passed through. Everywhere in the city the verbal strutting seemed to be standard learned behavior of males between fourteen and forty as an acceptable way to get the attention of the opposite sex.

"Hey, mama. Hey, fox. Ain't you gonna say hello?"

Leah ignored the tall, skinny youth who thought too much of himself. She'd seen him before. Was it that he didn't know any better, or that he didn't care? When Leah left the store moments later, the skinny teen fell into step beside her. He couldn't have been more than seventeen. His friends stayed where they were, joking and taking bets on his chances with her.

"Let me carry that for you," he began ingratiatingly.

"That's all right," Leah responded, swinging her bundle away from his reach. "You're not stronger than I am. I'll carry it myself." She quickened her steps home.

The comment caused the onlooking companions to crack up in laughter, slapping each other's palms, butting their knuckles. The skinny youth recovered quickly from the set-down, but Leah was way ahead of him down the street.

"I'm strong enough where it counts. And I know how

to use it. You should check it out sometimes . . .
sweet thang!"

Leah opened the invitation and read it once more.
One of Seventh Avenue's hottest young designers was
opening a western boutique on the ground floor of the
store where Gail worked. It was redoing what Ralph
Lauren had done years before. Fashion and trends were
cyclical, and nothing if not fickle. Everything came
back sooner or later, updated for those who'd missed
it the first time around.

Gail said she had made it her responsibility to coor-
dinate the opening night events: fashion show, reception, press and photo coverage. The right people had
to be invited, who would in turn bring the right people,
and on ad nauseam. Leah grimaced. She didn't want
to go. But even as she complained, she laid out her
outfit—appropriate western attire was expected—because she wanted the night to be a success for Gail's
sake. Gail had a plan for herself, and tonight's event
was only a step in the right direction toward reaching
her goals.

Leah recognized that while her sister was sometimes
resentful of how Seventh Avenue operated, it was only
because she herself wasn't yet in charge. What she
wanted was a line of designer clothes all her own, of
course. Leah envied her sister her single-mindedness
and dedication to purpose: making a name for herself
in fashion and pots of money along the way. Any offers
of help were greedily accepted, but Gail had no time
for anyone who wasn't in a position to do her some
good, who could help her dreams come true.

"I learned a lesson from those little white girls at
college," she constantly lectured. "And that's how to
position yourself to meet the right people and take ad-

vantage of the right opportunities. Seventh Avenue is going to know who I am in three to five years' time."

Leah understood. Time tables were very useful if everything went according to schedule. So far Gail was certainly doing okay, but it had taken longer than "three to five years." Out of school and into a marketing program at one of Manhattan's top stores, putting in time as assistant buyer in children's wear, then transferring to the Executive Training Division to add a little polish and business know-how. Finally winning a foothold in the exclusive group of people responsible for the high-priced boutiques and special lines at the store.

Leah couldn't help smiling. And feeling proud. Both of their wardrobes were filled with her sister's creations. Gail had designed the event for this evening, complete with props, such as cactus plants and wooden fences, ropes and cookout gear, a saddle, Stetson hats, and even the dried white shell of a Texas longhorn steer had to be located and displayed. The invitations had read, "don't forget your spurs," and Gail expected to see lots of tooled leather calf boots and fringed vests.

Leah arrived home from work to find Gail fussing to make her hair look both western and New York chic. Whatever that meant, Gail's thick nape-length hair would not cooperate. She settled on combing it straight back and behind her ears, which allowed her to don a Stetson. When she was finished dressing, she was wearing rust-colored suede jeans with a cream silk blouse, elaborately stitched red boots, and an expression that said *this* new trend was not her idea of fashion. But if anyone could carry it off, it was Gail. Still, she had no intention of being the target of snide comments or looks of amusement. She arranged for a car service to take her into Manhattan to the store.

When Allen called for Leah, she was similarly

dressed, and she felt equally as silly. Allen was far less sanguine. From the moment he entered the house he did nothing but complain.

"Woman is out of her mind," he muttered, although dressed pretty inconspicuously in jeans and a simple white western shirt with mother-of-pearl buttons.

"Allen, you look great," Leah reassured him, and she meant it. He was a handsome man.

Leah had always been impressed and moved by Allen's physical presence. You couldn't help but notice him. He was tall and broad-shouldered and carried himself straight, with a nearly imperial bearing. His hair was always neatly cut, with a thick and soft curl. His heavy mustache was the same, and he wore tortoise-shell glasses that gave him an air of intelligence and command. He was thoroughly masculine, Leah didn't deny, but she'd long ago observed that Allen had a tendency toward churlishness and lacked a sympathetic nature.

She could see that he'd drawn the line at cowboy boots. They really weren't his style. Allen's only concession to the theme Gail was promoting was a leather belt with a huge silver buckle in the shape of a horse's head. He was simply coordinated and the casualness of his clothing made him seem less restrained than he normally was.

"Maybe it won't be so bad." Leah tried to soothe him as he turned and fussed in front of a mirror.

"Look like some damned country yokel. I don't like this shirt."

"Why don't we try a scarf or something tied at the throat?" she suggested, but already Allen was shaking his head.

"I'm not going anywhere with some bandanna, or whatever it's called, around my neck."

Leah hesitated, feeling somewhat annoyed for trying

to assuage his ego. "Are you going to wear the Stetson?"

Allen gave her a quelling look that annoyed her even more. "Let's get the hell out of here before I change my mind."

At the store an hour later, it was clear to Leah that she wouldn't be competing with anyone. Everyone was dressed more or less the same way. A few outfits were outrageous or bold, like the young woman who easily stood at just under six feet tall, wearing a very short denim skirt that stopped an inch below her behind. Her black body suit had no back, and her knee-high suede boots were tangerine red. And she wore an Indian headdress complete with plumage and beads.

Allen and Leah didn't see much of Gail, which was to be expected. They did find themselves being continually swallowed in clusters of people until Leah began to feel claustrophobic. She became separated from Allen but spotted him some distance away in conversation with several people. No doubt exchanging business cards and nurturing a prospective new client. It was too much of an effort to try to reach him, so Leah wandered about on her own, nursing a glass of champagne. She slowly elbowed her way through the crowd, trying to see some of the displayed fashions and accessories that would go on sale the next day. She stopped by a lighted showcase with an arrangement of Southwest silver and turquoise jewelry. Her attention was caught and she stood fascinated by the craftsmanship of the individual pieces.

She was still staring when she heard a male voice behind her.

"Gail . . . look, hon, you can't just slip away like this. You're needed in the—" He stopped when Leah turned around to face him.

She stood facing a tall black man with several cameras hanging around his neck. He wasn't in costume like everyone else, except for a token red bandanna tied around his upper arm.

He stated the obvious, running his gaze quickly over her. "You're not Gail."

"You're right, I'm not," Leah smiled.

The man arched a brow, looking at Leah closely. "A sister?"

She nodded. "I'm Leah."

"Hi. Steven," he said, putting out his hand for her to shake.

"Gail's around here somewhere. Probably going crazy. You might check and see if she's with the models. I think it's almost time for their show."

But Steven wasn't listening. Instead, he seemed to be studying her, making Leah wonder with amusement if he was counting all her eyelashes. And he was holding her hand much too long. She pulled it free.

"Yeah, well . . . that's why I have to find her," he said, still scrutinizing Leah with unmistakable admiration. "I'm supposed to record this circus, but I need to know where the outlets are for the extra lights."

Leah shrugged. "Can't help you."

"Are you here alone by chance?" he asked with a caressing, hopeful grin.

Leah shook her head. "Sorry."

"Oh, you just broke my heart," he moaned dramatically and clutched his chest.

"As a matter of fact, I have to go find—"

"That's too bad." He slowly pulled himself together. "Gotta find your sister. But I'll see you again," Steven said significantly before turning away.

A runway had been cleverly constructed down the center aisle on the second floor of the store, between junior sportswear and petites. Leah, unable to locate Allen, was escorted to a solitary seat in the audience as the fashion show got under way. The music came on loud and fast and kept up a throbbing momentum for the duration of the show. She was certain that a speaker had been placed directly under her chair. Before long Leah felt the beginning of a headache pounding at her temples.

She finally spotted Allen in the front row of the audience to her left, seated next to Gail. They were laughing and Gail was trying to place a Stetson on Allen's head, but he wasn't going to allow it. Leah was grateful that for the moment her sister and Allen seemed compatible. Yet even as she watched them together, she felt isolation and envy engulf her. She didn't understand why she should feel this way. Soon Gail was called away to see after yet another detail of the evening, leaving Allen alone.

By the time the show was drawing to a close, Leah's head felt ready to fall off her shoulders. There was too much cigarette smoke mixed with the smell of spilled wine. Too many different perfumes and colognes in the air. Too much music and too many people. She was ready to go home.

When Allen brought his car around to the side door of the store, Gail was ready to leave as well, and she stood waiting with Steven.

"Can you give us a lift?" she asked Allen pleadingly.

It was obvious to Leah that that was the last thing Allen really wanted to do. But he shrugged.

"Where to?"

Gail took hold of Steven's arm and smiled up to him. "Steven's place."

Leah felt somewhat grateful that Steven was paired with her sister, if for no reason than she hoped it might quell his interest in her, which he didn't even try to hide. It irritated Leah that her sister would be attracted to someone so shallow.

"Did you enjoy the show?" Gail asked conversationally from the backseat.

"I thought the models looked like hookers," Allen offered dryly.

"I thought they were fabulous," Leah said with a yawn.

"Tired?" Steven asked her. Leah didn't answer.

"In other words, you didn't like the show," Gail said to Allen.

"Do you really care what I think?"

"Not especially," Gail admitted airily. "If you knew what you were talking about, you'd have my job and I'd be in banking."

"Is this a domestic fight?" Steven asked with a laugh.

Allen made an impatient sound.

"Could you turn on the heater? I'm cold," Leah murmured.

"As soon as the engine warms up a little."

Gail chortled and reached between the seats to turn the heater on. "If you drove a better car, we wouldn't have to wait," she said.

Allen made another impatient sound.

Leah settled into her seat with closed eyes, letting the petty argument drift around her. She didn't care what it was about. She just wanted to take some aspirin for her headache. She wanted the comfort of silence and solitude. She wanted her own thoughts and imagination to wrap herself in.

Allen made the stop requested on University Place in lower Manhattan, and then he and Leah drove back to the Brooklyn brownstone.

"I could really use something to eat," Allen hinted broadly.

Leah smiled benevolently at him. "If you're willing to do the cooking, be my guest." To her surprise, he did.

Leah helped and together, at nearly midnight, they

were having waffles with strawberry jam and hot coffee.
The second round of coffee was taken in the living
room as they sat on the sofa listening to a CD of Lu-
ther Vandross. Leah leaned against Allen's chest, feeling sleepy and more generous toward him than she'd
been in a long time. She'd forgotten how nice it was
to be with him sometimes, like now, when it was quiet
and romantic and he didn't talk too much, but just
held her.

Allen had rolled up the sleeves of his shirt and
stretched his legs out in front of him. Leah had her
head against his shoulder as she sat with her legs
curled up, touching his thigh.

"Ummm. This is nice. Very nice."

Leah just smiled to herself but didn't say anything.
She relaxed against him. She knew Allen well, knew
what would happen next, and suddenly she didn't really
mind. She felt in the mood. He would begin to stroke
her arm, and then work his long fingers up to her
shoulder and neck. With her head near his shoulder
she could listen to his deep breathing, which would
signal the beginning of his desire. The sweet fragrance
of his cologne would both tickle and annoy her nose.
Then Allen would turn his head and his lips would
press kisses to her forehead. His finger would rim
around the shell of her ear. Leah began to feel languid.

Then Allen would take off his glasses and fold them
away into the pocket of his shirt. He'd pull her abruptly
into his arms and begin to kiss her ardently, immediately forcing her mouth open to receive his aggressive,
rough tongue.

Guiltily Leah realized that her attention was drifting
away from her feelings to thinking about Allen's kisses
and his technique. Her state of arousal waffled.

Allen held her too tightly in his growing excitement,

and she was uncomfortable. She felt cramped and bunched up.

"Leah . . ." Allen moaned, kissing her deeply and breathing into her mouth as their tongues danced. He squeezed her breast and moved his mouth to her cheek and then her ear, and Leah could hear the wet kisses, the sound loud and not very pleasant. But Allen's lips also found the sensitive area under her ear, and a titillating sensation stirred to life within her. Allen stood up, pulling Leah with him. Together they silently turned off most of the lights. The coffee cups were left on top of the table. Leah absently hoped they wouldn't leave ring marks, or Gail would have a fit.

In Leah's room, Allen hastily removed his clothing, carefully folding them over the stool at the foot of her bed. They got under the covers, but in five minutes the bed linens were disheveled and pulled from the mattress in the frenzy of their lovemaking.

Leah closed her eyes and settled down into Allen's arms. She liked it when he stroked and massaged her breasts, especially her nipples, but he never stayed at it long enough. She rubbed Allen's back, feeling the play of muscles under her fingers. She concentrated on the feelings budding deep within her loins, the sensuous throbbing that made her feel soft and which would spiral into a wrenching release if it continued. Her hands moved down to Allen's thighs, and she heard the intake of air between his lips and teeth. Down his legs her hands went, and up again between them. He stopped stroking her.

"Oh . . . Christ . . ." Allen moaned and moved to settle on top of her, finding easily the object of his desire. He pulled Leah's legs up to circle his waist as his rigid penis drove into her.

Leah tried hard to let her body take over, to flow into Allen's rhythm as he moved within her. She wanted to share the euphoria, too. It was there, elusive, and she breathed slowly to make the sensation stay. Faster and faster, deeper Allen moved, his face buried against her hair. He had his own program, and her body simply did what he wanted it to do. Leah strained. Her breathing began to quicken, and her own moan escaped softly as she hovered on the brink.

Allen suddenly let out a heart-wrenching gasp as his hips thrust forward. His primal grunts and groans paced his release. He held Leah to him, so close to his sweating, quaking body that he squeezed her climax right out of her and it died. Leah groaned and closed her eyes tightly in frustration. Allen, thinking that she'd reached satisfaction too, sighed.

"Yeah, baby . . . oh, yeah . . ."

Much later, Leah heard movement in the room. She was more than half asleep, but the sounds were familiar and didn't fully awaken her. Soon it was quiet again, and she turned onto her stomach and went back to sleep. She only wondered if Allen had remembered to put the self-lock in position on the front door when he let himself out.

In her sleep she grew restless, drifting until a dream formed and another man came to mind. A stranger suddenly appeared within the private circle of her life. The reality-based dream, devastating in its details and physical effect, returned to Leah in the night. As usual, it was about the man in the stairwell. . . .

Except that in the recurring dream it was never a stairwell but a long, muted tunnel with a maze of adjacent passageways. She would always try to stay on the path straight ahead, because she didn't want to think about what hid in the other corridors. She could never really see very clearly anyway in the low lighting, but she always knew that she was not alone. When the laughter finally came, as it always did so suddenly and so close, she knew there was no escape.

There would be an overpowering need to groan, to make a sound of fear. He'd touch her. His hands were big and rough. In one hand was the knife. He'd clutch her, drawing her into the horrible smells and heat of his body. He had her. He was going to—

Leah jumped in her skin.

She hadn't been able to get the scream out of her mouth. It struggled in her throat as if some silent force were keeping it there. She could still feel the pain of the fear that had been part of the nightmare. Like a fist pounding in her chest. For the better part of the past two years Leah had been dreaming about a stocky black man who'd attacked her one summer night.

Leah had never told Allen about it. And she'd never told her father or Gail. She'd never been sure why. She simply lived with the dream the same way people lived with a chronic condition. She accepted it, managed it, and secretly prayed that one day she'd get strong enough for it to just go away.

When Allen had slipped away in the middle of the night, Leah had been glad. Earlier she'd fallen to sleep next to him with her body feeling like a mild electrical shock had been administered to her. Not enough to do her any harm, but more than enough to leave her on edge.

Leah floated up out of the darkness of the dream, feeling the terror sink beneath her. She wiped the damp perspiration from between her breasts. She heard the final faded strains of male laughter. His laughter.

Leah trembled reflexively, feeling exhausted. She turned her head toward the window, grateful that there was a flat plane of blue through the glass. It was the sky. It was daylight. She was awake.

*   *   *

Leah knew she wasn't dreaming when the smell of fresh-brewed coffee accompanied her down the staircase that morning. She was surprised when she walked into the kitchen at seven and found Gail brooding over her cup.

"Morning," Leah murmured in a tired voice. She got a cup for herself from the cabinet. "When did you get in?"

Gail didn't answer right away, and Leah turned a frowning expression at her sister's silence. Finally Gail put her cup down. "Around three. I met Allen leaving."

Leah poured coffee into her cup. "Did you?" she asked rhetorically, and joined her sister at the table. "Is that all?" Gail seemed unusually subdued, and Leah watched her shrug with impatience.

"I said good morning, he said good night. He made some snide remark about Steven being a jerk."

Leah kept her gaze on Gail's face as she sipped carefully from the hot liquid. "And what did you say?" Gail glared at her, and Leah found herself drawing back from it.

"I told him that's like the pot calling the kettle, black." Gail got up abruptly and topped off her cup. Then she stood leaning against the edge of the sink drinking.

Leah turned in her chair to look at her sister. "Was that necessary?"

Gail sucked through her teeth. "I don't understand why you let him treat you this way."

"What?" Leah asked quietly.

"Like you're a convenience. Like you're here for his pleasure and he can come and go as he pleases. The man is selfish and insensitive."

Leah frowned, although Gail's observations touched a nerve in her. "Why should you care? Who made you a monitor and judge of my business? You've never liked Allen and that's obvious."

"I'm just thinking about you."

"Thanks, but don't. I can handle Allen. It's not as one-sided as you think."

"I just don't like what he's doing . . . or the way he's doing it."

Leah couldn't argue with that. Instead she faced forward, wrapped her hands around the warm cup, and pursed her lips thoughtfully. "I suppose I should thank you for your concern . . . Allen's okay. He treats me well enough. Maybe he's a little self-centered. Yes, he complains too much . . . but there ain't a whole hell of a lot of choices out there. He's smart and good-looking. Like you, he's just very involved with his career right now. He'll settle down."

"Are you really willing to wait that long? For him to settle down? Do you love him that much?" Gail asked.

Leah shrugged indifferently. "Love isn't the point," she murmured cryptically.

She felt like she sleepwalked through work that afternoon. She should have been able to predict that it would happen. It was always the follow-through to a night of having been victimized in her dreams. It was always a stark reminder not to get too complacent and not to feel too safe. But it also made Leah angry. When she looked at her life, her routine, what was there to be so assured about? Her home? Her relationship with her sister? A life that was comfortable and relatively easy? These were givens. She just felt . . . needy. Sometimes so very needy. Was that Allen's fault? It seemed that her relationship with him should have countered everything, all the other doubts. He should have made a difference. But he didn't.

Leah left work that afternoon in pretty much the disoriented state she'd begun the day with. The wind whipped leaves around the streets. They made a crinkly orange and yellow mess behind steps, against buildings, and piled up in drain holes. But the colors were beautiful, like confetti being tossed around in the air.

As Leah left the subway for the usual walk home, the brisk, chill day reminded her that Thanksgiving was mere weeks away and she and Gail had not yet given any thought as to how they would spend it. And of course, Christmas was not far behind. She thought of calling her father to see if he could be persuaded to fly to New York for at least one of the holidays. Leah wondered absently if she and Gail would get an invitation out to Thanksgiving dinner, saving them the job of cooking.

A gust of wind caught Leah from behind, blowing her hair around her face. She was almost upon her doorstep before she realized there was someone standing—waiting, actually—in front of her. Using one hand to smooth her now tangled hair, she squinted against the wind and saw a man staring at her. He was white, of just above average height, dressed in jeans and a black turtleneck sweater with a brown corduroy sports jacket. He had both hands in his front jeans pockets, and, rather than seeing him as a threat as he stood with his legs braced apart and staring right at her, Leah was instantly struck by her sense of uncertainty about him. His look was intent and never left her face as she slowed her steps. He was blocking her path. Then she noticed the gray eyes. Her stomach lurched as she realized he was familiar. No. She recognized him. Jay Eagle.

"It's you . . ." Leah murmured in amazement. She quickly noticed the distinct differences in him now, from more than a month ago. There was an unexpected satisfaction in seeing that she'd been right. He wasn't homeless or a derelict. "I wondered what had happened to you," she added artlessly.

"Did you?" he questioned automatically.

She shrugged, watching him with interest. Leah was aware of an odd sensation, as though she'd been living with a ghost and it had finally materialized before her. She felt vindicated, in a way, that her defense of him when Gail would have called the police had been justified. They'd been in no danger from him.

And, Leah thought as she took in the whole presence of him, she no longer even considered him a real stranger. In his right mind, shaven, freshly dressed, and lucid, he was even more intriguing. She was relieved and surprised.

"You didn't seem too together that night. But I didn't think you were drunk."

"It was a rough night. I was only half drunk."

Leah tilted her head in curiosity. "What about the other half?"

The question made him only half smile. He glanced away briefly for a moment, as if trying to decide for himself. He lifted his shoulders in a vague gesture. "Lost."

Leah didn't need another explanation. She nodded. "Well, I can see you're okay now," she said, her voice trailing off.

"I'll live," he answered flippantly.

There was an awkward silence while they appraised each other. He stood as if he were expecting Leah to say something, some sort of signal as to how he should respond. But all Leah could think to do was try to find her house keys in her shoulder bag and pull up the collar of her coat against the cold.

"Do you live around here?" she finally asked politely.

He seemed suddenly nervous. "No, I don't."

"Then, what are you doing here?"

He didn't answer right away, and Leah watched as he turned to look toward a car double-parked at the curb. A bulky black man sat in the driver's seat. The man, while he might not have been able to hear the conversation, was nonetheless watching her intently. She was alert to his wary gaze, which was not friendly.

"I came to find you," the man in front of Leah responded, drawing her attention from the man in the car. "I wanted to thank you for the coffee."

Leah couldn't describe how his thank-you made her feel, but it virtually blew away the edginess of her day. Still, she shook her head. "You don't have to thank me. It was only coffee." The driver in the waiting car honked the horn. "If he's waiting for you, you'd better go." She took a few steps around him, headed toward the house.

He looked at his watch. "I'm supposed to be at work."

Leah looked at her watch. "It's six-thirty. You work nights?"

He lifted a corner of his mouth in a grin. "I work twenty-four hours a day" was the cryptic reply. Suddenly he blurted out, "I thought maybe we could go for a drink or something . . ."

Leah stopped dead in her tracks and turned to stare at him.

He shrugged. "Maybe coffee."

"Why?" Leah asked. She was more puzzled than suspicious.

"Why not? Like you said, it's only coffee."

"I would think you'd had enough of that."

"It's safer than gin," he said dryly.

"Look . . ." Leah began uneasily. "I'm glad you're okay, but let's leave it at that."

"Aren't you even the least bit curious?"

"About what?"

"About what was going on that night with me."

"Not really," she lied. "But I'm glad to see you're okay. Why don't we just call it square for the coffee?"

"How about Saturday? I could meet you at noon," he suggested, ignoring her previous answer.

It struck Leah that he was used to asserting himself. His tenor voice was nicely modulated. It was clear and firm. She thought about his invitation but saw no hidden meanings or suggestions. But there was also a sense of caution and danger. Much more than when he was down and almost out in front of her home. Leah didn't think for a moment that he was a deviant or perverted, but just talking with him this way made her suddenly aware of herself, and suddenly just as aware of him. The difference between them was suddenly stark.

She shook her head, again moving toward the house. "I don't think so." She began to climb the steps to the front door, key in hand, aware that he stood watching. Aware of a sudden spiraling of excitement within her. Danger. Leah felt a rush.

"Why not?" he called up to her.

Leah chuckled silently and gave him a look of exasperation. "Can't you just take no for an answer?"

"I'd maybe accept a better answer."

Leah lost the annoyed edge to her voice. It turned to amusement at his persistence, his ease in light of the only history that existed between them.

"Just because," Leah replied. "How's that?"

"Try again," he challenged.

Leah stood on the top step outside her front door and gazed down on him. There was something very strong and sturdy about the way he returned her appraisal. There was also confidence and sharp awareness in his eyes, and Leah sensed quickly, Jay Eagle was probably an honest man. She glanced at the waiting man again and wondered who he was.

"I don't go out with men who are in the habit of getting half drunk."

Her remark hit home. Leah watched Jay Eagle's expression change, as the narrowing of his eyes seemed to cut into her. Leah instantly wished she'd said something else. She turned away from his stare.

The car honked again. Leah slowly unlocked the door. Then she hesitated. She turned around quickly, her breathing suddenly short.

"Wait a minute, Jay Eagle."

He was already at the curb, about to climb into the passenger side of the car, when her voice stopped him.

"How about Sunday? I can do Sunday. One o'clock?" Her heart thumped. She was out of her mind.

He merely nodded, opening the door of the waiting car. "Fine. I'll see you at one, Leah Downey. Here."

Leah's eyes widened in real suspicion now. "How do you know my name?" she asked.

He didn't answer. He climbed into the car and it pulled away from the curb. As it reached the far corner and turned, Leah considered the burly black man's expression as he'd stared at her. It was censoring, probably because she was black and had just accepted an invitation from a white man. And maybe it also held a warning that Leah recognized and had chosen to ignore. She hoped that she wasn't making a major mistake.

Chapter Two

Saturday started out normally enough with a phone call to Melvin Downey in Chicago. His daughters had tried to talk him into flying to New York for the holidays. He was tempted, he answered, but really didn't relish the idea of juggling himself and his luggage around other people in the cold of winter. Leah and Gail knew that he had gotten comfortable in his solitary retirement in Chicago. He had his own circle of friends and his own routine. He no longer needed companionship simply because the holidays were approaching.

After the long-distance call to Chicago came the ritual of Saturday chores: running all the little errands that prepared for the week ahead while cleaning up after the mess of the last one.

"Are we expecting Allen to come over tomorrow?" Gail asked as she dusted the top of the piano in the living room.

Leah hesitated as she straightened pillows on the sofa. "We?" she questioned. "I don't think so. I have other plans anyway."

"What other plans?" Gail asked, looking over her shoulder at her sister.

"I'm meeting someone for coffee tomorrow."

"Who is he?" Gail asked suspiciously.

Leah raised her brows. "What makes you think it's a he?"

" 'Cause women don't meet each other for coffee," Gail responded dryly. "What's going on?"

"Well . . ." Leah began slowly and then stopped. She didn't want to lie to her sister. But how could she explain agreeing to meet a white man who, a month ago, the two of them had found on their doorstep like some abandoned pet? "Remember the guy in front of the house back in September?"

Gail stopped her dusting immediately and regarded her sister as if she'd suddenly started talking in tongues. "You have got to be kidding. You mean to tell me you have a date to see a bum, some street low-life—"

"It's not a date. And he's not a bum, Gail. He is just someone who was having a bad time."

"So? We all have bad times. That doesn't mean you become friends with every asshole who has a sob story. Why the hell did you agree to meet him? Did he come back here again and you didn't tell me? Did you dare give him our phone number? What is going on?" Gail's voice rose with each accusation.

Leah's patience grew thin under Gail's fiery attack. "There is nothing going on. He stopped by last week to thank me for the coffee."

"What coffee?" Gail nearly shouted, completely confused and irritated.

Leah shook her head. "Forget it. You don't know about the coffee."

Gail planted her fists on her hips. "Girl, you are out of your mind."

Leah turned back to the chore at hand. She was now exasperated herself, but only because she had no good reason for what she had agreed to. "What are you getting so worked up about? I'm not a fool. If I thought it was unsafe, I wouldn't do it." Her voice trailed off.

"Unsafe?" Gail repeated blankly. "There's something else that comes first."

"What?"

Gail stared at her with real puzzlement. "The man is white. What is going on with you? This is . . . so unlike you. In fact, this is just plain stupid, Leah."

Leah remained silent, unable to come up with an argument that made better sense. Gail shook her head.

"You don't know anything about him. Why, in God's name, would you even want to? And why with him, of all people?"

Why indeed. Except to Leah, who'd actually given it some thought since seeing Jay Eagle again, the answer was so simple it seemed silly. And yes, foolish. "Curiosity," she said honestly. But she also couldn't explain that it was like standing on the edge of a cliff peering down into a great depth below. She'd never done that, either, but there was something enticing about the challenge and fear. Maybe agreeing to see Jay Eagle was a thing she wasn't used to doing. But she wanted to do *something* that was different in her life.

Gail made an impatient sound deep in her throat. "You obviously don't recall what curiosity did to the cat one fine day."

Leah thought wryly that she certainly had more smarts than a cat. That was why she was going to meet Jay Eagle for coffee. Despite everything. Just because . . .

It turned out to be a beautiful day, typical of late fall. It was cold and breezy and sunny. Leah wore a knit hat and gloves, a concession to the changing of the seasons, and a thick sweater coat. When she saw Jay Eagle again, he was dressed the same as he'd been the week before except that his turtleneck sweater was white.

Anticipation knotted Leah's stomach while she waited for him outside her front door. She stood on the curb looking down the one-way street. But his hello finally came from directly behind her. She jumped. When Leah turned around, he was watching her carefully.

"I didn't mean to scare you. You have to remember to watch your back."

"I wasn't expecting a sneak attack," Leah responded tartly, a bit annoyed because his sudden approach had thrown her off balance. There had been no time for her to see him from a distance, and decide ahead of time what she would do and say. Leah felt as if he'd somehow taken advantage. Giving Jay Eagle what she hoped was a displeased glance, Leah fell into step next to him.

Several blocks from her house, near Prospect Park, they found an upscale coffee shop and took a booth in front near a window. An eclectic Sunday brunch crowd was out. Young couples with small children making a mess of pancakes and syrup; solitary *Sunday Times* readers; senior citizens on fixed incomes out for their weekly treat.

They hadn't made much conversation on the walk over, except for one or two comments about the weather and the park that were so benign and absurd that Leah could feel her tension disappear. She'd asked what kind of work he did for a living, but somehow he'd avoided giving her a direct answer as he'd rushed them across the street, dodging a car. Now seated at the window table he lit a cigarette, and Leah scanned the menu. She looked at him over the top of the laminated card.

"How did you know my name?" she asked bluntly.

He dropped the match into an ashtray. "I asked your neighbor. And I've watched you. I knew where you lived, remember?"

Leah was again a little annoyed, but also surprised. "What were you doing? Checking me out?"

He shrugged, not embarrassed or repentant. "I was curious. I wanted to see what you were like."

"So what am I like?" Leah asked flippantly.

"I'm not sure yet," he answered. "That's why I stopped to talk to you last week."

Leah played nervously with the sugar dispenser. His answer had disconcerted her again. It was an indication that he was curious about her, too. Somehow she hadn't expected that.

A waitress came and took their order. He asked only for a toasted bagel with cream cheese and coffee. Leah thought about it as the waitress walked away, as if what he had or hadn't ordered said anything concrete about him. She covertly looked him over. He seemed lean and solidly built, like an athlete. Leah wondered if he pumped iron or was concerned about his appearance. No, he couldn't be that shallow, she decided. Or else he would have hidden himself away back in September and had his crisis, or whatever it was, alone.

"Why are you staring?"

She blinked rapidly and dropped her gaze. "Was I?"

"Intently," he said, sounding amused.

Leah shifted in her chair. "Sorry. I wasn't really staring. I tend to go into a trance when I'm thinking about something."

He considered her answer and then nodded. "Yeah, I do that, too. So what were you thinking about?"

Leah quickly tried to gauge how much she could ask about that night, but he seemed willing to talk openly with her. "Just . . . where did you go after you left my house?"

His gaze shifted a fraction of an inch from her face, and Leah wondered what he was remembering. The cause, the event, or the result. She decided it must be all three. He dragged on the cigarette and then seemed to swallow the smoke rather than exhale.

"To a friend's."

She accepted that with a nod. It was clear that wasn't the right question, or the right territory to explore.

The waitress returned with their order, and as she placed plates and drinks, Leah glanced around and suddenly caught two black men seated behind Jay Eagle eyeing her sharply. She would have ignored them except both were openly watching her, one swiveled around in his chair to do so. Leah raised her brows in question, but she fully understood their disapproval.

"I have a question for you," he said, putting out the cigarette and starting to spread cream cheese on his bagel. "Why did you call me Jay Eagle the other day?"

"You mean, that's not your name?" Her gaze drifted back from the two men.

"Not even close."

Leah shrugged, confused. "It was on the back of your jacket. I thought it was your name."

"My jacket?"

"The day I left you the coffee you were wearing a navy blue windbreaker. On the back was the name Jay Eagle. I just thought . . ."

His look of confusion disappeared and he laughed lightly, causing creases to appear on either side of his mouth. "I get it. I use to coach a softball team in Queens. It was called the Blue Jays of Eagle Troop 14. Jay Eagle. Blue Jays . . ." he coaxed her into the connection.

Leah grimaced and shook her head at the misunderstanding. He grinned at her.

"My name's Jason Horn."

They made a fingertips handshake over their plates. Leah noticed that his hand was strong and veined. Lightly callused but not rough.

"Had all the letters fallen off?"

"Just about. That jacket and me go back a long, long way."

Jason looked off to the side and his smile slowly faded. Leah could tell that memories of some sort were playing in his mind, perhaps of that day more than a month ago when she'd found him on her doorstep. He had been sad and worn out then. For a brief moment, as they faced each other, he looked exactly the same way.

"You know," he began, pulling himself out of his reverie, "leaving that coffee was nice. I appreciated it. But . . . why would you do something like that?" Jason looked at her carefully. "A black woman giving something like that to a white guy parked on her door . . ."

Leah laughed. His bluntness took her by surprise, but she was also relieved by his honesty. He didn't skirt reality.

"I had to come back; I was intrigued. I wanted to see who was crazy enough." He smiled, studying her.

"What does my being black have to do with it? It was only a cup of coffee. And from the looks of you at the time, you probably needed it. If you'd tried anything funny, I would have poured it all over you."

"Most people wouldn't have offered coffee . . . they would have called for help," he persisted. "What you did was potentially dangerous. You know that, don't you?"

"The thought crossed my mind," she admitted as a brief panic swept over her. She suddenly remembered the deserted stairwell and the attack.

Leah knew that in many ways she remained a pris-

oner to an event which had had a better ending than
she should have hoped for. Nothing had really happened. But it was the *almost* which sometimes brought
on a cold sweat. Despite her bad experience, Leah
knew she was also not so self-absorbed as to be unaware of someone else's pain. Intuitively, when she'd
stood looking out her living room window that morning
back in September, with Gail imagining Jason Horn as
an ax murderer, every fiber of Leah's humanity told her
he was not. Something innate within herself sensed
only a troubled soul.

"Are you thinking or staring again?"

She shook her head ruefully. "I was just thinking
about what you said, about leaving the coffee. I guess
I'm not like most people. I like to think that I'm not."

Although Jason didn't smile, his eyes were bright
with scrutiny and awareness. "Yeah. I can see that
now."

Their first cup of coffee led to a second and then a
third, and then another round of muffins to justify the
long stay. The coffee shop clientele changed completely. Twice.

"However," Leah began and then paused for effect.
"You did make me nervous in one way."

"Did I? How?"

"When you said you'd been watching me. When you
said you'd asked my neighbor for my name."

He seemed to understand her point and nodded as
he lit another cigarette. "I didn't think you'd forget
that. I'm glad. But it was easy. You tend to daydream
when you're walking all alone. It was kind of nice to
watch because you also smile at your own thoughts."

"Oh, no ..." Leah groaned, astounded by his
observation.

"Hey, I thought it was great that you had happy
thoughts. But you still have to be alert."

"Why are you telling me this? Are you warning me that you're not safe?"

Jason raised his brows as if she'd made a point. He hesitated. "Yes and no. I thought you were very unpretentious, very open. But not everyone will be as honest about it as I am. Not everyone is going to be free of less innocent motives."

"Am I supposed to thank you?" Leah asked.

"Not necessarily. Just keep what I said in mind."

She found his comments a little unnerving, as though he knew exactly what he was talking about. How many other people did he just watch? Yet she was also well aware that her thoughtlessness had led her into a staircase late at night in a public building. It hadn't mattered that it was public; there hadn't been anyone else around. She had miscalculated her degree of safety, and she'd been a perfect target.

"Excuse me . . ." Leah suddenly murmured and got up hastily from the table. She didn't worry about what this man, Jason Horn, thought of her abruptness. She hurried off to the ladies' room. Not because she needed to go so much as she needed the time alone to think about what he'd said. Leah had found it profoundly alarming to hear just how vulnerable she'd always be.

She took a deep breath, examined her reflection in the mirror. She had to force away the unreasonable panic that made her doubt Jason. He hadn't been the least bit flirtatious, and she found him interesting. Even better, he'd already proven that Gail had been wrong about him.

Leah returned to the table expecting him to have questions about her sudden departure a minute ago. But if Jason was surprised or curious, it wasn't evident. He moved his ashtray out of her way as she sat down again, and waited patiently for her to make the next move.

"I-I had something in my eye," Leah lied but only received a vague knowing smile in return.

"Is it better now?" he asked.

She looked sharply at him and felt some relief. He *was* very quick, very observant. He must have realized that his comments about her had shaken her a bit. The fact that she'd returned to their table should also have said that she'd decided to trust her instincts where he was concerned. Leah nodded almost shyly. She did feel better.

"Do you remember the bottle of wine breaking?"

He looked totally blank and lifted his shoulders in a slight shrug.

"I was with a friend who bumped into you."

"I take it I owe you a bottle."

"It's not important. I just wondered how much you recall of that night."

"Almost nothing. What do you drink?"

"Sometimes sauterne. Sometimes Rhine."

"Sweet."

"You don't like sweet?"

"I like beer. A man's drink."

Leah looked at him, puzzled. But his expression was perfectly straight, and she instantly realized that he was teasing and being slightly sarcastic. The combination was another relief and made her laugh.

Leah began to tally up the things she was learning about Jason Horn. All in all he seemed a pretty normal, healthy, average white male. Not as cocky or arrogant as many she'd had to deal with in her life. And he was attractive.

Jason was taller than she remembered. He had a face whose masculine features showed some wear and tear, but also the expressiveness of someone not afraid of his own feelings. He was not a young man, but he hadn't hit middle age yet. He seemed a man who had done and seen a lot. His hair, still mostly a medium brown, had just the beginnings of gray here and there. It also had a tendency to fall into a natural off-center part, and was a bit long in back. He was clean-shaven, unlike the slightly scruffy shadow of a beard he'd worn when she'd first seen him. And his eyes, a haunting warm gray, were very direct. When Jason talked he looked right at her, unless some thought or idea or memory drew his gaze off into space. The most extraordinary thing about his face were his eyes—and a surprisingly ready smile.

All afternoon Leah waited for the signs that indicated that their initial curiosity had been satisfied, and they would thank each other for the coffee and say good-bye. But it didn't happen that way. The time passed with no inclination from either of them to end it.

They finally left the coffee shop and began walking along the perimeter of Prospect Park to the west. It was dark now; the sun had set over an hour earlier. Slowly they made their way back to Leah's street. She asked him what had happened after he'd finally gotten home in September. He said he'd gone to bed and slept until late Sunday night. And when she asked if he'd made it to work on Monday, he was silent and thoughtful for quite a long time. Finally, he shook his head in answer.

They passed four teenage boys in front of an apartment house near the corner, laughing together and goofing on the exaggerated sexual exploits of one of them. Jason and Leah looked at each other briefly with the same thought. They wouldn't want to be fifteen again for anything.

Once in front of the brownstone, they sat next to each other on the steps. Jason was still an encounter, albeit a unique and fascinating one. But she still didn't know him well enough to put out the welcome mat and invite him in.

Besides, Gail would have killed her.

Leah declined Jason's offer of a cigarette and sat quietly while he smoked. She thought the afternoon over. None of the mystery of that earlier September night had been solved or even much discussed. None of her questions had been answered. On the other hand, she'd felt too shy to be specific. Maybe there was no need to be. Jason Horn seemed fine now. Back to normal, whatever that might be for him. Still, it had been a surprisingly pleasant day, Leah conceded. Soon they'd say good night and wish each other well. *Fini.*

Leah was disappointed, and she hadn't expected that. But after all, what more was there? She'd learned that he lived somewhere on the border of Sunset Park. He'd mentioned his sister, so he had family. He could be a killer for all she really knew, although this was a terrible time to suddenly think of that. She didn't believe that, anyway. Leah pulled her sweater coat closer about her and hunched her shoulders.

"Are you cold?" Jason asked, noticing.

"No, I'm fine." She turned to look at him but couldn't see the details of his face in the dark. She could see the cigarette smoke curling over his head, an occasional flash in his eyes.

"What do you do?" he asked suddenly, as if the question had only just occurred to him.

"I do design work. Book jackets and ads. Promotion, some illustrations. I work for a publishing house in Manhattan."

"An artist," he commented, nodding.

"Not really. I'm a graphic designer."

"You're an artist," he repeated firmly.

She shrugged. "I like what I do. It's easy for me.

What about you? I already know you used to work with a scout troop, and you work twenty-four hours a day."

He looked sharply at her.

Leah grinned. "I'm a good listener."

Jason hesitated, taking another puff of the cigarette, almost nervously. "Me? I work with kids."

"Are you a teacher? I bet you teach something like gym and health ed, or coach a team sport. Right? You know, you don't look like a teacher."

He smiled at her quizzically. "What does a teacher look like?"

"Oh . . . harried. Overweight. Resigned. Orthopedic."

He chuckled in amusement and then grew silent. "No, I'm not a teacher."

Jason paused for so long that Leah knew he didn't want to answer and was hoping that the subject would just drop. But the long pause made her all the more interested.

"Well?" she coaxed impatiently.

Jason was looking away, across the street, down the block. Almost anywhere but at Leah. He began to crack the knuckles of his left hand. "I'm a cop."

If Jason was trying to shock her, he succeeded. She could sense that he hadn't wanted to tell her at all because he probably knew what the reaction would be. About that he had been right.

In Jason Horn's experience people reacted a certain way to the police. The reactions were never good. Except in an emergency. People see grim-looking men, mostly white, with guns and handcuffs. Even out of uniform something about them was a dead giveaway as to what they did every day. The police were seen as different. Police were "them" against "us."

Leah had never spoken to a cop in her life. They were people you approached if there was a crisis; you didn't have coffee with them. She felt herself withdrawing. She couldn't help it.

"Surprised?" Jason asked, still not looking at her. Perhaps he knew the look on her face would put them astronomical distances apart.

"Yes," she murmured tightly and felt uncharacteristic anger building. Some of it was unidentifiable and nebulous, but the rest was very clear. She knew how cops treated black folks.

"What are you thinking now?" Jason asked.

For a moment Leah couldn't answer. She just sat stiffly, not looking at him. "The truth? I'm thinking, what the hell am I doing here with you?" She turned to regard him openly. "And I'm thinking about a lot of young black men killed senselessly by police. White police."

Jason shook his head. "Not always senselessly. Sometimes there's good reason and you know it," he said unapologetically.

Leah was taken aback.

Of course. She knew that. But it didn't help. She sat silently as Jason calmly finished his cigarette and tossed the butt into the street. In a nervous gesture he ran his hand through his hair and half turned toward Leah.

"Look, we're the first ones you'd call if you were in trouble. How bad can I be?"

"I don't have a choice, do I?" she asked tightly.

"But I'd be there," he said softly.

I. Not *we.* Leah looked at him finally, seeing a man more sure of himself. He no longer needed sympathy. She no longer wanted to give it. Without any further response, Leah suddenly stood.

Jason reached out and grabbed her arm. Not roughly, but firmly enough to deter her. In that instant their eyes met. Jason wouldn't let go, and slowly Leah sat down again. The short silence that followed was needed, to let go of a tension that had built with astounding speed, and which had to dissipate somehow.

"Are you uncomfortable with me?" Jason asked quietly.

Leah's eyes widened with acknowledgment. "Aren't you?"

Jason half grinned. "No . . ."

Leah felt impatient. This wasn't going right. He should have taken himself off in some sort of defensive huff, the same way she would have a moment ago. But Jason just sat there, as if waiting for the steam to vent itself completely from her.

"What kind of cop are you anyway?" Leah asked.

Jason slowly leaned back against the wrought iron banister, and reached for another cigarette. "A good one . . ." he murmured.

Jason told Leah that he was a juvenile officer, a kiddie cop. Somehow the information allowed Leah to feel he was different from her image of the men in blue. Maybe because she wanted to believe otherwise. She sat and listened to Jason talk about what it was he actually did. Nonetheless, she made a feeble remark, a criticism that didn't come close to damaging his ego.

"I suppose you know you smoke too much."

He shrugged but lit the cigarette anyway.

"You don't look like a cop, either," Leah observed.

Jason grinned. "Still trying to convince yourself I'm okay?"

He was more than half right, and the fact that he could smile about it went a long way toward making Leah relax. She was no longer inclined to leave. She leaned back against the opposite banister from Jason and left all that space between them.

"Why juvenile work? Why not homicide, or narcotics or . . ."

"Some other disgusting vice?" Jason filled in for her. "It's all the same. Juvenile used to mean kids who got into trouble. Now it's criminals who are not of legal age. Everything changed."

"What do you do for them?"

Jason shrugged negligently. "Not much, really. I listen. I talk. I coach sports. It's physical and lets off a lot of energy. If they want to fight, they can fight with me." He smiled at her. "I'm bigger, so I usually win. It's better than having them go out and hurt someone else because they're frustrated and pissed off."

Leah did not know what she had expected Jason to tell her about his work, but it wasn't this. It didn't sound so much like police work as it did social work, a kind of therapy for problem kids. An intervention system between the kids and incarceration.

"Why?" Leah asked.

She could see Jason taking the time to consider the question. Once again he got that faraway look that told Leah he was looking for an honest answer.

"Sometimes I think Americans don't really like kids very much. We have them and then we don't know what to do with them. Kids take time, and they're often a lot of trouble. More and more people aren't willing to be troubled. So what we end up with, what I see too much of, is throwaway kids. I see an awful lot of abandoned, abused, neglected kids that nobody wants. I sometimes wonder, how did it come to this? How did people get from caring enough about each other to create a kid and bring it into the world, to one day deciding they just don't want to be bothered anymore?"

Leah was silent. She was surprised. And she had to admit she was impressed. She'd almost completely forgotten about her indignation of a moment ago as she listened to Jason. He certainly didn't talk like a cop. But she still wondered if he was really all that different from the other cops she'd read about or had seen on the nightly news.

"Do you shoot people?" she found herself asking.

Jason squinted against his cigarette smoke and was thoughtful. "If I have to."

"Have you had to?"

He hesitated and then looked squarely at her. "Yeah. Once."

"At least you're honest," she murmured. Then she felt an overwhelming need to move, to get away and be alone. "I've got to go . . ." she said, standing.

Jason stood as well. "I'd like to see you again," he said easily. "I feel I still owe you an explanation."

Leah shook her head. "You don't have to."

"I'd like to. I'd like to try to tell you what happened in September. I'm still trying to understand myself. How about we go for dinner Friday night and talk about it?"

His question annoyed Leah. He wasn't going to give up. Her expression must have shown that because Jason gave her a wry grin.

"The coffee brought me to my senses, but it didn't cure anything. Maybe I'm still a little out of it."

It occurred to Leah belatedly that Jason was not having any trouble at all with their being together under such odd circumstances. She wondered if she could trust her own sense that he was okay, and that having dinner with him was indeed, no big deal. Leah wanted to see him again because in truth, her curiosity had not abated at all with the afternoon. Discovering that he was a cop had only upped the ante—clear through the roof. Leah wondered if she would have felt the same if he'd actually been a teacher.

"You know, you're getting an awful lot of mileage out of one cup of coffee."

Jason lifted a corner of his mouth in a sad sort of smile. "Maybe. Maybe it wasn't the coffee at all, but the thought that was important. At least to me." He watched her and waited.

Leah finally agreed on a long sigh. "Okay." She began climbing the stairs.

Jason watched her. "It's been an interesting afternoon, Leah Downey."

"That's one way to put it," she said dryly. As she put the key in the door, she half turned to watch Jason as he started to walk away.

"I'll pick you up here at seven. See you Friday." With long, casual strides he was gone.

Gail was simultaneously reading a fashion magazine, watching TV, and polishing her nails when Leah entered the house. She did not hesitate for a second to satisfy her curiosity. "Well?" she began. "Did he get funny on you?"

"I had a police escort the whole afternoon. I couldn't have been safer," Leah responded.

Jason blocked out the babble of the station house routine. The noise no longer drove him crazy because there was never a peaceful moment. He had long since given up expecting an environment conducive to clear thinking and productivity.

A fellow officer had once told Jason that the general public should never get the idea that a police precinct was a pleasant environment. If people found themselves at one, it would not be an enriching experience. It was dreary, intimidating, and cold. It had no attractive rooms, no comfortable furniture, and a lot of skeptical men and women in uniform who'd seen it all, and then some. However, if asked, the officers, down to a man, would probably say that they loved their work. All for different reasons and with different expectations. It would take a lot to convince anyone outside the brotherhood that any of the reasons were altruistic. Being a cop was mostly about power . . . and control. Jason never tried to deny that.

The work was often dirty, boring, and routine. Most of the men never saw any of the adrenaline-pumping action that was fictionalized in movies or reported on TV. What the job gave him and most of the other members of law enforcement was the sense of rightness, toughness, and a perverse involvement in the worst kinds of human and personal tragedy people have to endure.

Yes, he liked being a cop, but he also wondered if he was really just like all the other guys in service. The police force could be seen, and sometimes was, as an exclusive club of misfits, some of whom were doing a truly thankless job. There were also as many cops who delivered babies with confidence, intervened and saved lives and were there when needed, as there were the other kind: those who exercised private vendettas of hate and prejudice and revenge.

And corruption still flourished.

Jason heard the commotion in the hallway before he saw what was going on. He also recognized the voices of the two people involved. One adult, the other a teenager.

The officer who lumbered down the hall toward Jason was of the latter category of cop who hated people just on principle, particularly non-white people. He had not been a high school football player, although he was built like a muscular tank. And he loved to throw his weight around.

Officer Theodore Spano maneuvered in the busy corridors of his station house with ease and authority. His reluctant companion was not as comfortable. Nor was he supposed to be. Spano had one beefy arm around the neck of a youth half his size and age. He pulled the boy by his head down the precinct hallway.

"Common, sucka. Get the fuck off my neck."

Spano dragged the teen carelessly along, and although the boy struggled, he was no match for the bulky cop. No one watching questioned the use of force, and no one had sympathy for the youth. He'd been in and out of the precinct before.

"Shut up, dickhead," Spano muttered as he approached a desk sergeant and handed him a folder of papers. The desk sergeant pointedly ignored the thrashing teen and his shouted curses and threats.

"Git off me, mother fucker. You gonna break my neck," the boy sputtered, his head and shoulders bent at a unnatural angle. His efforts to free himself were useless.

"That's the idea," Spano answered.

Jason stopped in the middle of the hall, directly blocking Spano's path.

"Hey, Jason, man. Help me. This sucka is trying to kill me."

Spano sourly faced Jason. Jason knew that there had never been love lost between the two of them, not even simple respect. He was fully aware that Spano hated him and the work he did. Spano didn't recognize the youth squad as legitimate police work. He considered cops like Jason a bunch of wimp faggots who were afraid to get out on the streets where the real danger was.

"Here's another of your little street turds, Horn."

Jason's eyes narrowed at the way the boy was being treated, and he knew Spano was waiting for him to say something.

"Where'd you find him?" Jason asked calmly.

"There was an attempted robbery of a convenience store this morning. Your boy here was brought in with two others."

"Charges?" Jason asked.

Spano shrugged. "He was there and a gun was recovered."

"That don't prove nothin'. I be outta here . . ."

Jason calmly took over the head lock on the boy, but didn't let up on the pressure or force. Spano turned to walk away.

"No one came to pick him up this time. I don't blame them."

"I'll take him home," Jason said.

"He don't need rehabilitation. He needs a fuckin' cage," Spano said over his shoulder.

"Yo' mama! Eat shit and die," the boy shouted after the retreating officer.

"Shut up, Slack," Jason advised as he pulled the boy into his office.

Jason abruptly released the boy and pushed him roughly toward an empty chair. Slack collapsed as he continued to curse Spano through the open doorway. Jason ignored him as he sat down behind his completely disorganized desk.

Slack rubbed his throat. "You saw him. He tried to kill me, man. I could bring his ass up on charges of police brutality."

Jason continued to ignore the young teen and began searching for something on his desk. He shifted stacks of papers and miscellaneous objects from side to side as he looked.

"Keep still," he ordered Slack.

"Mother fucker . . ." Slack muttered, his body tense with energy as he shifted restlessly in his seat. He glanced up at Jason from under his lids and made an impatient smirk. "Not you, man. That other dude."

"I thought we agreed you'd try to stay out of trouble, Slack," Jason commented, making a note on one piece of paper and starting to look for another.

"I ain't in no trouble. I was just hanging out."

"Why aren't you in school?"

Slack cackled at the foolish idea. "You know school is shit, Jason. I don't learn nothin' there."

"You have a choice. Stay in school or you go upstate."

Slack played with the zipper on his bright orange anorak jacket, indifferent to Jason's veiled threat. "I been upstate."

Jason gave him a brief, thorough once-over. "Nice jacket. Where'd you get it?"

"I didn't steal it. The Mex gave it to me."

"Just because he wanted to be a nice guy?"

Slack grinned broadly. " 'Cause I done him a favor. He owed me."

"You continue to hang out with Razor, Mex, and that bunch, and you're gonna end up dead."

Slack was unconvinced and sat sullenly staring into space. Jason handed him the paper he'd been searching for.

"You never showed up for counseling. What happened?"

Slack merely glanced at the paper. His butt was almost on the edge of the chair as he leaned against the wooden back. He sat with his legs spread wide apart, his knees rocking back and forth. He shrugged. "I was sick, man. Nobody called me or nothin'."

Jason eyed the petulant teen, trying not to lose his temper, trying hard not to just give up. He wanted to believe that Slack only needed time to realize that he was on his side. "I called. I spoke to your grandmother. She said she hadn't seen you in a week."

A sly and slightly embarrassed grin appeared on

Slack's oak brown face, adorned with straggling chin hair and a very thin mustache. "Oh, shit," he chuckled. "She gave me up. That's cold." He licked his lips and the grin disappeared. He'd been caught in his lie. But still he shook his head. "That ain't right. I was sick. I swear, Jason."

Jason sat back in his chair and watched Slack closely. The boy was incredibly street smart. Too smart for his own good, since he made so many stupid decisions. Jason sighed. He'd been having a hard time trying to get Slack to think before he acted out, to control his quick temper and his tendency to hurt and destroy. Jason pushed back farther in his chair and let it rock gently.

"So, I'm hearing that if I set up the appointment again, you'll keep it. Correct?"

Slack nodded but wouldn't look Jason in the face. "Yeah, man. I'll go."

"What about this morning?"

Slack was shaking his head again. "I was outside the store and I didn't have no gun. I'm not trippin' on you, man."

Jason said nothing but continued to stare and to gauge Slack coldly. The boy finally got serious. He leaned toward Jason and he put up his hand with the fingers spread.

"I'm telling you the truth. I didn't have no gun."

Jason dropped his gaze to the pen he'd absently been playing with. "You understand what I could do if you're lying to me?"

"Yeah," Slack said sullenly.

Jason let the silence and his disbelief stretch out until Slack stopped posturing and cut his game. The boy looked at him squarely.

"I didn't have no gun," Slack repeated slowly.

After another moment Jason threw the pen onto the desk. "Wait outside. I'll drive you home later."

Slack jumped up from his chair and headed for the door and freedom. But he suddenly stopped and turned back to Jason.

"Hey, man. You got a coupla dollars you can lend me?"

Jason hesitated but finally dug into his pocket for a five dollar bill. He extended the money and Slack grabbed for it. Jason held firmly to his end. "You'll keep the appointment this time, right?"

Slack sneered. "For five bucks?" Jason held fast. "Yeah, right," he said, snatching the bill and taking off.

He just missed colliding with a man coming through the door. Joe Wagner cursed as Slack adroitly ducked under the big man's arm, causing Joe to fumble several bags that he carried. His dark face, with its broad features, thick black mustache, and eyebrows, registered annoyance that was just as quickly gone.

Joe was Jason's office roomie and his sometime partner. He came into the office weighed down with a huge McDonald's take-out bag and an armful of file folders. He carelessly pushed an already existing pile of papers to one side of his desk to make room for his lunch. He sat down heavily in a wooden desk chair set on casters. The chair groaned and squeaked. Digging into the bag for a Big Mac, Joe looked at Jason.

"You realize you're contributing to the delinquency of a minor."

Jason picked up a basketball from the floor and tossed it to Joe. "At least he didn't steal it. I'm making real progress. It's an investment in his future."

Joe easily caught the ball and quickly returned it across the room. "He ain't got a future."

"You could help me on this one. Slack's a tough

case, but I'm not ready to throw in the towel, yet. Why don't you talk to him?"

Joe grunted, taking a mammoth bite out of his burger. " 'Cause it's too late to talk to him. I'm telling you, Jace. The kid is probably crazy. He can't be trusted." He took another bite of the burger and reached for the last two in the bag. He carelessly tossed one to Jason, who caught it easily. "So, how was Brooklyn?"

Jason's response was slow in coming, and even then his voice was uneasy. "Her name is Leah Downey."

"Don't matter. She's just conquered territory."

"I didn't conquer her," Jason defended patiently, opening the burger. "Besides, you only noticed 'cause she's black."

"You mean *you* only noticed because she's black."

Jason raised his brows. "You got something against black people?"

Joe scowled at him.

"Give me a break, okay?" Jason murmured. "I need this grief over a cup of coffee?"

"You don't know what grief is, man. First it's coffee. Before you know it it's something else. You comin' over for Thanksgiving? Nora got this big old sucka to roast."

"Now, that's mighty white of you, sah," Jason drawled.

Joe chuckled, nearly choking on the burger. "Fuck you . . ."

As soon as Slack thought Jason's car had left the block, he turned back from the entrance of his grandmother's building and headed toward the street. He knew he couldn't risk doing anything in the lobby. Too many people knew his grandmother, and knew his reputation. If the old lady had tripped on him once, she'd do it again. But Slack knew he had to get some bucks from somewhere. There was stuff he needed.

Slack stood under the deteriorating entrance arc with the name BATTENCOURT embossed in cement across the top. Much of the name, however, had been chipped or eroded away; all of it was covered with several layers of graffiti. Slack glanced up and down the street and decided there were at least three opportunities waiting for him. He picked the easiest one.

"Yeah," Slack drawled confidently. He walked to the narrow alleyway between his grandmother's building and the one next door. It was where the garbage was kept for pickup and reeked of debris, urine, food, and animal wastes. He carefully stepped over the mess and headed for the super's storage room. He found a clean garbage bag and, taking off his expensive jacket, carefully wrapped it so it wouldn't get dirty or noticed, and hid it away. Next, he turned his cap around so that the beak was in front and shadowed most of his face. Then he went back into the street.

Slack didn't have time for anything fancy. And he was impatient to be done, to make up for what he hadn't gotten that morning. As he scouted out his target again, he was feeling good. He felt righteous because he hadn't lied to Jason about the coat, and he had told the truth about the gun. He was ready to reward himself.

An old man crossed the street carrying a heavy shopping bag in one hand. He walked slowly and leaned heavily on a cane in the other hand. Slack stood unnoticed in the front overhang of a deserted building and watched until the old man reached another building a few hundred feet away. When he finally got inside the front door, Slack left his cover and quickly followed.

He reached the building as the slow older man was inside the lobby. He'd put down his bag to get his keys. Slack picked up the bag and pushed the door open.

"I got it," he said.

The man mumbled thank you as the door closed behind them.

"This way?" Slack asked. But without waiting, he headed to the back of the long hallway and the space underneath the staircase.

"Wait a minute. Where you think you're going with that?" the old man called out, hastening after the teen.

"Right here, old man. I don't want your food," Slack said.

But when the man caught up to him, in the darkened back of the hallway where there were no apartments, Slack threw the bag aside, spilling the groceries. He pushed the man into the grimy stucco wall.

"What—what's going on?"

"Shut up! Gimme your money."

"I don't have any."

"Bullshit!" Slack held the old man to the wall with one hand. He snatched the cane from his hand and dropped it. With quick expertise Slack located the worn canvas wallet with its Velcro opening in the inside coat pocket.

Within seconds Slack had withdrawn the bills and thrown the wallet to the floor as well.

"What . . . what you gonna do?" the man asked nervously, but Slack wasn't paying attention.

"Shit," he muttered in disgust. Twenty-seven dollars. Chump change. Then he remembered that Jason had given him five. Thirty-two dollars was better than empty pockets.

He pushed the old man once more, just for good measure. He casually folded the bills and stuffed them into his pocket. He left the building unseen. Slack went back to get his coat, turned his hat backward, and walked to Dunkin Donuts two blocks away to get something to eat.

It was only four-thirty when Jason got back to the precinct from taking Slack to the Bronx. Joe was sitting on the edge of his desk, bouncing the basketball on the floor between his legs. Jason stood for a second watching Joe. He'd learned a long time ago to recognize that when Joe had something to say, something touchy and personal, he fidgeted with things. Whatever was near at hand. Back in September when Jason had gotten the call over his car phone to return to the precinct, it had been to find his partner folding paper airplanes and sailing them across the office. Jason recalled that when he'd come into the office and asked, "What's up?" there had been about a dozen of them all over the floor and file cabinets. It had been very bad news that Joe had for him that day.

Seeing Joe toy with the basketball didn't particularly bother Jason. He figured nothing in his life could be as bad as that day in September.

"Something on your mind?" Jason asked as he returned to his desk.

Joe shook his head. "Didn't mean to lecture you about this black woman, man, but I can smell trouble gathering like storm clouds."

"You're seeing problems that are never going to happen. All I did was to introduce myself to her."

"You gonna see her again?"

"I don't know," Jason said evasively.

Joe stopped bouncing the ball and glanced at Jason. "Look, people are going to notice if you're interested in the woman. You can say it was just coffee all you want, but I know a man with an itch when I see one."

Jason sat back in his chair until the seat tilted at an angle. He propped his feet on the edge of the desk and, clasping his hands behind his head, listened thoughtfully. Joe let the ball roll off the tips of his fingers. It bounced once or twice more and settled in a corner.

"Know what I'm saying?" Joe added quietly.

Jason sighed. He knew. He'd found out about the few itches Joe himself had had over the years. Joe had even joked once that he knew which ones to scratch. But he had always stayed in his own territory. Then again, Jason considered, he had always thought Joe a damned fool for the way he'd hurt Nora, and almost lost her. After that he'd stopped fooling around with other women. But Jason wasn't married, and he knew there wasn't anyone he could hurt.

"Why are you so protective over someone you don't even know? Don't even like, far as I can tell."

Joe examined his hands for a moment and then looked seriously at Jason. "Tribal instinct. Shit like that. I know that a healthy, good-looking guy like you gets all kinds of offers. You can have your pick, Jace. But not with someone like this Leah person. People get crazy over that. And if you don't know any better, Leah Downey sure should."

Jason grimaced. He didn't believe any of that applied to him. This wasn't about hitting skin and becoming a ghost, Jason thought with amusement, using a turn of phrase he'd picked up from one of his incorrigibles.

"Are you speaking from your great wealth of experience?" he asked Joe with a crooked grin.

Joe sighed audibly in defeat and slowly got up from his perch on the desk. Jason watched him closely. Joe had been his partner for seven years, ever since Joe's old partner, Leon, had been killed. It had not been some tough on-the-job incident, either. Leon had drowned while on vacation one summer with his family.

Joe was well aware that Jason held no preconceived ideas about anyone. He took people at face value, gave them the benefit of the doubt until proven wrong. It made for a lousy character trait in a cop, Joe had once said—but made Jason an honest human being.

"Listen, Joe. You gotta trust that I won't do something really dumb, you know?"

Joe sat at his desk. He frowned as he thought about it. Finally he made a helpless kind of gesture, lifting his hands and shoulders. "Jace, I trust you with my life. But I don't trust your judgment where someone like this Brooklyn dame is concerned."

Jason sprang forward impatiently in his seat, dropping his feet to the floor. "You're blowing this whole thing way out of proportion. Nothing's going to happen, for Christ's sake."

"Let's not bring the Lord into this. Far as I'm concerned, he's kept a pretty low profile on what we do to each other down here." Joe leaned forward over his desk. He and Jason faced each other squarely. "I also believe that the Civil Rights Bill is mostly a piece of paper. Reality is something else, and I shouldn't have to tell you that not everybody's equal. Lots of folks ain't treated like they were. There is a brick wall out there that you're going to crash right into. Remember, you heard it here first."

Jason shifted his gaze away. It was clear that Joe understood only the bottom line. And maybe Jason couldn't blame him. Double standards prevailed. It had much less to do with what a person was at birth than what happened in all the years afterward.

He'd been forewarned.

Chapter Three

Jill tilted her head as she chewed thoughtfully on her sandwich. She studied the three mock-ups of covers that Leah had spread out over the conference table.

"What do you think?" Leah asked as she sipped from her can of soda.

"I'm thinking that we should have gone out to lunch so I wouldn't have to make a decision yet." Jill lifted the tissue flap on one of the boards and examined the work. "This one is interesting. The book is about office conflict between male and female co-workers. The idea of half the cover bleeding fabric that's supposed to be a man's suit, and the other half fabric of a woman's dress, is eye catching."

Leah shook her head. "Wrong."

"Why?"

"Because the page is divided exactly in half. Visually it's very disturbing. Graphically it's a cheap way out. And the colors . . . men wear gray suits. Women never wear gray. You will *not* find the color gray in their wardrobe, even for business."

As she talked, she pulled out a fourth board from under the pile. The cover showed one of the basic accouterments of work. She gave the board to Jill. "How about this one?"

"Neat. Simple. Clear," Jill said, nodding slowly. "This makes more sense. Two attachés . . . his and hers."

Leah chuckled and tapped the board. "Wrong again. One attaché and one tote. His and hers. Much more subtle but easy to recognize."

Jill pursed her lips. "You're right, you're right. Okay, go ahead and finish it."

"Thanks. If I'd known you were going to be so easy, I would have—"

"What do you think of Peter?"

Leah blinked. "Peter Condon? The editor? I don't know him very well. Seems nice, why?"

Jill sighed. "He asked me out."

"Did you accept?"

"Not yet. I'm thinking about it."

"What's to think about?" Leah asked.

"Whether or not I want to go through all that."

"I don't get it."

"Dating. Putting yourself out here. Starting over."

"Oh," Leah murmured. Jason immediately came to mind. But they weren't dating. They were just . . .

"I don't know if I can take the anxiety."

Leah grimaced and took a small bite of her sandwich. "I know what you mean."

Jill glanced at her. "How could you? You've been seeing one man for two years. You're set. You don't have to be out there anymore."

Leah felt slightly irritated that her life had been so neatly packaged. She and Allen hadn't come to any understanding. They hadn't made any plans. They'd never talked about the future. He was still free; so was she. She looked at Jill.

"What makes you think I couldn't get interested in someone else?"

Jill seemed taken aback. "Are you?"

For a second Leah thought about telling Jill about Jason Horn, but she wasn't ready to share that information yet. She had a desire to keep it private not because she thought anything was actually happening, but precisely because she believed that nothing was. She didn't want to explain a random encounter.

Leah shrugged. "It doesn't much matter. Gail says no one dates anymore anyway."

Jill chuckled in amusement. "Oh, really? Then what the hell is going on between men and women?"

Leah sat back in her chair and chewed on the end of the straw. "They circle around each other like predatory animals. They try to figure out who's going to make the first move."

"The guys still get to make the first call, I don't care what the women's magazines say."

"That's true, but we still get to say no if he's a jerk"— they looked at each other and grinned, finishing together—"like Mike."

"The thing is, if you wait until someone great comes along, you might never date at all," Jill lamented.

"There are some interesting guys out there," Leah said absently, thinking again of Jason. She was, nonetheless, experiencing trepidation and curiosity about what the coming evening would be like with him. "Peter Condon is probably an interesting guy."

"Maybe. But men expect so much."

Leah raised her brows. "Don't we? Shouldn't we?"

Jill was thoughtful for a time. "You're right," she finally sighed. "I'll say yes. What have I got to lose?"

What indeed? Leah repeated to herself several hours later as she stood in front of her open closet, eyeing the neat line of clothing. Her sage words of advice to Jill notwithstanding, she was beginning to feel something akin to panic. She was agonizing over what she should wear for the evening with Jason.

If this wasn't a date, what was it?

Was Jason likely to suggest pizza or Chinese? Did

he like Mexican or Japanese? Or would he want something more upscale? Leah sighed as she removed items of clothing almost randomly. She was going to be severely disappointed if there wasn't at least a tablecloth.

Jason took her to the kind of place that could be said to have atmosphere. There were candles in the center of each table, the soft lighting effectively disguising the slightly shabby but comfortable and laid-back setting. The tables were spaced far enough apart so that they didn't have to listen to the couple at the next table. The waiter didn't try to rush them through their dinner, and they were there for hours. Even better, it was in the West Village and no one paid any attention to the fact that they were a mixed couple. She wondered if Jason's choice of restaurant had been deliberate. It wasn't at all what she would have expected from him, but then everything about Jason had so far been unexpected.

All through dinner they kept to light banter and safe questions, but Jason ordered another bottle of wine, and the talk finally became reflective and personal. Leah made the first move.

"Where are you from originally?" she asked him.

He drew on the ever present cigarette and tapped the ash into the ashtray. "Pennsylvania. Harrisburg. My sister and her family still live there. My parents are both dead."

Leah lowered her gaze to the pale yellow liquid in her glass. Rhine wine. He'd remembered. She hoped Jason was going to tell her more. She wanted to know how he'd come to be in New York, why he'd become a cop. When she glanced at him again, she found Jason watching her, waiting. He was going to make her ask the one compelling question.

"Are you married?"

"Divorced. It's been about ten years. I was going to

be an engineer," he continued smoothly, "but became a cop instead. In between was Vietnam."

"You seem a little young to have been there."

"I was among the last in. One of the lucky ones to get out."

"Yes," she murmured softly.

"My son, Michael, was born while I was overseas," Jason stated. He didn't add that Michael was almost two when he'd come home or that his son didn't know who he was. Jason looked at Leah, saw a certain understanding in her eyes, and wondered if she really did. He also didn't tell her that after he got home was when his life really fell apart. He didn't tell her how all of his perceptions and his future had changed because of his tour in-country.

For a moment Jason's mind drifted back to the confusion of those first years back home with Lisa and Michael. Pursuing the engineering program had seemed pointless. When he came back to the States he saw an entirely different kind of war being waged on American soil. The results were the same. Children were being lost.

He joined the police academy and became a cop.

He found his way into the juvenile division and stayed. He also brought his work home with him at night. Literally. All the strays from family court and juvenile detention. It got so that the local precinct would call him first when another lost kid came through the door. His wife hated every one of them.

Lisa was quick to point out to him that he had a son now, and it was time he put his family first above helping others. Jason knew she was right. But Michael was safe with parents who loved him. The kids Jason came across every day had nothing. He tried to stop being a depository for problem kids, but it didn't happen soon enough. Lisa moved back to Pennsylvania, taking Michael with her. She filed for a divorce, citing unreconcilable differences. About that, at least, she'd been right.

Jason looked at the end of his cigarette and then at Leah. "I came to New York because I knew it would be tough. I knew the real challenge was here. I knew it was going to be hard to succeed."

"Have you?" she asked quizzically.

Jason nodded slowly. "Sometimes," he said quietly. But he'd never really been sure if he could be proud about any of it. After all, he had failed his wife and son.

Leah sat staring at Jason. She hadn't expected him to stop talking so abruptly. She sighed and took a deep breath, not even realizing that she'd been holding it. The ashtray between them was filled with butts and ashes. The second bottle of wine was almost gone. Leah was afraid to move or to say anything that would break the spell. And she was relieved and eager when Jason began quietly talking once more.

"After the divorce I'd try to see Mike as much as I could. It was hard. His mother didn't want him in New York, didn't want him being influenced and hassled by 'niggers and spics' . . ." He used his index fingers to put quotes around the phrasing.

Leah still reacted with a stiffening of her spine and narrowing of her eyes. Jason ignored it and continued.

"Lisa thought she could keep Michael safe and wholesome in Pennsylvania, but I thought when he got older, maybe he'd want to come and live with me anyway."

Leah was once again caught up in his story, except she could hear a tightening in Jason's voice. A strain that indicated emotions still hovering on the edge. He'd come so far and the end of the story was near. She suddenly felt an intense awareness.

"Jason . . ." she began very gently. "You don't have to tell me every . . ."

"In September I was just leaving family court when I got the call to return to the precinct. Mike had been killed in a school bus accident while on an outing. Three other kids died as well." The words were said calmly enough, but Jason lifted his head and rested his chin on clenched hands, the left one still holding a long-forgotten cigarette with the ash hanging precariously on the end. He looked at Leah with pain in his eyes, and she knew he wasn't really seeing her.

"I left the precinct alone. I shouldn't have, but at the time I didn't want anyone with me. Not even Joe, my partner. I was thinking, why did it have to be Mike? Why couldn't it have been me? I found a bar and had a couple of drinks. I thought I felt better, that I could handle it. Then I stopped somewhere else and had a few more. I lost count after that," Jason said, finally flicking his ash into the tray. "I don't even remember driving down to Pennsylvania that day. I don't remember coming back to New York," Jason murmured. "For the next two days I did nothing but drink and have bad dreams about kids." He took a long drag on the cigarette and shifted his attention back to Leah. He frowned slightly. "I have no idea how I got into your block. I don't remember it all. It's three miles from where I work. I do remember there were kids playing stickball in the street." Jason chuckled softly. "Do you know I never even heard of stickball until I came to New York?"

Leah knew there were no comforting words to say, nothing that would ease the loss. She signaled the waiter and ordered coffee. And she told him about Kenny.

Had her brother, Kenneth, lived he would have been forty-three. He'd been twelve years older than her, and he'd died in Vietnam. She and Gail, even their father, never talked much about Kenny anymore, Leah realized. She remembered him as an older giant in her life who'd been patient, protective, and loving. He'd wanted to be a lawyer, but was never to finish law school. Leah wondered aloud, for the first time, if her brother's aspirations would have changed if he'd survived the war the way Jason had. She did remember Kenny being angry about having to go to Vietnam.

"He was just like the rest of us, then," Jason murmured. "Confused and scared. I mean, nobody understood why we were there. Most of us were just kids, but we had some vague thought that we were supposed to wipe out the enemy, kick some ass and keep the world free of communism. While we were over there we didn't always understand who the enemy was. We just wanted to get home. It was a hell of a place. Hot. Wet. Miserable . . ."

"But you did come home," Leah reminded Jason quietly.

"Yeah. I came home," he whispered, lapsing into silence.

When Jason took her back to Brooklyn, Leah invited him into the house, but he said no. In a way she was relieved.

"Thanks for dinner. And thank you for telling me, you know . . . what happened. It must have been very difficult to share so much with a stranger." She had a sense of surrealism about the evening; it seemed odd that it had even taken place.

Jason just smiled. "We split two bottles of wine tonight. I don't think we're strangers."

In the soft lamplight his eyes were dark and unreadable, but he made Leah feel suddenly exposed. Yet there was a comfortable warmth to them as well. Absently Leah supposed that this evening would end their connection. Jason would go back to his wayward kids, perhaps doing for them what he hadn't done for his own son. But he took a step closer into her space, and alarm signals went up. He looked carefully at her.

"You *are* a good listener. I like talking to you. Am I going to see you again?"

Leah hoped that skepticism was branded like stone in her eyes. She wanted Jason to see it. She wanted him to see *her,* to see what this really meant. She knew instinctively there was danger ahead. How could there not be? She'd thought that Jason would say he too had enjoyed their dinner and a chance to get to know her. And then that was supposed to be it.

Leah shifted her weight from one foot to the next. "Jason . . ." she began, but then didn't know how to put into words her hesitation. Was he going to force her to be obvious?

"There's no commitment." He shrugged easily. "There can't be any harm. Have you ever been to a hockey game?"

Leah wasn't even sure she knew what hockey was. The question so completely threw her off guard that she only shook her head blankly. Hockey was not a sport that little black girls from Brooklyn knew anything about.

"Tell you what. I'll call you after Thanksgiving," Jason suggested. "Maybe we'll go."

Leah didn't answer him as he waved good night and turned to walk away. She couldn't. She just stared after his retreating form. Jason hadn't made any promises. He'd only asked a question, but then he'd left before getting her answer. Maybe he'd expected her to say no, Leah speculated. So why hadn't she? Because only now that Jason was gone did she recognize that inside her mind was a consideration born of a present hope and past disappointment.

In the cozy quiet of her darkened bedroom late that night, Leah knew that sleep was futile. She was curled up under the covers, but instead of being lulled into rest she was wired and alert and fully awake. Her eyes, as a matter of fact, were wide open, although she stared at nothing in particular. Just into space and blackened corners.

As she lay quietly and reflectively she admitted, with a kind of awed surprise, that Jason Horn was the most fascinating man she'd ever met. Their initial encounter and subsequent meeting seemed a complete fantasy, a bizarre twist of fate. They were actually getting to know each other. And she wanted to know more. To Leah, the black and white differences between them didn't seem to be an issue that needed exploration, since she had no expectations that their acquaintance was going anywhere. She could handle it. Obviously, so could Jason. However, she knew it wouldn't stay that way if she saw him again.

The recounting of Jason Horn's life had stirred the embers of her own past. And while she'd felt no need to air the details to Jason, she now lay awake with a score of characters and events appearing from the recesses of her life. Being with him tonight had begun the dredging, because a comparison was forming, despite her best efforts. There had only been a select few males that Leah had ever truly been interested in. Relationships that had all the earmarks and potential for being more than friendship. She had made emotional investments in each one with good, bad, and unexpected results.

When she had been fifteen years old, she fell madly in love with a boy in her ninth-grade class. His name was Billy. He'd never taken her out, never had lunch with her, and had only waited once for her after school. She'd fantasized that one day Billy would marry her.

Leah finally got over Billy at nineteen when he got married to a girl he'd met in church.

She lost her virginity her first year in college. Ron had been twenty-five and a graduate student working on a master's in political science. He was mature, worldly, handsome, and smart. He was also one very angry black man. Ron was verbose and eloquent about the historical injustices done to blacks in America, and spent a lot of time feeling cheated and vengeful. It had been exciting to listen to him speak at first, as he grabbed the attention of a group of coeds and fired them up with his rhetoric and ideas. But Ron ultimately had only one thought, and to Leah it had been singularly depressing. Things certainly weren't all that good for a lot of blacks in America, but to her mind it was by no means a hopeless situation requiring revolution and a call to arms.

In the final analysis Leah's relationship with Ron was mostly physical. She had enjoyed his lovemaking, had felt breathless with his inventiveness and willingness to teach her the pleasures of her body and his. But sex, too, was sometimes as quick and angry as Ron himself. They finally broke up when Ron decided that being nonviolent was not going to get him where he wanted to be. He also decided after a year and a half with her that she was bourgeois and an elitist, unaware and uninvolved. His accusations had stung deep. Questioning her loyalties, her priorities, her identity. Leah had spent the next two years marching and protesting on one advocacy issue after another to prove him wrong.

During the summer session in her junior year, Leah had met Philip. He was thin, wore glasses, was serious . . . and he was white. He'd sat next to her in Spanish class. She'd never even noticed him until halfway through the five-week session he'd leaned over her desk and asked for the translation of a joke the instructor had just recited. Leah had been the only one in class to laugh, being the only one who understood. That night Philip drove her to the subway, but after that, until the very end of the term, he took her all the way home to Brooklyn after each class. She'd lent him her notebooks so he could study, and still he found it hard to keep up. Leah had suggested that he switch to French.

Philip took her out one night on a date. Leah had agreed readily enough, feeling a youthful willingness to ignore conventions. Interracial dating had not yet caught on. They'd gone to Sullivan Street to see a play called *The Fantastiks*. They had dinner at an Italian restaurant and ran into a cousin of Philip's and her date outside the theater afterward. The cousin was pleasant, but Leah could see she was curious as to why Philip was out with a black woman.

When the two couples had separated later in the evening, Philip and Leah drove through Central Park and ended up in the dark near the boat basin making out. She had the hell bitten out of her bare legs by mosquitoes, but at the time she had not cared. She thought she might be in love again. It didn't bother her particularly that Philip was white and she was black. As a matter of fact, it was not mentioned even once between them.

Philip said that he wanted to take her to a famous tavern in the Village to celebrate the end of the semester, and Leah looked forward to it. They took the final exam in the college auditorium with three hundred other students. Leah finished first and then waited an hour for Philip to be done. They got into Philip's car . . . and he drove her home to Brooklyn. He said good night and promised that he'd call her soon. Leah never saw or heard from him again. For years after she wondered what she'd done wrong. Worse, Leah agonized if spending time with her had just been some sort of experiment for him.

She'd made an analogy between Philip and Jason the first time Jason had asked her out for coffee. She'd wondered if he'd really show up. When Jason had asked her out again, she had known by the time Jason had brought her home that all similarities had ended. Now she lay in bed wondering what she was getting herself into.

And, of course, there was Allen.

Two years ago she and Gail had met Allen at the opening show of silk-screen prints by an artist and mutual friend. Allen had seemed at the time more taken with Gail, but it was Leah he'd asked out and whom he'd begun to date steadily. Leah found Allen good company and intelligent, even if a little stiff and pompous at times. Allen treated her well enough and didn't make many demands. Neither did Leah ever have many thoughts of wanting more for herself. Allen became a pattern, a fixture, along with other things in her life, like her job and friends and family. He was comfortable to be with . . . and he was black.

What thoughts Leah had given to the patterns of her life and to the future didn't necessarily include Allen, but it didn't exclude him either. The pattern for the time being was set: routine, pleasant, and predictable. If she wasn't insanely happy she was, at least, content.

But Jason Horn was an almost perfect stranger whom, she was afraid, she rather liked. Jason wasn't what she was used to, and that was a big part of the problem. He didn't fit anywhere into the patterns. And if they were to go on meeting each other, she'd have to rethink *content,* and rethink the future and the patterns of her life. She would have to rethink expectations, and reconsider history. Leah recognized that most certainly her life would change.

The patterns would be broken.

Leah was not the only one with unexpected reflections on the evening. Jason walked away from the brownstone feeling a combination of surprise and confusion. Had he really just asked her out again?

Why?

He pushed his hands through his dark hair. The afternoon coffee a week ago with Leah Downey had been nice. Tonight had been even nicer. But Jason had not anticipated anything beyond that. It had just slipped out. Well, maybe not. *Am I going to see you again?*

Jason tried to remember the last time he'd been with a new woman without feeling he had to pretend to be someone he wasn't. Had he asked Leah Downey out again because he felt relieved?

He decided he didn't have the patience to deal with the subway again to get home. All that peeling back of scabs over the wounds of his life left him feeling exposed. And hyper. He decided to walk home.

He was astounded that he'd revealed so much of himself. He'd really put himself out there, on display. Voluntarily.

Again, why?

Because he knew instinctively that he could not be less than honest. Leah had already seen him at his worst.

His ex-wife, Lisa, came to mind. He thought of his son. Michael had had such promise, so much potential. He was a great kid. Had been. They'd seen each other just two weeks before the accident, and now Jason would never see him again.

Shaking his head to clear it, Jason took a deep breath. He could feel the tension quickly dissolving as it turned into remorse and reflection. Suddenly, all kinds of events from the past three months came rushing back to him, like a film playing in fast forward. That afternoon in particular when Joe had tried to ease the bad news to him about the phone call and Michael's accident. Jason's first thought had been to wonder why Lisa hadn't told him herself. And then losing himself for almost four days, to the pain of helplessness and guilt. To anger and regret.

Jason felt the pain returning.

He was walking not fast but at a steady pace. He was trying hard not to slip into melancholia over the past. Losing Michael. And other kids. He thought about something Leah had asked him at their first meeting, and suddenly recalled, in painful details, the black teenager he'd shot five years go while trying to separate a street gang fight. He was always to wonder if he could have done something else besides use his gun. Something else besides act on instincts he'd learned to use in war.

Once back in the dark of his apartment, Jason moved toward the refrigerator in his narrow kitchenette. He took out a can of beer and wandered back into the combination living room and bedroom of the studio apartment. His bed was a queen-size mattress on a wooden platform, low to the floor. He sat on the edge and felt his thoughts swinging dizzily back and forth between the past and the present. On a stool next to the bed that he used as a nightstand he reached for a pack of cigarettes.

His attention was caught by a propped-up postcard of the Golden Gate Bridge in San Francisco. It was from a redheaded dancer he'd met last spring at the precinct when she'd come in to report a stolen bike. They'd become lovers. Jason had been enthralled with her because she did things with her life. He'd loved her uninhibited freedom of spirit. She'd left for California in September to dance in a musical. Jason picked up the card and read once again the bright but impersonal message on the back. He put it down again. She had talent and was going places. She also had a temper. Jason remembered her passion and liveliness right in this very bed. He remembered her telling him that there were other men in her life, and she didn't want any heavy relationship. So he saw her when he saw her, and enjoyed their time together. It used to be enough.

Jason's thoughts switched back to Leah Downey. He'd never dated a black woman before. He didn't even know any beyond Joe's wife, Nora, and a few of the women officers at the precinct. But that was different. And he honestly wasn't sure if Leah's being black made a difference. Jason was aware of the prejudice—toward black people, and Latinos and Asians and Arabs and anyone else who wasn't white—some of his fellow officers shared. The talk had always made him uneasy.

He liked the way Leah Downey listened. Intently, with her eyes on him. That's the way he talked to his groups. He looked them right in the eye. Jason thought she smiled nicely, easily. Not coquettish. No games. No pretense. He liked that, too. She didn't ask a lot of questions, but she responded with her complete attention, to everything he said. That interested him. Which still didn't come close to any reason to ask her out again.

But he had. Jason finished the cigarette and lit another. He sat in the dark and sipped his beer while staring at nothing in particular as he tried to figure out if Leah Downey was really all that special.

Chapter Four

For Thanksgiving dinner Gail invited her photographer friend, Steven, and Leah was expecting Allen. The day was gray and cold, but the smell of a dozen different foods filled the house with a warm, homey aroma. Gail, who'd offered to do most of the cooking, was anything but humble and home-like as she emerged from the kitchen at noon hot, bothered, and ill tempered.

Leah tried to soothe Gail as she set the table. But with most of the work done, Gail sprawled on the sofa and eventually dozed off for a nap.

Leah left her there and went to start the dessert. The kitchen, as was usually the case when Gail cooked, was a wreck. Leah began to clean up the mess. She had just finished putting away a handful of freshly washed utensils when she got a frantic visit from Biddy Rosen. Her widowed neighbor, who had a tendency toward over-worry and theatrics, had worked herself into near apoplexy over her preparation for dinner. Leah knew, however, that it wasn't the cooking. It was that her son, Harold, who was gay, was bringing home his lover.

The older woman's cheeks were flushed. The absurd wig she wore to disguise thinning gray hair was slightly out of place, giving her what Leah thought was a distracted air. Leah had barely opened the door when

Biddy rushed through. She grabbed Leah's hand and stared up at her with a plaintive expression.

"Help me," Biddy wailed so comically that Leah burst into laughter and assured her neighbor she would.

Biddy launched into a nearly unintelligible monologue about pearl onions, white sauce, good china, and a fear of making decent gravy that bespoke sure doom. She was also complaining that she didn't have a roasting pan big enough for her turkey. She had dashed across the street in nothing more than an old sweater with a grimy apron tied around her broad waist. Biddy followed Leah into the kitchen, pulling her hairpiece into place.

"Honestly, I don't know why I said I'd to this. Harold is coming, and he's bringing a friend."

Leah smiled as she hunted around the kitchen for a pan to lend her neighbor. "You sound like Gail. You could have said no. Next year let Harold cook for *you*."

But it was clear from Biddy's harassed expression that doing everything right was important to her. She was anxious that she and her son celebrate the holiday as everyone else was doing, like other families. As Leah listened to a steady stream of nervous chatter she resorted to the cooking sherry, pouring the other woman a healthy glassful. Biddy sat in a chair fanning herself with a tail of her apron.

"You know, when Harold was a little boy, you could have given him a hot dog with mustard and he'd have been just as happy. What did he know from cranberry sauce and turnips? My husband's family would come over. We'd have a house filled with quarreling relatives and antsy kids, there'd be all this food, and Harold would only want a hot dog."

"So, give him hot dogs. Maybe nothing's changed."

Biddy looked aghast. "I couldn't do that. He'd disown

me. Worse yet, he'd probably say, 'How embarrassing, how unpatriotic' or something like that." Biddy did a perfect imitation of her son, showing with humor that she'd made her peace long ago with her only child's way of life.

Leah rinsed out a pan for Biddy, who, suddenly remembering she'd left potatoes boiling on her stove, grabbed it dripping wet to race out of the house. The slamming door awakened Gail, who came into the kitchen in a much better mood than when she'd left.

"Mmmmm, it does smell good in here. Did you make a sweet potato pie for dessert?" she asked, opening the oven to peek inside.

"No. Apple. If you're going upstairs to take a shower and change, will you please bring down some linen napkins from the closet? And some candles."

Gail grimaced. "Candles? For Steven? Why waste them?"

"It'll look nice. Besides, Allen likes candles."

Gail chortled as she left the kitchen. "He ain't worth it, either," she muttered behind her back.

When Steven and Allen arrived, there were fresh flowers in the hallway, den, and living room. There were candles burning on the sideboard and dining room table. Allen, remembering Steven from the boutique opening, took an instant dislike to him.

To Steven's credit, he was only amused. He shook hands with Allen after giving him a thorough once-over and proceeded to ignore him the rest of the night. Steven's only indication as to what he thought of Leah's boyfriend was to whisper to Gail, "The man is lame."

The four of them sat and had drinks. Gail was more charming than the evening called for, flirting back and forth between the two men, talking and laughing nonstop.

Steven managed to seat himself next to Leah and monopolized her attention. Leah decided that she didn't care for him very much for no other reason than he seemed to find everything and everyone so amusing. And she vaguely thought him disloyal to Gail for ignoring her. But Gail didn't seem to mind. As a matter of fact, she and Allen were getting on better than usual, for which Leah was grateful.

"So . . ." Steven began, his arm stretched behind her on the sofa back. "Tell me about yourself."

There's nothing to tell."

"If you're related to Gail, there must be," he said dryly, glancing briefly in Gail's direction. "Are you in fashion also?"

"No, I'm not."

"That's too bad. You'd make a terrific show house model."

Leah smiled politely.

"I'd really like to take pictures of you sometime. You've got good bone structure. Wonderful legs. Would you pose for me?" he asked smoothly.

It was such a bad come-on that Leah was inclined to think he was serious. "I don't photograph very well. Why not use Gail? She loves to have her picture taken."

"Yeah, I know." Steven chuckled. "Gail's real pretty. But you have something more."

Leah didn't give him a chance to say more of what. She tried to change the subject. And she tried to get up. "Would you like another drink?"

Steven curved his hand over her shoulder to hold her still. "Relax. Relax . . ." he said soothingly. "Just sit and talk to me. I won't bite, you know."

"I bite back," Leah responded at once.

Steven raised his brows in surprise, but he laughed at her sudden show of spirit.

"Is it fun working with all those beautiful women all day long?" she asked, listening as Allen and Gail laughed together across the room.

Steven shrugged. "Not really. And they're mostly girls, not women. A lot of 'em are bitches and a pain to work with. The white chicks have class but no style. The black sisters have style but sometimes no class," he commented openly.

"Sounds interesting," Leah said absently.

"It's a living. I'm really an actor between auditions."

"Oh, really?"

"I'm up for a part in a new series being shot here in New York. I got called back last week for another reading."

"What if you don't get the part?"

"I'll ask you again to pose for me." Steven smiled seductively.

Leah shook her head. "I hope you get the part."

"I got a couple of things going. Sooner or later I'll break out." He shrugged good-naturedly. "Maybe I'll just find someone to support me."

Leah couldn't tell if Steven was serious or not, but she used the moment to stand and suggest they all get seated for dinner. She focused her attention on Allen. But whatever flow of gregarious talk and humor he had been able to conduct with Gail before dinner suddenly came to a halt with herself. Gail had much less trouble switching her focus to Steven, and Leah had to conclude at the end of the evening that the only person who really seemed to have had a good time was her sister.

"How's the new position?" Leah asked Allen at one point. She knew he always liked talking about that.

"It's okay." Allen nodded, busy with turkey and cranberry sauce.

Leah waited for more. "I guess that means it's working out."

Silence from Allen.

Laughter from across the table.

"How are your folks?" Leah tried again.

"Fine, fine. I'll see them at Christmas."

Leah sighed. "Allen, am I boring you?" she asked bluntly.

Allen's expression was one of great patience. "Leah, I can't talk and eat at the same time."

Leah looked at Gail and Steven. How come *they* could?

Steven declined dessert and stood to leave when dinner was over. He thanked Leah and Gail for inviting him, and shook hands with Allen.

"I'll just run up and get my things . . ." Gail said to the room in general.

Leah looked surprised. "What things? Are you going out?"

Benign confusion furrowed Gail's brow. "Didn't I tell you? Steven and I have plans for the rest of the evening."

Steven neither confirmed nor denied the news. He stood quietly and patiently by the door studying the designs on the floor runner.

"I'll be right back," Gail said as she raced up the stairs.

Leah looked around at the remains of dinner. "It's okay. I'll clear the table," she said wryly, but the irony was lost since no one was listening. Allen silently helped to stack dishes, but they clattered so loudly in his hands that Leah was afraid her grandmother's china would break. She gently pushed him aside and told him she could do the job alone.

Leah was in the kitchen rinsing plates when Gail came in.

"Leah, I'm sorry I'm leaving you to clean up the dirty work."

Leah smiled. She couldn't help but feel there was a double meaning to Gail's statement. "I know you're sorry. But you're going anyway." Gail held her peace and put on her coat. "Are you seriously seeing Steven?

Gail shrugged. "He's on a short list of available escorts."

"He doesn't seem your type."

"He serves the purpose," Gail answered cryptically as she buttoned her coat.

Leah looked up sharply. "What purpose?" But Gail was already in the hallway headed toward the front door and the waiting Steven.

Steven surprised Leah by taking her hand and squeezing it gently in his own. "Thanks again for dinner. I'm sorry about the quick good-bye. I hope this doesn't spoil the rest of the evening."

"Don't worry about it. Gail's unpredictable. And she's full of surprises."

"Not all of them fun, I bet," he said dryly.

Allen hung back in the living room examining CD jackets, indifferent to the gathering.

Gail opened the door. "I'll talk with you later," she told her sister. "Good night, Allen," she yelled out, but when there was no answer from the living room Gail smiled broadly, shrugged, and left, with Steven right behind her.

Leah stood in the following silence with a sense that the evening had crashed resoundingly. It had changed at some point from being dinner into bizarre conversations with innuendos. She searched out Allen and found him in the dining room downing a glass of wine. Leah began to silently gather the dinner glasses when Allen suddenly reached out and grabbed her arm. She looked at him questioningly, but the light reflected in the lens of his glasses keep his eyes hidden.

"Leave that stuff," he said. Then he faced her fully and pulled Leah into his arms and began to kiss her.

She was completely unprepared and stood for a moment as he feathered kisses over her face. She pulled back, her expression puzzled.

"Allen, what are you doing?" she asked with a nervous laugh. She was very uncertain about this sudden directness from him. She was not prepared to switch emotional gears on a dime while holding a basket of uneaten bread and a pitcher of gravy.

But Allen only shook his head and continued to kiss her.

"Don't say anything," he mumbled, his mouth making its way along her jaw to her neck and throat.

Leah put the basket and pitcher down awkwardly, nearly spilling the contents of both. Allen started coaxing her backward toward the stairs. She resisted.

"Allen . . ."

He stopped. "What's the problem? What does it look like I'm doing?" he asked, rubbing her arms.

The caress only made Leah feel chilled. And she didn't have a more concrete answer than: it didn't feel right. She shrugged. "Can't you just slow down? Can't we sit for a while and talk?"

"We've been talking all evening."

"Not to me. You had almost nothing to say to me all during dinner."

"Your sister and that fool talked enough for all of us."

Leah frowned. "Why do you call Steven a fool?"

"Because he's a joke."

"Then why are you letting him get to you?"

Allen sighed and didn't answer. Instead he silently took her hand and led the way up the stairs to her room. Leah followed, but her trepidation was building. In her room Allen again took her into his arms, and his kisses became intense and demanding, not allowing her a moment to think.

Leah might have softened enough to get into the mood, but Allen began to pull impatiently at her clothing.

"I'll do it," she murmured, resigned.

Leah tried to slow him down. She helped to unbutton the dress and removed her underwear while Allen fumbled out of his own clothing and swiftly brought her down onto the bed. Leah thought that now Allen would proceed as he always did—building up his passion, trying to bring her along. She hoped that he would now pay attention to her. But he didn't.

With no preliminaries, no soft touches, Allen brought them together before her body was ready. Leah held onto his shoulders, her fingers digging into his flesh, bracing herself against his sudden hardness and the dry friction with each thrust of his hips. Leah began twisting her body, arching it to pull away.

"Oh, my God . . ." she moaned. She was uncomfortable. And scared.

She said Allen's name twice. He didn't seem to hear.

Allen buried his face in her neck, grunting and hissing. Leah didn't understand what demon was driving him. She didn't want to do this, and certainly not this way. Allen was not forcing her, but he was insistent. Leah couldn't stop him. She lay there beneath him totally left out and uninvolved, feeling the inside of her vagina burn and pull roughly against the agitation of his penis.

His mouth searched for hers, but Leah kept her lips pressed tightly closed, protecting the least vulnerable spot of her body. He was mumbling incoherently. Angry words, blurred and unintelligible as his mouth pressed to hers. He pushed into her one last time, and Leah gritted her teeth against the pressure.

"It . . . hurts. You're hurting me . . ." she whispered.

But it was all over. Allen collapsed on top of her and breathed heavily. After several minutes he rolled away, and Leah suddenly felt ice cold as the air in the room hit her skin. She lay stunned for a moment and then quickly struggled off the bed. She hurried into the bathroom in the hall and locked herself in.

There she washed herself over and over with hot water. She splashed her face with cold water until goose-flesh raised on her arms and legs, and she shivered uncontrollably. Rage churned in her stomach. She fought against being sick. Leah wrapped a robe around herself and slowly returned to the bedroom.

She found Allen seated on the side of the bed, holding his head in his hands, his elbows resting on his knees. Leah stared coldly at him.

"I want you to get dressed and leave," she said in a low voice shaky with emotion. "I don't want you to talk, I don't want you to say anything. Just get out."

Allen looked up. "Leah . . ."

Leah turned her back and squeezed her eyes closed. "Get out!" she said, covering her ears.

She waited in the hallway until she heard Allen finish dressing. He left her room and she followed as he descended to the first floor. Allen didn't try to say anything more as he got his overcoat.

He hesitated only a moment at the door that Leah held open for him. She hoped that he could see by her erectly held body, the closed expression, that to ask for forgiveness was pointless. He left quietly.

Something else had hurt Leah far more than Allen's indifferent use of her body, his total lack of gentleness. In his single-mindedness she felt she had become invisible again. Just like that time with the stranger who'd accosted her in a stairwell, who'd made her a victim. Allen was not a malicious person, or one given to violence, but Leah realized that she could have been anyone in that bed with him tonight. She had been the unwilling recipient of his frustration and of a desire that had nothing to do with her.

For that she could never forgive him.

Leah had nothing to say to Gail when her sister returned home the next morning. She had too many feelings of her own to work out to consider anyone else's. If Gail thought Leah's behavior odd, she did not mention it.

Leah spent two days working on the knots of anxiety in her stomach. She tried to understand what she'd done to provoke Allen's aggression and finally convinced herself that she'd done nothing at all. But the weekend after Thanksgiving was a nightmare of recriminations, and it wasn't until late Sunday night that she began to relax.

The phone rang at nine-thirty, just as the thought of soaking in a scented bath seemed appealing. Leah had managed to find her balance again, but when she answered the phone and heard Allen rush into an apology on the other end, she quickly hung up without saying a word.

Gail, with an arm full of freshly folded linens, stuck her head in her sister's doorway. "That was a quick call. Who was it?"

Leah wondered if Gail could detect her rapid heartbeat or her anger. "Wrong number," she murmured.

Allen called again on Wednesday at her office. Leah had just finished a production meeting with Jill, Mike, and several others. They were all pleased with the way the spring line of books was shaping up. The department was a month ahead of schedule, and bonuses for Christmas were promised to everyone. Leah had personally been complimented by a senior editor for an innovative jacket idea. So she was feeling much more charitable when Allen's call came in just before lunch. But that quickly changed.

"Leah? This is Allen. Please don't hang up," he pleaded.

Leah had been about to do just that but paused. She was curious about what Allen could say that would make things better.

"I'm sorry. I'm really, really sorry about last week. It was a shitty thing to do and . . . I feel like a bastard."

Leah took a deep breath. "Good. You were a bastard," she said tightly. "I don't know if I want to talk to you yet, Allen."

"Did I . . . hurt you?" he asked.

Leah turned her back to the studio, not wanting anyone to hear. "Yes," she hissed. How could he not know that he had?

"Look, I'll make it up to you. I really will, Leah. I owe you more than an apology. I know—"

"Allen, don't—"

"The evening was ruined and it was all my fault—"

"Stop . . ." Leah moaned.

He did. For a long moment there was silence on both ends of the line. Leah rubbed her temple. She wished he hadn't called. She wished she knew how to handle this. She wished there was someone to talk to about this. No, not Gail.

"Can I take you to dinner?" Allen asked quietly.

Leah wasn't sure she'd heard right. Dinner? He must be kidding. "No, Allen. I don't think so. Dinner is not going to make me feel better."

"Please, Leah. I know you're upset, but give me a chance to make it up. *Please* . . ."

Leah slowly raised her head. There was real anxiety

in his voice. Maybe he really was sorry. Maybe now he'd realize just how much he'd come to take her for granted.

"How about Friday?" he asked when the pause continued.

"All right," she whispered, giving in.

"Good. That's good. How about I pick you up from work? How's six?"

"Six is fine," she mumbled, and slowly hung up the phone.

She felt strange, as though all her feelings had left her body and she was nothing more than an empty shell. She would move and function and get things done. But it wasn't really all of her, present and accounted for.

Leah stared out the studio window at the river. The call from Allen had not helped at all. Perhaps her anger wasn't real. Perhaps all through the two-year relationship with Allen she'd kept it reined in. It didn't really seem that he was taking this seriously. Or her. Shouldn't he be more repentant? Shouldn't she be feeling more vindicated?

Leah wanted to run, to escape. She wasn't sure she and Allen could bridge her confusion and doubt. They'd have dinner to soothe his guilt. Leah would forgive him.

And then what?

"I'm going out with Allen Friday night," Leah informed her sister that evening as they stood in the kitchen trying to decide what to have for dinner.

"Oh? What brought that on? I can't remember the last time Allen took you anywhere," Gail said sarcastically.

Leah shrugged. She felt listless. "Then it's a nice change."

"Isn't he happy with your cooking anymore?"

"My cooking has nothing to do with it!" Leah snapped. She looked quickly at Gail, stunned at her own outburst. But although Gail did seem surprised, Leah gave her no opportunity to question her. "Why don't we order in for dinner?" she suggested, reaching for one of many takeout menus attached to the refrigerator door. Leah examined one menu's choices, aware that her sister stood behind her. "Do you have a preference?" she asked.

"It doesn't matter. Pick what you want." Gail poured herself a glass of water from the tap, took only a sip, and poured the rest down the sink. "Are you two celebrating something? Where is Allen taking you to dinner?" she asked.

Leah put the menu aside and looked at Gail with exasperation. "I don't know," she answered impatiently. "And you know what? It's not all that important to me. *Not*, apparently, as much as it is to you. Tell you what, as soon as I find out I'll make sure you know, okay?"

Gail shrugged. "You don't have to get uppity. I was just curious."

"Then I guess I just don't understand all this curiosity in where I might be having dinner with my . . . with Allen. I'm ordering lasagna and garlic knots. What do you want?"

"Shrimp with tofu in oyster sauce," Gail said.

Her exasperation growing, Leah turned on her sister. She was about to ask what was the problem when she saw the bright expression on Gail's face. It was playful and teasing. It had been a very long time since they'd both been contrary just for the sake of getting a rise out of each other.

"Girl, you drive me crazy," Leah said easily, tossing the paper menu at her sister. "I thought we were ordering dinner?"

"Pizza," Gail said with a sudden cheeriness that wasn't used often.

Leah laughed and nodded. "With everything."

Leah looked at the clock on the opposite wall from her worktable. It was almost five-thirty, and Allen would be there soon. She bent over her sketch pad again, finishing the caricature she'd started. It was based on a portrait of her father, and was one of a series she'd been working on for some time. It had started just for fun, but when word got out that she was good at it, she had found herself giving some of the sketches away as gifts. She'd been working for a while on a series of faces. Some were almost caricatures, like the one of Mike Berger with his worst physical qualities exaggerated. The over-styled hair, the pouch, the overbite. But at the moment Leah couldn't enjoy the humor or satisfaction of her work. She was too busy trying not to be nervous about seeing Allen.

When she heard the voices outside the studio door, Allen's and Jill's, Leah put the sketch away with the others she'd completed and cleared away her materials. It wasn't until Leah actually saw Allen that she realized that agreeing to dinner so soon had not been a good idea. He was impeccably dressed as always. He appeared sophisticated and urbane, personable and intelligent. He was the picture of desirable black manhood—and she didn't really want to see him. She was no longer angry with Allen, but she was wary of him.

Allen and Jill were talking amiably about a movie they'd both seen. Jill laughed at some comment and then called out to Leah, "Your prince is here."

Allen's expression was closed and he stood waiting. Leah knew she had to make the first move. Allen had apologized to her, but it was clear that he wasn't going to repeat himself.

"Ready?" was all she asked. Her smile was tight and her insides were in turmoil.

Allen did take her to a very nice restaurant, and it was obvious that, at least tonight, money was no object. He was very careful and solicitous of her needs. He played with her slender fingers and leaned close to her across the table. It was like when they'd first started dating and he'd made her feel so special. They lingered over dinner, and although the fiasco of Thanksgiving was carefully avoided in conversation, it was clear by the general strain of the evening that it was not forgotten.

Leah answered all of his questions automatically, or smiled at the appropriate moment to some remark he'd made. But while she commented on this and that, she took time to study him dispassionately.

She tried to see in him what it was she liked and didn't like. She was trying to figure out if there was any point in even continuing to see him beyond the evening. Leah used to have a halfhearted fantasy about Allen when they'd first met. She thought that he'd turn out to be just the person she wanted and needed in her life. Not necessarily marriage—Leah had never been sure that marriage was what she wanted—but at least that he'd occupy some emotional corner of her life. She thought Allen would be a companion, a good friend and lover. But Thanksgiving night had proven that companionship and friendship had never been established between them.

Dinner was almost over before Leah allowed herself to really feel comfortable with Allen, because it took her that long to remember that at the end of the night she could go home alone if she wanted.

"I'm glad you let me talk you into dinner," Allen said, smiling at her over the candle.

"Are you? Why?"

"I enjoyed this. We should do this more often, you know?"

Leah looked down into her wineglass, turning it slowly by the stem. It occurred to her that Allen had become too complacent too quickly. He'd already put aside what had really happened between them. She wasn't going to tell him that after he'd left her on Thanksgiving night, she'd spent more than two hours putting away leftover food from the dinner and cleaning the kitchen. Anything to avoid going back to her room. At one-thirty in the morning, she was changing the linens on her bed. And then she'd returned to the living room on the first floor and had spent the night on the sofa.

"Are you going to tell me about it, Allen?" she suddenly asked.

He looked puzzled. "What do you mean? Tell you what?"

Leah stared at him, trying to see if there was doubt or remorse in his eyes. She wanted to believe that Allen regretted what had happened. She sensed that he did. But Leah also sensed that, again, it had had nothing to do with her.

"About Thanksgiving, of course. Why did you do it, What were you thinking?"

"I thought you'd gotten over that," he said defensively.

"No, I haven't. I've forgiven you because I don't think you meant to hurt me physically. That doesn't mean I don't want an explanation."

"Leah . . ." he began reluctantly, and then stopped.

He used his index finger and thumb to smooth down his mustache while he silently regarded her. Allen, who was sharp and articulate, was clearly at a loss for words.

Leah was disappointed and she laughed derisively. "Did I really look so unbelievably great that night that you couldn't wait until dinner had digested?"

But that only made Allen withdraw more. He sat back and his mouth became grim and taut.

Leah bent toward him and whispered, "Did you think I was flirting with Steven? I wasn't. If anything I thought he was fresh. I—"

Allen was shaking his head. He sighed deeply. "No, no. That's not it. Steven is an asshole. I just wanted . . . I don't know. I guess I just needed to hold you and to know that you were there for me. You understand?" he asked.

Leah still stared at him. Slowly she shook her head. "No, I don't. Because I've always been there for you, Allen. And if you needed to be held, all you had to do was ask. You didn't ask, you took. And you took as if you had the right to."

His mouth grew tighter. He shifted his gaze angrily to the side, but didn't dispute her. He still didn't explain, or try to put her mind at ease.

"I know I handled it wrong," was all he said.

His response seemed shallow and irrelevant. Leah's chuckle was silent and incredulous. "I would say so," she murmured.

Things got awkward again when they reached Brooklyn, but Leah was thankful when Allen declined her hesitant invitation to come in. Yet he stood looking at the closed door to the brownstone as if considering whether he wanted to or not.

"No. I don't think so. It's not a good idea tonight," he chuckled ruefully. His hands were jammed into the pockets of his overcoat.

Leah knew that he wasn't going to touch her. Not even a kiss good night.

"It was a lovely evening, Allen. Thank you." She tilted her head. "Are you feeling less guilty now?"

Allen let out a sigh but said nothing.

"Never mind. That was unfair and I guess I shouldn't ask," Leah murmured. Then she relented and made it easier for him in the end. "Good night, Allen. I'll talk with you soon." She climbed the stairs into the house.

Leah found Gail in the den with her sketch pads and materials on the floor around her, where she sat working up dress designs.

"Hi," Leah said as she leaned in the doorway. "What are you doing?"

"Oh, just a couple of ideas I had for dresses."

Leah bent over her sister's shoulder and examined a design for a black cocktail-length dress that had a stunning wing-like pattern of rhinestones up the torso to the shoulders and sleeves. "I really like that one."

"You've got expensive taste," Gail said, putting the drawing aside. "That will cost a fortune to make."

"Yeah, but then you could sell it for a fortune," Leah reasoned, grinning.

Gail stood up from the floor. Immediately Leah noticed a cigarette burning in an ashtray on a small nearby table.

"So, how was the evening?" Gail asked pleasantly.

"It was fine. There were candles, flowers, and champagne," Leah said with a wide grin.

"Sounds very nice. Special occasion?" Gail asked quietly.

Leah sighed and took off her coat. "No. It was a nice restaurant, but not the Rainbow Room. I see you're smoking again."

Gail laughed nervously. "Just a little tense, I guess. Where's the man of the hour?"

Leah took off her coat. "He left. He didn't want to come in. What are you so tense about? Is it work?"

Gail blew smoke, squashing her half-finished cigarette out. "It's not important. There was a phone call for you. Someone named Jason. Who's Jason?" she asked with a frown.

Leah looked at her sister. She wasn't inclined to explain yet. "Just an acquaintance."

Gail dropped a pencil on top of her sketch pad. "Well, I'm going to bed. I have a staff meeting in the morning and a trade show to attend at the Javits Center in the afternoon. I just wanted to hear how tonight went. Are you coming?"

For whatever reason, Leah could sense a certain reticence in her sister. It was unusual. She was about to ask Gail if there was some sort of problem, but she decided against it. She had enough problems of her own to consider at the moment. If Gail wanted to talk, she only had to say so.

"In a moment," Leah said.

Gail nodded and went to put away her drawings. She finally called out good night and headed for her room above. After Leah hung up her coat, she began to feel small and adrift in the quiet of the first floor.

For a long moment she stood still with her eyes closed. A sudden overwhelming sense of loneliness came out of nowhere to wrap itself suddenly around her. She'd been serious when she told Allen the evening had been lovely. He'd certainly tried hard enough. But it hadn't been enough. The only problem was, Leah wasn't sure what had been missing. She felt lightheaded. And agitated.

She turned off the lights in the hallway, and halfway up the stairs the phone rang. Leah hurried back to the living room to answer. "Hello?"

"It. It's Jay Eagle."

For a moment Leah drew a total blank. Then she smiled. "Hello, Jay Eagle." She could hear a great deal of noise in the background. "Where are you?" she asked, holding the receiver away from her ear.

"Hey, you guys. Quiet down! Slack, get off the court," Jason shouted out of range of the receiver. "Sorry. I'm refereeing a basketball game. It's halftime."

"Oh, really? High school or a local team?"

Jason chuckled in amusement. "Spoffard."

"Oh . . ." Leah responded weakly, but she recovered quickly. "How was Thanksgiving?"

"Okay, I guess. I had to work."

"Picked the short straw, eh?" Leah teased.

"It wasn't so bad. No major crimes committed. I guess everybody was either pigging out on turkey or busy trying to steal one."

Leah laughed.

"And you?" he asked.

"The usual. Very traditional. My sister and I cooked for friends—" A whistle shrilled in her ear and she winced. She could hear Jason ordering someone named Slack back to the bench.

"Look, it's crazy here. I gotta go. I have some hockey tickets for next week, and I thought maybe you could come with me."

Leah was silent. There it was again. He wanted to see her. "That's nice of you. But I don't think it's such a good idea . . ."

Jason didn't get the hint.

"Come on. It's a fun game. If you don't know anything about it, I'll teach you. I'm a great teacher, you know."

"I'm sure you are, but . . ."

"I'd really like you to come," he said seriously.

Leah really couldn't imagine why. "Well . . ."

He laughed suddenly. "She who hesitates is lost."

Jason rattled off to Leah all the information she'd need before she could recoup and formulate a legitimate excuse.

"Jason, I—"

"Hey. I'm trained not to take no for an answer."

He hung up.

She sat holding the receiver. And then she began to laugh.

Chapter Five

On the night of the hockey game it snowed. Leah had made arrangements to meet Jason in front of Madison Square Garden at six o'clock. As the afternoon wore on and the weather grew messier, Leah began to see the possibilities of not showing up at all. In the end, guilt more than curiosity forced her to not leave Jason waiting. Unreasonably, she blamed her indecision on him. The bad weather had become his fault as well.

The snow, as it turned out, was not just a first snowfall for New York, a light seasonal dusting. It was a full-fledged storm complete with slush, traffic tie-ups, and train delays. Leah had never experienced commuter rush hour at Penn Station before, and she thought it was all totally insane. She wondered how Jason was ever going to find her in the crowd.

Allen had called earlier in the week, hoping to be invited to dinner. His unexpected forwardness threw her off guard. But the thought of pretending normalcy with Allen had made Leah uncomfortable. She was relieved when she could honestly tell Allen she had other plans.

Leah had the peculiar feeling, standing up to her ankles in snow, that the world was rushing away from her in some tremendous escape. She stood looking at intense, sober faces of working men and women as they passed her on their way home. At least she wasn't standing all alone. There was an over-padded Santa and a trio from the Salvation Army who were ringing bells and pleading for contributions.

A young man with lank blond hair passingly asked if she had hockey tickets to sell. He didn't wait for an answer, probably assessing quickly that it was unlikely that a young black woman would have tickets to scalp. Leah looked at her watch, annoyance building. Five more minutes and she was going home.

She was aware suddenly that someone else was standing just behind her left shoulder, and when she turned her head there was a black man eyeing her. Her heart lurched and she became alert. Leah knew he wasn't looking for tickets. She thought of moving, but forced herself to stay still, willing any threat she imagined to go away. Surely, he couldn't get personal or violent right there?

"Bad night, right?" the man said in a friendly enough voice.

Leah huddled in her coat. He was not dressed for this kind of weather. No hat, no gloves, a shabby coat, and he was wearing sneakers. Just seeing them made her feet feel numb. "Ummm . . ." was her noncommittal answer.

"I could sure use something to drink. Warm me up inside. Know what I mean?"

Leah didn't answer. She felt a hand on her arm. Her resolve to remain calm failed her. Her breath caught in her throat and she jerked away.

"How 'bout you and me—"

"The lady isn't interested," Jason cut in out of nowhere.

"Okay, okay," the man said quickly, moving away into the crowd.

Leah knew a flashing moment of profound relief.

"I'm sorry I'm late. I got stuck writing out a report. Have you been waiting long?" Jason asked.

"Too long," Leah said tartly. She was angry. "You know, I really hate just waiting. People get the wrong idea, especially around here."

"Did anyone bother you?" Jason asked pointedly.

"Just him . . ." Leah motioned in the direction of the still fleeing young man. She swallowed the rest of her wrath. Took a deep breath. Jason had shown up after all.

He was wearing a dark blue sweater pulled over an open-neck shirt, jeans, and western-style boots. He wore a short leather aviation jacket and a red baseball cap. He wasn't dressed for the weather, either.

"Are you hungry?" he asked, propelling Leah toward the entrance to the Garden.

"Yes. And cold." Her teeth were clenched.

"Good. I'm taking you to one of New York's finest. I discovered this place several years ago when I first started coming to the Garden. You are in for a treat."

Leah allowed Jason to guide her with the gentle pressure of his hand on her back. At the entrance gates to the arena, Jason produced two tickets and they melded with a slowly moving procession of people headed for their seats.

Leah's sense of the ridiculous was tickled when they stopped in front of a concession stand and Jason placed an order for franks, beer, and popcorn. They carried everything to their seats, and with a cardboard tray balanced on their laps, they had dinner. Leah couldn't remember the last time she'd had a hot dog and ate this one with delight, enjoying the spicy brown mustard that left her tongue tingling.

While waiting for the game to start, she looked around. She noticed that seating in the arena was differentiated by colors. Their seats were yellow, which was not as good as the red, but certainly better than blue or green, which were just under the rafters. The arena was fast filling up with fans, most of them male. She saw no other black faces, and it made her feel conspicuous.

Several rows in front was a group of about thirteen adolescent boys accompanied by two middle-aged men, probably the fathers of two of the boys. Leah noticed that Jason's gaze kept returning to the group, his expression tight and closed. She could easily guess what was going through his mind. He still saw his own son in every boy of a similar age. Leah touched his arm to divert his attention. She asked him about the rules of the game. Gratefully, and with more details than she cared about, Jason obliged.

He told her which two teams were playing, their standings in the league. He talked about the officials and penalties until it all made no sense to Leah. Jason pointed at the rink at the visiting players emerged through the a passageway and onto the ice. The crowd shouted halfhearted boos.

"See number thirty one? Right now he's got the best season average for saves on goal."

"What's a save on goal?" Leah asked, watching the skaters in the bulky, padded uniforms.

"That's when the goalie—the guy at the net—prevents the puck from scoring."

Leah turned her head to look earnestly at Jason. "What's a puck?"

"The puck?" he repeated blankly. The puck was the game. Jason wondered how he was going to explain that when he saw Leah's expression. Curious. Guileless. Teasing. He started to chuckle and felt a gentle purging of his distraction.

"Didn't mean to get so serious," he said sheepishly.

"I can see you're a big fan," Leah murmured with a smile.

The game began. While Jason yelled insults at the referees and cheered on the Rangers, Leah made a concentrated effort to follow the movement of the puck and players. It made her dizzy. Jason tried to explain an offsides, but Leah promptly gave up hope of ever seeing one. She surprised herself and Jason, however, by jumping to her feet and cheering when someone scored a goal. Not so much for the team scoring—it was the opposition—but because she was able to spot the goal at all. Leah put her fingers to her mouth and managed a shrill whistle.

Jason raised his brows in surprise. "Where did you learn to do that?"

"Kenny taught me," Leah boasted proudly. She could see that Jason was impressed. After all, whistling was not a girl thing to do. In that moment she began to enjoy herself.

Jason watched Leah become animated, and his uncertainty disappeared. When he'd first spotted her, standing stiffly and impatiently outside the Garden, he'd thought this whole idea of his was crazy. Plus Joe had harangued him all afternoon about taking Leah Downey to a hockey game. Jason glanced at her as her face expressed concentration, excitement, and surprise. He decided to make sure that the evening went well. She was the one on alien ground. . . .

The Rangers lost. He went on to explain why, but it was all way over Leah's head and she really didn't care about the details. The game had been visual. Incredibly fast. The fistfights had made her gasp and stare, fascinated at the rituals of a game that allowed for action to stop for a brawl.

When the game ended, there was a general exodus. Jason guided her out of the Garden, using his body to block the pushing fans rushing for the parking lot or the subway. His light touch, as before, continued. Leah recognized that it was not really possessive but protective. She glanced at Jason's profile and watched the way his eyes scanned the crowds; the cop in him was fully aware of everything and everyone around them.

Once outside, Jason looked at his watch and suggested they stop for a drink before heading back to Brooklyn. At a deli on Seventh Avenue they sat at the counter. He had a beer and Leah had hot chocolate.

Jason grimaced at her. "I don't think I know anybody who really drinks hot chocolate."

"Well, you know one now," Leah said, grinning. "And I'll be sober when I'm done."

"Touché," Jason said good-naturedly, lighting a cigarette. "How did you like the game?"

"I still don't understand it, but it was fun," Leah admitted. "You took a real chance, you know. I might have hated it. This could have been one hell of a long evening."

Jason watched her carefully, but he didn't seem offended by her comment. "Supposing you had hated it. What would you have done about it?"

Leah sighed. "Stuck it out. I would have looked stupid storming out and leaving you there alone."

Jason chuckled softly. "It's been done."

"Why did you ask? Did you think I might?"

Jason didn't even hesitate. "No," he responded. "It wasn't such a big risk. You strike me as a person who can still be surprised, who doesn't mind trying new things."

"Do I?" Leah asked, intrigued.

Jason nodded, exhaling smoke. "There's a certain wide-eyed look about you."

Leah rolled her eyes. "Sappy, I think you call it."

"No, not sappy. Just interested. Curious," Jason said, looking at her. "Curiosity will keep you young forever."

Leah half smiled at his observation. "I don't think I'll give up my pension fund on that basis. Sometimes I feel very old. Ancient."

"Yeah, so do I," he agreed with some sadness.

Leah sipped her chocolate. In her head she started drawing comparisons between Jason and Allen. She quickly stopped. It wasn't fair. She still knew next to nothing about Jason.

"So, I guess it's fair to assume you like sports. You're a jock as well as a cop. How macho," she teased.

Jason shrugged slightly and grinned at her. He nodded toward her half-finished cup. "I should have asked if you wanted anything to eat."

"No, thanks. If I eat this late I'll have nightmares." She immediately wished she'd made a different reference. When she glanced at him, he was closely studying her face and Leah hoped that he couldn't detect her nervousness. "The hot chocolate is fine, thanks. Tell me something about these kids you work with. How do they find you?"

Jason finished his beer and signaled for another. "They don't find me. It's the other way around. Referrals come in from family court, social services, schools, detention centers."

"Are they really . . . bad?" Leah suspected that she sounded naive. Judging from Jason's expression, he thought so, too.

"Worse. These are kids whose parents, assuming they have any and know who they are, stopped interacting with them around the age of four or five. By seven they're stealing from stores, from other kids, and getting into fights at school. By nine they've tuned out school but go because it's better than home. They start drinking beer and cheap wine, smoking, more stealing."

Jason stopped and narrowed his gaze at her. "Do you want me to go on?"

Leah could only nod, already speechless.

"Now they're being sent to detention, and the family is called in. At this point the authorities realize that no one is responsible enough or cares enough to do anything. But they don't have any answers, either. At age eleven they're probably carrying weapons, extorting smaller kids, working for older kids. This way there's someone who might protect them when they need it.

"At around fifteen or sixteen, when the state is ready to sweep them under the carpet, I get involved. There's an intervention program set up that tries to show these kids that there are other options to choose from."

"Sports as opposed to jail?" Leah questioned.

"It's cheap therapy."

"How successful are you?"

Jason spread out his left hand and banked it left and right. "I'd say about fifty-fifty."

"Is that all?"

"It's better than zero."

Leah shook her head sadly. She'd never known kids who lived the kind of life Jason had described. She'd never known kids who didn't have parents.

"Look," Jason said, lightly touching the back of her hand. "When I get them it's already almost too late. But if they get convicted of something and get sent away, then it *is* too late. We've lost them. Jail only makes them better at what put them there to begin with. Sports . . ." He lifted his shoulders. "It's physical. The guys get to work out a lot of stuff. They get a chance to win, for once."

Leah continued to look at Jason. Slowly she began to smile.

"What?" he asked.

"You sound so passionate about it."

He actually blushed but tried to cover it. "I wouldn't use the word passionate myself, but someone has to do something, start somewhere. The alternatives stink.

"The guys are okay. Many of them are smarter than they get credit for. But they can be mean, and you can't really trust them. And every once in a while there's a real hard case, like this one kid, Slack. You know you're not reaching him, and it's not clear he wants to be reached."

"Slack?" Leah repeated skeptically.

Jason nodded. "Right. As in, he doesn't give any."

Leah chuckled. She liked listening to Jason talk. He had a sense of humor.

He frowned at her. "Are you sure you want to hear this? We can talk about that new book by what's-his-name."

She chuckled again. "I'm sure. It wasn't a trick question to stroke your ego."

Jason exhaled the last of his cigarette, crushed it in the ashtray, and shook his head, bemused. "Most women I know wouldn't give a—" He stopped, realizing that perhaps he was venturing onto delicate ground.

Leah stared into her cup. She cleared her throat. "Do these kids from hell play hockey?"

"Sort of. Street hockey on roller skates. We get old pairs donated by a rink in the Bronx. They call it a white boy's game."

Surprisingly, they chuckled together. Then Leah gnawed her lower lip and then took a deep breath. "Did you ever take Michael to hockey games?"

Jason took a large gulp of beer. "Sure. Lots of times. We used to play when I went to visit him. There's a pond behind the school—his school . . ."

Jason stopped for a moment and Leah waited.

"It would freeze pretty solid in winter. We'd get together about fifteen boys and make up teams. We'd play by our own rules and always manage to find a spot for every kid.

"I once brought a bunch of guys from a detention center to a game. These kids were from Harlem and the Heights. They didn't get it. Loved the fighting, but the game was over their heads. They all wanted to be football players anyway, for the NFL." Again, his eyes got that faraway look. "Michael said he wanted to be a football player, but . . ." The thought trailed off and Jason shrugged. "He was going to spend Christmas with me this year. He would have graduated next June."

"What will you do for the holidays?" Leah asked quietly.

"Don't know yet."

"You shouldn't spend it alone."

"I'm not afraid of being alone," Jason said easily.

"That's not the point."

He smiled at her. "I'm afraid to ask what is."

Leah shook her head. "You're either being cynical or you're making fun of me."

Jason slowly shook his head. "I'm sorry. I'm not . . ."

"Then you're trying to tell me to mind my own business. Fine. You're right. I don't really care," she said with a vague gesture.

Jason began to smile again. It wasn't so much a smile of amusement as one of sudden awareness. "Yes, you do," he said. "Thanks."

They finished their drinks and took the subway back to Brooklyn. There didn't seem to be much need for more conversation, and Leah didn't mind the occasional lapses into silence between them. She was very aware of Jason's presence next to her, and very aware of passengers who sent covert or blatant glances their way. The curiosity seemed unnecessary, but Leah knew that some of their whispered comments and laughter among themselves was about her and Jason. Leah hated that it made her feel defensive. Like the men in the coffee shop the first time she and Jason had been out.

In Brooklyn, they passed the corner market. Leah noticed the usual contingent of teens hanging out, and the tall, skinny one in particular who always had something to say. This time was no different.

"Hey! Sweet thang. What you doing with that dude?" The teen began to laugh. "He all in your pants, right?"

Leah stared straight ahead and said nothing, feeling both angry and uneasy. Jason turned to look at the boy, and then excused himself to approach the teen. Leah felt her heart begin to pound. There was going to be trouble.

She didn't move. Leah couldn't hear exactly what was being said, but Jason was talking quietly. His hands were in his jacket pockets. His breath made vapor out of the cold air around him.

"Fuck you, man," the boy suddenly shouted defiantly.

Jason continued his low-voiced response. For a moment the boys seemed to be listening to what he had to say. They appeared impatient and disgusted, their body language indicating clearly that they were not intimidated by Jason, but there seemed to be a reluctant acceptance of what he was telling them.

The leader had one more parting shot to make, but Jason cut him off with a clear hand signal that they should leave. The boys had more to say but nevertheless ambled away from the corner.

Jason walked back to Leah, and they continued down the block to her house.

"I'm sorry," she muttered.

Jason frowned at her. "Do you know those guys?"

"Not really. They live around here, but . . ."

"Then why should you be sorry? Look, I deal with guys like that every day, all day long. They're wimps compared to someone like Slack. I'm not offended. You shouldn't be."

"What did you say to him?"

Jason grinned. "I told him he showed a lack of good manners. I told him that was no way to talk to a lady. Not in those words, of course. My ancestry came into question. And we both talked about doing certain things to certain parts of each other's bodies. . . ."

Leah shook her head and couldn't help smiling. Their steps slowed as they reached the brownstone. At the lamp post by the curb near her house they stopped completely. Jason wrapped an arm around the post.

"See this post? This is my lamp post. This post kept me upright that night when I thought I was going to sink into hell. See, here's my name." Jason pointed at some meaningless spot on the pole.

"I don't understand how you can joke about it," Leah said.

"What else should I do? Curse it? Kick it?"

Jason stroked the lamp post as if he'd developed some sort of personal relationship with it. He gave Leah a self-deprecating grin. "At least I had the good sense to stay from behind the wheel of my car. I might have ended up wrapped around this same pole."

Leah wasn't listening. She was watching Jason and building up the courage to speak. She knew that she was on the cusp of either withdrawing from her acquaintance with him or pulling closer. The words she felt like saying struggled with her common sense.

"Would you like to come for dinner sometime?" she blurted out.

Jason's eyes swung quickly to stare into her face, trying to gauge her. The grin never changed. "Feeling sorry for me?" he asked.

Leah lowered her gaze. "I don't know. Maybe."

"Don't," Jason whispered, his expression becoming serious. He studied her for a long second. "This is not like the time with coffee, Leah. Not anymore." He let go of the lamp post and stepped closer to her.

Leah made an impatient tsking sound with her tongue. "You know, already I'm sorry I said anything."

"Why? I didn't sound grateful enough?"

Leah turned abruptly away. Jason took hold of her arm and gently turned her back to face him.

"No, don't leave yet. I'm sorry."

"It's late, and I—"

"It feels a little strange, doesn't it?"

There was something in the hold Jason had on her arm. Leah glanced down at his strong fingers, then back at his face. There was something about his gray eyes and what she saw in them. Leah felt her heart begin to beat faster in agitation.

"Wha—what feels strange?"

Jason hesitated, but then he bent forward to swiftly kiss her.

As soon as Leah realized what he was going to do, she stepped back. "Don't . . ."

Jason put up a hand to stay her. "Schhh . . ."

They stood looking at each other, both of them asking, what next? Indeed, what next? It was an extremely important question because if there was to be a next step, it would begin now.

Jason reached out to Leah slowly. She wondered if he could see her confusion, could see she was poised for flight. But instead of saying a single thing to reassure her, Jason followed through on his impulse. Against her resistance Jason pulled her slowly toward him and kissed her.

Leah felt as though she were holding her breath. She closed her eyes and let a great sigh escape. It wasn't really a kiss. Jason just pressed his mouth to hers. That is, until he began to move his lips and gently explored the shape and surface of her mouth. But just with his lips. Leah's acquiescence was stiff at first and then softened. It loosened and became accepting, almost a natural response. With so much tenderness that she felt mesmerized, Jason coaxed her lips apart. His tongue quickly found hers and the touch was electrifying, although Leah couldn't tell if it was due to the surprise or the feeling. It *was* a little strange, a little mysterious. But not careless.

Neither of them remembered they were standing in the street under a lamp post in thirty-five-degree weather. Leah felt overly warm. Limp. This had been an honest kiss. A real one. And Jason didn't seem to be nearly as frightened of it as she was.

He finally broke the kiss and stood back to look into her eyes. It was impossible for Leah to tell what he was thinking. Jason's face seemed blank for the first time since she'd met him. But his eyes were dark and intense and not without feelings of some kind. Leah just continued to stare at Jason, hoping he would say something first. Leah hoped that in the dark he couldn't see her hands clutching together.

"I bet you've never had an evening quite like this one. Right?"

Leah merely shook her head.

"And never with anyone like me?"

She stared at him.

"There's a first time for everything," Jason said. He nodded in the direction of the corner and the market. "He was right about one thing."

"What?" she asked. "Who was?"

"That kid."

"I—I don't know what you mean."

"I would like to make love with you."

Leah felt her stomach tighten. Jason raised his hand in a gesture of a wave, turned, and walked away.

He was decidedly shaken.

He hadn't planned on doing that. But, after all, it wasn't as if he'd never kissed a woman good night after a date. There had been a natural timeliness to the kiss. It felt really nice.

Jason took a deep breath and counted to five, and then slowly let the air out. No. It had been something other than nice. More. Different. Did he know what he was doing? God, he felt odd. Confused. He wondered abstractedly if Leah Downey's silky brown skin had added a sense of the new and exotic to the experience. He didn't know. He really didn't want to know. He only knew that in that moment he wanted to really hold her much closer and let the chips fall where they may. He was too old to start questioning his judgment and instincts.

With an impatient shake of his head Jason wondered, what the hell was the big deal anyway? Joe had been on his case about Leah Downey from the moment he'd told his colleague about the woman who'd given him a cup of coffee. Joe's cynicism was legendary and understandable. He didn't trust anybody's motives about anything. Not like himself, who gave much more latitude.

Okay. So they had met under strange circumstances. They had become, in a way, very unlikely friends. Maybe it couldn't be called friendship at all. And now maybe they didn't even have that. Had he ruined that, too?

Jason knew that he was comfortable with Leah. Any way he looked at it, questioned it, dissected it and tried to make it something else, he came back to the fact that he really liked Leah Downey. He could talk to her, and she listened.

She made him feel his age. Not old, just grown up. Like it was perfectly okay that he goofed up and made mistakes and showed weakness. He had a job that she hated, but she knew that the job had to get done. She didn't have to hate him . . . just because. Together they'd managed to find this equal ground by more than mere chance, and deeper than just curiosity.

But Jason recognized that something else was happening.

In the ice-cold, now windless air of a December night Jason Horn had sweaty palms. That hadn't happened since he was a teenager when he felt all hands and feet and uncontrollable glands. He wondered if he was, indeed, getting old.

Leah walked aimlessly around the house for more than an hour. She could still feel Jason's kiss on her mouth, and it still made her feel strange. She was confused and just beginning to feel frightened. But she also felt light-headed. Too many possibilities flashed before her eyes. Leah knew that none of them were going to be easy.

She finally sat down in the den, melancholia descending upon her. She began remembering Philip and that summer in school. Fresh stabs of pain and humiliation assailed her, and she felt close to tears. She liked Jason. But she was not going to let this new thing with him, whatever it was, turn out the same way. She would make him go away. She would protect herself.

Above her a door opened, and there were footsteps on the second-floor landing.

"Leah? Is that you? It's late."

Leah got up and went to the door of the den. She

called up the stairwell. "I know. Sorry I woke you up. I'll be up in a minute."

"See you in the morning." Gail's door closed, and it was quiet again.

Leah continued to stand in the doorway. The silence of the house settled around her. It should have been a comfortable and safe feeling but was neither. She experienced a strong anticlimactic hyperness that made her feel both excited and terrified.

The phone rang, scaring her. She stared at it. Finally, Leah picked up the receiver, already knowing who was on the other end.

"Hello?" Her voice sounded thin and breathy.

"Hi," Jason said quietly. There was a silence while the mechanics of the New York Telephone company clicked in their ears. "I just wanted to thank you for the evening. I'm glad you came. It was fun."

"Yes . . ."

"I'm not home yet."

"I didn't think so. Where are you?"

"At a pay phone."

Leah wondered if she should be flattered. She didn't know how to respond. What did it mean that he couldn't wait to get home to call her?

"Are you okay?" he asked suddenly.

"No. Not really," Leah answered truthfully.

"Me, either. Do you suppose that's good or bad?"

Leah considered. She felt exasperated. "I don't know. I have no idea."

"Well, right now it's not important. Am I still invited for dinner?"

"Dinner?"

He chuckled. "How quickly they forget. You talked about Christmas, remember? You said something like I shouldn't be alone. Did you mean it?"

"Yes. Of course I did."

"Good. I'll bring dessert."

"That would be nice."

"Something chocolate."

Jason paused again and Leah realized that he'd made a small joke at her expense. She didn't know whether to be amused or suspicious.

"Leah?"

"Yes?"

"I meant what I said to you," Jason almost whispered. "Do you know what I'm talking about?"

The sudden tension in her chest was a dead giveaway that she did. Jason's admission played back instantly in her head. Her stomach roiled with the reality of being wanted in that way.

"Yes, I know," Leah finally whispered back.

For whatever reason Jason's confession stayed stubbornly with Leah. She tried not to think about it, not to conjure up a visual scenario of her and Jason together actually being possible. It was enough that her imagination wouldn't cooperate; neither would her senses. *I meant what I said* played over and over in her head. And over and over she felt an unexpected breathlessness at the clarity and boldness of what Jason wanted.

It had also seemed obvious that he had no intention of playing at seduction. She didn't know what his game plan was. Maybe he didn't even have one, which made his words seem like a promise. Or inevitable.

The very idea of it played in Leah's subconscious, but rose to the surface more than a week later when Allen appeared early one evening at the brownstone. She'd just arrived home from work. When she answered the bell and found Allen on the other side of the door, Leah realized she hadn't given him a thought since that night with Jason.

"Allen. What are you doing here?" she asked uncomfortably.

"I thought I'd surprise you," he said, stepping past her into the hallway.

Leah kept the door open and watched in rising annoyance as Allen put his gloves in his pockets and unbuttoned his overcoat. He was expecting to stay.

"We talked about going to Raintree's some night for dinner. I was free and I thought you'd enjoy it."

"You should have called," Leah responded flatly.

Allen straightened his shoulders. "You have other plans again?"

She watched him silently for a moment, debating her answer. Leah finally shook her head. "No. But I really don't want to go out tonight. I have some artwork I want to get done."

Allen pursed his lips. "Is that anything like having to wash your hair or something like that?"

"Allen . . ." she began patiently.

"Okay," he interrupted. "We can stay in. Look. I just wanted to talk to you." He gestured toward the door, and Leah closed it.

"About what?"

"You know, you're making it damned hard for me. I wanted to talk about the future. You and me. There's talk about moving me up into the international division of customer service, possibly as a V.P."

She crossed her arms over her chest. "Congratulations."

"It makes the company look good. Black male, Brown undergraduate, Yale MBA. Things are happening, Leah. And I thought it was time to—"

She began to feel hot. She felt her heart begin to race in anxiety. "You're pushing me, Allen. I'm happy about your prospects, but—"

Allen suddenly exploded. "Dammit, Leah! How do I

get through to you? How long are you going to make me keep apologizing?"

"Don't yell at me. I'm not making you do anything."

The door swung open, and Gail stood on the threshold.

"What's going on?" she asked, her gaze going back and forth between them. "I could hear you before I got to the door."

Once Gail decided that her sister was being bullied by Allen, she turned on him like a tigress protecting a cub. Gail misunderstood the tone of the encounter, and put her own spin on it. Leah wondered what the devil Gail was thinking to come at Allen, practically with her claws drawn, to demand that he leave her sister alone. She found herself between Gail and Allen acting as referee. If it wasn't so surprising it would have been comical to Leah—both of them fighting over her. She watched her sister's response, stunned.

Leah sighed and rubbed her temples. Another headache. And she felt tense. She knew Allen had tried to explain, before Gail had appeared with her righteous indignation, that he'd been thinking about them. It wasn't a discussion that Leah wanted to have just then, but as skittish and uncertain as she was about Allen, she didn't know how to make him stop. Leah grabbed Gail's arm.

"It's okay, Gail. Stop it. We weren't fighting."

Gail turned on her. "Don't let him treat you this way."

"You should talk," Allen shot back. "This is all your fault."

"Okay, enough! Gail, if you don't mind I can handle this. Allen's not staying." She looked pointedly at him.

"Good," Gail muttered. "Can't do anything right." She pushed past them into the house.

Allen stood controlling his anger. "You want me to go."

"Yes. I appreciate that—that you need to talk. But not now. Not tonight. I'm not prepared to."

"Then when?"

"I don't know," Leah said helplessly. "Soon."

He stared at her. "I'll call you," he muttered. He pulled open the door and left. The door rattled closed behind him.

Leah looked through the window next to the door, watching Allen's departure. He'd left his car farther down the block, and his purposeful strides, long and angry, carried him away from her in that direction. She felt sorry, but also relieved.

Leah approached the kitchen entrance and stood cautiously watching her sister. Gail was sitting at the table with a cigarette in one hand and a glass of orange juice in the other. Leah wondered if Gail had put vodka in it.

"What was that all about?" Leah asked.

But Gail glanced over her shoulder to give Leah a look with just the right amount of indignation and surprise.

"You tell me. I come home to find Allen looming over you, and I thought he was going to do something stupid."

"Temporary insanity?" Leah questioned sarcastically.

"I thought you two were fighting. I thought he was going to . . . well . . ." She shrugged.

"First of all, Allen wasn't looming over me, and second of all, we weren't fighting. 'Leave my sister alone'?" Leah repeated, both skeptical and incredulous. "What's the matter with you?"

"Okay. So I overreacted," Gail said, more skittish than contrite. "It sounded like he was about to say something to . . . to hurt you."

Leah didn't know whether to be touched, confused, or amused. Confused won out. "Like what?"

Gail drew deeply on her cigarette and delicately blew it out in a thin, vaporish stream. "Since he obviously didn't say anything significant, it doesn't matter."

"We've known Allen more than two years, and you're just now getting protective? He and I have had arguments before."

But Leah didn't remark to her sister that this time, while not exactly an argument, had been different. She'd always given in to Allen in the past, letting him win the point. The discussions had never been so serious that the outcome had mattered to her one way or another. Her ego wasn't on the line. But this evening's encounter had been about her, planning and doing things she didn't want to do. Maybe Gail had sensed that it was, too. Leah frowned at her sister as another thing came back to her. It had happened while their three voices had vied to be heard over one another.

"Why did Allen say it was all your fault?"

Gail looked at her for a long moment, the fine brows arched up. She looked like she was either trying to remember, or trying to think of how to answer. Finally she just shrugged.

"I have no idea."

Leah had to be satisfied that her sister did not.

"God, one more hour before we get out of here," Jill complained, looking at the mess on her worktable.

"Have a hot date tonight?" Leah asked.

"As a matter of fact, I do."

Leah heard the hesitation and looked at Jill. "Peter?"

"Yes." Jill nodded.

Leah was surprised to see her blush.

"What's he like?"

Jill got up abruptly from her chair again, and went to a supply shelf in search of something.

"Very nice," she said with her back turned. "I mean, he's okay. He likes to eat out . . ." She inadvertently knocked over a box of pencils. "We go to some nice places. Expensive, too."

Two glass jars of rubber cement clanked.

"Jill, forget that stuff. I want to hear more about him. You were so unsure when he first asked you out."

Jill turned around, but her chuckle was almost nervous. "Well, I got over it."

"What do you do besides go out to eat? You can skip the personal stuff," Leah teased, and Jill's smile was shy.

"We go to basketball games sometimes. And he's a hockey fan, but I hate it."

Jill continued on, but Leah found she suddenly couldn't stay focused. The mention of hockey immediately brought an image of Jason to her mind—the moment before he'd kissed her. Sometimes she could still feel the moment of contact, when the firmness of his lips had surprised her. Leah wished she'd stop thinking about it. She shouldn't have allowed it.

"Is Peter from New York?" Leah forced herself to ask Jill.

Jill laughed. "No one's from New York. Unless they're from Brooklyn. I think he's from Ohio. He's been an editor here for four years. Or did he say five?"

Leah frowned. "You don't seem to know an awful lot about him."

"I know enough. And it's early yet."

Leah sighed. "So, what do you think?"

She had only meant to tease, but she looked up from her work when Jill didn't answer, to find her apparently giving the question serious thought.

"I don't know. How do you know when it's the real

thing, Leah?" she asked quietly. "Does it count if when he kisses you, you wonder what happened to your ability to think?"

Sounded good to Leah, although she knew the question was rhetorical.

"Does it count if at first you didn't think much of him, but suddenly you can't stop thinking about him?" Jill let out a long sigh and made her way back to her desk to sit facing Leah. "Anyway, it's still new. Kind of sudden. I don't know if he's the one for me or if I'm the one for him."

Leah continued to watch Jill. It seemed so easy for her. She'd try this one, but if it didn't work out, well, maybe next time. What if she was in love with him? How could she ever consider anyone else?

"I'm sure it'll work out," Leah offered.

"Maybe. In the meantime he's fun to be with. How about you? What's new with you and Allen?"

Leah blinked. The question seemed to come right out of left field, and she had no real answer. She tried to show no particular expression, and made a vague gesture with her hand. "Nothing much. I haven't seen him recently."

"Really? Nothing serious, I hope."

"Well, it's just that . . . I don't know . . ." Leah gave up.

"Maybe it's time for a change," Jill suggested.

"What do you mean, a change?"

"As far as I know, you haven't dated anyone else but Allen. Yet your relationship with him seems so . . . so predictable, you know? Why not meet some new people? Make him nervous."

Leah was not the least worried about making Allen nervous. She was making herself very nervous, however, because she was no longer sure what she wanted from Allen. Or even if she wanted him. She'd also tried very hard to convince herself that she wasn't dating Jason. They were just spending time together once in a while. Like friends.

"Are you doing anything special for Christmas?" Jill asked.

"Not that I know of." Leah half smiled. "Gail and I probably won't be flying to Chicago to be with my father. Allen will spend the holidays with his family in Philadelphia."

She wondered again about Jason. Would he have to spend it alone? She was thinking of family, of course, but that didn't mean he would be alone. Leah quickly realized where her thoughts were taking her and shifted in her seat to break the spell. She glanced at Jill.

"We certainly don't sound very much in the spirit, do we?"

"Just another Christmas," Jill murmured, shaking her head.

"Like most of the others," Leah concurred.

"My New Year's resolutions are to find a bigger apartment, lose weight, and take a cruise."

"You mean, you're not going to hope that Peter is the man of your dreams?"

"Nope." Jill grinned brightly. "I'm only going to hope that he won't become my worst nightmare. What about you? What do you want for the New Year?"

The first thing that came to Leah's mind was that the new year wouldn't resemble the last one.

"To be surprised," she whispered cryptically.

Gail was writing out her Christmas cards. It was the least she could do to contribute to the spirit of the season.

She sipped from a glass of wine and watched a rerun of *The Bishop's Wife* as she wrote messages and addressed envelopes. When the phone rang she took her time gracefully unfolding herself from the sofa. She whispered hello absently, absorbed in the Hollywood magic of the movie. Suddenly a voice launched into pleas and apologies.

It was Allen.

"Leah? Look, baby, I know you're still upset, but we've got to talk about this. We have to try to work things out and go on with our lives, our future. Why can't I come over so we can deal with it?"

Gail realized the mistake at once and started to identify herself. And then she changed her mind. She had not expected this opportunity, and her thoughts raced as she quickly tried to formulate a plan.

"What is there to talk about, Allen?" Gail asked in a soft imitation of Leah's voice. It was close enough.

"About us!"

"Ummmm," Gail murmured noncommittally.

"I said I was sorry about Thanksgiving. What more do you want?" Allen asked peevishly.

Gail listened carefully.

"Leah, are you listening to me?" he asked impatiently.

"Yes . . . yes."

"Well? When do I get to see you? We can't let this thing just go on and on between us."

"All right," Gail said with real hesitation in her voice. What had happened at Thanksgiving?

"When? I'm leaving to spend Christmas with my folks next week. I want to see you before then. Can I come Monday?"

"No, not Monday," Gail hastened. "Make it Wednesday."

"Leah, are you all right?

It was time to get off the phone. "I'm fine. I was,

er, just in the middle of something, that's all. I really have to get off the phone."

"Okay. Then I'll see you Wednesday, right?"

"Yes, fine. Bye, Allen."

On December 21 Jason came to dinner.

Gail met him at the door. She raised her brows haughtily as she looked him over carefully. She had to admit there was no resemblance between the man in the doorway and the one who'd camped out on her doorstep several months earlier. Gail took her own sweet time before opening the door and stepping aside to let Jason in.

"You certainly look a lot better than the last time I saw you," she said tartly.

Jason grinned at the caustic greeting. "Hello," he said. It was going to be one hell of an evening.

Right off Jason noticed how beautiful Gail Downey was and that she was well aware of it. The second thing he noticed as he followed her into the house was that Gail Downey didn't much like him and was probably never going to.

When Leah came from the kitchen to greet him, Jason could see from the furtive look in her eyes that she'd developed doubts about the wisdom of going through with the evening. Was she sorry she'd invited him? He had a sense now, as Leah smiled a nervous hello, that had he called to confirm the dinner as he'd planned to several days earlier, Leah would have canceled. He was glad he hadn't called.

Jason noticed that Leah was an inch or so shorter than her willowy sister, and not as curvaceous. They were both pretty women very similar in facial features except, again, Gail had a sensuality calculated to start fires.

"I see you made it," Leah commented foolishly.

"Did you think I wouldn't?" Jason challenged softly.

Leah only looked at him, surprised how close he'd come to the mark.

Gail seated herself on the sofa. "Fooled you, didn't he?" she murmured.

"Would you like a drink?" Leah asked, indicating a chair for Jason. "Wine?"

"Beer," he answered, taking a seat opposite Gail. He wanted to keep her in full view. Leah disappeared into the kitchen, and Jason and Gail silently appraised each other. Neither wanted to be the first to blink.

Jason suspected that her silence was meant to make him feel ill at ease. She obviously didn't particularly like having him in her home. Jason only waited patiently for conversation to begin. But Gail was not like Leah. She wasn't going to be social. And she wasn't going to be polite.

Jason looked toward the kitchen as Leah came back with a tray of drinks. She was nervous. He could tell she was going to use her duties as hostess to keep a distance between them. Jason understood that Leah was retreating. *He* almost had. Especially after his confession the last time. But now that he was here, seeing her reminded him of that kiss. He could still recall the way Leah had hesitated, making him feel as though he had to teach her not to be afraid. And she hadn't withdrawn. He could feel the moment she'd begun to respond as well.

Leah smiled tentatively at him as she gave him the bottle of Molson. He accepted it, and with his other hand unexpectedly grabbed hers, pulling her to the vacant seat next to him.

Gail crossed her legs comfortably. "What do you do?"

Jason exchanged looks with Leah. He thought she would have told her sister everything about him. He was pleased that Leah might have kept some things private. He was also perversely annoyed that some obvious things about him Leah did not want her sister to know.

"I'm a cop."

"What?" Gail thundered.

She jumped to her feet, eyes glaring. Then she abruptly reached across the coffee table and pulled the bottle of beer from Jason's hands, stunning both him and her sister.

Leah came to her feet. "Gail, what are you doing?"

Gail fumed at her. "Are you out of your mind? This man kills people."

Leah took the beer back by force and returned it to Jason. The look she gave him expressed determination.

"I'm sorry, I—"

"Don't you dare apologize for me," Gail snorted angrily.

"Did I say something wrong?" Jason inquired easily, taking a sip from his beer. He got no answer.

He watched as Gail reluctantly reseated herself, her hands balled into fists in her lap. Jason suspected that she honestly didn't know if she wanted to slap him or her sister.

"I'll be damned," Gail muttered darkly. "Are you one of those guys with a Great White Hope complex? Or do you think you're everybody's Big Brother? Is being a cop just an excuse to carry a gun and use it on black folks?"

Jason settled himself back into the chair cushions. He could sense the helplessness and stiffness in Leah, seated next to him. He was tempted to touch her, to let her know he could take care of himself. But he was certain the move would just give Gail another reason to attack.

"Please, feel free to ask me anything," he said comfortably. "I'm not out to save the world if that's what you mean. I'm only helping out in my little corner of it. Yours, too."

"Screw that," Gail countered with spirit. "Your corner is white. And please don't hand me some bullshit about it's justice you stand for."

Jason shrugged. "All right. I won't. But if someone didn't defend your rights, too, you wouldn't be here." He gestured around him to Gail and Leah's middle-class environment.

"I got here," Gail argued, "despite the white man's best and worst efforts. You haven't done me any favors."

Leah suddenly stood up. "Now that we're all acquainted, let's have dinner," she said sarcastically. She gave her sister a pointedly annoyed look as she led the way into the dining room.

Once Gail had seated herself, she watched Jason with continued suspicion. "So you sobered up and came looking for my sister."

Jason swallowed his first bite and gave Leah a look he hoped she would understand was personal. "I just wanted to thank her."

"That was months ago. How long does it take to say thank you? And how the hell did you manage to get from that to dinner in my house?" Gail inquired, her anger building again.

Leah put her fork and knife down sharply, fed up with Gail's barbs. "For God's sake, Gail. Can't you just shut up, eat dinner, and be gracious?"

"Someone has to look out for fools and little children. So far you're behaving like both, sweetheart."

"And who looks out for you?" Jason asked quietly.

Gail had not expected any direct comment from Jason, and his question brought her up short.

"Excuse me?" Gail narrowed her eyes dangerously at him.

Jason looked directly at her. "I mean, has anyone ever told you to mind your own business?"

"Jason!" Leah rounded on him at once. Gail's mouth dropped open in stunned silence.

Jason calmly continued eating. "Leah is not a functional idiot or a child, and I'm not a racist. Well, maybe I am a little." he wiped his mouth slowly with his napkin and then looked squarely at Gail. "I really hate black people who hate white people who hate black people. It never ends, know what I mean?"

Leah and Gail just sat staring at him, neither of them knowing what to say next. Leah could see that her sister was in shock. This was a first. Leah knew suddenly that she had never in her life seen her sister speechless. It was quite a novelty.

Jason put his napkin down, feeling the oppressing silence beginning to weigh on him. He felt tired and edgy. He'd run into people like Gail before. He was just sorry that this particular person had to be someone related to Leah. He was really pleased that Leah had even thought to invite him for dinner. It would probably be the last time.

He looked at Leah, who cautiously returned his questioning glance. "Should I keep eating or would you like me to leave now?"

Surprisingly, Leah began to grin. "I would like you to stay. I'm anxious to see what else is going to happen tonight."

Gail gave Leah a murderous look, but calmly picked up her fork to finish her dinner. "A little competition is good for the soul," she murmured. "If Allen can survive, so can I."

The reference to Allen made Leah wince. She glanced at Jason but found him biting into a buttered slice of homemade rosemary bread.

"You're a good cook," he said to her.

"Thanks," Leah murmured, half expecting her sister to say something rude.

"It runs in the family," Gail commented.

That was it.

"Can I have the recipe for the bread?" Jason asked Leah.

She raised her brows and laughed lightly. "Do you cook?"

Jason grinned. "No. But aren't you supposed to ask for recipes when you go to someone's house for dinner? It's a compliment or something."

Leah shook her head at him and smiled. She loved the way he just bounced back. "I'll give you a doggy bag. You can take the rest with you. The recipe is a family secret."

"And it's not authentic soul food," Gail said dryly. "In case you thought it was."

Leah sighed. The truce was over.

"I didn't," Jason said easily, helping himself to another slice.

By the end of the evening, however, Leah was feeling let down. She didn't know what she'd expected dinner to be like, but certainly not the undeclared war between her sister and Jason. And she'd somehow thought it would be more cozy, more like when she and Jason were out together alone. After dinner, she and Gail cleared the table and Jason entertained himself with music from the CD player and another beer in the living room.

He could hear the conversation, or rather the debate between the two women, coming from the kitchen. He stayed put. Jason was girding himself for the next round with Leah's sister, but unexpectedly Gail made a surprisingly discreet retreat when she was finished in the kitchen.

She sashayed into the living room, where Jason was

looking at framed photographs arranged atop a piano. Leah was right behind her.

"Well," Gail sighed dramatically, "I've been told, in so many words, to mind my own business and to act nice. I can take a hint. I'm going to my room, so behave yourselves. I don't want to have to call the cops."

Jason and Leah silently watched Gail's seductive ascent up the stairs. Jason let out a low, long whistle and turned to Leah. "She's a real firecracker."

"Gail has always been right up front and believes in speaking her mind. Even when she shouldn't."

"That's okay. At least I know where I stand with her."

Leah was puzzled. "You do?"

"Not too close," Jason finished dryly.

Leah started to laugh. Jason was pleased that he'd managed that. He watched Leah for a moment, finding new things about her that he liked. Her hair had a kind of loose, twisty waviness to it, full and thick. She had a slender neck and small shoulders. Smallish breasts.

Jason's silent examination was making Leah nervous again, he could see, but he said nothing to her. Finally Leah turned and sat on the sofa. He smiled. She wasn't ready to end the evening, either. He followed Leah to the sofa but didn't sit too close. He lit a cigarette not because he really wanted one but because he needed something to do with his hands. He looked at Leah thoughtfully.

"Gail's very different from you."

"You noticed," Leah said with a laugh. "She's very strong. Very together. I wish I could be more like her."

Jason shook his head in disagreement. "She could stand to be a little more like you. Nice. Soft."

"A marshmallow?" she suggested flippantly.

Jason grinned. "Not at all. You're too hard on yourself. You're not that soft. But you have more . . . humanity."

Leah started to fidget. She didn't know what he meant. If it was a compliment, it made her feel strange.

Jason looked around the room. "This is a nice brownstone. It's got great details."

Leah glanced around. "I love this house. It actually belonged to an old spinster aunt. She left it jointly to Gail and me when she died."

"Where are your parents?"

"There's only my dad. He's from Illinois originally. When he retired he wanted to move back there. Gail and I have our lives here."

Jason nodded, glancing around. "Is the stairwell real oak?"

"The floors, too. There are six stained glass windows on the upper floors."

"I'd like to see them sometime."

The offhand comment made Leah look closely at Jason. She'd assumed that after what he'd been through with Gail, the last place he'd want to see again was the inside of this house. She quickly changed the subject.

"Have you decided what you're doing for Christmas?"

"I don't know. Maybe go to my sister's."

His answer was terse, and it was apparent to Leah that he didn't want to talk about the holidays. She remembered he was supposed to have spent it with his son.

"Is your sister married?" she asked.

He smiled fondly. "Very. She's got four kids. Her husband, Nick, is a great guy."

When Jason looked at her again, Leah felt a jolt through her body. She knew exactly what was going through his mind just then. She saw in Jason's eyes that loneliness and lingering pain, the kind that comes with loving people and then losing them. Was Jason thinking of Michael? Or his ex-wife?

But it was also frightening, that look. She knew instinctively it had less to do with loss than it did with hopefulness, wishful thinking. Need. Somewhere in this look Leah knew their relationship had changed again. She found that she couldn't look away from it. Jason couldn't, either. He reached out, and just touched her hand.

"I gotta go," he suddenly whispered, his eyes searching for something in her face. He got up abruptly, putting the beer bottle on the coffee table, and walked slowly to the door to retrieve his coat. He knew that Leah was following. "Thanks for dinner. It was nice. Tell your sister she missed her calling. Does Al Sharpton know about her?"

"I'm glad you could come," Leah said, feeling slightly depressed. She didn't really know why. "And I hope you have a good holiday. No matter where you spend it." She opened the door.

Jason turned to face her in the small entrance foyer. He pushed the door closed again. Leah couldn't see his face completely in the shadowed darkness of that spot, but she knew he was staring at her. She knew what was going to happen. The only question was whether or not she wanted it to happen. Jason took hold of her upper arms and began to pull her toward him. He bent to kiss her cheek.

All evening she had tried to treat Jason as nothing more than an invited guest to her home. A friend. But when he touched her, Leah felt a spark of anticipation ignite inside her. There was so much tension she could barely breathe.

His lips on her cheek began a journey toward her mouth, but Leah wouldn't let him. She didn't think she could bear that raw, naked feeling that would come with his kiss. She put both hands on Jason's chest and pushed him away.

"Jason, no . . ." She shook her head, lowering her gaze. "I don't think it's a good idea for us to get involved."

He lifted his head but didn't release her. "We're not involved. Who's Allen?"

The shift was jarring, and Leah squeezed her eyes closed for a second to focus her brain. "Allen . . ." She took a deep breath. She couldn't think straight. "He's my, er, I . . . he's someone I've been dating for a while."

Even as she said the words Jason bent forward again to kiss the corner of her mouth. Her lips briefly. He stroked her cheek.

"Is it serious?"

The calm of his question, the absurdity of the situation, immediately annoyed Leah. She stepped out of Jason's reach, jerking her head away from his hand. "If it was serious you wouldn't be here."

Unexpectedly Jason smiled at her. He reached behind his back and opened the door. He quickly leaned to kiss her cheek again, and before Leah could recover he was through the door and halfway down the steps.

"Wait a minute!" Leah ordered with a spurt of anger. "You never say good-bye. You just walk away."

Jason looked up at her from the foot of the stairs. He put on his red baseball cap. "This isn't good-bye. Merry Christmas, Leah."

Leah watched him walk away before she muttered a very satisfying oath under her breath. She stepped inside and shut the door soundly.

Chapter Six

Leah sat in front of the mirror and stared at herself. She saw a thin toffee-colored face dominated by a pair of sable eyes. Her hair, literally her crowning glory, was thick with highlights of red. This morning it was wild and tangled, but it added a certain sensuality to her face. Her nose was short, her mouth nicely shaped for her face. It was a pretty face, so she'd been told. But beyond the features she still wondered what people saw when they looked at her. Did they see a young woman who was attractive? Did they see someone with a history, questions, and doubts? Or did they just see someone black?

Leah examined herself thoroughly in the mirror as though she'd never seen herself before. She was well proportioned and everything functioned. Why, then, did she get so many different responses from so many different men?

Philip's unexplained rejection of her had done much to undermine her sense of being just a woman, albeit a very young one. Leah had no particular ill feelings toward Ron. She attributed that failed relationship to too little experience and know-how on her part for someone like him. Ron had been focused on something more important to himself than she had been. Some ideology that was impossible to compete with. The man in the stairwell that time had had a face. It was con-

nected to a person whom Leah didn't know and who
didn't know her. Nonetheless, he'd left a profound
mark on her life. For as long as Leah continued to
have the dream, *he* would be like some poor distant
relative who remained unmentioned and in the shadows of her existence.

Allen?

Allen she'd had more hope for, but they'd spent two
years in a netherland-like limbo where any depth of
feelings, and future, had never been stimulated or
encouraged.

And then there was Jason.

Standing naked in front of her mirror, Leah closed
her eyes and sighed. She thought of Jason's sorrow, of
his sense of humor, which set off her own. Of his
attention to her, which made her feel special. Of her
attention to him, which was more than curiosity. She
very much needed to feel special in *someone's* life.
What did it mean . . . what *could* it mean that that
someone was Jason?

She hugged herself against the cold morning air.
Goose bumps rose on her skin. She kept her eyes
closed and allowed herself the memory of Jason holding and kissing her. She had no right to welcome it.
He had no right to offer it. Or had he? What was he
doing in her life to confuse her all over again?

Last night in her dreams she'd run miles again, in a
murkey tunnel with that man hot in pursuit. She could
no longer tell if he was closer or father away, but he
was behind her, and he still held the knife. It seemed
like such an effort to outrun him, to outsmart him in
one corridor and then another. Her body had gotten
so much heavier and slower since the last time he'd
tried to catch her.

In her head Leah imagined the grating pitch of his

laugh, and it got more hysterical, louder in her ears. She was still in a maze and she ran along the hall again, heading toward the tunnel opening. He wasn't close to her yet, and she felt that maybe this time she could get down the corridor and head toward the entrance. She was elated. It was getting easier. The light at the opening was directly in front of her. Her hand reached out before her, stretching beyond its natural length. Her heart pounded. Oh, God, she was going to make it. Her fingers touched the sun. But another hand, one from behind her, tapped on her shoulder.

"No, no . . ."

Just a few more inches and she would have been free.

"No. No . . ." Leah moaned in her sleep.

"Leah, wake up. Wake up!" Gail ordered softly, shaking her sister's shoulder.

Leah rolled onto her back as the dream slipped away. Her heart raced. She forced her eyes open and stared into the frowning face of her sister. She collapsed against the pillows. "Was I . . crying out again?"

"It's all right."

"I thought I . . ."

"Bad dreams?"

Leah silently nodded.

"I thought we'd outgrown those. You've been having a lot of them lately, haven't you? Do you know I can hear you groaning from the next room?"

"I'm sorry I woke you up."

"What's wrong? What's causing these awful dreams?"

Leah didn't answer.

"Want to talk about it?"

"No." Leah shook her head sharply. "I'm awake now. Really. I'll be all right."

"Why don't we do something together?" Gail suggested brightly.

"What do you mean, something?"

Gail narrowed her eyes and considered. "I don't know. A play? Or you can come to our office party. The head buyer gives great gifts." Gail straightened abruptly. "Or let's do our Christmas shopping together."

Leah blinked at her, trying to focus on the present, the question, and her sister's proposal. They hated shopping together. She smiled crookedly.

"That could be fun."

"Yeah. And we'll grab some dinner somewhere, and—"

"Tonight?"

Gail's face fell. "I can't tonight. I was thinking maybe tomorrow?"

Leah shook her head. "End of the year production meeting. I'll probably be at the office until after six. How about the day after tomorrow? It's my last offer," Leah teased quietly.

But Gail was deep in thought. "I'd really like to, but . . ."

Leah's smile was tired. "You have a date that won't wait."

Gail sighed and shrugged.

Leah didn't suggest that her sister might cancel the date. She patted Gail's hand. "Thanks anyway for the offer. It was a nice idea."

"We can still do something together over the holidays," Gail coaxed with her most persuasive manner. She stood up from the side of the bed. "It's almost time to get up anyway. Why don't you take a shower? You'll feel much better. I'll go make some hot chocolate. It's cold in here!" she declared, hugging herself as she left the room.

It took a little longer for Leah to pull herself together and out of the bed that morning. She had to first gather all the parts of herself that had been scattered in the night.

Now Leah stared at her reflection, looking deeply into the dark centers of her eyes. For a brief moment there was a sort of veil that held the residue of the dream; the only difference was that in that light at the end of the long corridor she'd heard her name called. It had echoed back to her . . . in Jason's voice.

In the quiet darkness of his apartment the energy of the day lingered for Jason. The residual adrenaline pumped into his brain, jumbling all the events together.

He'd had a bad day at the precinct. One of the kids he'd been working with through family court had been shot dead by a shop owner. The proprietor said the kid was trying to rob his store. Jason had not only gone to the morgue to see the boy's body, but had been asked by his supervising officer to notify the family that, two days before Christmas, their son was dead.

Maybe the kid was dead because of Christmas, although that was only Jason's guess. The boy had been sixteen, with no money to buy gifts for his family or even his new son. The family would have no tree or decorations. Jason could put the two bits of information together and figure out how all of it would have to end.

Then a game that he'd coached that week on Riker's Island had broken out into a brawl between the two teams. All future games had been suspended until further notice. A report had come in about a seventeen-year-old mother who had apparently grown tired of the responsibility of her child and of herself. She had drowned the infant in the kitchen sink and then had slit her own wrists. But she was going to live.

Slack, born Jerome Findlay, had tried to choke a male attendant at the group home where he'd been assigned and housed. There was no place for Slack to go for the holidays. There was no one who wanted him. The fragments of his family had been divided up among many of the city's social agencies: jail, state hospital, foster care . . . Potter's Field. Jason tried to find someone to take charge of the sixteen-year-old, even for one night. But Jason knew that Slack was too difficult, too hostile. Too prone to unpredictable violence. He had found several hours to go and spend with Slack, trying to talk him into staying cool. It worked, but it had only been a stopgap measure. Jason still believed that if he could just find the right combination of time and activities, of attention for the boy, that Slack might still be turned around.

All he tragedies of the day made Jason also remember Vietnam and all the children he'd seen die there.

'Nam had been desperate and frightening and surreal. Of course, there had been atrocities all the time on all sides. But he'd never been able to get used to the way children were used. As shields and messengers, as decoys and bounty. As disposable commodities in a situation that was not of their making. He would always remember the first time his unit had come upon a small roadside village, mostly bombed out and devastated. But in this village all the young men were away fighting in the war. Area guerrilla activity was still known to be fierce, and protected by sympathizers. These people's lives had already been so invaded, so violated, that now, as the unit approached, they just sat waiting without movement or sound or expectations. Old men and women . . . and the children.

Whatever happened to them happened. There were no longer good guys or bad guys. There were only, always, the soldiers. The old people and children sat squatted with distended stomachs from lack of food and proper diet.

Jason and his men had been looking for a small band of Vietcong known to be in the area. The only trouble in a country like this was that the enemy could look just like the people he and his men were trying to protect. But following the routine, the men searched the entire village, checked for ways they knew the guerillas had been known to hide and disguise themselves. It was clear after fifteen minutes that there were no fighters there. One of the men in Jason's unit, however, had discovered a young girl half hidden among the squatted silent group of villagers. They'd been shielding her from the soldiers. But the men had been in and out of the jungle for too many weeks, and they knew. They could smell her. She might have been as old as fifteen but looked younger because she was so small.

"Hey! Look what we got here. Hey, you guys. Right here. She ain't too dirty, neither," the soldier joked, pulling the reluctant girl into the open.

"Lay off. Let's just get the hell out of here," Jason tried, nervous that there might yet be a trap. "Can't you horny bastards see she's just a kid?"

"So what? Hell, she's got all the parts she needs, right?"

"Come on, man," another began. "She could be your sister."

Yet another of the soldiers grabbed the girl by the hair and shoved her into the dry, tall grass. "No gook could ever be my sister," he said with a snort, pushing her to the ground, egged on by several of his buddies. A few of the men turned away to squat and smoke cigarettes; most waited their turn. Some of the men didn't care one way or the other, but no one came to her aid. No one moved. She never wept, never struggled, but lay there silently as young men had their way.

The old looked down at their bare feet. The children fought in the dirt for scraps of rations thrown carelessly by some of the waiting soldiers. In the tall grass there was only grunting. Jason wandered off, not wanting to be a witness but doing nothing to stop it. Off in the distance he could hear the pop-pop of single-shot gunfire. Smoke appeared in the air all around him.

The last man, now finished, hitched up his pants and called the men together.

"Jesus, that was good," he crowed as they all slowly moved out and continued beyond the village on their search.

Jason hung back. Slowly he had approached the dry grass, looking for the girl. Maybe she'd just get up and one of her people would take care of her. What Jason spotted first was the red of her blood. She was stretched out, eyes staring blankly into the space over her head. Her ragged pants had been pulled down around one ankle. Her top was pulled up to expose an undeveloped chest with rib bones pressing against her skin. Jason stood in a trance and watched the blood ooze from between her thin young legs. She was dead.

Jason turned away and was sick. He hadn't help her. Maybe he wasn't supposed to help her. His mission, after all, was to stay alive. But he might have done something more than just be a soldier. He might as well have been one of the men who'd raped her.

Jason felt his pain increase, because the scene segued into one of a Christmas spent in 'Nam in a muddy trench. There had been no dinner to speak of, and the mere thought of family and presents, and goodwill toward men, seemed completely out of place. In his depression and loneliness of being away from home and surrounded by the constant fear of dying, Jason had found a young Vietnamese girl and spent the night with her. It was only because he needed so badly to believe that someone else felt as lost as he did. And if they were that vulnerable, too, maybe they could trust each other.

He'd fallen asleep afterward only to awaken and find her pointing his own gun at him. The Christmas truce of goodwill was over. One of his men looking for him that holiday morning had blown her brains out before the girl could figure out how to work the gun.

And, Jason finally thought, this time last year he had been helping Michael raise the Christmas tree in the living room of his mother's house. Michael had said to him, "I'm real glad you're here, Dad."

Jason closed his eyes and leaned back against the pillows on his bed. He was tired. And he was lonely. Why was he thinking about the precinct and dead children? In the dark Jason smoked until his throat burned. He tried to dim the nightmares in his head. But the nicotine wasn't enough, and he got up and searched around his kitchen until he found a hall-full bottle of gin and one of scotch. He thought he wanted someone there with him, someone he could take to bed and hold and love—just for the night—to get him through the dreams. He thought of a half-dozen names and rejected them all. It was much better just to get drunk instead. Alone. Jason decided he didn't want to see anybody he had feelings for tonight, because tomorrow's hangover might wash them all away.

Christmas Eve at the precinct wasn't much different than any other day of the year. There were still loud voices, protests from the holding pen, phones ringing. There had been a laughable attempt at decoration. Silvery streamers were hung on the wall behind the front desk. A Christmas tree, a "gift" from a friendly street dealer, stood brightly lit opposite the first-floor elevator. At least most of the men would get to go home early to be with their families.

The very idea sank Jason deeper into the hole of his depression. He had so little family left. He felt his stomach churn. It heaved every time he thought about all the holiday drinks he'd had so far that afternoon. It was the office party. He hadn't been very sober to begin with from the night before. He should have forgotten about the scotch.

He'd lost two kids this week. Where the hell had he been? He was still feeling that there should have been something he could have done to prevent those deaths.

Jason sat slouched in his desk chair, his eyes bloodshot and tired. He hadn't bothered to shave that morning, and no one had even noticed. Except maybe Joe. Joe had seen him like this before.

"Don't you know it's the season to be jolly and all that shit? Come on, man. Lighten up. It's Christmas, for Christ's sake. No pun intended," Joe cackled.

Jason didn't look up from his methodical efforts to loop paper clips together into a chain. He dropped several of the clips, but thought better of trying to bend to retrieve them from the floor.

"Do you ever wonder if it matters, Joe? Do you ever say to yourself, what the hell are we doing here anyway?"

Joe sighed deeply and leaned back in his squeaky chair. "Here we go again," he muttered. "Every time you get drunk you get philosophical. No, I don't think about it 'cause it don't matter. I don't think I make a damn of a difference. What happens, happens, man. With or without us."

Jason dropped more clips and in frustration tossed the link chain onto the already messy desk. "Then why bother? Why don't we just sit back, let everyone handle their own problems? We could just sweep up the victims afterward. Save a lot of time and energy."

Joe chuckled. "Now, that's a great idea. I know a couple of people I'd like to get rid of."

Jason glared at Joe's sarcasm and slammed a drawer shut. "All right. So it was a stupid idea."

Joe stopped laughing and sat forward. "Look, man. It's just a job, not a calling. Simple. You win some and you lose some. Most people don't give a shit what we're trying to do. Hell, sometimes we don't give a damn what we do. I put in my eight hours, and I collect my check."

Jason stared at Joe. "So that's the answer? Don't take it seriously?"

"Sure, you can take it seriously. Just don't take it home with you at night. You got to learn to turn it off when the buzzer sounds. Else you're dead in the water, man. You'll never reach retirement."

"And that's more important?"

"Damn straight."

Jason knew that Joe was right. Maybe. Jason looked at his partner and envied him. The world was made for people like Joe: just the facts, thank you. The gray areas were for someone else to gnaw over.

Joe sighed in exasperation. He threw himself back against his chair, and the spring action threatened to topple him backward to the floor. But the chair held and Joe comfortably rocked. He shook his head at Jason.

"Come on, Jace. Why do you do this to yourself?"

"Do what?" he mumbled.

"Tear yourself up inside, man. Care too damn much. People get hurt when they care."

Jason smiled at the irony. "That's how I know I'm still alive, I guess. I can't let go."

Joe shook his head again. "You don't need to have your guts turned inside out to know that. You thinking about those two stiffs from yesterday?"

Jason grimaced at the cold description.

"Too late. Can't do nothing for them that's dead and gone. You want to worry about something? How about how *not* to let it be you?"

Jason nodded absently. It was the only way to get off the subject. Joe just didn't understand. He didn't respond the same way.

"So what are you doing for Christmas? Not staying alone, are you?"

Jason blinked at him, and shook his head. Leah had asked that same question. She'd cared. "No. Soon as I get out of here I'm on the road to P.A. My sister's." He didn't add that he planned on visiting Michael's grave, maybe with Lisa. They didn't have much to say to each other anymore, but they had a grief to share.

Joe suddenly sprang forward again, snapping his fingers sharply. "Almost forgot!"

From under his desk he pulled out a huge, gaily wrapped box. He put it on a vacant chair that was on casters and, with a push, sent the chair rolling toward Jason.

"This is from me and Nora. It's a great gift. There's a cooked turkey in there and everything."

Jason gave Joe a halfhearted smile. "Thanks."

"Nora said thanks for the portable CD player. I told her it didn't fall off the back of a truck."

Jason looked at Joe and slowly a grin broke out on his tired face.

"Look, Jace," Joe began softly. "We can't save the world. We don't know how. I'm not even sure it's worth it."

Jason sighed. "I hope to God you're wrong."

*   *   *

Leah and Gail had their tree up and decorated with ornaments collected in their family for almost three generations. All the presents were piled under the tree, a colorful kaleidoscope of paper and ribbons, waiting to be opened.

On the way home from work Leah stopped next door with two small gifts for Joy and Bobby Chen. She stayed to have coffee with Sarah and to gossip. Sarah gave Leah a piece of antique Chinese embroidery of a phoenix on silk fabric, outlined with ornate brocade ribbon. Leah thought it would look wonderful framed for the dining room.

It was almost nine-thirty when Leah headed for home. Music was playing softly from the living room. She came in the front door quietly, and while she stopped to remove her coat she heard voices coming from the den. She knew Gail's voice at once, but was surprised to recognize Allen's. The voices were muffled and unintelligible down the length of the hallway, but raised in argument. Leah moved toward the room, thinking to join them, glad that Allen had stopped by before his drive down to Philadelphia. She could give him his gift now. She wouldn't have to spend more time than necessary with him. She wouldn't have to be alone with him in the house, with her bedroom just above them. Leah stopped in the hall just outside the entrance when she heard that Gail and Allen were apparently arguing, in part, over her.

"You're an absolute shit, Allen. Who do you think you're fooling? All that crap about *your* career and *your* future and *your* image . . . what about Leah and her future?"

"That's none of your damned business," Allen could be heard growling. "Leah and I are doing just fine."

Gail chuckled. "Oh? Does she know how she fits in with your plans? Do you ever discuss anything with

Leah about what she wants? You want to marry her just to make yourself look good. Well, your fantasy sucks because it's one-sided and it's built on lies."

"You forget that Leah loves me."

"Oh, please . . . Leah doesn't know what love is, and I *know* you're not in love with her. You wish you were."

"Shut up, Gail. Like I said, it's between me and Leah. At least it would have been if you hadn't lied to me. I thought she'd be here and we'd have a chance to be alone and talk."

"Talk about what? About what happened at Thanksgiving, Allen?"

From the hallway Leah could hear an angry sound from Allen.

"What did she tell you?" he asked Gail.

Leah knew her sister well enough to know Gail would bluff.

"Enough," Gail answered softly. "Why don't you tell me your side?"

"Why the hell should you care? You'd already left to spend the night with that—that . . ."

"Oh, oh. Now I get it," Gail laughed softly. "This meeting with Leah wasn't about anything more than protecting yourself. The only person you've managed to fool besides yourself is Leah."

Leah stood rooted, afraid to move or even to breathe normally now that she'd committed herself to eavesdropping. She felt a certain kind of morbid willfulness to stay invisible as secrets were being exchanged.

Her sister's voice lowered, lost its flippant control and sharpness. It became soft and seductive . . . and sincere.

"I don't give a damn about Steven, or any of those guys I dated. I know you think I've slept around. But I've been waving them under your nose like a carrot to get a reaction out of you. And you know what? You not only took a bite, you swallowed the whole damned thing. I knew that sooner or later it was going to get to you if you thought all those other men had me and you couldn't. You wanted to convince yourself that I was unworthy of you. You thought it would be so easy to settle for Leah. She wouldn't give you the hard time that I do, and she'd act the way you wanted. But Leah is not me. You put on your airs and act so superior— who do you think you are? When are you going to stop pretending? You don't want Leah. You only think you should. And if you really loved her, we never would have had that weekend together last September. Your big mistake was in thinking that two nights would get me out of your system."

"You acted like a common tramp," Allen said angrily.

"You loved it," Gail threw back at him. "You're crazy about me, Allen. What you like about me is that I will do exactly what I feel, exactly what turns you on." She laughed softly. "You can play at being conventional during the day, but at night you're no different than other men. I know what you like in bed. If you had any guts, you'd admit it right now and let Leah go."

"And what makes you think I'd want to marry you instead?"

There was silence for a moment. Leah could imagine her sister moving toward Allen. She could almost see Gail looking up at him with her seductive eyes and smiling mouth. She was probably standing very close to Allen now, her gaze smoldering through thick lashes. Leah had seen Gail do that before. Get close enough to bewitch and beguile. She'd use her heated sensuality to capture and hold fast her prey.

Leah shivered. Why was she just standing there listening? Shouldn't she burst in or something? When Gail finally answered Allen's question, her voice was a husky whisper.

"Because I'm your fantasy, Allen. Every time you hold Leah you wish she were me. You and I are one of a kind. We bring out the worst in each other. But think about what it would be like if we brought out the best. We belong together . . ."

Outside the door Leah felt like a ghost. She wasn't eavesdropping. She was saving her life. But the effort had opened up a hole right in the middle of her body, and all her bewilderment poured out in silence. There it was. Said out loud and clear. She was not an object of desire. She was, had been, convenient.

"I knew the first time I saw you. I knew that someday . . . I'd have you," Gail whispered. "You knew it, too."

There was a pause, and Leah knew that they were kissing because she could hear their lips separating on moist little sounds. She began to feel embarrassed.

There was another small movement and Allen mumbled.

"You bitch . . ."

When Leah heard no more sounds she knew precisely what was happening. Allen had grabbed Gail to him and was kissing her passionately.

In a way Leah was glad that it had come to this. It was not unlike what had happened with Ron or Philip, or even her very first crush on Billy. The men in her life had never demonstrated an ability to love her. Perhaps it wasn't even their fault but her own. She was starting to believe that maybe she didn't have the stuff of which great love and commitment were born. Didn't she rate devotion? Didn't she at least rate honesty? Leah felt numb, but also in that instant surprisingly composed and calm. Like she was floating. Detached and free.

She must have made a sound, for Gail and Allen were suddenly at the den door staring in disbelief at her presence. She was pressed back against the wall.

If Leah could have melted into the wallpaper she would have. Instead she stood there facing the truth and letting it burn deeply into her soul.

Gail's expression was defiant, like that of someone who'd done something wrong but who would still have you believe otherwise. Allen's expression was remorseful. He also seemed relieved and oddly triumphant. It was that last look that pierced Leah's heart. It was as though Allen was saying he'd won after all.

The floating sensation quickly drained from Leah and then she felt leaden. All those months, two whole years, and Allen had only been testing her out. Trying her on for size against his own determination to make sure he'd gotten the best.

And she wasn't the best.

Leah stood with her hands buried deep in the pockets of her wool slacks. Allen and Gail stared back at her, as if expecting a demonstration of outrage. Leah looked from one to the other in the stifling silence.

"Merry Christmas" was all she could think to say.

Leah could tell that Gail thought she was going to create a scene by ranting and raving, crying and pointing an accusing finger. But she merely stared at them both with a puzzled and curious expression on her face. Allen looked appropriately ashamed for just a moment. That was good enough. But he hadn't humbled himself.

"I guess this would have happened sooner or later," Leah whispered.

"Leah, I—" Allen began.

"Don't say anything. Please."

"What happened was—"

"Shut up, Allen," Gail ordered sharply, her eyes never leaving her sister's face.

"Don't tell me to shut up," Allen thundered. But when he looked at Leah again, the anger was all gone.

"It shouldn't have happened this way, Leah. You didn't deserve this."

Leah curled her lips at him. "I seem to remember you saying the same thing several weeks ago. But it keeps happening, doesn't it?"

Allen didn't answer.

"I used to wonder if you would ask me to marry you. I'm not sure I would have been flattered, Allen. Of course, you understand why I'd say no."

Still there was no answer from Allen, and no more response from Gail.

Leah abruptly turned away, murmuring, "I'm going to my room. Good night . . ."

It seemed like the best thing to do. She was the awkward side of the triangle; only she didn't have anyone to champion her. Leah began to feel numb and disoriented. She didn't immediately feel hurt or betrayed, just very foolish.

The Hallelujah Chorus, sung in sweet, wrenching harmony, played all morning and afternoon, mixed with the ringing of the doorbell and the telephone. In between Leah responded to good wishes from neighbors, and tried not to succumb to despair. She drank hot eggnog laced liberally with rum and nutmeg. Or she watched the neighborhood kids from the living room window as they tried out a variety of toys, bikes, trikes, footballs, and rollerblades.

At one point Leah went into the kitchen with the idea of making some sort of dinner. But her heart wasn't in it, and she didn't really feel like eating anyway. Gail had talked her into calling their father long-distance, as though their mutual mission to wish him a Merry Christmas would magically bridge the distance between the two of them. Leah succeeded in sounding believably cheerful, but after the call she slipped once more into the privacy of despair. Most of the day she sat in her room staring at the wallpaper. And drinking rum and eggnog.

At least Gail respected her silence. She went about her own celebration, trying to pretend the previous night's fiasco hadn't happened. Surely Gail recognized that some of what had happened was her fault. Leah wondered if she had made it harder on all of them by being so blind to what was going on under her very nose. How ignorant could a person be? All the beautifully wrapped presents remained unopened under the tree, an embarrassing reminder of how ill-used this season and all it stood for had been.

They ate dinner in virtual silence. Gail did most of the talking, guilt making her bear the responsibility, as well as a dread of the long silences. While Leah patiently and politely answered any questions, she volunteered nothing, and later she would have no recollection of what was said. Her mind had gone blissfully and protectively blank.

Sarah Chen called late in the afternoon to invite them for drinks. Gail said she'd love to come for a while, inwardly feeling grateful that she had an opportunity to escape the silent house.

Leah was very happy to be left alone. She mixed an eggnog toddy and sat in the living room with nothing but the tree lights for illumination. She listened to the holiday music and felt like a fraud. She couldn't understand her inability to cry, or even why she felt so little hurt. Nothing. She felt hollow. She didn't want to talk and didn't want anyone to talk to her. Leah wished that the holidays were over so she could get back to work. She knew that eventually she'd have to face her sister, adapt to the changes. But right now, right this instant, she was feeling light-headed and sleepy from the rum.

Leah thought of Jason suddenly, and remembered that stupor she'd first seen him in months ago. She understood clearly now how easy it was for a person to get lost and not to care about anything. She could empathize with a need to disconnect and tune out, to put up invisible barriers that would separate her from the things that were destroying her.

"Merry Christmas, Jason," Leah said softly and raised her glass to the dark room. She hoped he'd had a Merry Christmas. She hoped that someone, somewhere, had had a Merry Christmas. Her eyes wondered to the tree under which were spread the presents she and Gail would have exchanged. Presents from their dad, little things from friends and colleagues; her present to Allen, his to her. She was never going to open it.

God, this had been one hell of a year for holidays and sharing. How could the New Year possibly top the last few months?

Leah knocked on the wood of the coffee table, and a silly laugh escaped her. No point in tempting fate. She felt depression settling in now that the rum had relaxed her body. And she also felt a little sick from all the sweet eggnog. The last thing she needed was to be sick. A little unsteadily she walked to the hallway and slowly made her way up the stairs and fell to sleep across her bed.

It was not until several days after Christmas that Gail and Leah finally sat and talked, and even then only because Gail couldn't stand the silence any longer. Early in the evening, after she'd smoked herself into a state of anxiety, Gail finally approached Leah. She found her sister in the den sketching caricatures. Upon entering, Gail caught a brief glimpse of images of Allen and herself, Jill and the Chen kids. However, Leah quickly covered them when Gail came into the room.

"Leah . . ." Gail began cautiously. "I think we should try to talk this out."

Leah smiled vacantly. She suddenly remembered Allen wanting to do the exact same thing after Thanksgiving. "Talk what out?"

"Come on, Leah. How can you ask what? This silence. And the whole scene from Christmas. You do remember Christmas Eve, don't you?"

"Everybody always has so much to say after the fact. Okay, let's talk," she said warily.

She got up from the desk in the den and preceded her sister into the living room. There was more space in there. Gail followed and sat on the sofa. Leah stood by the window and waited patiently for Gail to begin.

Gail sighed. "Look, if I had thought Allen really cared about you, I never would have made a play for him. I know I can be a bitch sometimes, but you are my sister."

"That didn't stop you," Leah pointed out.

"I know, I know. It's just that I've always been attracted to Allen. Right from that first time we saw him. I thought he was one fine-looking black man. Handsome and smart. We kept looking at each other and there was . . . this sort of spark. You know what I mean. But he asked you out, not me. I was confused, but I thought, hey, that's that." Gail stopped for a moment and regarded her sister.

"But then, every time we were in the same room together, something happened. All we did was fight and hiss at each other. I couldn't figure out why. I only knew I was crazy about him one minute and wanted to scratch his damned eyes out the next."

"Sounds like you were both in heat," Leah murmured dryly.

Gail shot her an impatient glare. She lit a cigarette and exhaled raggedly. She sat staring into space.

"It took me a long time to figure out what was going on. I thought maybe I'd been wrong. Maybe he really didn't like me. Then I finally realized he was fighting *not* to want me.

"I got all turned around inside, Leah. I couldn't have him, so I did all kinds of outrageous things to make him notice, and to try to make him mad."

Gail puffed furiously on the cigarette, and then put it out half finished. She immediately lit another.

"And then one night after he was here for dinner, he kissed me good night. You'd gone to get his coat or whatever. He said something about how I'd styled my hair that night, and I shot right back with an answer. Suddenly we were both laughing. It was like . . . like . . . how come we always fought before? Over what?"

Gail impatiently put the second cigarette out. She hated this. She hated having to explain herself to anyone. But when she looked at her sister, she didn't see resentment in Leah's eyes. Only a kind of mild curiosity. Gail sat back and tried to relax.

"When Allen kissed me it wasn't just good night, Gail and a friendly peck. It was a kiss. And right then we both knew."

Leah averted her gaze. She guessed she should be grateful that it hadn't been a night when Allen had stayed to make love to her, and then leave to go home. But all those other nights afterward . . .

Leah shook her head impatiently. She wasn't going to think about that. She wondered if Gail or Allen ever had.

"I hated that Allen was hiding behind you, using you."

"He wasn't honest with either one of us, and you still wanted him?" Leah asked, somewhat astonished.

Gail chuckled. "Honey, this isn't supposed to make sense. It's not about logic, it's about glands," she said ruefully. "I thought sooner or later you'd pick up on what was happening."

"And make it easier for you by just letting Allen go. Be polite and step aside. The only problem, Gail, was that I didn't have a clue."

Gail frowned. "And you never even suspected about that weekend in September?"

Leah's expression was completely blank. "What weekend?"

Gaily slowly shook her head. She suddenly felt sorry for Leah, and a little angry for how little she'd suspected. You can't defend yourself if you don't know there's a reason to.

"It doesn't matter. It happened. Allen and I spent a weekend together."

Leah turned her back, feeling the heat of embarrassment warm her face. Something about the fact that it had been so easy for both Allen and Gail to fool her suddenly hit home. That she had detected nothing particularly different in Allen's behavior afterward—all the way up until Thanksgiving—made Leah feel like she was shrinking. She took a deep breath and paced several feet between the window and the fireplace. She wasn't going to let it happen. She wasn't going to forgive them and allow herself to disappear.

"Why couldn't you just tell me? Either of you?"

"Because I was trying to get Allen to admit he didn't love you. I didn't want to confront *you*. I wanted to get to *Allen*." Gail shook her head sadly. "Leah, I'm sorry. I really didn't mean for it to come out this way. I just couldn't stand much more of this pretending. I decided to confront him and just take my chances."

"If I'd been in love with him, tough, right?"

Gail shook her head positively. "But you weren't in love with him."

"No, I wasn't," Leah admitted softly.

And she felt relief. It was unexpected. As if she'd let go of a burden of having to make a difficult decision. She watched as Gail got up and slowly approached her near the fireplace. Leah observed Gail dispassionately, admiring her presence, and grace. Her guts. Leah understood exactly why Allen would be more attracted to her sister.

"I hoped that you and Steven would like each other well enough to—you know, get together. He thought you were sweet. And he guessed that something was going on between Allen and me. He warned me that you could get hurt."

Leah stared at Gail, annoyed. There was no point in pulling her hair, or staring at her as if she was demented. Leah knew she had to be responsible for protecting her own feelings.

"How come Steven knew and you didn't?"

"I told you. I thought you'd figure it out. I couldn't believe you didn't know something was going on. Then, when Allen called here looking for you last week, he sounded really desperate. Something about Thanksgiving. Did you two fight?"

Leah watched Gail narrow her gaze on her.

"What happened between you and Allen at Thanksgiving?"

Leah crossed her arms over her chest. "That's between Allen and me. I'm not going to talk about it."

She was glad that at least Allen hadn't further disgraced her by relating the incident. Gail gave her a sideways glance that was both innocent and contrived.

"You and Allen didn't have plans for New Year's Eve, did you?"

"We hadn't talked that far in advance."

Gail sighed. "Well, at least he didn't screw that up. His firm is having a blow-out affair at the Marriott Marquis. He asked me to go."

"Good for you. Sounds like fun," Leah said without much emotion.

"Are you very angry with me?" Gail asked contritely.

"I'm not angry, Gail. really. I'm just very tired of the whole thing."

Gail touched her hand. "I wish it could have been a happier Christmas."

Leah didn't shake the hand off, as she was inclined to do. But she resented, in a way, that Gail so quickly thought the matter settled. She had eased her conscience. And she had won, as Allen had.

"Me, too," Leah said quietly.

Jason returned to New York feeling better but also very restless. The redheaded dancer called to say she was in town and wanted to come over to visit. He declined even though he was lonely. He was tired of feeling that way. After a few cigarettes and a can of beer, Jason knew exactly what he wanted to do.

At ten-thirty that night he called Leah.

"Hi. It's Jason."

"Oh. Hello."

"You don't sound so hot. Is this a bad time to be calling? Or, didn't you expect me to call?"

"No, no. This is fine," Leah assured him, but he'd heard the surprise in her tone. "How was your holiday? Did you go to Pennsylvania?"

"Yeah, I did."

"I told you that was a better idea than being alone. Did you have a good time?"

"It was difficult. But good. And yours?"

There was a momentary silence. "Difficult," she repeated thinly.

"Should I ask?" Jason inquired alertly.

"It's better if you don't."

Jason sensed that something was wrong, but thought

better of pursuing it. "Too much partying, no doubt," he suggested.

"Not enough," Leah responded wryly.

"Well, we can do something about that. Do you have plans for New Year's Eve?"

"No. Not really."

Jason could hear her hesitation. "Then how about going to a party with me?"

"A party?" she repeated blankly.

Jason chuckled. "You do know what a party is, don't you?"

"Of course I do," Leah said, annoyed.

Jason knew she was searching for an excuse to say no, and he suddenly didn't want her to. "Are you going to tell me you have nothing to wear, or you don't want to go?"

"It's not that . . .."

"If you have nothing to wear, I'll lend you something," he said outrageously.

Leah laughed. "Of all the people you know in this city, you can't find a date for New Year's Eve?"

"Sure I can," Jason said quietly. "But I'm asking you."

Leah lounged back against the pillows on her bed. She thought of Thanksgiving and Christmas Eve. She thought of Gail and Allen and everyone in the whole world celebrating New Year's. Except her. "Okay. I'll go."

"You will?" Jason perked up. He had expected more resistance.

Leah's laugh was nervous. "Don't change your mind, now. It would have been a lot easier to say no."

Jason chuckled. "No, no. It's just that . . . well, great. We're going to have a good time. I promise."

"Sure," Leah said with some skepticism. But she was still glad that she wouldn't have to be alone while others celebrated. "So, should I dress for Times Square or for dancing to a live band?"

"Somewhere in between. It's a private house party."

"Fine. I'll even bring some champagne."

"Bet. And I'll bring the noise makers. And the noise."

Chapter Seven

Leah didn't tell Gail what her plans were for New Year's Eve. She wouldn't say with whom, where, when, or how she was spending the evening. It gave Leah a sense of control again and she was pleased that there was an area of her life that Gail knew nothing about.

She thought carefully about what she would wear. She wanted to make herself feel good. She wanted to look attractive again. And she wanted Jason to notice. Leah decided on black velvet pants and a black sweater. Over this she wore a bright red Japanese kimono printed with orange and yellow flowers. She'd bought the kimono on impulse three years earlier because the combination of colors were so striking and bold. But Leah had never worn it and, actually, never had any idea how she would wear it . . . until now.

She twisted her hair into an off-centered topknot and stuck red lacquered chopsticks through the bun. She wore a pair of dangling silver earrings temporarily pilfered from her sister. Leah was happy with the results, and her anticipation of the evening made her feel bold and adventurous.

Just before Gail was to be picked up by Allen, she came into her sister's room and watched, bemused, the elaborate preparations.

"Well, wherever it is you're going, you're certainly

dressed to celebrate. I hope you have fun," Gail offered.

"I plan to . . ." Leah murmured, concentrating on the application of her lip gloss.

"I don't suppose you know when you'll be home?"

"No idea at all. Maybe I won't come home tonight."

"Look, I'm just concerned."

"Don't be. Frankly, Gail, whenever you're concerned there's no guarantee you're really thinking about me."

"I'm beginning to get worried about you. You're not acting like yourself anymore, Leah."

"And what is that exactly?" Leah asked, amused.

"The way you used to be. You're behaving like a—a rebellious teenager."

"Good. All in all, the way I used to be didn't do me much good. Don't worry about me. Go and have a good time and I'll see you next year," Leah said flippantly.

She got up from the vanity stool and approached her sister, who stood, uncharacteristically indecisive, just inside the bedroom door.

"I can take a hint," Gail said dryly.

"I knew you would. You look great," Leah said honestly, quickly assessing her sister's mini silver tank dress worn under a black beaded bolero jacket. "I wouldn't have the nerve to go out in that."

Gail laughed with a shake of her head. Leah could detect a sigh in the laugh, a little like relief.

"Girl, we're even. I wouldn't wear that, either," she said, gesturing to the bright kimono.

Leah turned to examine the full effect in a mirror. "It is bright, isn't it? Do I look like a neon sign?"

Gail came to stand behind her sister, her hands lightly on Leah's shoulder. The two oval faces framed together in the mirror showed the clear differences, as well as the strong similarities, between them.

"No, but you will certainly be noticed," Gail said. "And you do look terrific."

Their gazes met in the mirror.

"Thanks," Leah murmured.

She turned around. Gail pecked her on the cheek.

"Happy New Year, Leah. I'll see you later."

Gail quickly left the room, and Leah sensed that her sister had come as close as she was ever going to to apologizing for her part in the failed holidays.

After Gail departed, Leah finished her grooming, checked her hair and outfit once more, and went down to the living room. It was almost nine o'clock. Until now she hadn't allowed herself to think much about Jason or the coming evening. She only wanted to have a good time. She was going to keep it simple. Jason was simply a nice-looking guy she knew. She was going to a party with him with lots of other people and lots of noise and gaiety. She wasn't going to remember what he'd said to her the last time they were together. She wasn't going to put a lot of emphasis on a few good night kisses. She was going to remember that he probably dated a dozen other women and that she was just someone else on his list.

Don't assume anything and you won't be disappointed, she told herself. Take it moment to moment. Don't try to question it too much; just go with it. Leah had made the decision that she was going to be like Gail for a while—thinking only of herself. She would smile and be bright and tease and have fun. With champagne and a toast, Leah would drink the past into oblivion.

The bell rang and slowly Leah went to answer. As she pulled the door open, a final surge of apprehension swept through her. It was too late. There stood Jason dressed casually for a party in charcoal gray slacks and a black knit polo shirt, the short leather jacket, and his red baseball cap. He said nothing at first, but Leah had to smile as he looked her up and down. All the thought and care had been worth this one moment. Jason let out a low whistle.

"You look great."

"You mean I haven't before?" she teased.

"No, that's not it. You have, but . . . you look *great*," he repeated.

"Thank you. Come in."

Leah led the way into the living room, aware that Jason was still staring at her. He reached for her hand and slowly turned her around. Such open admiration again surprised Leah, and unnerved her. Jason was so bold, so open with his feelings and thoughts. It made her feel that he was moving too fast and she couldn't keep up with him.

"I sure hope this was all for me."

"Only for tonight. Tomorrow I turn back into a pumpkin."

"No, it's the coach that turns into a pumpkin, not Cinderella," he laughed.

Leah stood poised with her hands on her hips. "There are no black Cinderellas, Jason."

He shrugged. "Why not?"

Leah only shook her head. She might have known he wouldn't just accept her word for it.

"Never mind. Would you like a drink?"

"I think we better get going. The traffic is going to be crazy. Besides, my car is double-parked out front."

"If you get a ticket, I know someone who can fix it for you."

He frowned in a playful manner as he helped Leah into her winter coat. "You've been watching too much TV," he said.

As they headed through the door Leah checked herself and stopped. "Wait a minute. I almost forgot the champagne."

She ran back to get the silver-wrapped bottle from the dining room table.

Jason's car was an older model Volvo that looked like it might have been red at one point. It was now a combination of scratches, rust, dents, and dried mud. The interior was black and the backseat was piled with an assortment of papers, sweats, and sports gear. He politely helped her into the front, hastily flipping a book that had been on the passenger seat into the back. As they moved into traffic, Leah suddenly pulled off Jason's red cap and added it to the pile behind them. Jason laughed and combed his hair with his fingers.

Leah settled in her seat to enjoy the ride as they headed toward the expressway. Jason, reading her thoughts, offered, "We're headed for New Hyde Park. You don't have to get back to Brooklyn too early, do you?"

"There's no place I have to be until Monday morning," she found herself saying.

He looked quickly at her before once more concentrating on the road. He was quiet while he drove, and Leah wondered what he was thinking. It occurred to her that there had been no initial awkward moments between them. Jason had come for her and they had left the house together as if this was okay, and they were now used to being together.

The room was smoke-filled and noisy. There were small groups of people sitting on any available flat surface, including the floor. Leah had a glass of white wine, and she sat on a stool in front of Nora Wagner, listening as the woman described all her Christmas gifts. Nora was a big woman. She wore glasses and sported three pairs of earrings. She had a boisterous laugh and a hacking smoker's cough. Leah had liked her instantly.

It was from Nora that she learned that the kind of work Joe and Jason did was not as benign as just working with kids in jeopardy. Nora was a concerned cop's wife. She was stoic, sometimes flippant, but it was clear to Leah that she masked her worry from Joe, who went out every day with no certainty that he would return at night.

It was one thing for Jason to tell her he was a cop. It was quite another for Leah to make the connection between the newspaper horror stories, the violence, the danger, and Jason. There were men and women here from his precinct, an odd collection of individuals who looked like they had nowhere else to go. Leah could believe that they didn't. And it was odd to see holstered guns casually worn as part of their normal daily attire.

Joe had greeted her and Jason at the door. Leah remembered Joe from the parked black car that had waited at the curb the first time she'd officially met Jason. Behind the wheel Joe had seemed cold. He wasn't that much warmer now. Almost immediately he started calling her Brooklyn.

"My name's Leah."

"Hey . . ." Joe said expansively. "What's in a name?"

Everyone seemed to know Jason, and he was quickly pulled from one group to another in the crowded little house.

"Hey, y'all. Listen up," Joe shouted. "This here is Brooklyn. She's with Jason tonight, so be cool and watch your language."

"Leah . . ." she tried to correct into the noise, but it was doubtful that anyone heard her, or really cared.

There were some good-natured remarks and laughing. A drink was thrust into her hand and her coat quickly confiscated. Joe placed a heavy hand on her shoulder.

"You'll catch the names later. Check everybody out."

Nora had found her quickly, befriending her when Leah felt so out of place as Jason was swallowed in a circle of colleagues. Everyone was nice to her and wanted to know what she did, but Leah knew she was the outsider here. All of these people had something in common, and she knew so little about it. Nora spent some time filling her in, but Leah became more interested when Nora got around to discussing Jason in particular.

"Jason's good people," Nora said. "I noticed right away, and said so to Joe. I said, you stay with him. He's different, but he'll never let you down.

"He's had some bad times. Losing his son like that. What a shame," Nora said, shaking her head. She squinted at Leah through her glasses. "I never seen Jason with no black girl before. I know all of Jason's girlfriends," she boasted. "If they don't pass my approval, they have got to go. Told Jason so," and she laughed heartily.

Leah suspected that Nora was not joking, but quickly corrected one misconception. "We're not dating, actually. We're just friends."

Nora's chest rolled with silent laughter. "Lord have mercy, child," she choked. "That's how it starts. Where'd he find you anyway?"

"He didn't. I found him—"

She would have explained further except that Nora became suddenly distracted. Looking beyond Leah, she gestured with her hand. "Jason, you get yourself in here and come dance with Leah. She don't want to hear me run my mouth."

Jason obeyed, silently taking Leah's hand, pulling her from the ottoman and leading her to the cleared dance floor. Most of the guests were moving in a dark sea of swaying bodies.

The music became slow and Jason pulled Leah into his arms. The few earlier kisses notwithstanding, they had never been this close before. Leah was aware of his lean, hard body, his arm around her narrow waist, his hand holding hers. She tried to concentrate on the music, on the guests she could see over Jason's shoulder. Joe was standing talking to another man, but his eyes strayed to her and Jason as they moved together.

There was an unexpected grace to his movements. Leah knew, with some amusement, that she could dispel the myth of cops having two left feet. He led her smoothly and she followed, all the while concentrating on how their bodies touched and where. He smelled different from Allen. Allen liked men's colognes and aftershave scents. Leah didn't have to search to find that natural essence of Jason, just himself. It made her feel peculiar inside, as if they were melding together, or she'd found out something intimate about him. Jason somehow seemed so masculine without anything extra to enhance him.

She looked into his face, and found that he was studying her carefully. The look seemed too personal and too warm. Could he tell what she'd been thinking?

"I don't think Joe likes me very much," she said suddenly.

Jason's grin was slow. His arm tightened just slightly. "Doesn't matter. I like you."

This will never do, Leah thought. But when the dance ended Jason continued to stand with his arm about her, staring into her face. She felt a rush of relief when the music started again and she was claimed by Joe for the next dance. He, too, showed smooth movements for such a big man. He twirled and led Leah through some sensual, soulful turns as if testing her. She stayed with him step for step. Actually, dancing with Joe was easier. They knew exactly what to expect from each other.

At 11:47 Nora came into the room with a tray loaded with fluted champagne glasses. "Okay, everybody. Take a glass now. Only a few minutes left to the old year."

"Thank goodness," someone sighed and received laughing agreement.

Jason took two glasses from the tray and gave one to Leah. "This is probably your champagne," he reminded her.

Joe was passing around streamers and confetti. Jason disappeared into the bedroom where the coats were piled and quickly returned with two noise makers from the pocket of his jacket. The TV volume was turned way up so that they all could hear and watch the lighted ball drop in Times Square. Jason and Leah stood with their noise makers and champagne along with everyone else counting down the last ten seconds. At twelve o'clock Joe flicked the overhead light on and off. Confetti snowed everywhere and the cheers were deafening.

Leah toasted Jason and tried to sip from her glass. She got jostled and the champagne spilled down her chin instead. She started to giggle. Jason tried to wipe the liquid away, but someone slapped him on the back in good spirits, inadvertently pushing him into Leah. Very naturally they kissed as everyone else was doing. Quickly. Safely. They quietly wished each other a Happy New Year.

It was almost dawn when they left the party. Jason had had his share to drink, but seemed in command of the car and soon Leah stopped worrying. They weren't in any hurry, and the drive back to Brooklyn was slow on the nearly deserted streets and roads. With her eyes closed and her head back against the headrest, the laughter of the party still reverberated in Leah's head. She tried to focus on that, and not on the image of Jason or the look in his eyes when he'd found her alone in the kitchen pouring more glasses of soda at 2:30 in the morning.

The way they'd looked at each other had pushed open another door of possibility before them, closed some of the old ones behind. It was the champagne, Leah thought. She shouldn't have had so much champagne. But it might not have made any difference anyway, considering how Jason had casually put his arms around her and kissed her again.

No asking, no hesitation. No tentativeness but a full kiss that connected them and fused their lips and made Leah feel surprisingly languid and giddy. His tongue in her mouth was still a strange thing. Even with her eyes closed Leah was aware that it belonged to someone white. But the eeriness of this actually happening only added to the eroticism of the moment. For Jason was demonstrating a desire and need and enjoyment that was catching. Leah gave in to it, liking the way the kiss was tender and slow. It had been beyond the celebration of New Year's, beyond a drunken liberty. He hadn't been drunk. And she hadn't bothered to stop him. . . .

"I gotta stop at the precinct before I get you home. Do you mind?" Jason yawned.

"Uh-um." Leah shook her head slowly. She didn't open her eyes. She didn't mind much of anything just then.

The station house was a surprise. It was ugly.

There were squad cars parked into the curb on the dreary Brooklyn street, and all the activity was inside. There were two very young girls lounging around the front desk, joking with the on-duty clerk. The girls were garishly dressed, none too subtly advertising their youthful bodies to whoever was interested. The desk clerk and a few other officers were interested. The young women greeted Jason by name as he and Leah entered and passed on.

"Neighborhood groupies," Jason offered as an explanation as they continued down a series of corridors.

Leah noticed that the walls of the precinct were dirty and painted two shades of institutional green. There was wire mesh in the glass of all the windows. They passed an elderly couple seated on a bench complaining to a cop. There were two Hispanic women struggling through thick accents to be understood by yet another officer. There was a grizzled, smelly drunk, someone crying somewhere, yelling. . . . Leah hurried to catch up to Jason, trying to curb her discomfort. She felt as though she'd stepped into a parallel universe.

Jason took her into a room marked YOUTH OFFICER and indicated a desk. That desk and another across the room were piled high with papers, folders, and an amazing collection of gadgets, toys, and things.

"I have to get something from my locker. Have a seat and I'll be right back." Jason waved briefly and left Leah alone in the chilly room.

Leah stood for an uncertain moment before stiffly sitting on the edge of a wooden chair. She wondered if the chairs were intentionally uncomfortable. Looking around the small room, she found it grim and bare except for the stuff on and around Jason's desk. On the wall between the two windows were a number of drawings and paintings done by young hands. Leah got up to examine them close up. One showed an institutional building with lopsided windows. The other was a picture of a man. The head was oversized compared to the body, but when looked at carefully, Leah could see it was meant to be a portrait of Jason. The artist had even added the red cap.

Below the drawings was a yellowed piece of lined notebook paper with several lines written on it:

> when i was locket up
> and could not see
> wat it was i want to be
> you come and sit me free
> now i am some body.

Leah was touched. Whatever it was Jason did, he must be very good at it. The drawings and poem were testimony to that. She looked at his desk. There was a switchblade knife wedged between the phone and a book, a half-eaten pack of M&Ms. There was a softball and two framed photos of a boy. Leah knew it was Michael. One showed him about five years old and seated on Jason's shoulders. Michael looked very much like him except for his blond curly hair and dimples. The other picture showed Michael about age thirteen, his face starting to look less babyish. He was wearing a Flyers 16 T-shirt.

While still examining the photos Leah heard voices behind her. She turned as an officer came into the room. He looked at her in momentary surprise, and then his face grew annoyed.

"What the fuck are you doing in here?" he asked bluntly.

He was tall and husky, with a thick, dark mustache, florid cheeks, and a stomach that extended over his gun belt.

Leah, also taken by surprise, was stunned by his tone. "Excuse me?"

"You know you don't belong here."

"I'm here with—"

"Look, you know the routine. Get your ass back up front." He grabbed Leah by the arm and jerked her toward the door.

Leah immediately resisted, her surprise gone and anger replacing it. "Let go of me. What do you think you're doing?"

The officer shook her. "What do you think you're doing," he mimicked her. "Don't give me that shit. Your pimp can post bail, else you're here for the duration. Now move it."

Jason came through the door carrying a small, brightly wrapped box. He stopped at what he saw.

"Jason . . ." Leah cried.

"Let her go, Spano," Jason said clearly, blocking the door.

"You know this woman, Horn?" Spano asked, not letting go of Leah's arm even when she tried to pull free.

Jason stepped into the room right in front of Spano. "I said, let her go." His tone was hard and direct.

For a moment Spano looked like he wanted the confrontation to go further. But he abruptly let Leah go, pushing her slightly off balance. "Another one of yours, eh? You better be careful, man. You turning on us?"

"You pig," Leah said scathingly.

"You fuckin' nigger whore . . ." Spano turned to her.

Leah was too angry to move.

"Shut the fuck up! Get out of here, Spano. While you still can," Jason ordered dangerously.

Spano puffed up his chest, but then thought better of whatever he was going to do. He backed off. "Fine with me. To each his own, man." He pushed roughly past Jason out of the room.

It was suddenly too silent.

Jason looked down at the box he held. He wanted to put it down quickly. To hide it. Then he heard Leah move, and as he turned to face her she rushed past him out the door. He started after her.

"Leah . . ."

She was too angry to cry. Too indignant to feel anything but cold rage. She wanted to get out of there as fast as she could. Leah ignored Jason's call and frantically tried to remember which corridor led to the exit.

"Leah, wait a minute." Jason ran after her.

No one tried to stop her, but several officers and other civilians paused at Jason's raised voice and the young black woman hurrying down the hallway.

"Leah . . ." Jason got hold of her arm and forced her to stop.

"Let go of my arm," Leah said, breathing heavily.

"I'm sorry, Leah. I—"

"That bastard thought I was a prostitute. He had no right to talk to me that way."

"I know. It's just that we don't usually get a lot of women around here unless—" Jason stopped.

"Unless they're hookers, junkies, thieves, or victims. Or like those girls up front, right? Then why did you bring me here?" she asked, bewildered. Her heart was pounding in anger.

When Jason didn't answer immediately, she shook his hand off and again headed for the door.

"I'll take you home," Jason said after her.

Leah kept moving and Jason had to run to catch up to her. He moved to block her path. Leah stopped.

"I don't want you to take me home. I'll get home by myself."

Leah pushed roughly at Jason's chest and he grabbed her arms firmly.

"Leah!" he said forcefully, shaking her.

Leah finally stopped struggling and stood still. Her breathing was ragged and deep. When she didn't resist anymore, Jason let go of her arms. "I'm taking you home."

Leah didn't argue.

The ride back to her house seemed interminable. Leah felt a knot of outrage twist her stomach. It combined with too much wine from the party. Too much confidence that the worst was over. Too much hope that the new year might really be different. Leah couldn't forget the hostility and disrespect, that had been hurled at her by the officer. She was trying not to let him undermine the chance she'd been willing to take with Jason.

She was furious. And disappointed. She was tired of feeling both. Leah knew, however, that the damage had been done. All she could do for the moment was not let it build up inside, not sure of what would happen to her if it was released.

I told you so . . . I told you so . . .

Leah rubbed her throbbing temples and wondered what in the world she thought she was doing here with Jason. But she knew. When he reached out to clasp her hand, giving it a squeeze, she jerked it free. Jason captured it again and held it tightly.

"I'm sorry," Jason offered again. He knew it wasn't enough for her.

They entered the silent house as the sun was coming up. There was going to be a bright beginning to the new year. To Leah it seemed absurd. The timing was way off. Jason followed her into the living room. But she wanted the good-bye to be quick and short.

"Thanks for the party. I had a wonderful time," she said automatically. Her voice was flat.

"I'm really sorry, Leah. It shouldn't have happened. Spano is an asshole."

"It wasn't your fault," she said tonelessly. "You don't have to explain."

Slowly he approached her. He gently touched her shoulder, taking the box out of his jacket pocket. "Here. I had something for you. It's not much, really."

Leah looked at the offered box and almost recoiled. "I don't want it."

"Take it." he pushed it into her hand.

Indifferently Leah began to tear the paper from the box. She lifted the lid to find a coffee mug inside. She stared at it blankly, puzzled. She looked at Jason.

"What is this?" she asked impatiently.

"I thought that . . . if you ever have to leave me coffee again . . ."

Leah couldn't believe what she was hearing. What did he mean, *again?* Wasn't he paying any attention to what had happened just now? Was he so insensitive not to know that what his fellow officer had put her through mattered?

The injury was compounded because for no reason, Leah vividly recalled walking into the den and finding her sister and Allen locked in each other's arms. Just how many times was she supposed to forgive and forget? How many more humiliating moments before someone realized that her feelings, her needs, mattered, too?

"Again? You've got to be kidding." She started to laugh.

And Leah couldn't stop laughing; she wasn't even sure what was so funny. *She* was. *Jason* was. The world was hysterical. The laughter hurt so much she started to cry.

Jason knew too late the gift was a dumb idea. He felt like a jerk with Leah laughing like that, like he didn't get it. But he should have, he told himself. How was he to have known that the trip to the precinct would turn out as it had? The mug had been meant as a private joke just between him and Leah.

"Leah . . ." Jason crooned, touching her arm. She knocked his hand away, dropping the box in the process.

"Don't touch me!"

He watched as she walked away in the direction of the den. Then she stopped. She didn't go in.

Leah turned around and Jason stood watching her. Waiting for her. He knew what was happening and he couldn't just leave. It began to get to him, her face distorted with hurt and anger. He suddenly hoped to God that Leah wasn't going to blame him.

Jason slowly closed the distance between them. He reached out to pull Leah to him in one fluid motion. He gave her no time to say anything as he quickly kissed her. The kiss, completely unlike the others, was demanding and possessive. It was meant to overwhelm and obliterate. It was meant to protect and to give and say, "I'm sorry." It was meant to bring them together before they were torn further, and forever, apart.

Leah felt desire and panic sweep through her, each fighting for dominance. The kiss was like a drug, stripping her of all resistance. It was invasive. She began to respond, to return his ardor. Suddenly everything else was wiped out. This had nothing whatsoever to do with the incident at the precinct. That was quickly set aside because the issue wasn't Spano and his ignorance. It really was just about her and Jason.

Leah forced her head to the side, trying to catch her breath. Tears rolled down her face.

"What are we doing?" she asked, bewildered. "What are we doing?"

"I thought we were doing a pretty good job of kissing each other," he whispered. He angled for her mouth again.

Leah turned in the circle of Jason's arms, her back against his chest.

"No, no. What are we doing like this? You and me," her voice shook. "Why me, Jason? What is it with you anyway? Is it because I'm black? Do you have some sort of bet with the guys at the station? Am I the—the next conquest?"

"Leah, it's not like that. I swear it isn't. I like you; can't you tell? I've never known anyone like you."

"What does that mean, like me? I'm not so different. You could have anyone you want, Jason. Anyone."

Jason vividly recalled a similar remark from Joe. He turned her around and looked at her. He could see she was agitated and scared.

"Look, I find you attractive and I like being with you. I don't want to stop seeing you because of what happened. Or because of anything else. I'm not just trying to jump your bones."

Leah pulled away from him.

"I'm trying to get to know you. It's important to me. So how do I convince you I'm for real?"

"Maybe you can't. Maybe it's just not possible. To-night is a good example of why it's not. Nothing changes, Jason. Ever." Leah looked beseechingly at him. "Everything I've ever heard, ever been taught, ever saw or read says we shouldn't be here like this. This just can't happen. Not after so much history and hate."

"You're giving me more power than I deserve." Carefully he reached out and took hold of her hand. "What we do should matter to no one but us. What we are to each other shouldn't be decided by some committee or by history. It's only our business, Leah. Yours and mine."

"It's everybody's business!" Leah said wildly. "What do you think that incident was about the night you brought me home from the hockey game? Remember those black teens on the corner? Remember that officer at the precinct? Don't you get it, Jason? It's not just you and me."

"Okay, so maybe me being white and you being black is a problem for other people."

Leah looked at him, incredulous, and laughed shortly.

"But I'm not the whole world. You only have to deal with me."

"We can't . . ." Leah moaned.

"The first thing you do is to forget Spano. He and I have never liked each other. He knows nothing about you. Do you really care?"

Leah wanted to believe him. She blinked rapidly.

Jason tightened his hold on her and stepped closer to Leah. "You and I have not committed any crimes. What happens here is of our making. That's enough of a responsibility. Don't let a history we've never lived get in the way. I don't know about you but I wasn't here a hundred years ago . . . fifty years ago . . ."

"You think it's that easy, eh?" she whispered.

"Why not? I'm not the enemy, Leah." When she said nothing Jason tugged gently on her hand. Fresh tears began to fall. "Do you want me to leave?"

Her stomach roiled. His thumb was rubbing over the back of her hand. Leah looked into his gray eyes. They were slightly red but perfectly focused. She could see that Jason wanted her. And she knew in that instant her answer to Jason was not going to be what it should be. She didn't want to think beyond the moment. And for the moment she didn't want to be alone.

"No." Her voice was almost inaudible.

Then slowly Jason began to ease the coat off her shoulder and down her arms. Leah stood still like an obedient child. Jason threw the coat onto the sofa and added his leather jacket. He turned back to her and, holding her very carefully, started to kiss her again.

Leah's heart raced, and she felt like she was slipping down the side of a glass incline. The trip was fast and smooth and felt exhilarating. She couldn't stop and she couldn't detour. She would never recover. Leah put her arms around him. As her own desire and her need for control fought each other, a flood of disconnected thoughts flashed through her mind. Allen on Thanksgiving night. What Gail would say. What her dad would say. Leah was consumed with confusion, guilt and fear . . . but she knew she wanted Jason, too.

"The den . . ." Jason mouthed hoarsely against her cheek, pressing her close to his body.

He was already aroused. He was hard and the feel of him pressing against her stomach seemed to make her spine flex.

No! Not the den . . .

"Upstairs. My room."

In her room the shades and curtains were drawn against the morning and the rest of the world. Jason got the bright kimono off her shoulder, and it slid to the floor. He took off his gun holster, and it landed on the vanity cushion with a heavy thud. His eyes were heavy-lidded and soft with passion.

Leah could feel his body heat standing so close to him. She was aware of every nuance of their mounting desire. Jason gingerly pulled the lacquered sticks from her hair, but the knot was secured in place.

Jason was enjoying the soft, pretty look of her, her eyes bright in the half-darkness of the room, her breathing softly hurried . . . her skin warm and smooth. He touched her throat. Looked long and carefully at her body. He touched her breasts, her nipples, his gaze coming back to her eyes for reaction. Leah let him see all he needed to see.

Jason took his time. He wanted the moment to last as long as possible. Gently he cupped his hands around her face and brought his mouth back to hers. Leah closed her eyes. Jason's mouth wandered over the planes of her face, to her ears and to that extremely sensitive spot under the lobe. He lingered there and she melted against him.

Neither of them would remember later how their clothing ended up strewn about the room, or who closed the bedroom door. They were both filled with so much passion that every other consideration was crowded out. They climbed under the sheet and coverlet and came together. Jason's gentle hands seemed to be everywhere. In her mind and with her body Leah could clearly outline his weight, his stomach pressed against hers, and the hard, thick feel of his penis. He pushed her legs apart and settled between them. He continued to administer kisses until Leah felt helpless beneath him. Everything about him felt hot. His skin, his mouth—the darting assertiveness of his tongue as it danced with hers. His hands exploring and stroking. Her tears now, trailing from her eyes into her temples, were because of a profound sense of relief, an astonishing surprise.

She was totally open and helpless, but Jason made no move to push into her right away. Gradually Leah began to adjust to the weight and feel of his body on hers. His chest hair was soft. The feel of his thighs and his muscular calves made her feel safely contained. She felt him shift and fumble awkwardly between their bodies, rolling his to the side for a moment. He was putting on a condom.

Her mouth quivered with tears. She couldn't seem to stop crying. Leah was stunned by his consideration and awareness. She was so far gone that she hadn't even given a thought to protection. Allen had never used condoms. She'd never asked him to. A sob escaped and Jason began to rub the length of his body against her in an erotic fashion. A spiraling sensation of desire shot through Leah's groin.

"Please don't," Jason pleaded, brushing the tears away.

He looked down at her breasts, fascinated by the dusky aureoles, the milk chocolate of her skin. He bent toward a nipple, closing his eyes. His tongue touched the peak and slowly drew it into his mouth. Leah sighed deeply and arched her hips. She drew Jason's head closer to her body.

They were color-blind in the dark.

Leah's head buzzed. She couldn't believe what was happening. She felt delicious eddies and swirling heat in her body. Hope. She twisted and heaved beneath Jason. Her body rejoiced while her heart hoped that history wasn't repeating itself.

"Oh, God . . ." she cried. Jason pulled her closer to his heat, comforting her, his hands moving over her back and sides. He stroked and touched and kissed her gently and loved her all the more. Jason suddenly lifted his hips, balancing his weight on his forearms. He kissed her again and thrust deeply, gently into her.

And she was lost.

It was a summer day.
Her body was propelled through the air, over tree-tops that were full and green. The trees disappeared and fell away to reveal wonderful space, causing her stomach to take a dip. She thought she would fall back to earth in a crash, killing herself for daring to presume she could fly free. But she was perfectly safe, held in place by a magic chair. . . .

The dream paled and Leah's eyes fluttered open. For a moment she didn't know where she was. Something was holding her. She was lying on her side, and realized that Jason's arm was around her. Her body was curved into his, back to front, and Leah could feel his steady breathing in her hair. She tried to shift position.

Her movement caused Jason to roll onto his back away from her. Slowly Leah turned over to find Jason sleeping soundly next to her.

It was a bit chilly in the room, but he'd managed to kick away most of the covers, leaving both of them bare, and giving Leah her first full look at him. His hair was gently tussled, his cheeks and jaw dark with overnight stubble. He was all pale skin, long and nicely built. His body hair was not as dark as his head, and the hair under his arms was almost blond. His chest hair was partially gray. There were a good number of scars, one in particular along his right collarbone running to his throat. There was another down his left thigh. Leah looked at his limp penis, lying curved against his leg. His genital hair was long and also almost blond. She had touched him there and found it soft.

Jason suddenly rolled his head on the pillow in her direction and slowly opened his eyes. They were still red and blurry from sleep, but in a moment he was focused on her face. A half smile lifted one corner of his mouth. His morning beard had gray in it, too.

"Good morning . . ."

"Good afternoon," Leah corrected softly. She no longer felt afraid but suddenly shy. She felt drowsy . . . and safe.

Jason shifted slightly so he could look at her stretched out next to him. His large hand caressed Leah's breasts, down her stomach and thighs. He rolled again until he was completely stretched out on top of her once more. He wrapped his arms around her and buried his mouth suddenly in the side of her neck. Jason gently nuzzled, rubbing his nose and mouth on her warm skin. Sleepily he undulated his body against her and moaned quietly.

Leah let her eyes drift closed and her body became

soft and pliable again, adjusting and accepting his weight. She stroked his back.

Jason used his index finger and pushed the matted hair off her forehead, finding a scar at the temple.

"Where'd you get that?" he asked, running his thumb over it.

"Cowboys and Indians," she answered.

He grinned. "Somebody tried to scalp you?"

"Gail."

"Doesn't surprise me," he said with lazy humor.

Leah reached out and touched her finger to the scar at his throat. "Where did you get that?"

" 'Nam. There are others."

"I noticed."

"Can't be helped. It comes with the job." Jason wiggled his hips against her. "All the important parts work." Leah couldn't be persuaded to smile. Jason shook his head. "It's not as bad as you think."

She touched the scar again. She swallowed hard as a sudden realization hit home. Leah gazed seriously into his eyes which, as they returned her gaze, were drowsy with desire. "Jason . . ."

Jason pressed her back into the bedding and kissed her forehead; he bent lower to her mouth. "Not now," he mumbled hoarsely.

He began to make love to her again.

Later, when Leah came out of the shower wrapped in her robe, Jason was no longer in the room. Her heart gave a lurch as she immediately thought he'd dressed and left. But his gun and holster were still on the vanity stool, although all their clothing had been picked up from the floor. Leah heard sounds from downstairs and followed them to the kitchen, where she found Jason rummaging in the cabinets and refrigerator. The towel from his shower was wrapped around his waist, not concealing an awful lot, and his hair was damp and spiky. Leah let her fear subside and automatically began the coffee maker.

"I feel like I haven't eaten in a week," Jason groaned, his head deep inside the refrigerator.

"What would you like to eat?"

"Everything."

Leah joined him at the refrigerator, but Jason used his hip to bump her aside. "Get out of the way. I'll make breakfast."

It was three o'clock in the afternoon.

Gail called at one point to say she'd be home in the morning, but Leah didn't even ask her where she was.

Afterward she and Jason returned to the room upstairs, but only to lie in bed talking. They talked about almost everything but what had happened between them. They also did not talk of Leah's apprehensions because it was nothing they could settle in just one night together. They talked about themselves. They were hungry to know each other in a different way now.

They had passed another barrier.

Leah had given herself up totally to the night, and forced herself not to think about later or tomorrow. She was filled with a nice warmth and quiet happiness at what she'd experienced with Jason, and she was determined that no matter what, it would be enough.

The first time they'd made love she'd been unable to climax. She'd used all her energy vacillating between the joy of Jason's stimulating touches and the fear of what they were doing together. She had, nonetheless, given herself up to the reality of that moment at least reveling in the feel of his hands and kisses on her body.

And then just a little while ago, all that she'd held in abeyance, combined with a languid acceptance of Jason's possession of her, had finally released her to fully share in the experience with him.

"Would you like to see what I do?" she asked suddenly.

She climbed off the bed to retrieve her portfolio, leaning against a nightstand. She unzippered it and spread the contents over her lap and Jason's.

"These are books I'm working on for the summer and fall."

Leah leafed through the pages slowly, explaining each one. Jason remained silent but interested. He seemed to get a particular charge out of her caricatures of people she worked with. He told her the one of Gail didn't quite work.

While she was talking, Jason began to stroke her arm and shoulders. Leah looked at him, stopping in mid-sentence. His eyes were soft and caressing, and she sensed that he wanted to hold her. Leah put the portfolio on the floor and he took her into his arms again, sliding them down flat on the bed. They didn't talk and they didn't make love. Soon it was Jason's steady breathing that told Leah he'd fallen back to sleep.

Much, much later, when she was alone, she would think in detail about the last twenty-four hours, what it had given to her and what it had taken away. Jason had taken her within the circle of his life, beyond his being a cop and someone she'd seen in a sad moment. She'd met his friends, danced with him, made love with him. The time they'd spent together more than balanced the incident with the officer at the precinct. When Leah thought about it, it didn't even hurt so much. Jason had dispelled the surprise and replaced it with tender, loving care.

For Leah, many things would be different in the future from this fresh beginning, which had taken on the dimensions of a surreal fantasy.

PART TWO

Chapter Eight

The next time Leah walked into Jason's precinct it was with trepidation. The incident of New Year's Eve had been a stupid and unfortunate experience. She had not forgotten the officer named Spano, and she was wary of encountering him again. More than that, however, returning suddenly threw her back to the event of the mugging and her decision at the time not to make a report to the police, or to tell anyone.

The precinct was busy, and there were cops and civilians everywhere. Leah was a bit stunned at the number of people who seemed to need the intervention of police in their lives. For a moment she saw the rituals of law enforcement, and the dealings that went on with individuals. But all those years ago she had believed that there would be no help for her beyond a written and filed statement, and certainly no one who would understand how her sense of self had been stripped away. She hadn't wanted to be a statistic. Leah had only wanted the fear and humiliation to go away.

Leah walked into the dreary interior and approached the officer at the front desk. Seeing so many men and women in blue made her feel that she'd entered a private club. Indeed, she drew so many curious glances that she felt she didn't belong here. But she had been the one to ask Jason if she could come again. He'd seemed hesitant at first, making her feel that somehow

she was invading his territory. Leah quickly guessed
that he, too, was remembering the last time she'd
been there.

She had research to do. Her latest freelance assignment was a book by a retired cop about gay officers
on the force. She wanted to look around the station
house, observe the officers on duty, how they inter-
acted with one another and with the public. Leah
didn't need to talk to any of them. That's what the
manuscript was for. But she needed to get a handle
on the environment that the author had portrayed in
order to conceive of a design for the book and its cover.

Leah told the desk officer she was there to see Jason
Horn. She tried to sound professional and detached,
but he seemed so interested in her, even while he was
dialing Jason on his line, that for a moment Leah wondered how much he, or anyone else at the precinct,
knew of their relationship. She suddenly felt conspicuous, as if all her secrets were on display. For an awful
moment Leah remembered the accusation she'd
thrown at Jason the night they'd first made love, that
she was just a curiosity to him, but her fears had
proven to be groundless.

Yet when Jason appeared several minutes later, Leah
didn't recognize him. He was in uniform. Who is this
man? she wondered. She barely recognized Jason in
the dark slacks and blue shirt with its black and silver
accents. He appeared unexpectedly formal, and it made
him seem even more a stranger. Even when he smiled
at her it was not truly personal. When he led her away
from the front desk, Leah realized that she still had
not connected Jason with his job. They'd spent all their
time together when he was off duty, a civilian. Just a
man. Her lover. Had Jason returned to meet her back
in November dressed as he was this moment, they
might never have gotten beyond the initial encounter.

Maybe he'd known that, too.

"I had to be in court this morning," he said to her.

Leah nodded, accepting the explanation, but it did nothing to remove her sense of disorientation. She kept giving him covert glances. The uniform made Jason seem intimidating, authoritative.

Jason glanced quickly around. He took Leah's arm and pulled her into a small office off a narrow corridor. She turned to face him, but he didn't touch her. Jason's eyes were serious and bright as he gazed at her startled expression.

"Leah, it's me. It's *me*."

Leah gnawed her lip, feeling heat rush to her face. "I know," she said quietly.

Jason shook his head. "No, you don't." He took a quick look out the door and closed it. "I'm not supposed to be doing this . . ."

"Doing what?" Leah asked, watching him with a frown.

Jason's grin was boyish. "Fraternizing with the public."

He cupped her face and brought his mouth to hers. The kiss was soft. Leah closed her eyes and let him kiss her until she recognized the touch and the taste of him. The distinct movements of his lips and the thrust of his tongue. She sighed. Jason briefly deepened the kiss before releasing her. He stepped back.

Leah opened her eyes. She saw Jason. She began to smile in relief. "I—I'm sorry."

"I've seen the same reaction from lawyers I've met in court who don't know me if I run into them off hours. Some of the guys I coach freak when they see me in my blues."

"Do they all get a kiss to make it better?"

Jason chuckled silently as he opened the door. "Not a chance. I'm selective."

He led her back to the central area and asked what she needed for her research.

"A seat somewhere out of the way where I can just watch. Will anyone mind?"

Jason shrugged and shook his head. "They know who you are, Leah."

She stared at him.

"Does that bother you?"

She glanced around at people going about their routine. She looked back to Jason, back to the man she'd known before he dressed in a blue uniform. "Not if it doesn't bother you. You work here."

"Don't worry about me," Jason responded, indicating a chair for her to sit in.

He decided that there was nothing to be gained by telling Leah that there *had* been initial curiosity about her. Jason knew that it was Spano who'd probably got the story rolling, and thereafter Jason had found himself defending his decision to date a black woman. He hadn't expected that.

"I'll come back in about a half hour. Will that be enough time?"

It was more than enough, although Leah's observations soon had less to do with her assignment than it did trying to get a feel for the people and place where Jason worked. These were more than just men and women dressed a certain way who legally bore arms. They had a shared mission, a shared philosophy, and it all seemed foreign and incomprehensible to Leah.

At one point an officer approached and introduced himself as Officer O'Neill. He asked if she'd like some coffee or a soda. She was surprised and accepted, although she found herself unable to lower the invisible wall that separated her from him. It was a protective barrier against the unknown.

When Jason returned, Leah was relieved. His presence made her feel less obvious. But he was not alone. There was a sturdily built black youth with him, walking with a slow gait that clearly stated the boy's indifference to his surroundings. He seemed tough and unresponsive. He might have been seventeen. He was wearing a black T-shirt with TOUGH SHIT written in gold foil on the front, under a neon bright orange down jacket easily two sizes too big for him. There were scars on his neck and face, home-done ink tattoos on the back of his hands. He wore a black knit ski cap pulled way down on his head.

The tattoos were what grabbed Leah's attention. Those and his eyes. She couldn't help staring as she realized that she saw nothing beyond their flat brown surface. *Nothing.* Her stomach suddenly churned because that man, the one who'd attacked her, had had eyes like this. Behind them there didn't seem to be any emotion. No sustained thoughts, or right and wrong. Leah realized with sharp accuracy that, like the other man, this boy did not see her as a person, a human being, but simply sized her up as an opportunity or an enemy. There was no middle ground or other criteria. Not even the fact that they were both black.

To actually meet someone with such limited capacity for feelings astonished Leah. What in the world had happened to him and his life? How had he gotten this way?

"How's it going?" Jason asked Leah.

She couldn't even answer right away, so stark was her sense that this boy could strike out at any moment for any reason—or no reason at all.

The teen slumped against the wall and glared at her. His stare was cold, and Leah had the feeling he'd already made up his mind about her. He didn't like her. Was it just because of her or because of her connection to Jason?

"Fine," she responded absently, trying to answer her own questions.

Seeing the direction of her attention, Jason beckoned to the boy. With an obvious lack of interest the youth pushed himself away from the wall and took two very slow steps forward. Jason put his hand on the boy's shoulder and urged him to his side.

"This is Slack," Jason announced with a slight emphasis.

Leah again examined the boy closely. She remembered the name. Someone Jason worked with. The difficult one.

"Hi, Slack," she said quietly, looking at him. She even held out her hand. "I'm Leah."

Slack shifted from one foot to the other. He looked at Leah's hand and then off into space. "Yeah," he uttered in a tone that was empty.

"Hey," Jason said in a sort of warning signal to Slack that they both understood.

With a calculated effort meant to show his boredom, Slack extended his right hand and merely touched Leah's fingertips, but didn't take hold of them. His hand dropped again to his side.

Leah looked at Jason and smiled tentatively.

He shrugged patiently. "He's not housebroken yet," Jason responded dryly. "Lighten up, man. You can't remember the last time someone this pretty looked at you."

Leah might have been amused by Jason's remark, but when she looked at Slack again, any amusement vanished. Beyond the dislike she'd discerned before, Leah thought she could also detect resentment.

"You wait here," Jason instructed Slack firmly. He walked away to the desk sergeant.

Leah had her mouth open, but there was no chance to say anything to Jason before he was gone. She didn't want to be left alone with this boy. But in case she'd been wrong, she looked into Slack's eyes again. He was about her height, and he had a way of looking with his head tilted slightly back that it appeared he was looking down on her. His eyes were dark and impenetrable. There was a wall around him meant very clearly to keep everyone at a distance.

"Where do you live, Slack?" she found herself asking. Just to see how he'd answer.

His head tilted back farther. "What the fuck you want to know for?" he asked scathingly.

Leah stared round-eyed at him. His response was all the more bewildering because it was so instantly angry. He smirked at her.

"How come you know him?" he asked, referring to Jason.

"We're friends."

"He gettin' coochie from you?" he asked.

The question showed such a lack of discipline and respect that she couldn't answer. Leah couldn't seem to take her eyes from him. A sudden dreadful chill literally shook her from head to toe. "That's none of your business." The differences between her and Slack felt suddenly deep and solid. But looking at Slack she also saw the mugger. They were not the same age or size. The other man had been much bigger, but the limits of their lives were the same. She was anxious to get away from him. His presence evoked too many fears of her own vulnerability.

Leah decided not to say anything to Jason, probably because Slack's posture suggested that he expected her to. But mostly Leah didn't want to seem like a tattler and like she didn't know how to handle him.

She didn't, but that was her problem.

"Jason talks about you a lot. He seems to care about what happens to you, you know."

"He ain't my friend. He's a cop."

Leah felt even more foolish. She wondered if Jason really understood what he was dealing with in this boy. She was relieved when Jason finally returned, and she tried not to let her expression indicate her discomfort in Slack's presence. Jason spoke low, only for her to hear.

"Look, I'm giving him a ride back to his center in the Bronx. Am I going to see you later?"

Leah forgot about Slack for a minute and grinned at Jason. "I don't know. Am I going to see you later?"

He checked his watch. "Can you make it to my place? Around seven?"

"See you then."

Jason nodded and turned to Slack. "I'll get my coat." He strode away down the hallway, leaving her alone once more with Slack. She tried not to be intimidated but sensed that Slack could read her and knew she was afraid.

"What you lookin' at?" he asked scathingly, catching her in the act.

She shrugged uneasily. "I was just wondering why you don't think Jason's sincere about helping you."

"Nobody gives a shit, and I don't trust no cops. Jason thinks he knows me. And you look at me like I'm a fuckin' freak." Slack shook his head with eerie sly amusement. "Jason not your friend, neither. You still just a nigger. Just like me. Only he gettin' it from you," he laughed. "Dumb bitch . . ."

Leah swallowed hard, feeling angry and impatient. Anything she said would be inappropriate, ineffectual. "I feel sorry for you."

"Fuck you," he said indifferently.

Jason approached. "Let's go," he said, and Slack turned and bopped off slowly toward the exit.

Leah looked at Jason as he stood in front of her.

She stared because she could still only see the man she liked and trusted. She smiled. His blues gave him something extra.

"Want to be dropped off somewhere?"

"No. It's easier if I get on the train."

"Fine. So I'll see you later."

"Yes . . . Jason?" He stopped, already at the door of the precinct. "Be careful," Leah said hesitantly. He winked at her and left.

Leah knew the moment Jason opened the door to let her into his apartment that he'd had a bad day. He'd gotten there only fifteen minutes before she had, and already he was on his second beer. She'd grown to recognize the signs of stress and annoyance in him. She'd learned to know when just the politics of the precinct set him off into a short tirade of dissatisfaction. When he was pensive he got quiet and withdrawn. It could be a particular case or youngster, or some other relationship . . . something personal that began it all.

"Are you all right?" she asked when she saw the line of tension between his eyes, the reflexive muscle in his jaw that meant he was restless.

"Yeah, fine," Jason murmured. In his bare feet he walked into the open living room and stood with a hand on one hip, sipping from the beer.

His silence made Leah feel insecure and uncertain. Was it about her, them? Was he unhappy? She put her jacket away and dropped her purse on the floor. She eased out of her shoes and joined Jason, standing quietly behind him. She tentatively put her hand on Jason's back, feeling the hard play of muscles. She rubbed caressingly up and down, and actually knew when he began to loosen up and flex with her touch.

"Feel like talking about it?"

Jason slowly turned around to face Leah. He saw the concern and thoughtfulness in her eyes. But he knew he could not go into the details.

Leah had her hair pulled back into a ponytail, and the style made her look considerably younger than she was. She looked more defenseless and confused than he felt. But no, he didn't want to talk to her about his encounter with the redheaded dancer, or her unexpected irritation with his unavailability for the evening. Instead, Jason put his arms around Leah in a loose embrace, careful not to spill the beer.

"No," Jason shook his head at her question. "Believe me, you don't want to know."

"Then, what can I do?" She touched her hand to his bristly jaw. He rubbed his cheek against her.

"Just be with me."

"I'm here," she grinned. Leah took the bottle out of his hand. "I could give you a back rub, but a cold shower might do you more good."

Jason was amused by her simple solution. "Promise?"

"Promise," she nodded.

Even though it was her idea, Leah was surprised when Jason went off without further comment. Usually his mind would have been more creative, his need more physical and immediate. He was often more likely to say, "I have a better idea." But she watched as he unbuckled his belt and opened his jeans. He peeled off the T-shirt and headed for the bathroom.

Maybe he really would rather be alone, Leah thought. But when the bathroom door closed and the water started, she pensively wandered around the apartment, her imagination playing overtime with speculation and doubt.

Jason's studio apartment was on the fifth floor in the rear of a building, which gave him a view of the Brooklyn Bridge. The apartment opened onto a small foyer.

Just off to the left was the bathroom. Next to that, the kitchenette. He had constructed a counter perpendicular to the sink and stove that served as a work area/ desk/dining table with two stools drawn up.

Two things had caught Leah's attention the first time Jason had brought her here. One was the number of photographs of foreign lands, children, and pictures of Michael that covered the walls. The other was the queen-size bed, a mattress on a low platform, in the main room. Suddenly all Leah could think of was that Jason had made love to other women there. Leah had walked around the apartment, to inspect this space that was his. Jason had silently watched. She'd looked at the pictures on the wall taken in 'Nam and California. She stared so long she could almost conjure up a picture of Jason twenty years younger, tramping through the steamy jungles of a foreign land. Some of the pictures of Michael showed him with a very pretty young blond woman who could only have been Jason's ex-wife. Leah felt a bit chilled inside as a new insecurity attacked her. In light of such wholesome blond prettiness, she wondered what it was Jason saw in her.

Sometimes it seemed to Leah that Jason just needed her company. Sometimes it happened that when they were together he seemed to be drawing from her some reserve of strength and stability. After meeting Slack, Leah was not surprised.

Tonight it might again be about Slack . . . or something similar. Jason was again distracted but, she reminded herself, he still wanted to be with her.

Jason eventually came out from the bathroom, casual in his nakedness as he donned a pair of white Jockey shorts and ran his hands through his damp hair.

"Look, I just want to rest a while. You don't mind, do you?"

Leah had no time to think about it as Jason stretched

out across the bed. She did mind, but it wasn't until Jason had fallen to sleep that she could think why. Being left awake made her feel isolated. Leah needed the certainty of his being with her when he touched her, finding pleasure in loving her. She'd already discovered that Jason's greatest strength was his gentleness. He was sensitive enough to recognize that when she held herself aloof from him, which sometimes happened but never lasted for long, it was still out of a sense of fear that he might hurt her.

Leah was determined not to fall into their affair so deeply that there was no chance of her getting out unscathed. Besides which she knew that somewhere deep inside Jason was still hidden his own secrets and pain. Each time she let herself give in to the passion that he aroused in her, she felt guilty and uneasy. She was too confused between her personal satisfaction with him, someone who was white, and a sense that she hadn't given enough or tried hard enough with the men in her past who were black.

Making love to Allen had been pleasant but predictable. Jason was another story completely. He came right out and asked her: did this feel good, did she want to be touched there. Through Jason she discovered her body as something to marvel over and enjoy unclothed. Not in a lascivious way, and not as when she was an adolescent and she and her girlfriends had giggled over the way their bodies changed, how they were different from boys. Leah soon gave up questioning and analyzing for the sheer enjoyment of being with Jason. Even this way. She sat in the chair near the window and stared with blank eyes out into the night.

When Jason awoke two hours later, Leah was in the kitchen thinking about food and dinner. It required a lot of ingenuity since he apparently didn't see the need to keep more than beer on hand. It was a moment before Leah realized that Jason was awake and silently watching her.

"Hi, Jay Eagle," she smiled. She sat next to him on the platform bed. "You must be getting old. Can't make it through a whole day without taking a nap."

He grinned slowly at her.

"Look, the best I can do about dinner on short notice is an omelet. Do you like omelets? I hope so 'cause you have plenty of eggs. And beer. Do you eat like this all the time? White men don't cook either, eh? You should be dead, you know, with a diet like yours."

Jason suddenly took Leah by the arms and pulled her clear over his body onto the bed next to him. She let out a small surprised yelp, and Jason laughed lightly.

"Be quiet," he whispered, and kissed her.

Leah curled up against him as his lovemaking became gentle and lazy. She decided that she needed to stop worrying. She was just afraid to let herself feel so happy.

As Leah sat at her drafting table in front of the window, she could hear the occasional gusts of wind whipping through the canyons between the buildings near the river. It was no longer necessary to wear wool and corduroy and knits and boots. It was the end of April, and she was impatient for summer and the freedom it provided. Winter had made her feel too confined, although it meant private time with Jason. The winter had also been connected to some of the most spiteful and intrusive criticisms of their relationship that either she or Jason had ever had to endure.

Leah got up from her worktable and put away her artwork. It was almost five o'clock and she was ready to leave. But she wasn't ready to go home. Leah wandered into Jill's office, a small, cluttered cubicle at the end of the studio, and found her also preparing to leave. Jill turned to her and smiled.

"Hi. Leaving?"

Leah nodded. She played with the strap of her bag. "Got plans for tonight?"

Jill shook her head with a grin. "Nope. And I can tell neither do you. Want to go for dinner or a drink?"

"A drink would be fine," Leah said.

Jill raised her brows. "This must be serious."

Leah laughed nervously. "It's not. I just thought it would be nice to chill out and gossip."

"Ooooh. I'm all for that."

They went to a small café that was a favorite hangout with people from the office. But Leah was just as happy that she and Jill were able to find a table in the back of the room, away from the noisy front bar. They'd already had a few good laughs over Mike Berger, and shared knowledge about an office affair, when Leah turned the questions on Jill.

"How is it going?" Leah asked.

"How is what going?"

"You and Peter?"

"Oh. Okay, I guess."

"That's it? Just okay?"

Jill shrugged. "Well, you know how it is with men. Up and down and then up again."

"Yeah. But does that mean it's not working out?"

Jill grimaced and hedged. "It means we're working on it. It means," she sighed, "I'm trying to decide if I'm doing the right thing, being with this man."

Leah felt that Jill was talking for both of them. Everything was changing. Everyone was changing. Maybe it was spring fever. Maybe minerals in the tap water. Swamp gas.

"But don't think I haven't noticed that you're pretty dreamy yourself," Jill said speculatively.

Leah laughed nervously. Had everyone noticed?

"Me?"

"Yep. You have the breathless, awed look of someone in or about to be in love."

"Well, I'm not in love . . ." Leah said nervously.

"You . . . don't love Allen?" Jill asked, ignoring the firm statement. She scrutinized Leah through narrowed eyes. "You haven't said a word about Allen in weeks. What's going on?"

Leah's smile was furtive. "Nothing. We're not dating anymore."

"You're not? You mean you two broke up and you never even said anything?"

"I was a little preoccupied at the time," Leah said dryly. "And I felt funny just walking in one day and announcing, Allen and I have broken up."

Jill shook her head in surprise. "How come? Did he meet someone else?"

Leah hesitated. "Yes."

"And what about you? How did that make you feel?"

"Well, the truth is . . . I met someone else, too."

Jill's brows shot up. "How convenient. Which came first?"

Leah thought about it but decided it was too complicated to track. And it didn't matter. December was a long time ago. She shrugged. "I don't know. It just happened."

"You mean to tell me you've been seeing someone new and probably exciting, and you never said anything?"

Leah sighed and swirled the ice in the bottom of her Drambuie. "Well, it's been a little difficult."

"Oh. Not working out, eh?"

"No, that's not it. Jason and I are fine. I mean, I think we're okay, It's just that . . . well, he's white and—"

"White?" Jill interrupted blankly, as if the concept didn't register. "You mean he's . . ."

"White," Leah said, watching the other woman. Jill simply stared at her. And then she lowered her gaze to her glass and seemed unable to speak.

"Oh," Jill said quietly.

Leah felt uneasy with the reaction. "You said that."

Jill looked at Leah finally, but her expression was a little guarded, her eyes questioning. "How come?"

Leah frowned. "Excuse me?"

"How did it happen?"

Leah still wasn't sure she'd heard correctly, and was now uncomfortable with Jill's reaction to the news. "What do you mean, how did it happen? We met, liked each other, and he started asking me out."

Jill's mouth tightened and Leah realized that she'd never considered the possibility that her co-worker and friend would disapprove. Suddenly, she might just as well have been sitting opposite a complete stranger. Which made the situation suddenly so unreal. She and Jill knew each other. It seemed odd that they should work so closely, so long together, and Leah had never suspected that Jill might have a bias or two that would surface and come between them.

Jill shrugged. "I don't know what to say."

Leah pushed her glass aside. She'd had enough of the sweet liqueur. "I think you've already said it. You don't approve, do you?"

Jill laughed nervously, smoothing her hair behind an ear. "I guess I'm just shocked."

"Why?"

"Because . . . because you're just asking for trouble. I mean, why make things so difficult?"

"What is it you don't like, Jill? That Jason asked me out or that I said yes?"

Jill got over her initial shock and stared at Leah.

"Look, I'm sorry, but I just think it's a mistake. What are you trying to prove?"

Leah was disappointed. There had been no one she could openly talk to about her relationship with Jason. She'd hoped that Jill would just have been a friend and listened.

"I guess that it's possible for two people to really like each other and color not be an issue. Like you and Peter, we're just trying to work out an honest relationship. Jason and I are fine with it. It's everyone else in the world that's getting on our case."

"Leah, I'm sorry. I didn't mean to sound so hard, but . . . do you really think it's going to work?"

"I don't know if it will or won't. But it would have been nice to have someone say, I hope it does. I'll get this. I have to get home."

Leah reached for the bill on the table as Jill stared open-mouthed at her. Before she could gather her wits, Leah was already slipping into her blazer and gathering her tote and purse.

"Leah, wait. Let me try to explain how I feel."

Leah turned on her. "Jill, I already know how you feel. But this isn't about you. I'll see you tomorrow."

With that Leah hurried toward the front of the café. She had paid the bill and left before Jill had a chance to catch up to her.

Leah guessed she should have known better. She had, back at the beginning. At the moment, however, she was perilously close to caring for a New York City cop named Jason Horn far more than could possibly be good for her. She was, all at once, both miserable and happy. Happy with the time spent with him. Incredulous with how good they seemed together. Miserable because it had no place to go. And everyone was telling her so.

"You are so comfortable," Jason had said recently to her. "You make me feel like I do everything right."

But there was more to a relationship that just making love. Sometimes Leah would allow herself a daydream in which a future presented itself with Jason. But it was always confused and unreal. Pointless, because she couldn't see an ending. Frightening, because she was sure she didn't want to.

Leah stood a dozen yards or so beyond the finish line. The small area was already busy with people waiting for the first of the runners to arrive. There were time keepers and park officials, a waiting medical unit—just in case—folding chairs and cots, and a table set up with cups of Tang, Gatorade, and water.

Leah kept out of the way and hid behind her sunglasses, protecting her anxiety and annoyance. The anxiety was because she knew Jason was really too tired to have run the race this Sunday morning. It would have made more sense for him to have slept in late, especially after what he'd called one hell of a night. The annoyance she hadn't gotten around to examining yet. And she'd had no luck convincing herself that she'd overreacted to Jason's canceling of their date the night before.

She scanned the distance, down the path and between the spring-leafed trees, looking for the runners in the Prospect Park May Day 10K. A sudden cheer went up, and Leah shifted her attention from the phone conversation with Jason the previous night to the sight of runners approaching the end of the race. She spotted him in the first group, his Day-Glo orange entry bib visible with the number twenty-four printed front and back. She forgot about all other considerations except that Jason had made it. Joy and worry surged in her chest. He was going to finish eighth.

Leah waved to Jason, hoping to mark her position, but she didn't think he'd seen her as several officials reached him to note his number and finishing time on a chart, to ask how he was feeling. She felt another rush, this one of pride. He wasn't even winded although Leah had noticed an almost imperceptible limp. She watched as Jason conversed with a volunteer as he was handed several items. He accepted a cup of Gatorade, and shook out the long, muscular leg that apparently troubled him.

She gathered up his sweat top and red cap, her tote, and started forward through the growing crowd.

"Jason," Leah called out.

He glanced up quickly and his eyes searched her out. He grinned and gave Leah a thumb's-up sign. The other emotion she'd been grappling with since late the night before disappeared.

The finish line area was now packed with runners, their friends and families, as Leah walked toward Jason. Then she heard his name called out in a feminine voice, and saw a young woman suddenly emerge in front of Jason, and the two of them embraced.

Leah stopped where she was, watching the encounter and feeling like she was witnessing the union of an old relationship. The woman, also dressed as a runner, hugged Jason as they laughed together over the coincidence of their meeting. She was a brunette with a lithe build that bespoke fitness. She was lively and attractive, and she spurred to life within Leah, as she watched the two of them, a sudden rise of apprehension.

Jason finally looked around for Leah and, seeing her, beckoned her forward. She came to stand next to him, a smile coming automatically to her lips. She was again glad for the shield the dark glasses provided. Jason put a damp arm around her shoulders.

"Leah, this is Cindy Walken."

"Cindy Walken-*Schott*. Hi, Leah." Cindy smiled, and they shook hands.

Leah found her grip firm and forthright. She seemed very friendly.

"Cindy used to be on the force," Jason informed Leah.

"Emphasis on the used to," Cindy laughed.

"Why did you quit?" Leah spoke up.

Cindy looked briefly at Jason and shrugged. "It was crazy. I decided to go back to school and study law. I think I'd rather prosecute than arrest. It's a lot safer."

Jason squeezed Leah's shoulder. "Cindy's husband worried about her, but she can take care of herself."

"Thanks, Jason." Cindy nodded, somewhat surprised by his observation.

"How did you place in the race?" Leah asked, already impressed with the other woman's vitality.

"Fifteenth," she announced happily. She poked Jason in the ribs. "Kept up with you big guys."

Jason grinned at her. "Told you you could take care of yourself."

"Congratulations," Leah murmured.

"Thanks. Look, I'd better go find my husband. It was nice seeing you, Jason. You're looking good. Nice meeting you," she said to Leah and waved as she walked away.

Leah put her arm around Jason's waist. It was a possessive move, one meant to connect them physically for the moment. One meant to dispel the sometimes ephemeral feel of their relationship, when Jason was involved in other areas of his life that she couldn't take part in. What they shared was substantial, and because it was Leah found herself trying to divine the future beyond the physical joy they both claimed and enjoyed in each other.

Jason was sweaty and warm. He smelled hot and male. Virile. Leah suddenly smiled secretly to herself, finding his vigor stimulating. She heard him sigh.

"Fifteenth. And I thought I was running at a good clip. Man, she's in great shape."

Leah kept her voice smooth. "She's also about ten years younger."

"Thanks a lot," Jason chuckled good-naturedly.

"How's your knee?" she asked as they walked and separated from the milling crowds.

"Okay. I think I pulled it a bit on the last mile."

"Will an ice pack help?"

"A cold beer sounds better, but the ice won't hurt."

"Let's get you home," she said.

"Great. I'm beat," he groaned.

She glanced at him again. His face was only slightly flushed, but perspiration gleamed from his forehead, arms, and shoulders. Under the running bib, which he now removed and discarded, his tank shirt was soaked, and his chest hair was matted to his skin.

Leah had found out early in January that Jason also liked to jog. She'd awaken one morning in his bed and found him gone. It was not quite seven. She was bewildered as to where he had gone—obviously not far; he'd left his gun—when he'd come in sweaty but full of energy . . . and lust. They'd made love instead of breakfast, and both had been late for work. But it didn't take long for Leah to also figure out that the running, the pushing of his body to the limit, worked off excess frustration, stress, and lingering sadness. When he began asking her to attend the short races he'd enter, Leah did. Except for the one time half a dozen of his fellow officers from the precinct signed up together and it was an occasion for male bonding.

"So what do you get for running a Ten-K and crossing the finish line in the top ten?"

Jason grinned as he used his forearm to wipe sweat from his face. "My ego stroked, a sore body, and a T-shirt." He held up his other hand to show the white folded cloth. He gave it to Leah. "Here, this is for you."

"I don't wear T-shirts," Leah reminded him.

Jason suddenly kissed her, leaving her mouth smudged with his salty dampness. "Use it as a night-shirt. You can leave it at my place."

Again Leah smiled at him. She blinked behind the sunglasses, glad that Jason couldn't see her whole face, her expression just then. She was sure that everything was hanging out, exposing her, leaving her defenseless against the pleasure of being with him.

They got into Jason's car for the short drive back to her house. Every time they drove his car, Leah was reminded of that first time when they'd gone to the New Year's Eve party at Joe and Nora's. She glanced at his profile, thinking how far they'd come in four months. Still, they never really talked about where, exactly, they were, much less where they were headed. They hadn't gotten much past wanting to spend time together. And wanting to make love.

She was suddenly acutely aware of his physical presence next to her. In her life, her dreams. Leah put her hand on his hairy thigh, feeling the muscle underneath, knowing every inch of his body and its responses, most especially when they were together.

"Cindy seems very nice," she ventured quietly.

Jason detected the query in Leah's statement. The unasked question. He'd never been involved with Cindy, but it had come pretty close once. Before she'd gotten married and left the force. He decided to skirt the broader issue in Leah's remark. He laced his fingers with hers.

"I'm not into jockettes," he murmured, amused. Leah chuckled and he squeezed her fingers. "I like my

THE COLOR OF LOVE

woman soft and concerned. And I don't like them to run faster than I do."

"Well, that certainly lets me out."

"Except for the soft and concerned part," he corrected.

He released her hand and slid his slowly up her denimed thigh. His fingers curved to the inside of her leg with a caressing firmness. At the traffic light Jason turned to look at her.

Leah finally took the glasses off, not caring what Jason saw in her eyes or in their bright gaze that opened up the window to her heart.

"Can I stay tonight?" he asked softly.

She thought about him asking. They still only saw each other three or four times a week. Sometimes there was a weekend at her house or his apartment. Once, a weekend away in March when Jason had attended a special class in D.C., Leah had known that it made her life feel choppy and disoriented, as though she didn't have just one place to be, one place that was just theirs together. Jason seemed perfectly happy with things the way they were. And Leah knew it couldn't be her to ask why it felt so incomplete and temporary. She liked that Jason asked, that he never took it for granted. Still, it was that very same thoughtfulness that made her feel that there was distance between them.

"Yes," Leah answered his question.

While Jason showered, Leah made an ice pack in a Zip-loc bag, and wrapped it in a linen towel. On her way to the kitchen she'd passed Gail in the living room, making evening arrangements over the phone with Allen. They briefly acknowledged each other, but Gail was usually combative when Jason was in the house, and Leah worked at keeping them apart. However, as Leah was heading back to her room, Gail met her at the foot of the stairs.

"I hate it when you wait on that man hand and foot."

"I'm only taking him a beer and an ice pack. I haven't sworn servitude," Leah said dryly.

"It's early yet," Gail responded.

Leah made an impatient gesture and started up the stairs.

"What excuse did he have for standing you up last night?"

The question, unfortunately, renewed the ambivalence Leah had been living with all day. Whether or not to make an issue with Jason over a ruined dinner, a postponed evening. A lonely night. She stopped to look down at her sister, momentarily tempted to tell Gail to mind her own business, but knowing that Gail would just ignore her.

"He didn't need one. He said he couldn't make it, and he must have had a good reason."

Gail's smile was satisfied, just short of an "I told you so" smirk. "I'm sure he had a reason. But will it be a good enough one?"

"You don't have to deal with it, do you?" Leah asked, but didn't wait for an answer as she continued to her room.

She was aimlessly sorting through several recent drawings when Jason returned from the bathroom. She didn't turn around to face him.

"How was the shower?" she asked calmly.

Jason advanced into the room, toweling his hair and body. "Wet." He tossed the towel onto the vanity stool.

Leah pointed to the ice pack. "You should sit with that on your knee for a while and let it—"

"Still mad at me?" Jason interrupted. He was right behind her.

She slowly shook her head, turned the sketches face-down. "About what?"

Jason wasn't fooled. He came close enough to feel

her shoulders against his chest, her buttocks against his groin. "About last night."

"No . . ."

He put his arms slowly around her and pulled her to him. "Liar."

"I wasn't angry, really."

"Disappointed?" She merely nodded. Jason kissed the back of her head and hugged her gently. "Me, too."

Leah felt surrounded by him and, for this moment, safe and special. Jason began to rub and massage her stomach through the cotton fabric of her blouse.

"It was Slack. I didn't have time to go into it last night. Something happened at his grandmother's house. I got a call from her that Slack and one of his uncles were fighting. She was afraid that someone was going to get hurt. I didn't want it to be her."

Leah listened quietly and wondered if her doubts had been of her own making. She sighed and closed her eyes, reached down with her hands to just rest them on his legs.

"I didn't really have a choice about last night. I wanted to be with you like we planned. I know I messed up, but when Slack messes up, it becomes my problem."

"I know. You work twenty-four hours a day." She repeated his often used explanation. But already her stiffness was melting.

Jason's hands grew exploratory. He popped open the snap on her jeans and pulled down the zipper. He grew hard against her back, his penis rising. He slid his large hand into the opening of the jeans and splayed it over her navel and stomach. Jason leaned forward to kiss her ear and the side of her neck. "I'm sorry . . ."

"It's okay."

Slowly he turned her around and began kissing her as his hand released the buttons on the front of the blouse. His lips and tongue teasing and coaxing as he swept away her doubts, his guilt.

Leah let him capture her lips, needing him to be assertive and to show that he wanted her. Her tension quickly dissolved into desire. Jason kissed her with that purpose in mind. He stopped just for a moment, while he gazed thoughtfully into her face.

"I don't want you to forgive me, Leah. I just need you to understand."

She blinked at him, suddenly thinking that there was another meaning to his request, but only satisfied that Jason was comforting her and trying to make it better. She spread her hands over his chest, the hair now dry and springy, and his skin smelling of soap and shampoo.

"Of course I understand," she whispered.

Jason smiled slowly at her and began to kiss her again. "Thank you."

They got the rest of her things off, and there was finally nothing between their bodies but heartbeats and heat. When Jason lifted her from the floor, Leah held tightly around his neck and wrapped her legs around his hips. He turned, holding her, and made the short journey to the bed, where he lowered her to the mattress. Leah's hold around his neck brought Jason down on top of her.

She absorbed his passion into her body and let it flow delightfully to all her limbs. When Jason drew his legs up slightly, as he buried himself inside her body and began to move slowly, she touched his face and sighed in concern.

"Jason, your knee . . ."

But he kissed her fingers, her nose, her mouth. He looked at her, his eyes slumberous with longing. There was still humor in his eyes. "My knee is not what you should be thinking about."

He surged forward, and Leah moaned softly, undulating her hips against his entry. She decided to take his advice. She let her body take control and resolutely pushed her concerns to the back of her mind. She couldn't deal with them at the moment. She didn't even want to.

It was, nevertheless, overwhelming enough to accept that she and Jason did not belong to each other. That there might be competition for his time, attention, and loving: a sixteen-year-old youthful offender—and other women.

Leah squinted against the early evening light, but loved the warmth of it, which seemed to melt and flow over her skin. She closed her eyes and just listened to the babble of conversation from other diners, from passersby as she and Jason sat at a sidewalk café finishing dinner. She and Jason had discovered Milo's shortly after it opened, and they both loved its pasta specialties.

Besides its good but simple food and its unpretentious ambiance, Milo's had also become a neutral zone where many of their serious conversations took place. If a problem came up, Leah had discovered it wouldn't get discussed at the brownstone or at Jason's apartment. They always ended up in bed. Their lovemaking was always good, but it also masked everything else, delayed dealing with real issues. It was one of the things that had first concerned Leah about their relationship, that she and Jason might never really get beyond the purely physical.

They'd already finished dinner, and the conversation reached a lull. Jason was preoccupied. Leah understood enough about him to know that sometimes he mulled over things before deciding to talk about them.

Jason turned and smiled absently at her. Leah frowned. It seemed almost as if he wanted to say something. He hesitated, played with her fingers. She looked clearly into his gray eyes.

"What?" she quietly coaxed.

He glanced slowly at her, but he never had a chance to answer.

There was a muffled anguished cry that tore through the evening air. In unison everyone in the café turned their heads in the direction of the unmistakable sounds of pain and fright. At first there was nothing to see. Just a street off to the left that was lined with a number of older tenement buildings and local stores. At the far corner was a check-cashing establishment.

Leah frowned briefly at Jason as if to ask, had he heard something, too? Jason was alert and already his attention was carefully directed to the movement on the street. Then a middle-aged woman staggered from the check-cashing operation crying plaintively for help. The side of her face and head were red, the blood dripping onto the pink cardigan sweater she was wearing.

"Stop them! Help me! Help . . ." she cried in distress.

Several people hesitantly went to her aid as she pointed down the block. "Please stop them. My money . . ."

Jason was on his feet. "Stay here," he ordered Leah, never taking his eyes from the dozen or so people on the opposite block.

He didn't wait for her response, and she watched as he casually crossed the street, placing himself in the path of the flow of traffic away from the store where the woman stood.

Many people stood looking around, trying to figure out what was going on or trying to spot who was responsible. Only two young men seemed unaware . . . or indifferent. They were both wearing loose over-size denim coats. Totally unnecessary in the warm air of early May. Leah saw them and knew that Jason had picked them out as well.

Leah had never been able to tell an undercover or off-duty cop from anyone else in the street, and never understood how others picked them out so easily. But something about Jason must have alerted the two young men, because in a flash they broke into a sprint, separated, and dashed off in different directions.

Leah jumped to her feet, shocked and mesmerized by what was happening before her eyes. Adrenaline started to rush through her in excited disbelief. This was not a movie. This was not a report on the eleven o'clock news.

She knew Jason could not hope to catch both men, and he had to make an instant decision. She watched as he shifted positions on a pivot, shouted sharp, uncompromising orders. She next felt as though her heart had leaped into her throat with a forceful surge of anxiety.

Leah recognized what lay behind the woman's screams for help. The terrible fear that forced the sounds past her throat and through her lips. For Leah, a long time ago, her sounds had been absorbed into gray walls with no one around to hear or help. Her heart constricted with the memory of calling for help and getting no answer. She suddenly recognized the pursuit being carried out before her as inherent in Jason's life. He was totally concentrated on his efforts to apprehend the young men. Leah was breathless and shocked at his willingness to do so with no thought for himself. The potential danger began to tighten her throat.

The heavier of the two men cut across Jason and disappeared around the corner. Jason let him go, and went in pursuit of the smaller man, who held his coat closed with one hand as he tried to run.

Jason quickly shouted his orders to stop. He pulled his concealed gun and held it down as he ran. The young man jumped over the hood of a car, tripped, and fell on the other side. The coat fell open and two thick wads of currency tumbled to the sidewalk. He quickly scrambled up, forgetting the money as he awkwardly tried to regain his footing.

A woman screamed. People came out of shops and buildings at the commotion and stood open-mouthed at the action unfolding before them.

The man tripping gave Jason the time he needed, and he rounded the rear end of the car and placed himself squarely in front of the perpetrator.

"Freeze!" Jason demanded in a thunderous voice.

Before he could take aim, the young man was up and had rushed him straight on. Jason crashed backward onto the ground with the suspect trying to continue his escape clear over Jason's prone body. But Jason grabbed hold of the attacker's leg and held on as the wiry man twisted and tried to kick his way free.

A crowd gathered at a safe distance, watching but making no attempt to interfere. Leah finally hurried forward as the crowd blocked her sight of Jason. She forced her way through and found Jason wrestling his suspect down. His red cap came off and was kicked to the side. Leah edged her way around the gathering and retrieved the cap from beneath someone's feet.

Jason had the advantage now. He pulled the flailing young man to the ground and flipped him over onto his stomach. Then he ruthlessly planted his knee in the center of the perp's back. The man yelled.

Leah was transfixed at the power of one human being over another. For a moment it didn't matter that one of the men involved was Jason doing his job. And then it mattered most of all.

A police car came around the far corner, without

sirens but with lights on. It made several short siren blips, however, to clear a path.

Jason was panting. With his knee planted in the man's back, he put his gun away and slammed the suspect's head to the ground to make him stay still. Again the man screamed.

"You got anything on you?" Jason asked as he awkwardly frisked the man.

When two uniformed officers approached, hands on their guns, Jason looked up. "I'm a cop," he said loudly.

He reached for his ID and shield. Another patrol car arrived and more officers surrounded them.

When the suspect tried to lift his head and an arm, Jason's knee dug deeper. "Don't move!"

Leah visibly jumped at the control and hard authority of his voice.

Her world suddenly tilted and she literally felt dizzy, thrown off balance. She had seen all sides of Jason—except this one. This one that was capable of pain, violence, and power. She wondered, suddenly, about what else she didn't know about him. All of Leah's earlier fears, when she'd first found out that Jason Horn was a cop, came back in full force—like the nightmare. Her sense of helplessness increased. She felt threatened and shaky and couldn't dispel the notion that Jason and the man who had mugged her were somehow linked. It was their ability to control and manipulate. Their size and strength that was a power unto themselves. It threatened to sabotage Leah's intimate knowledge and experiences of Jason, and for a moment she saw him only as a stranger again.

Jason looked up as the uniformed officers asked questions and relieved him of the suspect. He used his forearm to wipe half his face of the perspiration generated during the collar and looked around for his hat. He had a superficial abrasion on the side of his hand,

and his chambray blue work shirt was dirty from the sidewalk. He did a double-take when he spotted Leah's face in the crowd. Her expression was not passive like most of those around her. Instead, Jason saw that her eyes were wide with horror . . . and revulsion.

But he couldn't go to her yet. He had to finish with his suspect, fill in the other officers. He braced himself against the withdrawal in Leah's eyes and turned back to the business at hand.

An ambulance was called for the woman. The two bundles of money were recovered: five thousand dollars. Another roll of money was found on the suspect. A description was given of the second suspect. In just thirty-five minutes the crowd had cleared, the suspect had been handcuffed and carted away, and the injured woman was on her way for medical care.

Jason held his anxiety in check. Not for anything he'd just been through—it had all been routine and had gone smoothly, given the circumstances. But now he had to face Leah. As soon as he could, he excused himself from his colleagues, letting them take over the arrest.

She had returned to Milo's. Her back was to him, and as he approached he saw that she was paying the bill and accepting her change.

"Leah . . ."

"I know. You have reports to fill out and a man in custody."

"Leah."

He reached her and took her arm. She was shaking. She handed him the red cap and kept a distance between them.

Jason looked at the cap blankly before taking it and stuffing the bill in the back pocket of his jeans. "I'm done. The other officers will take over. They don't need me for an arrest."

"It's okay. I'll go home. I'll—"

"Leah," he said calmly. "What's wrong?"

When she didn't meet his gaze, he felt his annoyance level rise, although he didn't show it.

"Nothing. I just want to go home."

"Fine. I think we could both use a drink. I think I have some wine, and we can relax—"

"No! I want to go home."

Leah pulled her arm free and tried to walk away. She turned and crashed right into a bistro table and knocked a chair over.

Jason righted the chair, and while he did so Leah began walking away. Jason cursed under his breath and sprinted after her. When he caught up, he circled an arm around her waist and forcibly steered her into the recessed entrance of a clothing shop already closed for the night. He didn't say anything and Leah didn't try to move. He stood close to her and could actually feel her fear. He could smell his own sweat and the calmer, cleaner fragrance of her body talc. Leah was breathing hard.

"Talk to me," Jason demanded patiently.

"I . . . it was . . ." she struggled.

Finally she looked up into his face, and Jason's heart constricted at the look of stark terror. Her eyes were filling with tears. He didn't touch her.

"I don't think I can do this."

"Do what?"

Leah shook her head. "I just can't, Jason . . . it was so awful. So scary." She had no idea how to explain how painfully vulnerable the incident had made her feel. She could feel the way the mugger had placed his hands over her mouth, cutting off her breathing. She could recall the way he tried to force her down. . . .

"And violent? Yes, it is. Some people are violent. Sometimes there is violence."

"What you do is violent, too," she said accusingly.

"You're right. Sometimes. It can't be helped. But I also try to keep people from getting hurt. I'm sorry, but the two go hand in hand."

Leah shook her head from side to side. "I can't . . . I can't."

Jason took firm hold of both her arms. "What, can't you? What?"

"I don't think I can handle knowing . . . that can happen." She indicated with a tilt of her head the direction of the arrest. "That you could be involved."

Jason pulled her closer until there was barely two inches between them. "This is my job," he whispered urgently. "This is what I do. But this is *not* who I am, Leah. No one should realize that better than you. I don't use force unless I have to. I don't get off on power or hurting people."

She just closed her eyes and shook her head, tears spilling down her face. She swayed and braced closed fists on his chest.

"Did you have to pull your gun?"

"He had a weapon," Jason said softly.

He watched as her eyes opened and her vision glistened brightly. Leah tried to assimilate the information and to process it to a logical conclusion. At least, Jason hoped that she would. But he could see that the fear remained in place. Jason just kept his hold on her and waited until she finally focused on him.

She opened her fists and ran her palms over his chest. His skin was damp and hot under the shirt; it was marked with perspiration. And it was dirty. She abruptly stopped crying.

"Your shirt is torn," she said in quiet observation. She looked into his face, examining it with a frown. "You . . . have a scratch. Here . . ." She lifted her hand to touch it.

Jason waited.

"Hey, Horn!"

Leah jumped again.

He half turned from the recess, although he kept his position shielding Leah, his hands on her.

"Yeah?"

"You want to come and claim this one?"

Jason shook his head. "You take it. You guys can owe me one."

He turned back to find Leah still staring at him. Her expression was thoughtful and considering, recuperating from her shock. Her hands pressed against his chest.

"Oh, Jason." She breathed out his name. She rested her forehead on his chest. He held her in a loose embrace.

The moment was bittersweet to him.

"After I get cleaned up, I'll take you home," Jason said softly.

He hoped she couldn't see his own fear and disappointment.

It was the first time they'd made love that afterward Leah felt that something was missing. She'd not been able to get back to that place where she and Jason felt perfect together. Where he filled her senses and she believed anything was possible between them. For the first time there was caution and hesitancy, and nothing to hold them together after the climax. Leah had not been able to feel Jason's satisfaction with her, even when he was inside her and his body strained to spill itself.

Leah had not expected that they would make love when he'd brought her home. But Jason had said to her, "Let's go upstairs," and she'd not questioned it. In her bedroom it had all happened quickly and mechanically, and a terrible fear gripped her afterward.

When Jason finally got up to use the bathroom, Leah curled up, wondering what they would say to each other when he returned. But she never knew when that was because she fell to sleep. And fell right into the dream . . .

An hour later, Leah groaned and wept her way out of sleep. Jason, lying quietly but awake next to her, watched as she struggled.

"No. Noooooo," Leah moaned. Her body twisted. "Don't. Please . . ."

Jason leaned over her, holding her shoulder. "Wake up, Leah. Wake up. It's a dream." She sprang halfway up, her face contorted. Jason captured her in his arms and again murmured to her, "Hey. Take it easy. It's just a dream. And it's all over."

Leah went limp in his arms. Her body was warm and damp. "Is he . . . gone?" she whispered nonsensically.

"What?"

She opened her eyes and looked beseechingly at him. It surprised Jason to see the depths of her distress. She blinked rapidly, finally realizing where she was and with whom. But Jason puzzled over what she'd meant.

"You just had a bad dream. That's all," he whispered, brushing her hair from her face.

She shook her head. "It never feels like a dream."

"What were you dreaming about?"

Again she shook her head. "Could you please . . . just hold me?"

Jason did so silently. For a long time. The moment struck him as odd and different. Not because he held her, but because Leah had asked him to. It occurred to Jason that in all the time he'd known her, Leah had never asked anything of him.

It seemed an astounding realization, and Jason wondered why she had held herself back from him in that way. Was it his fault? Did she not trust him enough? Did he not care enough to notice? It made Jason feel helpless in a whole new way. Scared, even.

Other than Michael, no one had ever needed him before.

Chapter Nine

"Leah? Hi."

Leah hesitated before answering. She sometimes had a moment of ambivalence when Jason called. "Hi. How are you?"

"A little hectic. I hate this new schedule," Jason confessed contritely.

"What's wrong with it?"

"It shoots my social life to hell, for one thing."

Leah made no comment. It was the first concrete statement she'd had from Jason that his social life didn't always include her. She tried to use the information as a way of protecting her feelings, but it didn't always work. "Want to come for dinner?" she offered.

"I can't tonight."

"Oh . . ."

"I have to coach an indoor handball tournament in the Bronx. I called to find out if maybe you'd like to go."

Leah was amused. Another sporting event. It made her wonder what Jason had done on dates with other women. Had they been taken to concerts, or shows, or long drives while she got the locker room tour? Leah laughed softly at the irony of it. She guessed it didn't really matter. They still got to be together.

"What's so funny?" Jason asked her.

"What would I do at a handball game, Jason?"

"You could cheer."

"I could stay home."

"Please, Leah. Nobody should have to go to the Bronx alone. Keep me company?"

"Just what did you do before you met me?" she said, unable to keep the impatience from her tone.

"Complained a lot. But I went."

"All right, all right, I'll go. Are we having dinner?"

"No, you go ahead and eat, but I'll be there to get you in an hour and it's another hour's ride from your place."

"Fine. I'll be waiting in front of the house."

Despite her less than enthusiastic agreement to attend the tournament, Leah was glad of a chance to be away for the evening. The atmosphere at home was more than a little chilly between her and Gail. Leah hung up the phone and sat still for a moment. She felt a surge of annoyance for not telling Jason that she didn't want to travel to the Bronx, either. She wasn't in the mood to sit in a cold gym and watch a bunch of foul-mouthed teens work out their aggressions by hitting a ball against a wall. But her annoyance did nothing to dispel the accompanying anxiety. She did want to be with Jason. And he was calling all the shots.

Leah got up from the sofa in the living room and headed for the kitchen. She nearly collided with Gail in the hallway.

"Jason?" Gail asked with raised brows.

"Yes. Why?" Leah responded, realizing almost immediately how defensive she sounded.

Gail scoffed and made an impatient sound. "He certainly knows which buttons to push. All he has to do is call and you drop everything. How pathetic."

The accusation cut deeply, but Leah forced her expression to stay blank. "I know you don't like Jason, so

I'm not going to bother to answer." She tried to move around her sister.

Gail chuckled. "That's because you know I'm right."

Leah turned on her. "It's interesting how quickly you forgot what Allen put you through for two years."

Gail's smile was superior. "But I gained the upper hand. And I got what I wanted. Jason can't do anything for you, and you're going to get hurt."

But Leah didn't need Gail to raise doubts in her head about Jason or the wisdom of their affair. She was having enough doubts of her own.

On the drive up to the Bronx, Leah listened while Jason complained about his case load and work hours. He seemed tense and a bit curt, but Leah just chalked it up to work-related anxiety. And her annoyance grew because she was suddenly unwilling to be a sounding board for his problems. Leah interrupted him:

"You're doing a lot of extra stuff you don't have to do. You're taking on difficult cases that are hopeless."

"No kid is hopeless," Jason countered impatiently.

"What about Slack? I think he's dangerous."

"I can handle Slack."

"Well, you can't bring home every tough kid. Don't you see that sometimes you can't turn them around? What is it you're trying to prove to yourself?"

Jason sighed. He thought instantly of the kid he'd shot and killed. Leah's question echoed in his head, and he didn't have an answer. When she suggested that perhaps he wasn't getting enough rest, he impatiently brushed it aside and she said no more.

At the Bronx gym were boys from a nearby youth shelter sponsored by a Catholic church. To Leah, most of the boys, black and Latino, looked much older than their years, worn by the kind of lives they'd lived. Leah noticed at once, however, that the boys held Jason in a kind of cautious respect and admiration.

When Jason walked into the gym his whole demeanor changed, and so did theirs. He walked to the group and did a street handshake with several of them. They didn't so much say hello as they sort of acknowledged each other's presence and right to be there. Jason was accepted.

"All you homies are here to play tonight, right?" Jason asked comfortably. He pointed a finger at one youth who had a bandanna wrapped around his head. "No shit, hear me, Mex?" The boy shrugged indifferently. "I'm telling you straight up," Jason said to all of them, laying the ground rules for the evening.

Leah observed their ritualistic behavior in fascination, the way they treated one another and the way they listened to Jason. He *was* very good with the boys, somehow able to reach them on a level that didn't strip them of their pride, or not take them seriously.

Two boys started roughhousing, as if they were above Jason's commands. Leah saw the potential for the pushing to escalate as neither wanted to back down. Jason continued to talk while casually approaching the two teens. He suddenly grabbed one boy by the wrist, bending it back and applying enough pressure to make the teen uncomfortable. Jason, still talking, led the boy to an isolated bench and pushed him down.

"Oh, shit," the boy chuckled, embarrassed. But he stayed put and paid attention.

Watching, Leah felt contrite for the way she'd responded in the car. He was right not to give up. But she also remembered the brief exchange with Gail. She had been right, too.

And Slack was there.

Leah glanced at him briefly and then away with an even briefer smile. Despite the swirl of tension from seeing him, Leah was prepared to acknowledge him as part of a circle of youths that Jason was concerned with. But Slack's cold stare discouraged any familiarity.

She could feel his dislike of her as a tangible, three-dimensional thing that might lash out at her at any time. Slack seemed so angry. She wondered what he did with all of that anger. Where was it directed? For a foolish instant Leah considered the possibility of reaching out to him. After all, Jason had. But why? To be his friend? She decided quickly that she didn't want to be Slack's friend. The truth was, he made her feel as that man had that night on the stairs.

The boys got a little testy when Jason introduced her around.

"Ah, man, what you gotta bring her for?" Slack called out.

"She's a visitor. Say hello to the nice lady or I'll break your arm," Jason muttered.

"You know women is bad luck for our game, man. Even if she's foxy," someone else called out, followed by some loud chortling, whistles, and slapping of palms.

Leah felt challenged. She held her breath and faced them all squarely. "Jason said you were good players. I think he was trying to be nice," she said casually, staring them down.

Jason watched her in surprised silence, but Leah merely turned away to walk to a bench.

"Fuck her," Leah heard one of the boys mutter. It was followed by silence as she knew they waited for Jason's response.

"In your dreams," Jason shot back.

Again, some of the boys collapsed in laughter. But her challenge stood and some of them took up the dare.

"Bet!" they chorused, bopping away to form team

sets. "We'll show this bitch how we do the *do*. Wait 'til we through, Jack."

There was much shouting and joking as the teams were paired off and Jason got the games started. There were many other teams, other referees, and Leah suspected that some of them were off-duty cops as well. Slack played on the team from the Catholic shelter that housed him. When he played, he was aggressive and quick, but he bounced back and forth between an interest in the game and a need to show off. He kept yelling abusive remarks at the other players, and it was clear that not many of them were his friends.

Jason watched mostly in silence, only occasionally shouting an order or correcting a player, once ending a dispute over a call that nearly ended in a fistfight. The boys were tough and brash, not giving in too much and standing their ground stubbornly. Leah admitted to herself they played well, although it might have been just to show her up. She could also see that they loved this game. When their bare palms slapped the small ball against the back wall of the court, they were quick on their feet and clever with their opponents, and obviously impressed with themselves. They were in control of their hard, young bodies, aware of the muscles they'd formed, the evidence of their budding manhood: the walk, the talk, the attitude. And Jason had been right. This was one of the few places where it was possible to be who they were and still win.

Then Slack, angry at a point, took the small ball and, with a violent curse, threw it across the room. The ball hit Jason on the side of the head, knocking him clear off his feet. Almost immediately he struggled to get up. Leah jumped to her feet and began running across the wooden floor to his aid. She'd felt the contact in the pit of her stomach, as if she'd been hit herself.

Jason staggered dizzily for a moment, and Leah

grabbed his arm. The games stopped as the boys waited to see how Jason was. He made an effort to get his bearings.

"Jason . . ." Leah said quietly. He shook his head and gently pushed her aside.

"Goddamn it, Slack. This isn't baseball. What the hell you throw the ball for?" Jason groaned, but there was more surprise than anger in his hoarse voice.

"Sorry man. You just got in the way," Slack apologized defensively.

"Just stick to the game. You got a problem with the score, we'll work it out later." Jason waved the others back to their games.

Leah slowly made her way back to the bench. She realized she probably shouldn't have rushed forward the way she had. It only made her look foolish. And female. Nobody else had made a big deal of Jason's getting hit, including Jason. But Leah was now surprised at the degree of her emotions as she'd watched him being hit and crumbling to the wooden floor. She knew he was probably more hurt than he'd let on, but it was clear he had no intention of stopping the games. There were two more matches, with some boys being switched so that everyone had a chance to play.

Finally the session was over. Leah watched the boys return to the bench, where she'd stationed herself. They gathered items of clothing that had been discarded and strewn around the floor as they played. She retrieved her own tote bag and congratulated them on a nice effort.

"Bullshit," Slack said scornfully. "We was great."

Leah laughed nervously. "You lose points for trying to kill the coach."

Everyone laughed at Slack, singling him out. He didn't like it.

"What does she know?" he said. "She can't play this game."

Leah spoke before thinking: "Anybody can play this game. I played when I was a kid."

"Then the next time you come with Jason, you play me!" Slack said, and the other boys agreed wholeheartedly.

Jason promised to set it up even after Leah tried to give him what she hoped was a look of terror and regret. But Jason didn't get her off the spot. She decided not to push the point, since it was clear from Jason's pale countenance and tightly drawn mouth that he was in pain and just wanted to leave.

When Leah said good-bye to the boys, she made no special effort to include Slack. He made her uncomfortable, and she suspected that it was deliberate. And she didn't know if she wanted to work so hard to understand him.

"Are you planning on learning how to play handball before I bring you up here again?" Jason asked her as they made their way to the exit and his parked car.

"I'm hoping you'll think up something and save me from my big mouth," Leah said dryly.

Jason looked at her as they walked down the street. "You know, you were good with them. They liked you."

"How can you tell?"

"Let's just say their social vocabulary goes into the toilet when they don't care what you think of them."

"They called me a bitch."

"That's the way they talk."

"What do they call you?"

Jason chuckled. "You don't want to know. Besides, it can't be said in polite company."

Leah hesitated, thinking carefully about how to approach the subject that had most concerned her. "Slack doesn't seem to like me very much."

"Don't worry about it. He's suspicious and doesn't really trust anyone." He arched a brow at her. "Including me. Slack's got a lot of pride and that's good. It might be enough to save him if it doesn't kill him first. It's a real catch twenty-two."

"You really understand him, don't you?" Leah observed.

Jason shrugged with a deep sigh. "I've known others like him. He wants respect. But he doesn't know how to earn it or how to give it."

Leah frowned as Jason unlocked his car and carelessly tossed things in the backseat. "Has it ever occurred to you that you might not reach him?"

"No," Jason said unequivocally. "I can't think that way. Not for him. Not for myself."

As Jason opened the passenger door of the car, Leah asked if she should drive. Jason looked at her in surprise.

"I didn't know you could drive."

"You never asked."

"Please . . ." he said eagerly. Jason climbed into the passenger seat, giving her quick instructions as to the peculiarities of his car. Then he sat with his eyes closed, rubbing his temple as Leah headed back to Brooklyn.

When they reached his apartment, Jason was much worse. Leah made the decision not to leave him for the night and called Gail to tell her where she was. Jason apologized for not being in shape to drive her home, and Leah wondered if that meant he hadn't anticipated staying with her otherwise. She tried not to make an issue of it, but she was starting to feel peculiar inside. As she had earlier in the evening when he'd called, like an afterthought.

He stripped and fell into the bed after Leah gave him aspirin and water. He was out almost immediately.

Checking on him later, Leah saw a black and blue welt was appearing on his temple. His breathing was even, however, and he slept deeply. She got a towel and folded it with ice cubes and spent the next hour and a half pressing it against his head. He fidgeted once or twice but didn't awaken.

A little after midnight, the phone rang and Leah ran to answer, afraid the noise would awaken Jason.

"Hello," she breathed softly into the mouthpiece. There was a momentary silence, and then a strong, irritated female voice spoke up.

"Who's this?"

"Who is this?" Leah came right back.

"Is Jason there?" the voice demanded.

"He can't come to the phone. He's asleep."

"Well, tell him Peggy's on the phone. He'll take the call."

Leah felt uneasy again. "Jason had a small accident this evening coaching one of his teams. It's not serious, but he just needs to sleep."

"And I suppose you're nursing him back to health?" the voice asked.

"I'm just a friend who was there at the time," Leah said tightly, resenting the need to explain. "Do you want to leave a message? I'll see that he gets it."

"Will you? Then tell him I called. Tell him don't forget about our date tomorrow night. I'm looking forward to it."

"Fine," Leah said in a small voice. Her stomach somersaulted.

"Thank you," the voice now cooed. " 'Night, friend."

Leah could recognize a proprietary tone when she heard one. More than that, the female caller had extended her feline claws instinctively at having another female answer the phone for Jason. She understood that, too. But she somehow felt as if she'd just been put in her place again.

She thought about having told this Peggy that she was a friend. It bothered Leah that she had no other word to use. She'd found herself suddenly hesitant to say significant other, girlfriend, main squeeze . . . whatever, because she and Jason had never defined what their relationship was. It had just happened and moved along on a momentum that hadn't, as yet, taken on any particular direction. They were committed to each other, but Leah felt there were no parameters. And no forward progress.

Peggy was obviously a friend, too. But how good a friend, how intimate? Leah agonized over the possibilities. She thought of her sister's comment about Jason pushing her buttons and felt confused and insecure. And the phone call had undermined her.

She got a glass of orange juice and sat in Jason's chair by the window, alternately watching the lights on the bridge and Jason on the bed as he slept. She sat there well into the night, not being able to lie next to him and sleep herself. Not if tomorrow night she'd be replaced with someone else in his bed.

At four in the morning, Jason woke up with a soft groan. Leah made him take more aspirin and water, which he accepted silently, taking her presence for granted, and then he promptly went back to sleep.

At six-thirty, Leah washed her face and hands and straightened her clothes. She felt stiff and exhausted. She hadn't been able to get a minute of sleep. She began to gather her things, digging in her purse for a comb. It was then that she discovered that her wallet was missing.

It wasn't her wallet, actually, but a small leather folder that snapped closed. It contained her Social Security card, AAA membership, a driver's license, and an emergency twenty-dollar bill. She never carried credit cards, and money was kept in a separate zippered compartment of her bag.

Immediately the handball session came to mind: sitting on the bench with the boys' things dumped around her. Slack. But it could have been any of the boys. Leah frowned over the possibilities. Any one of them could have seen her as an easy mark. The question was now, should she say something to Jason? Would it start an investigation of the night's events and get the boys into more trouble? Was the twenty dollars worth it? Did she want to be the target of worse derision?

Leah had money to get home. Her ID's could be replaced. The thought of awakening Jason and asking his help never entered her mind, but a terrible sense that she was all alone again did.

Leah checked on Jason once more. The swelling had gone down, but the black and blue bruise he'd have to live with for a while. She closed the window shades to redirect the morning sun, and set a clock radio to wake him up at eight. Leah wrote out a short note on a paper towel, including the message from Peggy. Taking a last look at Jason, she left the apartment.

Jason awoke with the sounds of Tone Loc rapping in his head. He still had a headache, but the acute pain and dizziness of the previous night were gone. He guessed by the silence that Leah must have left early this morning because he remembered her presence all night long. Not seeing her, however, made Jason feel let down and annoyed.

He sat on the side of the bed, holding his head in his hands and thinking about why Leah would have left. He couldn't find a satisfactory answer. What did occur to Jason was that he was in a bad mood and he couldn't figure that out, either. He just wished that

Leah was there. It wasn't as if he was only now realizing how good it was to wake up and find her quietly nearby, or how nice to roll over and reach for her to make love. Leah made him comfortable. Even when they were apart, it only seemed temporary and he didn't usually mind. Only right now did he feel strange.

There was a ghost of her that lingered, an essence that Jason admitted was part of his life and he'd become used to. He took it for granted.

He went to the bathroom and saw the note only on his way back to the bed. He read it through twice and cursed under his breath. He'd almost forgotten about his meeting with Peggy. He wished now that she hadn't tried to reach him. He wished he hadn't agreed to see her. He felt uneasy with Leah having taken the call. It was too complicated.

Jason groaned and impatiently tossed away the message. His head was killing him, and he couldn't seem to think straight.

The date with Peggy was short-lived and a mistake.

It was hardly a date at all, since it never got started. That was probably Peggy's fault. Jason picked her up from her banking job on Flatbush Avenue in the Flatlands section of Brooklyn. Immediately Peggy asked about the "friend" who'd answered the phone the night before.

"So who was she?" Peggy asked, her blue eyes startling and beautiful in a pale face surrounded by a mass of very dark, wavy hair. She was petite and very pretty.

Jason shrugged impatiently. He never handled this part very well. Other women's curiosity about other women. "A friend. Just like she said."

Peggy reached into Jason's windbreaker pocket for his cigarettes and helped herself to one. She took her time lighting it, throwing the dead match out a crack of the open window.

"Can you be more specific?"

"Her name is Leah," Jason answered smoothly. He intended for that to be enough information. "You're looking great. How have you been?" he asked, glancing briefly at her.

"Don't change the subject. I'm not through yet." Peggy smiled sweetly.

Jason sighed. "Drop it, Peggy."

"Well, did you take her to one of your games?"

"You hate sports, remember? And the guys on my teams."

Peggy thought it over. "And you got hurt and she sat up with you?"

"I told you she was a friend."

Peggy gave Jason a very wry look. "Men don't have women for friends, Jason. That's a myth." She exhaled from the cigarette before tossing it out the window half smoked. "Are you fucking her?"

Jason's foot slammed on the brakes when he realized he'd almost run a red light. He stared at Peggy dumbfounded. "Jesus Christ, Peg. What the hell is this?"

"I'm only interested in my competition."

"She's not your competition because she's none of your business," Jason answered in irritation. "I haven't seen you since last summer. I didn't become a recluse. I met someone and I like her. That's it."

"You still haven't answered the question," Peggy persisted, her tone getting a tad testy.

"I'm not going to answer the question."

Peggy pouted and stared out the windshield. "You're fucking her."

"Look . . ." Jason tried to be patient, unable to comprehend how they'd ever gotten started on this conversation. "We never had any holds on each other. No contract, no promises, no commitments. We never expected our affair to go anywhere—"

"It was a relationship, *not* an affair," she said, annoyed.

"I didn't get bent out of shape when you went back to your ex that time, did I? Or when your boss tried wining and dining you? It's your life and it has nothing to do with me."

"I just didn't expect a woman to answer your phone, that's all."

"So what? It could have been my sister."

"But it wasn't."

"Leah was there because I wanted her to be. Sorry if you have a problem with that."

Peggy continued to pout, restlessly shaking her foot. "Leah. Sounds exotic."

Jason nodded slowly. "Yeah, I guess."

"So if she's so wonderful, how come you made this date?"

Jason's mouth quirked cynically. "This is not a date, and you called me. Something about needing my advice. Is it your ex again?"

Peggy grimaced. "I lied."

She turned to Jason, letting loose the full force of her charm. She smiled beguilingly and stroked her hand along his thigh. "I really missed you. I wanted to see if you felt the same."

Jason frowned and eased his shoulders back against the seat. "Peggy," he began cautiously, "it's been a long time."

"I know. But it could be good again if you give it a chance," she pleaded sweetly.

Jason glanced briefly at her and shook his head. "I don't think so."

Peggy crossed her arms and stared out the window. "Is it this Leah? Is she pretty?"

"Yeah, she is," Jason responded. He again glanced at Peggy. "As a matter of fact, she looks a little bit like you."

"Nobody looks like me," Peggy said, arching a brow seductively. "How?"

"She's slim. Has wavy hair."

"Does she have blue eyes, too?" Peggy asked with a laugh.

Jason frowned. "No. Actually, Leah's eyes are very dark."

Peggy settled back into her seat.

"She's black . . ."

Peggy's head snapped around in Jason's direction so quickly her dangling earrings slapped against her cheek. "What did you say?"

Jason could tell he'd said something to upset her. "I said she's black. Why? Is that a problem?"

"Is that a problem? Are you crazy?" Her eyes were wide with disbelief.

"What's the matter with you?" Jason asked, trying to keep his eyes on the traffic.

"Of course you're fucking her. What a stupid question." Peggy's voice rose. "Stop the car. I said, *stop the car!*" she screamed.

Jason cut off another car, its horn beeping angrily, as he pulled over in front of a fire hydrant. "Shit," he muttered, putting the car in neutral and turning to face Peggy. She was pressed back against the passenger door, glaring at him.

"Peggy, what's going on? What is the matter with you?"

"You have some goddamn nerve, Jason, calling me for a date now."

"What are you talking about? I didn't call you," he shouted impatiently.

"I'm talking about your black girlfriend, that's what.

How dare you screw some nigger tramp and then expect me to go out with you?"

Jason was stunned. His mouth dropped open and he struggled for words. "She—she's an artist. Leah is . . ." he said, trying to make sense of what was going on.

"What the hell difference does that make? She's probably been in and out of more beds than you can count. What if she's got AIDS? What if she infected you?"

Jason just stared at her. He couldn't believe what he was hearing. Was this the same woman he'd known for almost three years, saying these things, suggesting these things?

"She's not a tramp," he responded tightly.

"She's black and you're fucking her. What do you think that makes her?" Peggy ranted.

Jason felt his mouth clamp tight. He felt a vein in his neck fill with hot blood. A muscle worked reflexively in his jaw. "You're white and I used to fuck you," he said through clenched teeth. "What does that make you?"

Her eyes narrowed. "A damned fool. I can't believe you've actually been touching, kissing and"—Peggy's mouth twisted with horror—"and sticking it to some dirty black female. I don't want to have anything to do with you. No way am I going to follow an act like that. It's disgusting!"

With that Peggy struggled to get the car door open and quickly climbed out. She slammed the door and began hurrying away. Jason had no problem letting her go. But he sat in shock in the suddenly quiet car, staring after Peggy until he couldn't see her anymore.

Then he faced forward and stared just as long out the windshield. He felt as if he'd just been kicked in the stomach. His hands were clenched into fists, and the muscles in his thigh quivered. Jason dug for his cigarettes and lit one. He was annoyed to see his hand shaking slightly. He seemed to have trouble slowing his breathing. The vein in his neck felt like it was going to burst. He was too angry to think straight. He couldn't even say what he was angry about.

When Jason finally pulled away from the curb, he didn't know where he was going or what he was going to do the rest of the night. But for the moment the only place he felt safe was locked in his own car.

He spent a miserable night tossing and turning and scrambling the bed linens. When the sun rose the next morning, so did he. There were dark circles under his eyes and the feel of cotton in his mouth. He showered, shaved, and stared at a face that was still a few years short of middle age. His hair was turning gray over his ears, and this morning lines seemed deeply etched around his eyes. Too many lines that were evidence of too many wars, and he sensed there was another battle on the horizon.

He had to get out of the house. He got into his car and drove without hesitation to Leah's. He rang the bell gingerly and listened for sounds inside. Minutes later, when the door finally opened, two heads and two pairs of questioning eyes appeared in the doorway. It was now 6:00 A.M.

"Oh, for God's sake . . ." Gail muttered darkly, and disappeared inside again.

Leah looked with suspicion and surprise at Jason standing in her doorway. She pulled her robe closer around her and silently motioned for him to enter.

The first thought that entered her mind, however, was what had happened the evening before with Peggy. Finding Jason on her doorstep didn't necessarily reassure Leah. It was a surprise to see him like this, and she wondered if it was possible that Jason had somehow been aware of her restless night of doubts. Did he have some of his own?

"What's wrong?" Leah asked as soon as the door was shut. "Has something happened?" she asked quickly, looking at him as if expecting to see bullet holes or a stab wound.

Jason felt an odd relief at her concern. "I'm sorry. I thought maybe you'd be up having breakfast already," he said lamely.

But if Leah thought this sounded weak, she gave no indication of it. After a second she padded toward the kitchen in her bare feet, Jason following slowly behind.

He stood watching as Leah got two cups and prepared instant coffee. Jason sat at the small round kitchen table and took off his jacket. Leah glanced at him over her shoulder.

"I'm always finding you on my doorstep," she mused.

"And always saving me with coffee." Jason took the offered mug he'd given her on New Year's Eve. He watched Leah as she took a seat opposite him.

"And what am I saving you from this time?"

"Things that go bump in the night?" he offered nervously.

"I don't buy that," Leah murmured, resting her chin on a curved fist. "I don't think you're afraid of anything. You've been through too much."

"You're wrong. I'm afraid all the time. There are lots of things I can't handle. Lots of things I don't know about."

"Then you're no different from anyone else. Maybe that's not so bad. Maybe that's what life is all about. Just trying to handle all the stuff."

"Maybe . . ." he said softly, staring in the cup.

She shifted in her chair, staring at her hands. "How's your head? I see the bruise is almost gone."

He shifted, too. "I'm okay. I probably deserved it."

Leah frowned. "I don't understand."

His chuckle was dry and silent. "Every now and then a good knock upside the head should shake some sense loose."

"Did it?"

Jason looked at her, slowly and carefully examining the features of her face, the bright eyes that always gave him her complete attention. The full mouth that when she smiled . . . "I don't know," he murmured, blinking.

"Jason, it's the crack of dawn. Do you realize we're talking nonsense?"

She'd meant it almost as a joke, but when Jason looked at her, she was surprised at the serious intent of his gaze. She wondered why she was being carefully examined, and she fussed with her robe. He never answered, just stared at her.

"I look awful," Leah said, standing. "I better go and put something on. Comb my hair . . ."

"I know you think I'm crazy, showing up like this."

"I wondered. Are you sure you're all right?"

"Yeah, I'm sure."

"Well, if you want to wait I'll make some breakfast when I'm dressed."

"I have to be in court by ten. Can I drop you by your office on the way downtown?"

"Sure. That would be fine," Leah said slowly. Jason had done that only once before.

On the ride to Manhattan, he told her about the case that made it necessary for him to be in family court. There was no talk about why he'd shown up so early, or even when she'd see him again. But as Leah started to get out of the car, Jason held her arm and leaned to kiss her.

Something *was* wrong.

The kiss was fleeting and uncertain. His jaw tensed,

and his eyes looked bleak. She kept her gaze on Jason as she saw the struggle within him. Leah had no idea what he wanted to say, and she was ambivalent about her own feelings. What he thought mattered. But she felt the need to be self-protective and wary. To be prepared, just in case.

"Leah . . ." Jason watched her breathing under the pretty rose-colored sweater. Did she seem agitated and upset? "Last night with Peggy . . . it didn't mean anything."

Leah averted her eyes and stared out the window. She watched the rush-hour swarm of people and wondered, distractedly, where did they all come from? Where were they all going? Jason touched her shoulder in a gentle squeeze.

"You mean, the date turned out badly?" She couldn't believe how calm she sounded.

"It wasn't a date," he said stiffly. She was making it difficult for him. "It was . . ." Jason shrugged. "She used to be a friend."

Leah smiled slightly. "You have a lot of female friends."

Jason was reminded of Peggy's comment on that point, and realized that Leah knew that the relationship had been more. "We're not close anymore, but she wanted to talk." The lie felt awful and he hoped Leah wouldn't look too deeply into his eyes.

"Then there's no need for you to explain to me."

"There is. You know there is."

"I don't," she insisted, shaking her head. Leah looked at him and couldn't disguise either her anger or heartbreak. "I thought I did, but maybe I had no right to."

"Don't say it's not any of your business. Don't. It is, but . . ."

"I forgive you. I think that's what this morning's visit was all about, right?"

Jason looked helplessly at her. He couldn't answer directly, and he couldn't deny it.

"The truth is, Jason," she began carefully, slowly, so that her voice wouldn't shake, "you don't need my forgiveness. We don't belong to each other. There's no commitment carved in stone, written in blood."

He continued to stare at her, again hearing similar words that he'd said to Peggy. Only now the scenario was different. Jason narrowed his gaze, trying to decide if Leah really cared so little about their relationship, and then realized he was being unfair. After all, Leah was not the one who'd put it in jeopardy. He had.

And she was right. He did want her forgiveness.

Jason also knew suddenly that he couldn't tell Leah about Peggy's outburst. It had been too ugly, too cruel. And it hit him, like a cold splash of water, that she'd heard it all before.

"You mean a lot to me, Leah," Jason whispered, and even to his own ears it seemed weak. Inadequate.

Leah tried to smile. She reached to pat his hand awkwardly where it lay on her shoulder. "And you mean a lot to me." She wanted to put a hand up to stroke Jason's face, and ask him, "what did he see when he looked at her this way?"

"I want to see you tonight," Jason stated quietly.

Leah blinked at him. She thought about what *she* wanted and finally made a decision. "I can't. Gail and I are attending something at F.I.T. It's her alma mater."

He nodded, disappointed.

Her smile continued tentative and sad. "Call me?" Then she murmured a breathless good-bye and quickly got out of the car.

Chapter Ten

Somewhat violently, Gail tossed a handful of chopped lettuce leaves and Bermuda onion rings together in a bowl. Leah could hear her sister's long lacquered nails against the bottom and sides of the glass bowl, and they made a grating sound, like chalk on a blackboard. Leah watched the hand movements in absentminded fascination, her thoughts actually focused on the fact that she had not seen Jason in two weeks. She had been trying to analyze if the separation meant anything, but had only succeeded to making herself anxious and irritable.

She grabbed a carrot and, munching it, went to have a look at the roast in the oven. Leah frowned as she noticed that it was cooking too fast, but refrained from mentioning it. She and Gail were spending far too much time lately dickering over nonsense. Leah had come to believe that the less said about anything, the better. She nonetheless turned the oven temperature down and went back to her chair at the table.

The preparations were for dinner with Allen and two of his co-workers. Leah had offered to help with the cooking, but the offer had been brusquely declined. At any other time Gail would have been delighted to relinquish a hot, steamy kitchen to her sister, since they both knew Leah was the better cook.

Just when Leah was about to give up and wander off to do something else, Gail started to speak.

"How's the new love life going?" she asked tersely.

"I suppose you mean Jason."

"Are you seeing someone else I don't know about?"

"I can't do anything you don't know about," Leah responded.

"Is he any good in bed?"

Leah exclaimed in exasperation, "Do you mind? That's not up for discussion. You're unbelievable."

"Well, he must be doing something for you," Gail said in amusement. "You have a certain look about you. Hard to define. Dreamy, maybe thoughtful . . . maybe dumb. But it's sure not like any look Allen or that guy Ron had ever given you." Gail added shredded carrots to the bowl.

"Jason is different. He's . . . okay," she said quietly.

"What's it like dating a white man?"

Leah sighed. "No different than dating a black man," she answered.

But that wasn't strictly true. The things that entertained Jason and which were so new to her, Allen wouldn't have tolerated. The time spent making love would have bored Allen as well. She and Jason took a long time. Once Allen was satisfied he'd want to sleep, or get up and leave.

"And how do his parents like the idea of you two?"

Leah was defensive. "Jason and I aren't children. We don't need anyone's permission. Besides, his parents are both dead."

"How convenient. Have you wondered what Daddy would say about this? Do you realize you're behaving like a fool?"

Leah stiffened. No, she had not really considered what their father would think. That had been deliberate on her part.

"Then we're even," she said shortly. "You certainly carried on over Allen."

Gail glared at her. "You are going to get yourself hurt, Leah."

"Is that what you hope will happen? Just to prove your point?"

Gail pushed the salad bowl away. "Dammit! Don't pretend not to understand what I'm saying to you. You encounter the same people every day that I do. You have to take the same crap every day that I do. You can figure it out. White men don't look at black women the same way they look at their own kind."

"Jason's not like that. I think I would know it if he was," Leah defended quietly. She threw away the rest of the carrot.

"You think!" Gail shouted in surprise. "Honey, if I was sleeping with the guy, I'd damn well want to know for sure. And if race doesn't matter, he wouldn't be afraid to talk about it, would he? What do you think he sees when he looks at you?"

Leah nearly stopped breathing. Hadn't she wondered the same thing?

"I'll tell you," Gail said obligingly. "He sees a pretty black woman. She's available. And she can be had. Some white dude out there"—she jabbed her paring knife in the direction of the kitchen window for emphasis—"is not going to look at us and see *us*."

"I'm only interested that Jason sees me," Leah responded, agitated.

"It's never going to happen. They can never seem to get past the color. That hasn't changed in more than two hundred years, Leah."

"Will you stop exaggerating? That's not an argument anymore. People have choices now. I have a choice, and I've made mine. You're the one being biased. You're not even willing to give Jason a chance."

Gail's voice softened. "You're giving up willingly what has always been taken by force. Don't you have any pride, any sense of self?"

Leah felt her chest tightening. The doubt was spreading throughout her whole body, and it added horrible substance to her own fears.

"He'll never take you seriously," Gail pressed, watching the doubts cross her sister's face.

"You haven't even asked if I'm happy. Did you ever think that with Jason I might be happy?"

"Are you? Just how long do you think that will last? You have to think about what will happen when he's decided he wants some blond, blue-eyed all-American beauty after all. Where does that leave you?"

Leah looked at her sister with some surprise and pain in her eyes. Gail had managed to put a hole in her daydream, but probably no deeper than the one Leah had been plugging up herself over the last two weeks trying to convince herself that everything was okay.

"The same place it left me when you and Allen decided you wanted each other. The same place it left me when I found out he and you were screwing around behind my back. Alone, to work it out as best I can," she whispered.

The knot in her throat made it hard to talk. But Leah at least held off crying until she was alone in her room.

It was pouring rain outside. It was gray and windy, and the sudden gusts blew beads of water against the windows of the precinct house.

At his desk Jason absentmindedly glanced through the juvenile case folder that had made it necessary for him to be in court that morning, for the third time in as many weeks. He sat in his chair, rocking it back and forth on its hind legs. He had one foot propped against an open drawer of the desk. Every now and then he'd glance up to look out the window, but his expression was brooding. He sighed and combed a hand through his hair, still damp from his sprint through the rain from his car to the station house.

From the other desk Jason knew Joe took furtive glances at him, aware of his nervous movements. But Jason was trying to avoid talking to Joe because the subject would only come around to one thing. The fact that he was involved with Leah Downey. Jason was tired of hearing that no good would come of anything between him and Leah. He was tired of hearing the odds against it, as though their relationship was some sort of spectator sport to be bet on. He was tired of being told that if other people's attitudes didn't wreck it, the differences between them would.

Peggy came briefly and despairingly to mind.

Jason stole a glance at Joe, who pretended deep interest in the daily paper. Jason supposed that he should be grateful that Joe had warned him of the buzz around the precinct, that some of the talk was nasty, that Spano was the biggest instigator. On the other hand, O'Neill, Maddi, and Thompkins liked Leah and didn't give Jason a hard time about her.

Suddenly, Joe closed the paper and leaned on his desk, staring across at Jason. "Want to talk about it?"

"Talk about what?" Jason asked vaguely.

Joe shrugged indifferently and sat back in his chair. "Okay. So you don't want to talk about it. Want to toss for who goes for lunch?"

Jason looked up with a slow, skeptical smile. "Only if we use my quarter." He glanced out the window. "On second thought, I'm not up to going out again. I'm sick of getting wet."

"Suit yourself. We could order in from the Chinese

place. You know, Nora has been after my tail to bring you home for dinner soon. Says she needs to fatten you up. Bring Brooklyn with you."

Jason's eyes narrowed as he carefully regarded his colleague. "Why? Nora want to fatten her up, too?"

"Just thought you'd want to bring her, that's all. Nora likes the lady."

Jason continued to scrutinize Joe. "And you don't."

"Ain't none of my business, man."

"Sure you think it's your business. And don't give me any bullshit like it's because Leah is black." Jason got up abruptly and headed for a file cabinet, pulling open a drawer.

"Okay, since you mentioned it, why the fuck don't you leave the woman alone? And it ain't because she's black, but because you're white. You ain't gonna do the woman no good, man."

"How do you know that? Maybe she wants to be involved with me. Maybe I want to be involved with her. How about that?"

"What do you get out of it anyway, huh?" Joe asked angrily, getting up to confront Jason by the file cabinet. "Nothing but some black nookie from a better class of woman then you're used to—"

"Fuck you . . ." Jason suddenly exploded, throwing his file folder at Joe.

Joe reacted quickly and pushed Jason violently against the cabinets. The metal unit rattled loudly against the back wall. Jason quickly righted himself and shoved Joe back, pushing the bigger man off balance.

"I don't need any goddamn advice from you. Just back the hell off, okay?"

"Why not? 'Cause I'm just another nigger who you think don't know shit?"

The shoving between the two escalated until Joe

grabbed Jason's swinging arm in a lock that stopped him from moving. Jason struggled.

"What you need is a kick in the ass. Listen up, man!" Joe thundered. Jason suddenly stopped resisting, and Joe pulled him around and then pushed him away abruptly. "You don't know what you're messin' with. I'm telling you. You're into something you can't handle. Why you gotta make things so hard?"

"Why the hell do you care so much? Am I some sort of threat? Is it that I don't have the right? *She* doesn't? Who told you you could decide that for me or Leah?"

Jason and Joe glared at each other, and now that the initial angry heat of explosion was over, they both were surprised and regretful. They were friends. Partners. Why were they both so angry anyway? Neither one could put it into words. Neither one could understand what had just happened. Jason stood with his hands on his hips, breathing deeply.

"Shit!" Joe shouted again, and kicked a wastepaper basket so hard it sailed across the room and crashed into the opposite wall. The door to the office opened quickly, and several men appeared in the doorway, ready for trouble.

"Get the fuck outta my office!" Joe stormed, pointing a finger at the officers, who stood staring in open curiosity. "Out!"

The door slowly closed again. Tense silence remained in the room with the two men. Except for the annoying repetitive patter of the rain outside.

Jason slowly sat back in his chair. He braced his elbows on the desk and rested his head in his hands.

"You don't really care about her, Jason. She's just another lay to you. You know that's all it is. That's all it could ever be."

"Leah is different. I've *never* treated her like other women. You don't know what we're like together. It—

it's a whole lot more," Jason murmured, but he sounded confused.

"Is it?" Joe asked.

"Why can't it be? Who are you or anyone else to say it can't be?"

"It ain't me, man. It's the world. It's life. That's just the way it is."

"Drop it, Joe. Just let it go. I don't want to fight with you," Jason said wearily.

Joe looked at Jason sadly, and he too sat heavily in his chair once again. "It ain't gonna go away. I don't want to fight you either, man. But one of these days you're going to find yourself in deep shit."

Jason didn't want to admit that maybe Joe was right. And he didn't particularly like any of the feelings of unease he'd been living with recently. He didn't know how to sort it out. He found himself suddenly cautious around people, as if expecting comments or criticism. He was constantly on edge and defensive.

Spano's comments were proving irritating and persistent. And it was more than Spano. It was the two weeks of having had only brief, uneasy phone conversations with Leah. It was Jason doing something that profoundly disturbed him. He'd been involved in an arrest, called in as part of a backup team on a night when cops seemed to be needed everywhere.

Jason remembered he had one suspect down on the ground handcuffed, and another leaning on the trunk of the squad car in the position. There were a half-dozen cops and cars all over the street. Curious bystanders watched as if this was a show staged for their benefit. No fear here, just resignation and familiarity. This scene was commonplace in Bed Stuy.

Jason had another pair of handcuffs ready and used his foot to knock the suspect's legs farther apart.

"Okay, nigger, spread 'em. I want to know what you got up there besides your balls . . ."

A sudden rush had gone over Jason, and he'd stood stone still. He felt as if he'd just crashed head-on into a wall. *That* wall. The one Joe had told him about months ago. The words echoed in his head. He'd felt the instant hostility they'd evoked, the insult to identity and pride. Jason had turned around to look at all the dark faces staring at him. Everyone was still and angry. But they weren't surprised. They were used to this, too.

But it wasn't what the onlookers might have been thinking that bothered Jason. It was how easily the word had slipped through his lips—the careless racial slur taken for granted. It had come out without a second thought, and it bothered him. Jason thought instantly of Leah.

Is that how he thought of her?

God, no . . . no!

He'd tossed his extra cuffs to another officer. "Here, you do it," he muttered angrily. He'd walked a few feet away. His hands were shaking.

What had he been thinking?

Jason remembered that awful scene with Peggy, her virulent disgust and objections because of Leah.

What had he been thinking. . . ?

"Shit," Jason mumbled in irritation.

He turned his back on the fight, on Joe's warning, and picked up the phone. He dialed a number and waited impatiently until a female voice answered.

"Hi. It's Jason."

"Who?"

"Jason."

"Who?"

"It's Ja—okay, okay. How've you been, Carol?"

"As if you cared. Do you mean today or the last six months."

"I know," Jason said contritely. "But it's been a real busy time."

He tapped nervously on the desktop, and when he looked at Joe, it was to find the other man listening openly and without any apparent surprise.

"Look, I thought maybe I could take you to dinner tonight. You can tell me all about the last six months. Are you free?"

"Would it matter if I wasn't?"

"That's up to you."

"You don't give much advance warning, do you?"

Jason ran his hand through his hair. He laughed nervously. "I'm sorry. I told you, it's been real busy. Well? How about it? It won't be a late night. Promise."

"Already I don't like the sound of this. But curiosity has the better of me. What time?"

"I'll see you at seven."

Jason hung up the phone. Joe just sat staring at him.

It was six-thirty before he could clock out, and it had been a day full of irritations. The long day followed Jason right into the locker room, where there were other officers in various stages of undress. Some were coming on duty, most were going off. Jason was too deep into the earlier confrontation with Joe and his own problems to notice the sudden lack of conversation with his appearance. He approached his locker, walking between Spano and another officer. While he worked the combination on the lock, Jason heard someone say, "Nigger lover."

Jason didn't recognize the voice. It was followed by silence, but he didn't turn around or acknowledge the comment.

Someone else made the sound of a monkey, and this was followed by snickers from several of the men.

"Come on. Knock it off," someone advised.

Jason slowly pulled the locker door open, but then

he abruptly slammed it shut. The sound was loud and grabbed everyone's attention. He turned around to face the room, and a few men turned away from him. Spano sat down on the bench and bent to untie his shoes.

"Any of you assholes have something you want to say to me?" Jason inquired quietly.

"Yeah," Spano began boldly, "how's the spook? Had any lately?" He grabbed his crotch in a rude gesture.

Several men moved away from both Jason and Spano. Some laughed softly, but none wanted to actually get in the middle. Without warning Jason stuck his foot under the end of the bench and pulled. Spano went down heavily onto the floor when the bench toppled over. All laughter died.

Spano tried to get up, but Jason quickly applied a foot right to his throat.

"You mother fucker . . ." Spano choked, wrestling with Jason's foot.

"How about you, Spano? What was that you wanted to say?"

"Come on. Ease up, Jason. It was just a joke, man," someone said.

"Get the fuck off me, Horn. She's nothing but a—"

"Do you, asshole?" Jason gritted angrily through clenched teeth, pressing harder with his foot. He felt an uncomfortable rage building. He wanted to grab Spano by the throat. He wanted to hurt him. He wanted to hurt someone.

An officer moved toward Spano, as if to come to his assistance, but Jason merely raised a warning hand and pointed a finger at him.

"Stay out of this." He turned his attention back to the man on the floor. "I'm waiting," Jason shouted angrily. His foot pressed harder.

"No . . ." Spano sputtered. "I . . . agh . . ."

"What was that? I can't hear you."

"I said no, goddamn it. I ain't got nothin' to say."

Jason slowly lifted his foot and felt his calf muscle contract instantly into a cramp. Every fiber of his body was stiff. The adrenaline in his system made him hot and dizzy. He glanced down at Spano and then at the men around the silenced locker room. He tried to catch his breath.

This had been a mistake.

These were men he had to rely on. They might someday have to save his life, or he theirs. It was supposed to be a brotherhood, but he'd been kicked out of the fraternity.

Very slowly conversation picked up again. Spano struggled to his feet, and two colleagues restrained him from going after Jason.

Jason didn't care. He got what he needed from his locker. He was tired and depressed and totally pissed off. He wished, too late, that he'd never tried to keep the date for that night two weeks ago, or that he'd never let Peggy get to him. Jason wished that he and Joe had never had a fight.

As Jason exited the locker room, he wasn't at all sure what he had left.

He got no satisfaction from the evening, either. It only added to his general bad mood. He wondered why he felt as though his life was falling apart all around him.

Carol was a counselor for a school in the same district as Jason's precinct. She was tall, curvaceous with frosted, short blond hair. And although not technically pretty, she was sexy and attractive and had a quick, dry wit. For a moment as he waited for Carol to get into his car, he had a painful flashing image of Peggy and the last time he'd seen her. He wasn't going to make the same mistake tonight. One good thing about Carol was that she never asked a lot of questions.

"For chrissakes, Jason, this car is filthy. When are you going to clean it or buy a new one?" she complained, dusting off her hands once she was seated in the car.

"Pretend you don't see it. With the windows open, it will all blow away anyhow."

"Very funny. You could plant potatoes in your backseat. I bet you don't even know what's back there."

"You're probably right." He quickly glanced at her in appreciation. "But you don't want to talk about my car. How've you been?"

"A girl could starve to death waiting for a date for dinner."

"You know my number," Jason teased.

"As if you're ever at home. Are you still coaching games on Riker's Island and playing Daddy to all those street urchins?"

"You mean the ones you can't keep in school?" he quipped.

Carol laughed good-naturedly, and Jason began to relax.

"Jason?" she began quietly.

"Uhmm?"

"I—I heard about your son, and the accident. I just wanted to say I'm real sorry. I know it's a tremendous loss."

Jason's hands tightened on the wheel of the car. He didn't want to discuss Michael with Carol. He'd gone a long time without slipping back to those memories. He didn't need or want them tonight.

"Thanks," he said shortly, and Carol wisely let it drop.

Jason drove into Manhattan to one of his favorite restaurants. It was a Vietnamese place with no atmosphere but great food and service. It was run by a large, cheerful family who'd long ago come to expect Jason as a pretty regular customer. The menu they were given was in Vietnamese. This was the only time he got practice in the language, and he furrowed his brow in concentration trying to remember the right words and sounds.

Carol and Jason spent dinner in easy conversation, just catching up on months of absence from each other. Unlike Peg, Carol wasn't interested in whom Jason might have dated in the interim. She picked over her food, grimacing at the unfamiliar vegetables and spices, and complained that pork and abalone were fattening. She chuckled and wondered out loud why he hadn't taken her to a French restaurant, where at least the unpronounceable names were romantic. Jason responded that this week's budget didn't run to French food. Besides which he didn't want to have to wear a tie.

He finished eating and sat back in his chair, smoking a cigarette. He watched Carol as she continued to pick, and at some point was only half listening to her flow of idle conversation. Jason suddenly found himself comparing Carol to Leah. He was remembering dinner here with Leah several weeks ago.

She had been impressed at what had seemed to her Jason's easy command of a difficult tongue. She'd asked him to name everything on her plate, and he'd done his best, cheating a bit when he couldn't. She'd asked him how to say wonderful, and all through dinner Leah had repeated it to herself, trying not to forget. And when the meal was over and the waiter brought the check, Leah had turned to the waiter and uttered the hard-learned phrase, causing the waiter to giggle and beam in appreciation of her effort.

The thought stayed with Jason as he and Carol left

the restaurant, walked around lower Manhattan for a while, and then drove to her place.

Much, much later, while Carol showered and coffee perked in the kitchen, Jason sat in her bed smoking, lying back against the rumpled mess of the bed linens. They hadn't made love.

He couldn't do it.

He'd wanted to touch and feel a woman's skin. He'd wanted the soft giving of her body to cushion his confusion and wrap him in solace. He'd wanted to slip slowly into desire and excitement and fulfillment. But he and Carol had never gotten beyond foreplay. He'd never even gotten properly hard. So they'd just lain in bed for an hour talking, but not talking about *that*.

Finally, realizing that nothing was going to happen, Carol had kissed him lightly and gotten out of bed. Jason had hardly noticed.

He found himself thinking of Leah. He wondered what she was doing tonight. Once he'd begun seeing her regularly, he'd been pretty certain that Leah was seeing only him. The possibility that she might have had a date, or been with someone else in the past few weeks, had not fully occurred to Jason until this instant. The very idea made him nervous and restless with jealousy.

In one graceful motion, with the cigarette clamped between his teeth, Jason got up and began to dress. He managed to sit still for two cups of coffee with Carol before maneuvering his way toward the door. He'd forgotten that one of the things he'd always liked about Carol was her ability to see things clearly, dispassionately, and without fluff. She used her insight now as he was about to leave.

"You know, Jason, you were never one for pretending. You yourself always said you're too old for that."

"So?" he prompted.

"So stop pretending that you're fine and we're fine and everything's fine."

"I don't know what you're talking about."

"Sure you do. Want to talk about it?"

Jason grinned and leaned against the wall. "You know, suddenly an awful lot of people are interested in what's on my mind."

"Maybe they're trying to tell you something. Anyway, I'm only interested in tonight," Carol corrected.

Jason hesitated. "There's nothing to tell, Carol. I guess I'm just tired. I realize tonight was . . ." He couldn't think how to say it. "Look, maybe I'd just better go."

"You've been edgy and absent all evening," Carol observed, standing with her hands on her hips and looking at him with her head tilted. "And if you were really here, maybe there would have been a chance for me to really talk with you. Only, I don't think it would have made a difference.

"You know, all evening I felt as if there were someone else with us, particularly in bed. Someone else you were trying to make love to. I didn't like the feeling, Jason. I didn't like being a substitute," Carol said softly.

Jason lifted a hand helplessly before it dropped again. He couldn't go into it. He couldn't take the chance again. Not after Peggy. "It's just that . . . I'm having a bad time at work."

"Are you sure that's all?"

He nodded. Then he looked at her. "I'll call you, Carol," he whispered.

"No, Jason. Do us both a favor. Call me when you want to see me, not when you need to work off some frustration." Then she opened the door, blew him a kiss, and gently pushed Jason through the opening.

In his ancient car, feeling rather ancient himself,

Jason rode aimlessly around Brooklyn. It was almost two. He thought of calling Leah and quickly dismissed the idea. What would he say to her? Instead he found a bar and quietly sat in a corner drinking and smoking and staring blankly into space. Jason was oblivious to the coaxing glances of the two ladies sitting several stools away.

Finally he drove home, and in the dark of the apartment he recalled the whole, long, miserable day.

"Damn you Spano," Jason muttered in the dark, angry that someone so meaningless to him had managed to get under his skin. He was angry and he didn't understand why. Things were happening to him that he'd never experienced before, and he didn't understand any of that, either.

When Jason called to remind Leah about dinner at Joe and Nora's house, she was no longer sure she wanted to go. Jason had sounded as if he, too, was rather sorry that he'd accepted the invitation. They had not seen each other in more than two weeks, and the phone conversations had not been satisfying.

Leah felt defensive. Maybe it had to do with not being flattered any more at being carted off to Jason's team events, surrounded by sweaty teens, smelly equipment, and uncomfortable chairs. Maybe it was because she felt hidden among the other refuse of Jason's daily life—just another one of "his" as that jerk Spano had suggested. Maybe because she sensed that Jason was in hiding, too, that somewhere he'd stopped dealing with her openly and she was just another warm body in his life. Maybe Gail had been right after all, and the novelty had worn off—because her color certainly wouldn't.

Every day Leah didn't see Jason was a day she was prepared for their relationship to end. In a way she wanted it to, so she could stop wondering what it was Jason wanted from her, so she could stop wondering what they were becoming. Maybe they hadn't really made that decision at all. Maybe it had just happened.

They were cool to each other when Jason picked her up for the drive out to New Hyde Park. She wore a dusty rose linen sheath dress. She wore her hair loose and full, making her face seem small and her eyes enormous. The pink of the dress made her skin look velvety smooth and soft and rich. When he saw her he had sudden memories of New Year's Eve. For a moment he just wanted to hold her slender body close to him and forget about dinner, forget about the world.

Instead they climbed into his car for a stiff, almost completely silent ride out of the city. The gap widened between them.

There were eight other people at the house besides Joe and Nora. As Jason walked into the house everyone screamed, "Surprise," and the light switch was thrown off and on rapidly. Leah had not known this was to be a birthday party, and when Jason turned to look at her questioningly, as if she'd had a hand in this, she merely shrugged.

They got separated early on as Jason was obliged to spend time talking to his hosts, guests, and friends. Leah didn't seek him out during the evening, and he chose to interpret that as meaning she didn't want to. One young handsome black man, a lawyer Jason knew from court, took it upon himself to keep Leah company.

Ross Bennett was very nice and he was interesting, but Leah could barely keep her mind on what he was saying, feeling false as she smiled and laughed at the appropriate moments.

None of this was lost on Nora, who had known the moment Jason and Leah walked in the door that something was wrong between them. Nora and Joe had exchanged looks. "Uh-oh," they'd both muttered in unison.

There were not so many people that Jason couldn't have found a moment for Leah, or that she couldn't have joined any of the small groups he moved among as he held court. But more than stubbornness and pride kept them apart.

"Lord, Lord . . ." Nora tsked to Joe. "I told that girl she and Jason couldn't just be friends for long."

"And I told Jason to be careful and not think with his—"

"You hush up," Nora scolded, cutting Joe a telling look. "I'm very fond of Jason, but if he hurts that child, so help me I'll whip his behind myself!"

Nora had provided plenty of food and booze. Leah was glad to see that unlike New Year's, Jason didn't seem inclined to drink freely. Later, there was a huge cake with gaudy pink, blue, and yellow iced flowers. Despite his avoiding her, Leah was pleased to see that Jason was very touched by the attention and time Nora and Joe had taken on his behalf. He engulfed the other woman in a tight, affectionate hug.

"You're too good to me, Nora." Jason kissed her cheek.

"I'm not the only one," she answered caustically. "I think you're worth it, Jason. Just don't prove me wrong."

Jason blushed and pretended ignorance of her meaning.

It was well after midnight when Leah and Jason left to drive to Brooklyn. A box with the remains of his birthday cake was balanced on her lap.

"Did you have a good time?" Jason asked.

"It was pleasant."

"I noticed you got along well with Ross Bennett."

"Did you?" Leah asked indifferently.

"Do you like him?"

Leah looked at Jason pointedly. "He was the only one who spared me any time."

"I'm sorry. I couldn't just sit in one place, stay with you. I had to spend time with everyone," he explained calmly.

Silence prevailed for the next mile.

"Ross is a nice guy. He's a real straight shooter."

"He seems to be," Leah sighed impatiently.

They were five miles from her house.

"I suppose he asked you out," Jason said quietly.

"Who?"

"Ross."

Leah was hurt. "What if he did?"

Jason shrugged. "I don't mind, you know."

Leah turned her head to stare in bewilderment at Jason's profile. "Well, I don't care if you don't mind," she said, her anger building.

Jason turned to look at her as he waited for a light to change. "I'm only saying I understand that you want to date other people. I understand—"

"You don't understand a thing, Jason. Ross Bennett is black, is that what you're trying to get at? Are you trying to fix me up with one of my own kind?"

The car pulled up in front of her house, and Leah immediately got the door open. "Happy Birthday, Jason. Good night."

"Hey, wait a minute," he said in irritation. "Why are you so angry? What did I do? What the hell is going on with everybody?"

Leah faced him, her face stiff with anger but her real feelings and fears well hidden.

"Color isn't an issue when men begin to act like assholes. When you're being stupid, you're all pretty much the same."

Leah thrust the cake box in his arms and got out of the car. "Don't worry about what's going on. I'll make it easy for you; *nothing's* going on anymore."

She slammed the door and ran up the stairs to the house.

"Shit!" Jason exploded in rage. He hit his fist against the steering wheel. Then he angrily tossed the cake box into the passenger seat, unmindful of the damage to its contents. He heard Leah's front door slam.

For a moment Jason considered going after her, but instead shifted into drive and pulled away from the curb with a screech.

"Fuck it," he said through clenched teeth, wondering why he had even bothered at all.

Chapter Eleven

The perfectly modulated voice at last announced American Airlines flight #507 departing gate thirty-one for Chicago's O'Hare International Airport. Leah stood up and gathered her handbag and carry-on tote. She checked to make sure she had her boarding pass and, taking a deep breath, turned to Allen and Gail. She had not had much to say to either of them coming out to LaGuardia, and even less to say now as she was about to leave.

A red angora beret was pulled down over her thick hair, matching the high turtleneck sweater she wore with black pants. Her coat, designed and sewn by her sister, was thrown over an arm. Gail was standing to the side, shifting from one foot to the next with impatience. She'd been angry that Leah had gone ahead and arranged to visit their father without including her. They'd planned to travel to Chicago together for a week sometime during the Spring or Summer, but in the last five days Leah had made her reservations, taken ten days off from work, and concluded her plans before Gail ever knew what was happening. All the arguments and shouting afterward did nothing to make Leah change her mind.

"I don't want your company," Leah had told Gail. She wanted to be with the one person in the world she knew wasn't going to judge her.

Allen took Leah's carry-on bag, and the three of them headed to the security check. Leah was just as happy that he and Gail couldn't go beyond this point.

"I really don't understand why you're doing this," Gail said, her personal grievance overshadowing them all. "Why couldn't you wait two more goddamn weeks so I could go, too?"

"This trip is for me. There's nothing to stop you from planning your own trip later."

"You're just being selfish."

"Yes, you've said so several times," Leah reminded Gail. "I just want some time to myself, away from New York."

"And me? This is pointless. Don't you know you can't run away? He'll still be here when you return," Gail said bluntly.

Her alluding to Jason immediately caused the tension to surge through Leah again, as it had for the past several days of reliving her last meeting with him. There was a tightening in her chest that threatened her breathing. She was getting away not a moment too soon. Perhaps everything would still be in place when she returned to New York. But it was also possible that she would have changed and it wouldn't matter.

"Thank you for your insight," Leah murmured. Gail turned away impatiently as Leah took her tote from Allen. "Thanks for the ride to the airport. I appreciate it."

Leah could see that her appreciation only embarrassed Allen. He'd listened to the exchange between the two sisters and obviously knew he had no place in their argument. Leah could tell that Allen wished that Gail would just let the whole thing drop. And it wasn't her problem if he was uncomfortable with the subject.

Allen knew about Jason. When Gail had first told him she was dating a white man, his reaction had been one of affront, as if she was doing this to him just to get even. Leah could well imagine that Allen had felt betrayed and angry. What could Leah see in a white man? A cop, of all people? Why would she do this to herself, and to her friends and family? Leah grimaced and shifted her coat on her arm. She'd been betrayed, too.

Allen shrugged. "No problem. If there's anything else I can do—"

"There is. Get Gail out of here before I get violent." With that Leah said good-bye and passed through the security check.

From the time she boarded the plane until she disembarked two hours later in Chicago, Leah remembered nothing of the flight. She was emotionally and physically exhausted, and sat silently in her seat. The last several days had been a nightmare of anger, hurt, recriminations, and sleeplessness. Everything had gotten out of control.

By all dictates of good sense Leah knew that she had gotten herself into an impossible circumstance. But she was already emotionally attached to Jason and couldn't seem to get around that. And despite the suspicions that had caused them to rail at each other the night of his birthday party, her feelings had not changed. Things would have been so much easier if they had.

Her father met her at the baggage claim. Melvin Downey gave his daughter a bear hug and warm kisses of welcome. Sixty-eight years old, he was the same height as his daughter, but had gotten a little round in the middle since retiring from a federal job a number of years ago. His smooth brown face was without lines, and although his hair line had long since receded, he still had very little gray hair. Only the full mustache was heavily peppered.

Leah felt an immediate sense of security, of safety, and finally began to relax. She felt as she had as a little girl. If something had disturbed her, she had automatically come home so that Daddy could make it all right. She never doubted that he could then, and that was exactly what she hoped for now.

For the first few days she did nothing more than be with her father, reestablishing her relationship with him and becoming the daughter again. She passed peaceful hours listening to her father talk about the changes in the family—cousins and aunts and uncles—changes in the neighborhood and with people she'd known since childhood.

Leah indulged him by cooking large, rich meals her father would never trouble with for himself, living alone as he did. She filled his freezer with her baked rolls and breads, casseroles, and meats. Her father laughed at all her fussing and finally confessed that he had a friend who made sure he ate properly.

It had never occurred to Leah that her father would ever consider having a relationship with a woman since her mother had died. In his gentle way he informed her that not only was it possible, it was a relationship he enjoyed. Leah was surprised. Not by any jealousy or threat on hearing that her father had a girlfriend, but by the twinge of envy. Everyone in her family seemed happily involved with someone. Everyone but her.

She explored the creaky and settled old house that she, Gail, and Kenny had spent their summers in with their grandparents until they were almost teenagers. She'd loved the high-ceilinged bedroom she'd shared with Gail, remembering the fights they'd had over who would get the bed nearest the window. Leah peeked into the room her brother had used, but all reminders of him had long ago been removed.

And after Leah had spent time unbending her taut nerves and becoming reacquainted with the familiar, the evening came when her father did what she'd expected him to do.

They'd settled in the living room after Sunday dinner with a plate of Leah's lemon cookies and cups of black coffee. Melvin Downey reached for one and looked at his daughter over the top of his reading glasses.

"You're going to ruin my schoolboy figure with all this good cookin'."

"Your schoolboy figure is retired. Enjoy yourself." Leah smiled.

Mr. Downey chuckled and took a large bite of his cookie. "Ummm-uph! Just like your mama used to make."

Leah sampled one. "They're not bad. But Mama's were better. That's 'cause—"

"I know. They were your mama's." He looked carefully at the slowly disappearing cookie. "What did you think of the sermon this morning?"

Leah curled up on the ancient overstuffed sofa. "It was vintage Reverend Mackie. I'm sure I heard that same sermon the last time I visited. And the time before that."

"Yeah, but it's comfortable. Most of us don't expect any surprises from the Bible. Besides, if he changed a word he'd lose half the congregation."

"A little challenge might be good for him. Keep him on his toes."

Mr. Downey finished his second cookie and settled back in his high-back chair. "He's too old for that. Might confuse him." When Leah did not respond, in fact seemed to be distracted, her father studied her closely and said, "So, what brings you here? It sure ain't Reverend Mackie's sermons. It's not a holiday or my birthday and no one's died. . . ."

Guiltily Leah glanced briefly at her father. She shrugged. "Gail and I have been fighting a lot recently."

Mr. Downey stretched out his legs and crossed them at the ankles. He rested his clasped hands on his stomach. "Well, she always was the tomcat of you two."

"Her nine lives are about to run out," Leah said forcefully.

Her father laughed and nodded. "Good . . ."

"I don't think it's good. We haven't said a kind word to each other in weeks."

"I remember when you wouldn't have said anything at all. You'd get all mad and pout and everything, but Gail would still get her way. What's changed?"

Leah thought. "Maybe I have. I don't appreciate her meddling."

"Yeah, Gail always did think she knew better than anyone else."

"Well, I'm tired of it."

"Then tell her to mind her own business."

She looked in surprise at her father. "You don't seem particularly concerned. How come you understand?"

"For one thing, I'm not the one who's mad at her. And for the other, since I'm not mad at her I get to see the whole picture. I know how difficult Gail can be sometimes. Don't forget I used to live with her, too." Leah smiled. "She's full of lip and sass and won't back down from anything or anyone. Remember the scrapes she used to get into? That kind of brass can be a good thing. She'll always be able to take care of herself. But it's a bad thing, too. Gail wants to run everyone's life like she does her own. *Her* way."

"Her way is not the only way. It's not my way—"

"Then just tell her so. She can be stubborn, but Gail's not stupid. You just make it clear you want her to back off. She'll get the picture."

"But what if she doesn't?"

"Then you don't believe strongly enough that she should. You're not willing to really fight her for what you want. Maybe"—Mr. Downey eyed his daughter with speculation—"maybe you're not really sure what it is you want."

Leah looked at him and met the questioning glare of his eyes. One thing at a time. . . . "Allen and I aren't dating anymore," she whispered.

"I wasn't going to ask . . ." he murmured.

"We broke up in December. Actually, we didn't just break up. He and Gail decided . . ."

"I see."

She was embarrassed and averted her gaze. "I didn't see it coming. Suddenly they were all over each other."

"And you were left standing with egg on your face," Mr. Downey concluded angrily.

Leah stared at him, surprised at his vehemence and wondering who he was annoyed with.

"Did you fight back?"

Leah's eyes widened. "No. How was I going to do that?"

"And why not?"

She blinked because of course he'd misunderstood. "Daddy, I didn't want Allen. I wasn't really in love with him, I guess. I got hurt, but not because of what they did. It was the way they did it. Behind my back, and not telling me until I saw—" she stopped. "It was no loss to me. They deserve each other," Leah said simply, and suddenly her father broke out into laughter.

"Well, don't tell Gail that. She might think she didn't get such a bargain after all." He continued to shake his head in amusement. And then the grin slowly faded. "But you didn't fly out here in a tear without Gail just to talk about her. Something else is bothering you."

The peaceful days had not been enough to keep the

feelings at bay, and with apprehension gnawing at her, Leah curled tighter into the corner of the sofa.

"Come on," Mr. Downey coaxed gently. "Tell Daddy what it is."

Those were the magic five words, the very ones that had always succeeded in prying free the details of her troubles. Well, she was older now, and inclined to keep some of the details private, but the words worked.

"I met someone. Actually, I met him before Allen and I broke up. He's a cop. A Vietnam vet. And he's divorced."

Mr. Downey raised his brows. "A cop? How in the world did you meet a cop?"

"Over a cup of coffee." At her father's puzzled expression Leah shook her head and went on, "Don't ask. The whole story isn't important. The thing is he'd just heard about the death of his son . . ."

"And you were there to console him?" Mr. Downey supplied.

"Sort of."

"Do you love him?"

The question brought Leah's head up with a jerk. She knew that somewhere along the way she'd stopped being casual about the relationship with Jason. She'd come to care, even to hope for more between them, but to be afraid of that hope.

"I could love him," Leah admitted slowly.

"How about him? Does he feel the same way? Does he love you?"

Leah sighed, closing her eyes and recalling the last vitriolic encounter between her and Jason. "I don't know. Sometimes . . . I feel like he needs me. At other times it seems like an impossible relationship and we're both just using each other. It's convenient. We have fun together," Leah confessed in some wonder, as if that had just occurred to her. "But up till now it hasn't been a very deep relationship."

Her father shifted in his chair impatiently. "Okay, okay. So he hasn't declared undying love. What's the problem? It is because he's a cop, or because he's divorced—"

"Daddy," Leah whispered urgently, "he's white."

There was a long silence while Mr. Downey stared at his daughter. Then he grunted and sort of sank into his comfortable chair with the burden of so many years of racism weighing heavily on his shoulders. Slowly he shook his head.

"Umph, umph, umph. Lord have mercy," he said warily.

Mr. Downey suddenly was indignant. And confused. As a parent he'd never told his children whom they could date or be friends with. As a black parent he'd only hoped that in their integrated environment his children would associate with people who treated them at least as equals. He remembered Leah's passing attachment to some white boy named Philip when she was still in college, but Mr. Downey had always been sure that it would never come to anything and therefore had not been concerned.

His children had gone to integrated schools, moved comfortably between two worlds because he and their mother had believed that it was healthier to see the world as it was becoming: neither black nor white but some, hopefully, cooperative mixture. He didn't want his children to be angry and black, but black and well prepared.

Also as a parent Melvin Downey had assumed that some day each of his kids would marry and supply him with grandchildren to joyfully indulge in his old age. He had assumed further that they would marry one of their own kind because it made sense. But nothing made sense anymore: Kenny dying in the war and all his potential lost. Gail might marry someday, but she didn't have the patience for children. Then there was Leah, who'd never spoken about either marriage or children. Allen had been so steady in her life, however, that Mr. Downey had thought that it was just a matter of time before they settled in together as man and wife.

He thought briefly of his own wife and wished suddenly, as he hadn't for a number of years, that she was here to advise them both. He wished that Ann were here to assure him that he had done a good job of raising their children and now that they were adults, their lives were their own.

History had done this, Mr. Downey thought angrily, and people repeating history with their foolish prejudices and senseless hatred, perpetrating it forever, sending his daughter home in confusion because she might choose to care for someone not of her own race.

He felt powerless to help her.

He didn't think Leah needed to be reminded who and what she was. The world at large would never let her forget. But her feelings had already been placed whether or not she realized it.

"Does it matter that he's white?" he asked.

Leah looked carefully at her father. "Does it matter to you?"

Mr. Downey chuckled and slowly shook is head. "Baby, I'm not the one in love with the guy."

"I never said it was love."

"Then it's something pretty close or you wouldn't have come running to me. You're scared, aren't you?"

"I'm confused. I don't know what I'm doing anymore. We're fine together. But when there's other people everything gets so crazy. You know, the remarks and the looks, and I keep thinking it's somehow all my fault. I hate that."

"And this guy . . ."

"His name is Jason Horn."

"What does Jason do?"

"Mostly he seems to ignore what's going on. It's so awful when people get up into your face and tell you what they think. But we haven't really talked about it much. I can't decide if it's because he doesn't care, or he doesn't know how to handle it. Maybe that's part of the problem, like Gail said. Jason and I haven't talked about being an interracial couple and what that means."

"Do you have confrontations all the time?" Mr. Downey asked in some surprise.

Leah let out a deep breath. "No. Not really. Sometimes nothing happens at all. But . . . it's the anticipation."

"There's no guarantee you'll be safe from all the crap that gets thrown at you, Leah. I don't think you can make him responsible for that. Maybe there's less to deal with than you think."

"Not to hear Gail talk. She's really down on Jason and thinks I'm being a fool. Do you think I am?"

Mr. Downey frowned. "No. No, I don't. You're never a fool for wanting to believe the best of someone. But I want you to be careful. I don't want to see you get hurt, either."

"Jason is a good man. I know that."

"Then that's good enough for me. I trust your judgment."

Leah sighed, fingering her hair nervously. "I sure hope I don't disappoint you."

"You'll never do that, baby. Stop being so concerned about what I think or what your sister thinks. Just don't disappoint yourself. You have to live with your conscience. We don't. I only ask that you be sure about what you want."

Leah stared into the distance, far beyond the walls of the living room. "What I want I don't think is possible. I've been thinking maybe the best thing is to break off now before things go any further."

"What you feel won't go away if you run," Mr. Downey said sagely.

It almost annoyed Leah that her father and sister could come up with pretty much the same sentiment. In other words, she could expect no easy answers.

"Look, you probably don't have a whole lot of information on how to handle this relationship. But neither does Jason. He doesn't know any more than you do what should be done. Therefore you both have to go on what you feel for each other. You both have to know if it's worth the risks.

"I bet he doesn't know how you feel. I bet you don't know what's going through his mind. Talk first. Things could be very easy for you two or very hard and miserable. But it all begins with you."

Leah sat silently for moment and then hazarded a probing look at her father. He had given her calm, sensible reasoning. He'd been fair. "But what do you think, Daddy? How do you feel about this? Honestly."

Her father thought carefully, and his expression became soft and sad. "What choice do I have? Maybe things have changed, and you and Jason Horn can work out what you feel for each other. But my experience over the years tells me otherwise." He reached over to pat her knee. "Be careful, baby. Just be real careful."

Leah sighed. Well, none of this mattered anyway. It was all too late. She and Jason had last parted in anger with a chasm of misunderstanding between them. There didn't seem to be any possibility for reconciliation, and perhaps things were better left as they were. She could deal with the undeveloped feelings eventually, and there would be no more need for second guesses.

Leah returned to New York, calm and rested, thinking this was true.

Jason sat staring at the loose change on the counter. He looked up at the pay phone to his right, lifted the receiver, and put it down again.

It was all Leah Downey's fault.

That's what Joe had said, and Jason was sick of hearing Joe say it. He was tired of hearing that he and Leah were out of their minds. But Jason had decided that maybe only he was. Joe kept telling him how he didn't understand why anyone would deliberately set about making life more difficult than it already was. But then Joe saw things coldly for what they were. Either black or white with no gray areas. Jason also knew that Joe's primary concern was to make him, as Joe said, "pull his shit together."

That was asking a lot.

The fact was, Jason didn't know what he was doing and was miserable doing it. After he'd last seen Leah he had been all put out, although he wasn't really sure why. He'd wanted to soothe his wounded ego in the arms of the redheaded dancer, but she, like Carol, was too smart to be used that way. And they proved to be good enough friends to send him home to deal with his problems himself.

Jason realized that he should just call Leah and try to find out what had gone wrong between them. To his great irritation Gail had answered when he'd finally called, and run interference.

Jason played with the coins. The voices and laughter around him were mostly male. He was in a smoke-fogged bar two blocks from the precinct. Only cops hung out here. Even the groupies knew better than to come into this sanctified territory. This was a different kind of clubhouse. It was where many of his colleagues dropped in randomly, whenever one of them needed to be reassured that they were not alone and that their doubts about their job were legitimate. Here they could all complain, could feel safe, could hide.

Jason had been considering getting drunk when he decided to make the call. His eyes were already red and watery from the cigarette smoke. The room was noisy and smelled of cops and beer. Jason looked at Joe, who'd been pushing him to make the call for the last hour and who'd even given him the coins to do so.

"Go on and call the woman. 'Cause you're making me crazy with your bad mood," Joe ordered, although he didn't believe a phone call was going to solve anything.

Jason dropped the coins into the box and dialed.

"Hello?"

"Um, is Leah there?"

" 'Fraid not," Gail answered indifferently.

"I have to talk to her. This is Jason."

Gail sighed, bored. "She's away. As in out-of-the-city away."

The possibility of Leah being completely unreachable had not entered his mind. "Are you sure?" Jason persisted.

Gail hung up on him.

Jason did what he was supposed to do, but he did it by rote, and without the enthusiasm and hopefulness that had always made his work a challenge. He bowed out at the last moment from coaching a game at Riker's. He got stabbed in the arm breaking up a domestic fight while in family court. And he knew the kid who'd died over a warehouse shipment of VCRs.

It had rained that day, which made it seem worse.

At the scene Jason lifted the tarp covering Razor's body and watched the boy's blood being diluted by the rain and washing away along the street. In death Razor looked a lot younger than sixteen. They always did.

Jason dropped the cloth and turned to Slack standing, indifferent and without expression, with several plainclothes cops and two other boys who'd been apprehended. Jason walked over to Slack, angry to find him at the scene.

"What happened?" Jason asked.

"He fell," Slack shrugged.

Beyond where the body lay covered was a warehouse. A rope ladder extended halfway down the side of the building from the roof. There was a broken window through which two additional officers were viewing the scene below. A rotted fire escape hung at a skewered angle, broken away from the building, and several VCR boxes with contents were smashed on the sidewalk near Razor. Jason turned back to Slack.

"Were you in on this?"

"I wasn't inside."

Jason stared at the boy. He was smart. Wily. He'd probably taken the easy job of lookout, Jason guessed. He pointed at the body. "That could have been you."

Slack looked away and shook his head. "I told 'em VCRs ain't worth it."

Jason sighed wearily. "They're going to take you in with the others. I'll talk to you tomorrow," he said in annoyance, turning away. He wondered what else it was going to take to finally reach him, to make Slack, and all the others, realize that there were other choices.

But tonight Jason didn't berate himself for maybe falling somewhere short of the mark himself. His thinking cleared up just long enough to realize what he was responsible for and what he wasn't. Sometimes there were no answers, and things weren't always fair. But his gut instincts would rarely lead him wrong, and he only had to trust them. Whether it was with his job . . . or Leah.

Jason got four days off between tours and put all his pent-up energy into driving to Pennsylvania and spending time with his sister and her family. He went fishing with his nephews and helped his brother-in-law repair part of the roof on his house. And he mostly didn't have much to say. Jason's withdrawn state was not lost on his sister.

Nancy Collins never asked, but she did wonder who the woman was who had captured Jason's attention enough to make him thoughtful, restless, and perhaps a bit scared. Nancy watched him work hard, his concentration on tarring and shingling, the power behind each hammered nail a testimony to emotions he still kept inside.

Jason came back to New York feeling no calmer for having decided that he needed to talk with Leah. He was still scared, but he knew that all those earlier feelings had been real, the ones he had had before running into that wall.

Leah was queasy about coming home. She had been gone almost two weeks, and she knew that nothing had changed. If anything, the time away had only pointed out that she couldn't get far enough away from Jason to forget him.

She didn't ask Gail if Jason had called while she was away. In a well-intended but misguided attempt to save her sister grief, Gail also didn't offer up the information that Jason had called. Gail had always believed that an end to the relationship was inevitable, and her contribution was to help it at every turn.

It was Thursday night with a long weekend ahead before Leah had to return to work the following Monday. She'd spent a few hours cleaning dead leaves from the base of the trees in the backyard. She'd then gone to dinner with Gail and several girlfriends. When they returned to the house, Gail gathered some personal things and said she was going to stay with Allen until Saturday. Leah couldn't help laughing as her sister shouldered her leather tote and called for a cab.

"What's so funny?" Gail asked suspiciously. She didn't like being laughed at.

"You can tell Allen all is forgiven. He can stop avoiding me now," Leah said dryly.

"He hasn't been avoiding you."

"Gail, Allen hasn't been in the same room with me for more than fifteen minutes since Christmas. He's flattering himself if he thinks I'm still angry."

Gail postured with a hand on her hip. "What have you got to be angry about?" She shot back testily. "You certainly didn't let dust gather around you for very long. Maybe he feels about you dating Jason the same way I do."

Leah stared at her sister, her eyes narrowing with annoyance. "I'm not dating Jason anymore. We had a fight. Do you want me to tell you that you were right after all?" she asked softly.

For just an instant Gail looked embarrassed and uncomfortable. Then a car horn beeped from outside, announcing the arrival of Gail's cab, and she looked hard at her sister. "There wasn't any other way for it to work out, hon. At least now you've come to your senses." Gail opened the door.

"I'm not happy about it," Leah confessed with a stubborn lift of her chin. Her sister hadn't won yet.

Gail grimaced. "What was it about him, anyway?"

"Nothing complicated. I liked him, that's all."

Gail shrugged and swung out the door. "You'll get over it."

In a pair of faded jeans and an oversized shirt she'd confiscated from her father, Leah cleaned a closet. It was better than watching TV until time to go to bed. It was less nerve-racking than thinking. At least when she was finished she'd have something to show for it.

The doorbell ringing a little after nine o'clock made Leah think it was Sarah Chen or Biddy Rosen. But all words of greeting died in her throat when Leah opened the door and saw Jason standing there. There was a funny moment of him looking unfamiliar again, as when she'd returned to his precinct house and seen him in uniform. Then there was a surge of relief because she had believed she was never going to see him again—and here he was. To say hello seemed foolish. So Leah said nothing. Jason looked unsure of himself. And defensive. But he was here.

In that first moment Leah couldn't think of why she'd been attracted to Jason in the first place. And then she looked into his eyes and it all fell into place. She was also aware that perhaps for the first time they were both assessing each other honestly.

Jason could see that he'd caught Leah completely by surprise. He hadn't known what he expected to happen at first, but this was not it. He didn't know that they would stand speechless, staring a each other in this way, as though they were strangers. What grabbed at him, however, was a sudden jolting sense of loss for what had been between them before.

"Hi, Leah. You're back."

Leah gripped the doorknob, using it for support. She stood very straight and stared right at him. "What are you doing here?"

Jason squeezed his hands into nervous fists. The

knuckles cracked. "I was hoping you'd invite me in for some coffee."

Leah's mouth tightened. "Jason, this is not a halfway house for troubled cops." She began to close the door, but Jason quickly grabbed the edge with his hand.

"All right. That was a stupid thing to say. I wanted to see you."

"Let go of my door. I don't want to see you," she said evenly.

Jason let go of the door, but stood in the frame so it was impossible for Leah to shut it. "Maybe that's true. But let's talk first and then you can decide."

Leah looked at him. "I don't think there's anything more to talk about. I think it was all said the last time we saw each other."

Jason slowly moved into the entrance, forcing Leah to take steps backward to avoid contact with him. "We didn't talk last time. As I recall, we were both pretty hot under the collar and did a lot of screaming. You weren't really listening to what I was saying, and I wasn't listening to you. I think we both deserve a second chance."

"It won't make any difference."

"On the other hand, it might make all the difference."

"What's the point?" Leah asked impatiently.

Jason shifted from one foot to the other. He stuffed his hands into the front pockets of his jeans. "The point is, maybe this time we can be honest with each other. About how we feel. About everything."

Leah didn't pretend not to understand. It would seem that all the pretending was over. She shook her head slowly. "I thought that everything ended that night of your birthday party, Jason. Maybe that was a better idea. The truth is, we never should have started."

"Not started what? Not begin to like each other? What was so wrong with that?"

"It went beyond that. What we did was have an affair against all the rules. And whether or not you were paying attention, we got clobbered for doing so."

"I'm paying attention now. I mean, it came a little bit late. That's what I want to talk about."

Leah's gaze roamed over Jason's face, trying to gauge his sincerity. He met her gaze steadily, and she knew she wanted to believe him. She turned and slowly walked into the kitchen. With a great deal of irony and resignation she began to make coffee. Jason leaned in the doorway watching her.

"So," Leah began somewhat dryly, "what great insights have you come to?" She could hear him settling against the entrance to the kitchen, using the frame for support.

"Just that you and I becoming friends and then lovers wasn't a mistake. It was just harder than I thought it would be. I thought it was no big deal, the black and white thing. Then the real shit started to hit the fan—"

"And all over you. Don't worry, it washes off," she offered tightly.

"It leaves a smell. It was like some sort of signal that there were people who couldn't accept the two of us together."

Leah laughed lightly and, flipping on the brew switch of the coffee maker, turned to look at him. "You didn't really accept the two of us together, either."

"Neither had you," he reminded her softly. "So what if you warned me? You stood and waited for the bombs to drop because you knew they would. You waited to see if I would stumble and fall, and I did. You know why? Because I really didn't believe that you being black was supposed to matter. I just didn't expect to get blown away because of it."

"Well, you weren't the only one being attacked, Jason. Everyone was telling me you couldn't be serious, that you were just using me."

Jason slowly straightened from the door frame, and his jaw tensed in annoyance. "Who's everyone? What did you say to them?" he asked softly.

They stared at each other, uncertainty and a possible finality of purpose hanging ominously between them. "Family. Friends. I told them all they were wrong. And then I prayed that they weren't right. I fought with my sister and defended you—"

"I didn't need defending."

Leah sighed and searched for two coffee mugs from a cabinet. She poured coffee for them both. "They were right about one thing. Our worlds are too different."

"We're not so different, and that's not the point anyway. The problem wasn't you and me, it was everybody else. I never expected so much . . ."

"Hate. The word you're searching for is hate."

Jason shook his head. "No. The word is ignorance."

Leah put the mugs down on the kitchen table and faced Jason squarely. "But it began to make sense, didn't it?"

"No," he said shortly, stepping up to the table close to her. "It began to scare me. It made me angry because I didn't know what to do. People I really cared about, who I thought were friends and cared about me, were suddenly . . ." He shook his head in bewilderment. "I didn't know how to handle it," he confessed.

Leah sat down heavily in her chair. Jason cautiously sat opposite her. "There was no reason why you should have," she offered sadly. "I've never been able to deal with it. I've had more practice."

Jason shook his head, looking carefully at her. "You

did better than I did. I think about it now, and maybe you had more at risk than I did. If I walked away, Leah, everyone might have considered the whole episode a joke. But for you . . . you might have been condemned forever. By your sister, your community . . . other black men . . ."

Leah smiled wryly. "See? You do begin to understand."

Jason actually blushed and stared into his coffee, his hands circling the cup tightly. "I'm sorry."

Leah shrugged. "What for? For being honest enough to try with me? For being honest enough to come here tonight and admit you'd gotten in way over your head?" She looked into Jason's face, into the expressive eyes with their depth of feelings, much more honest than most people. Through them she might have been able to see into his soul, to explore the depth of his being, to fall into an abyss of caring from which she might never return. . . .

Her gaze dropped for an erotic moment to his mouth. She remembered passion that had been pure, surprising, unrestrained with no consideration beyond mutual need. That's when it had been just the two of them without the rest of the world—an impossible situation, as she'd always known. Leah sipped her coffee and felt her throat closing in again. She didn't want to cry now. She didn't want it to matter this much.

"I'm sorry, too. I knew it would come to this," she whispered. She was afraid to talk louder because her voice would lose its strength, or her strength would fall apart.

Jason stared intently at her. "To this? What?" he asked, frowning.

"The end. *Fini* . . . good-bye."

"Good-bye . . ." he repeated blankly. Jason reached across the table and grabbed her wrist, almost causing

Leah to spill her coffee. "Wait a minute! Look, I came to tell you I finally realized what you were trying to say to me way back at the start, that a relationship between us would be hard and there's a lot against it. I came to tell you you were absolutely right. But I didn't come here to say good-bye." His voice was urgent, almost angry. "I took a lot of shit from the guys at the precinct. Even Joe had a lot to say about you and me."

"I'm not surprised," Leah said. "Joe, of all people, would have a lot to say."

"Joe's my partner," Jason responded angrily, shaking Leah's arm in his agitation. "He's my friend and I have to depend on him like nobody else. Maybe I lost a friend, someone who couldn't stomach the thought . . ."

Leah tried to pull her arm free. "That's the way it is sometimes. So what do you want? That I should apologize to you?" she asked bitterly.

"I just want you to hear me and to understand . . ."

Leah finally freed her arm. "Nobody understands better than me, Jason. If I hadn't understood, we never would have gotten past last September. There never would have been New Year's Eve."

Jason looked defeated and just sat looking remorsefully at Leah. "I'm not like the others."

"Well, neither am I. But the world still treats me and sees me as just another nigger, and Jason, you're from that world."

"Doesn't it mean anything to you at all that I didn't treat you that way? Yeah, I got confused. I even got angry. I got suspicious as hell. What the hell is a nigger anyway? Can you explain it to me?"

Leah suddenly stood up, her chair scraping across the tiled kitchen floor. Jason quickly stood as well and reached for her again.

"Can you?" he asked again, desperate in his desire to reach the bottom of their differences.

"It depends on your point of view."

"Leah . . ." Jason said loudly, holding her arms and forcing her to look into his face. His fingers pressed tightly into her arms, and Leah squirmed. "I haven't got one!"

The pressure of his hands hurt. That combined with the stress of their meeting worked to bring Leah's anxiety to the surface. She felt tears begin to fill her eyes.

"Jason, just go. We were both better off the night of the party. It's over between us and you'll soon forget. She tried to walk past him, but he held her steadfastly.

"Dammit! I don't want to forget. I don't want to walk away."

"Then forget what you and I want. Look at the odds. Do you really want to continue being an outcast because of me? It is worth losing friends and family?"

"Maybe it is."

Leah's eyes widened as she saw stubbornness stiffening Jason's body. "Then you're crazy."

"I'm not just going to walk away. . . ."

Silence fell between them. Tension clumped the muscles in Leah's stomach. This was a challenge. This was a gauntlet being thrown down, and it threw her off guard. Somehow it was now being directed at her. Her heart pounded.

"Then I'll walk away."

Jason quickly blocked the entrance to the kitchen. "Don't run!"

Slowly Leah's head came up. This was the third time she'd been accused of running away. How convenient of everyone to forget that she had taken a stand at the very beginning. That she had put everything on the line and stood her ground because she believed in Jason. She was livid.

"I'm not running!" she said tightly.

She got mad because Jason was standing in her way.

She reached up both fists and slammed him in his chest. "I'm not running, I'm not running . . ." she shouted. She forced her way past Jason and headed for the living room.

"Then where the hell are you going? And if all of this is just bullshit, then why are you crying?"

Leah stopped in the middle of the living room, realizing that there was no place else to go. She whipped around to face Jason, her face distorted and anguished and wet with tears. Her arms raised in supplication as she sobbed.

"Because . . . because I don't know what you want from me. Why can't you just let it be? Why did you even bother coming tonight? Go away and leave me alone."

"Leah, listen to me," Jason said softly, very slowly approaching her, but afraid that she would once again go into a tirade. Jason swallowed away his own emotion because he had a sudden realization. Leah had not once blamed him for anything. She had just not dared to expect anything of him. She had been taught too strong a lesson, and she had never been sure she could trust him with her feelings. He took even more care trying to reach out to her. Leah was like a wild animal poised for flight, and Jason didn't want her to run away from him.

"Listen . . ." he coaxed.

Leah stood breathing hard, angry that she had lost control and Jason was still confronting her. She was tired. She was weary of having to be careful, of not being allowed to feel what she really felt. She closed her eyes.

Jason gently touched her shoulders. Cautiously he lifted his hands to touch Leah's neck and then they framed her face. Her skin was damp and hot. It instantly reminded him of how pliant and feminine Leah always felt against him. She grabbed Jason's wrists but didn't try to pull away, or to shake his hands off.

"What do you want from me?" she croaked.

Jason's eyes roamed over the features of her face. He knew every facet of it, all her expressions, and he could read her better than he had thought. Even now he suddenly could see beyond this moment into a realm of possibilities that seemed both fearful and exciting. For whatever reason, Leah had touched him deep inside. Jason knew that he couldn't walk away. He didn't want to.

"I want you," he answered seriously. "I just want another chance with you."

Jason then closed her slowly into the circle of his arms as if he was afraid she'd start to fight him again. Leah accepted him stiffly, her arms straight down at her sides and her forehead resting on his chest. Tentatively Jason stroked her back and slowly she relaxed. He took a deep breath and let it out. The tension in his shoulders and neck began to loosen. His chest tingled from where Leah had pounded him, but the memory only made him smile. He felt as if he'd finally gotten an impossibly heavy door open, and had quickly passed through. Now he was on the other side into freedom.

Leah realized that some questions truly have no answers. She didn't understand why things are the way they are; they just are. She might believe in things, trust in people, and it was because of nothing more than instinct. Yet if she couldn't trust her instincts, then she had nothing to go on at all.

At the moment it made as much sense as anything else she'd thought recently. Even in this instant she recognized that she and Jason had weathered a hurricane and survived better than they might have hoped for. Despite everything he had come back. And he had stayed.

Leah was curled up beside him on the sofa. His jacket and baseball cap had been discarded on the floor. It had taken a while for her to calm down, and even now not much more had been said.

Jason hadn't really known what he was going to say to her when he'd arrived earlier. There had just been this urgency to face her and see if they still had a chance.

"Jason . . ." she began drowsily. "Please don't make any promises."

His thumb was stroking the side of her neck and jaw. He sighed. "All right. I promise not to make any promises."

"I'm serious. They're too difficult to keep."

"I know," he agreed. "I don't know where this is going."

"Then you know as much as I do. At least now we're even."

He turned his head to glance down at her. "As far as I was concerned, we were always even."

"Uh-uh." Leah disagreed. "You had the upper hand. You may not have realized it, but you did. White men do."

Jason chuckled silently and shook his head in disbelief.

"Right from the beginning we were headed into troubled waters. I knew that if things got too rough I'd probably drown, and you'd backstroke your way to safety," Leah murmured dryly.

"But you didn't say no," Jason reminded her softly.

Leah was quiet for a long time. "I guess I didn't really want to say no."

"Even though you were scared?"

She nodded against his chest. "Even though I was scared."

Jason considered that. "Do you realize that I'm scared, too?" he asked.

Leah frowned thoughtfully. "No. I guess I never thought of that. You know, you can still walk away."

"I can't. I finally realized that you're important to me."

"You have other women," Leah said smoothly.

"I don't suppose it would do any good to say they're just friends. How about being my main squeeze?" He grinned, nuzzling her cheek with his nose. Then he angled his head down and pressed his mouth to hers. There was an instant charge, as if they were kissing for the first time. Jason closed his eyes and his mouth became more intimate and possessive as she responded to him. He could feel the heat begin to rise in his body. He groaned deep in his chest.

"You don't feel any different."

"What are you talking about?"

"I wondered how you'd be in bed. You know why? Because you were so slender and your breasts were small. Your legs were long and your hands warm and delicate. I kept thinking of your hands and how they would feel on my chest, how tight your legs would wrap around my hips—"

"Jason . . ." Leah exclaimed in shock.

His fingers pressed to her lips to silence her. "Your eyes show you care, and your smile starts from here,"— he touched her brow—"and goes right to here"—and her chin. "I wanted to make love with you because I felt safe. That's pretty much how I wanted you to feel with me, Leah." He studied her closely, his brows furrowing, and he ran a finger firmly down the side of her face. "I can't do a damn thing about your being black, so I'm not going to worry about it."

"It does matter, Jason. Don't pretend like you don't see it. That's how we got in trouble in the first place, not dealing with it. Whether we like it or not, the world is color-coded, and that probably won't change in our lifetime. Swimming upstream is hard."

Jason grew sober and thoughtful. He massaged her neck, and tensed his jaw. "Then I guess we deal with it. I need you, Leah. It took a long time for me to see that, and maybe I was just scared of the responsibility. But the bottom line is I'm not anymore."

Leah stared at him, amazed at Jason's admission. "So what am I to be to you? Another friend? Another lover?"

"The one and only."

Leah didn't ask the obvious next question. She wasn't going to try to divine the future. She was hoping it would surprise her.

Jason took hold of her hand. "Did you tell your father about us?" he asked carefully.

Leah glanced briefly at him, somehow not surprised he'd known that she'd gone to visit her father in Chicago. "Yes, I did."

"What did he say?"

"He was careful not to say how he felt. I don't think he's exactly happy about us, but it has nothing to do with you personally, Jason. My father just doesn't want to see me get hurt."

"I don't want to hurt you."

"But you can't protect me from getting hurt, either," she said ruefully. Slowly she sat up and faced him. "What happens now?" she inquired softly.

Jason looked at her and smiled. He stroked her hair and trailed a finger from her throat down into the opening of the shirt, into the valley between her breasts.

"We tell everyone else to go to hell. We stop wor-

rying about what other people think and hope they
choke on their hatred. We try to be honest with each
other and let the chips fall where they may." He released Leah and stood up, retrieving his jacket and cap.

"Right now I'm going to work. I'll catch a bad guy
or two and keep the streets of the city safe for liberty
and other forms of democracy," he said flippantly. He
turned to Leah and snaked an arm around her waist,
hugging her to his side. Together they headed toward
the front door.

"We take one day at a time and forget the crap. Let's
not look for trouble, but let's not run away from it,
either. What do you think?"

"It sounds pretty simple."

They stopped behind the door and faced each other.
"It does, doesn't it?" He opened the door and under
the entrance light he caught the shadows on Leah's
face, the sparkle of her dark eyes, wide and questioning. Jason lifted her chin and planted a kiss on her
mouth. "Don't worry. I'll be back when I get off duty,"
he whispered, and then closed the door between them.

Chapter Twelve

Gail noticed the change in her sister. She knew that Leah had heard from Jason.

She felt she'd lost the battle for her sister's soul, and a white devil had captured it and held it fast. Leah had always listened to her in the past, always accepted her sister's advice and guidance. And Gail had always enjoyed the privileges that came with being the elder. She recognized that Leah had changed the balance, and now they were both equal. She heard all about the resurrection of the relationship with Jason, and endured Leah's buoyed spirits.

On that Sunday as they returned home together from church, Leah, in an animated voice filled with drama and amusement, told Gail about Reverend Mackie's service on redemption and salvation that she'd heard in Chicago.

Gail was not amused. "Well, you would have been a lost cause. Poor Reverend Mackie would have dropped dead on the altar if he'd known about you and Jason."

Leah smiled to herself. "Progress. At least you didn't call him 'that white man.' "

Leah gazed across the street to the lush greening of Prospect Park. She shook her head slowly. "Reverend Mackie wouldn't have condemned me. Daddy didn't. He told me to make up my own mind about Jason."

"Then I guess you have."

Leah stopped walking and touched Gail's arm to face her. "Look, Gail. You have to understand something I just figured out all by myself. I am the only one who can decide my identity. And the only person who I care about offending is God. I'll work it out with Him. All right?"

Gail stared at her sister and knew that Leah meant every word. She merely shrugged. "So what happened the other night?"

Leah thought. What had happened? Maybe her life had been saved. Maybe she'd regained possession of herself . . . and her soul. But certainly it was much more than that. It had to do with happiness.

Leah didn't tell Gail everything.

When the bell had rung at seven o'clock that Friday morning, more than eight hours after Jason had left her for his work tour, Leah had been in her robe, nervously trying to plan her day. Just in case Jason didn't return. The bell made her jump, and her hands were icy cold as she walked down the hall to the front door. She opened it slowly, and found him silhouetted against the bright morning sun. Leah couldn't see the details of his face, only the motion of Jason running his hands through his hair as he removed the red cap. A hesitant grin broke through the shadows of his face and he murmured hi. Leah smiled in utter relief.

She moved back so that Jason could step into the entrance, but he reached out to take her hand and stop her. He closed the door, leaned against it, and pulled her into his arms. Leah could feel his weariness in the slow movements of his hands.

With a studied intensity Jason kissed her and began to explore her mouth with his own. Leah pressed closer, her inhibitions disappearing as Jason deepened the kiss with a hunger that seemed shocking and

THE COLOR OF LOVE

erotic. His tongue danced with hers, explored slowly to reclaim her, and sought the kind of response from her that had always stirred him. His hands roamed her body, from her shoulders to her spine, down to her waist and buttocks. Jason arched Leah still closer. He managed one hand in between them to squeeze Leah's breast through the fabric of her robe in a blatantly masculine, possessive gesture.

Jason pulled the robe belt until it loosened and the robe fell open. Leah pulled her mouth free of his, but Jason only transferred his kisses to her chin, and then her throat and neck while he had pushed the robe aside and slipped his arms around her warm body, awkwardly trying to bring their passion together. They were still standing in the hall.

"Jay . . ." Leah got out breathlessly, bracing her hands against his chest and pushing to separate them. He slowly let her go.

"Jesus . . ." Jason moaned, and in that one blasphemous word was the depth of his feelings.

Leah took his hand and moved toward the stairwell. The robe fell around her, and Leah simply stepped out of it, leaving it on the floor. She had on only a pair of panties.

If their first time together had been extraordinary, this time was beyond description. They had discovered from the beginning that they were sexually suited to each other. Now the physical coupling was aided by feelings: real and admitted and enjoyed. This was better than before. The hard edge of doubt was not totally gone, but the genuine need was deeper and more stimulating. The softer allure of caring seeped in. Leah felt an intense, happy rejuvenation of her spirit and soul, her mind and body.

They didn't wait because they'd been waiting too

long. Everything now became basic and elemental. Their bodies had worked together as nature meant them to. Rocking and riding together, fused. Jason thrusting and Leah opening and lifting to receive him. They couldn't get close enough. They gave in to the power of the moment, the sheer bliss of release, and blended into each other. Her climax was so strong that she was to believe later that she'd held everything in, waiting just for him. But afterward, with her body languid and trembling, Leah felt also a brief rush of guilt. She was suddenly sure that feeling this good was a sin and she would have to pay for it later.

For a very long time afterward Jason lay collapsed on her body, his face buried in her hair and neck. His breath was hot, labored, and ticklish against her skin. Slowly Leah's legs relaxed and stretched out, and she let the full male weight of Jason's body cover her. Her hands took liberties they never had before: the simple gesture of stroking his hair, fingers teasing his buttocks. Reflexively Jason squeezed his hips against her, then relaxed again with a deep moan. He slid limp and damp from within her body.

"I missed you," Jason whispered simply. "I really missed you."

The words overwhelmed Leah.

"You only want me for my body," she teased, and was rewarded with a soft laugh.

Slowly Jason lifted his head to look down at her, his gaze slumberous with satisfaction. "Now I know what brown sugar really means . . ."

He wanted her again. He cupped her breasts, causing the nipples to tighten into buttons and swell. He let his hands stroke down Leah's rib cage and to her stomach, continuing along her thigh. Jason kissed her cheek and lowered his torso to Leah's chest.

"You have pretty skin."

Jason cupped his hands beneath her bottom and lifted her. He was hard again.

It was Leah's turn to moan.

"Yes. Yes . . ." Jason responded before slipping his body into hers, joining them together once more.

It had been slower and longer that time. Less urgent and desperate, more tenderness and thought. And in that time together Leah had forever banished the doubts and fears of the past. She had set about the business of basking in the affections of Jason Horn— cop, friend and lover—who accepted her as she was.

Leah had prayed fervently that the handball tournament she'd been foolish enough to instigate had been forgotten, but she had no such luck. When Jason informed her that he'd arranged a night of handball play-offs, Leah stoically agreed and kept her apprehensions to herself. On a mid-summery Wednesday night she and Jason drove up to the Bronx once again.

"Relax," Jason said to her on the drive up. "These guys are tough, but they have a strange and unpredictable code of ethics. They might take the game lightly and not try to make you look bad."

Leah chuckled. The very idea that they might patronize her was ironic. "Or, I might actually fool them all."

"Are you playing to beat them?"

"No. I'm going to play to *win*."

Jason nodded. "Good. They don't get a chance often enough to interact with someone like you, Leah. You have a normal life. You aren't within the circles of the criminal justice system."

"Well, I want to show them something else," Leah murmured thoughtfully.

Jason shot her a brief questioning glance.

"I want them to know I don't think they're worthless."

"They're still going to give you a hard time. It's part of their profile."

"I can handle it," she sighed confidently.

Leah had not played handball since junior high school, when her body was fearless and moved without feminine consciousness. She was no match for these young bloods, but she was going to try not to make a fool of herself.

On the sidelines at the gym, several of the boys were already bored and snickering with their assurance of beating her. Leah could barely contain her disappointment when Jason paired her opposite Slack. She could only guess that if Jason had, in any way, sensed her trepidation about being around the boy, he might well try to end the hostility by making them team players. Leah decided to stick with the lineup, even though it was clear that Slack was unhappy about it, too. They both knew it wasn't going to make a difference.

Leah glanced apprehensively at Jason, but of course he knew nothing of her feelings about Slack, or of the gnawing fear that he was capable of stoking. Leah fought it. She was going to play this game because now she *had* to play it. She was clearly on her own. She'd done nothing to prepare for the game because she'd hoped it would never happen. But when Leah had taken her place and the first game began, her body immediately assumed the proper form and position. She lost all awareness of herself, except that she felt her body move automatically to play the game. It was like riding a bicycle after many years; she hadn't forgotten how.

Leah had only intended her challenge to show the boys that she was game. In a way, she wanted a little of the respect they'd readily given to Jason. But she underestimated the power of their ego. Slack played not to just win but to punish her.

He gave no quarter to her being a girl, and more than once he bumped or pushed her as he stretched for the ball. Leah didn't know if it was deliberate or not, but the hard, damp contact with Slack made her feel bullied. Her heart raced. She struggled to maintain her distance. And lost the first game.

In the second Leah got knocked to the ground. An elbow jab to her side sent her to one knee, but she was up again before anyone could react, before Jason could intervene. She turned her wide, alert gaze to Slack as she regained her footing and found him daring her with his expression to do anything. Complain, retaliate, or back down. Leah played on. And lost the second game.

Jason blew the whistle.

"All right, that's it. Game. Match."

Leah walked away feeling as if every joint in her body had been hit with a stick. Her right arm especially felt numb, and her hand was slightly swollen from contact with the hard ball. Leah expected some comment, recognition, praise, from the boys. It never happened. There was only a muttered remark or two, not even meant for her to hear.

"My woman only worry 'bout sweatin' and her hair nappin' up."

"That's 'cause your woman is jive," a boy named Tall added, and the boys cracked up in laughter.

There was weak applause from the benches. Leah had no idea who or what it was for, and just then she didn't care. Her side hurt with every breath. She felt brutalized. Slack had done his best to put her in her place. And he'd succeeded. She was rattled and feeling shaky.

Leah got her tote and towel. She'd been careful this time not to have anything more in her possession than what she needed for the game. She felt a cool familiar

hand on the back of her neck, and still she jumped
skittishly. She returned to face Jason.

"You were terrific. I didn't know you were a jock.
What else can you play?"

"Oh, Old Maid. Checkers, and Scrabble. That's it,"
she responded with forced levity.

Jason frowned at her. "You okay?"

She nodded, taking a deep breath. "Yeah. Fine. I just
need—where's the ladies room?"

Jason relaxed and gently squeezed her shoulder.
"Out the door to the left, down the hall and left again."

Leah acknowledged the directions and began to
walk away.

"Leah?"

She stopped and turned, gazing blankly at him. His
voice sounded like an echo. Jason slowly approached
and stared into her face. "Did you get hurt out there?
Did Slack step over the line?"

She hesitated but then shook her head, determined
to see the night through and not to let Slack's hostility
get to her.

"I'm okay. I'll be right back."

The hallway was cool and unadorned. Just cement
walls and two naked ceiling bulbs for light. Leah could
see down the hall and it was empty. But the adjacent
junction at the end suddenly made her nervous. She
considered that maybe she didn't need to use the facili-
ties at all and could wait until she was home. She was
being silly. Nothing was going to happen to her here.
He wasn't here.

The bathroom was small and not particularly clean.
She hurried through washing her face and changing
into street clothes. She began to feel an unreasonable
anxiety building, that she was going to be trapped in
the bathroom in this unpleasant section of the hall and
no one would find her. Leah's throat felt blocked. She

scrambled to get out of the bathroom, throwing plain sense to the wind. She just wanted to get back to the dilapidated open gym where there was light . . . and Jason.

She got to the first junction and turned right. There was someone there, walking toward her. She stopped and her throat completely closed. It seemed so simple to just call out, ask who it was, but she couldn't. For there followed a long moment when the hallway changed dimensions and shape, and even the person coming toward her grew larger and larger and more threatening.

Leah stopped walking and put a hand on the wall, as if that would keep it from closing in on her. The approaching figure walked in a slow, cocky gait. She heard a cackle of laughter. Slack. Leah couldn't decide if he'd deliberately followed her, or if it was a coincidence he planned to take advantage of. She stood still, feeling trapped again. She felt overheated and had a terrible flashback of being caught in that stairwell. Leah could smell Slack. He tuned sideways to slide past her, and he suddenly stopped right in front of her. She kept her gaze down.

" 'Cuse me," Leah said, slightly breathless. She wanted to inch away toward the exit.

"You scared of me," Slack said with obvious pleasure. Leah shook her head. "No . . . I just don't like you very much."

"I don't fuckin' like you, either, bitch."

She turned from him, free of any possibility of touching him. She stumbled over her own feet and fell.

Slack laughed uproariously. "Have a nice trip?"

Leah took a deep breath and stood up again. The question inadvertently stilled the panic. She turned to face the nightmare, but there was just Slack. Beyond him, Jason came rushing forward.

"What's going on here?" Jason demanded, forcing his way through to her.

"She tripped, man." Slack chuckled unsympathetically.

Jason turned on him. "Did you try something?"

"Man, nobody did nothin' to her," he said, annoyed.

Leah touched Jason's arm to stop the accusations. She tried to laugh although it warbled.

"It . . . was my fault. Great footwork on the court; total spastic off."

Jason looked at her as if he doubted the explanation, but after a moment he turned to Slack. "Okay, this isn't a show. Where are you going?"

"To the joint," Slack responded.

"All right, go."

Slack squeezed past and disappeared around the corner, still chuckling. Jason turned back to Leah. Her eyes seemed overly bright and too wide.

"What happened out here? I thought I heard you scream."

Her smile was self-deprecating. She didn't have an explanation that could justify the disorientation. "I fell," she answered. "Just like he said."

Jason accepted that. He put an arm around her shoulder and led her back to the gym.

"You're not used to this kind of exercise. Your legs feel like rubber, right?"

Leah nodded absently. "Right," she whispered.

Everyone started to leave. The boys traveling home or escorted to shelters and group homes. To her surprise a few even acknowledged her with good-byes, after a fashion.

"Hey, Jason. You givin' me a lift home?" Slack asked when he returned to the gym.

Leah felt her exhaustion becoming heavy and oppressive. She waited.

"Not tonight. I asked Bob Chasen to drop you off."

Leah sighed. She didn't dare look to see Slack's reaction.

"Hey, Jason, man," Tall yelled after them as they made their way to the exit of the gym.

Jason looked back over his shoulder.

"She your woman?"

Leah looked up at Jason for his response and saw him blush. He smiled and reached to hold her hand. That was all.

Tall nodded. "She all right, man."

Leah was watching the efforts of a toddler as he pushed away the attempts of his young mother to direct his curiosity. He stumbled after pigeons, pulled on the grass, tried to climb into his stroller alone. He squatted to pick up a leaf from the ground and aimed it straight for his mouth.

"Uh, uh, uh," Leah heard the mother say, taking the leaf from the child and replacing it with a cracker.

The scene made Leah smile. She was both curious and fascinated. She didn't know many children, knew no one who had babies. She wondered about the couple in front of her. How had they come together? When had they decided they were in love? When had it led to a life together? And a child?

Leah turned her head and saw that Jason was also watching the threesome. She knew that his thoughts were different from her own. Did the young couple and their child remind him of Lisa and Michael? Leah tried to discern from Jason's steady gaze how much longing or regret lay behind the gray eyes.

She sighed and gave her attention absently to other people in the park. She and Jason never spoke of permanent. They never spoke of love. Leah wondered if it would ever come up. She turned her head to watch

Jason for a second, studying the movements of his lips, the way he held his cigarette. She always knew when Jason was thinking about his past and all his losses, his mistakes. Leah knew she couldn't change what had been, so she tried hard to concentrate on the now. Smiling, she reached over and pulled the remaining length from Jason's mouth and tossed it away. Jason glanced at her, incredulous, but flopped back down with a shrug and chuckled.

"You're going to stunt your growth," Leah said breezily.

Jason rolled onto his side, facing her, propping his head in his hand. "I never realized you were so bossy," he murmured.

"I'm not bossy. But I'm not going to waste my time on you if you're determined to die of cancer," Leah said tartly.

Jason's chuckle was dry and ironic. "That's the least of my worries. Lots of other things can do me in, sweetheart."

He rarely used endearments and when he did, Leah always felt that that was when she was closest to him. She could feel Jason's gaze upon her. Leah turned to meet the scrutiny and found a lazy, warm interest.

"When was the first time you fell in love?" Jason asked abruptly.

The question surprised Leah and made her wonder why he asked. She arched a brow. "Still trying to find out all my dark secrets?"

"Do you have any?"

"None that are interesting. Nothing I could be blackmailed with." She sighed inwardly at the thought of Billy, then Philip, Ron, and Allen. "Anyway, it wasn't love. It was infatuation. A deep crush that I thought at the time I would never recover from."

She turned her head to look at Jason. He was watching her intently. How had the question of love come to mind?

"When did you first have sex with a girl?" Leah blurted out suddenly.

For a split second Jason was stunned, then he burst out laughing. "That's not what I asked you."

"But I want to know."

He continued to laugh, shaking his head. Then he shrugged. "I don't know. About sixteen, I guess. I did it with a cashier at the local market. I remember I kept going back for soda, for cigarettes, anything, for three days just to make sure I was reading her invitation right. It happened after she got off work one night. In the back of her car. In the store's parking lot. She was twenty and gave me a lot of wet dreams for months."

Belatedly Jason looked sheepish and gave Leah a wry glance. "I guess you don't need all the details."

"I didn't know boys needed a reason to have wet dreams," she murmured, looking at her hands. She saw smooth brown skin with slender, tapered fingers. Leah imagined that the cashier was probably blond, real or otherwise, with freckles and pink breasts.

"A ready, willing, and able older woman helps a lot," Jason commented dryly. He sighed softly and looked off into the distance of the park. "The first time I thought I was in love was with Lisa. We met in high school. I'd drive her to classes, we'd meet for lunch, she helped me with English comp, baked me ginger snaps."

Leah closed her eyes. "Sounds romantic and . . . sweet," she said.

"We were too young to know anything. I proposed to her during halftime in the last football game my senior year. We went for pizza afterward to celebrate."

Leah wrinkled her nose.

Jason grinned and nodded. "Told you I didn't know anything."

Leah suddenly felt tension spring to life under her rib cage. She wished the subject hadn't come up. She looked at Jason, wondering where the conversation was leading. Was he trying to tell her something? She forced a light laugh so that her fears wouldn't show.

"Only been in love once in your life?"

Jason lit a fresh cigarette. "I don't know. I'm still trying to figure out what love is. Sometimes . . ." He left the rest of his thought hanging.

Leah's tension sank to her stomach. "Well, you're still one up on me. Never been married, never been engaged. Never been asked."

Jason stared into space. "Ever have fantasies?" he asked softly.

"Lots of them."

"Yeah. I guess girls do," he murmured teasingly, letting his index finger stroke and outline her chin. "But . . . I think I was a big disappointment to Lisa. She didn't think I was romantic . . . or sweet. I had to grow up before I knew about romantic."

There was no sadness, no regret in Jason's reflections. Leah could tell he was just reviewing the ways inexperience, hope, and love can lead a person into things, disappoint you and ruin your plans . . . and then save the day.

"It's doubtful I've learned very much in all these years."

Leah shook her head slowly and smiled at Jason. "You're wrong, you know. You show real potential, Jason Horn."

"You think so?" he asked. Then he grew quiet and pensive. "I don't know. Maybe I'll never get it right. Maybe it's too late."

Leah didn't answer right away, because along with the jitters in her nervous system that had been set in motion by the whole subject of love, she hoped desperately that Jason was wrong.

There had been a funeral for a fallen officer, and Jason was in full uniform. The service had been held at nine o'clock in the morning at St. Patrick's Cathedral. Whatever personal differences might exist between officers, today they were all united, drawn together by the death of one of their own. The tragedy of being killed in the line of duty happened just often enough during the year to make each of them angry, and vulnerable.

In summer blues they were dotted up and down Fifth Avenue, the rest of the citizens diverted to other streets. The enforced segregation made them all feel even more insular.

Joe and Jason had come in from Brooklyn in a black unmarked car, parking it illegally on Forty-eighth Street. Afterward Jason asked to be driven to Second Avenue to the building where Leah worked. Jason hated these funeral processions. It took too long afterward to stop thinking, *it could have been me.* He'd only ever been to three of these in all the years he'd been a cop. But this funeral was the first time that Jason felt the need to admit to someone he got scared and wanted reassurance instead of cutting himself off and working it out in isolation. He had no idea when the need had changed.

It was Gail's idea to organize a small dinner party so that the two couples could get together. Leah didn't say no, but she also thought that nothing good could possibly come from putting Jason, Allen, and her sister together in the same room. To put off a meeting, however, which Leah knew to be inevitable, would give the wrong signal. So she hoped against hope that all would go smoothly.

When Jason and Allen finally came face to face, there was a tentative and cool appraisal on both sides. They shook hands and tried to stare each other down, but neither would give in. Jason sensed, as only an adversary can, that Allen's obvious disdain of him was more than male posturing.

"I've heard a lot about you," Allen said by way of introduction.

"Sorry. Haven't heard a thing about you," Jason replied.

After that they understood each other perfectly.

Gail stood next to Allen, holding his arm. Leah was afraid to touch Jason, afraid that Gail would say something cutting, as was her wont. But after introductions Jason turned to slip an arm around her waist. He gave her a quick kiss. The kind where his mouth lightly captured hers and then slowly let go.

"Hi," he whispered. His gaze was probing but warm and personal.

Leah returned his smile. But she could detect Gail and Allen's disapproval.

"Easy, big guy," Gail whispered with a smile, taking Allen's hand and leading him to the sofa. They sat and she draped herself against him, stroking Allen's arm. "That was only the starting bell. It's going to be a long night."

"You know," Allen began in a conversational voice, "When we heard Leah was seeing a white cop we got worried. We thought maybe she'd lost it."

Jason let his jaw tighten as he regarded Allen openly. He saw an attractive and strongly built black man with presence and self-assurance. But Jason also discerned arrogance and intolerance. Just like Gail.

Jason slowly sat forward in his chair. "Look, I've already been through this. I don't think I want to be interrogated a second time."

Allen leaned forward. "Take it easy, my man," he said as if he were talking to someone who was about to become uncontrollable. "I'm just telling you how it comes down."

Jason's chuckle was dry and cynical. "You haven't a clue how it comes down. It's not Leah you're concerned about."

"Oooops," Gail said softly.

Allen's eyes narrowed. He adjusted his glasses. "What does that mean?"

"Here," Leah said quickly, pressing a beer into Jason's hand. For a moment their eyes met. She didn't want Jason to have to act a certain way, or to be careful . . . or to be compromised. She didn't want to be attacked, either. And Leah didn't want another testy evening served up with the baked Virginia ham.

Jason relaxed and nodded imperceptibly. He sat back again with his beer. He took a thoughtful sip. Leah turned away to serve drinks to Gail and Allen.

Jason put the beer down and took his time lighting a cigarette. "Why does it bother you? Me and Leah?"

Allen frowned, not disguising his resentment. "You know why. It isn't acceptable. We're her family. We have a right to be concerned," he voiced authoritatively.

Leah set down the tray sharply. "Excuse me?" she directed to Allen with an affronted look.

Allen sat back, sighing in exasperation. He took a deep breath and mulishly became silent.

Leah stood with her hands poised on her hips. "I want you all to stop talking about me as if I'm invisible, okay?" She looked pointedly at Allen. "You are not family. Let us not forget from whence this all came."

"Round one," Gail whispered. "Isn't this fun?"

"Stop it, Gail," Allen said in irritation.

"I'm going to check on dinner," Leah said. With an annoyed jerk of her head she left the room.

"What kind of beat do you work?" Allen asked. And then he smirked. "I bet you even have a black partner. Guys like you always do."

Jason began to grin. He liked the way Leah had suddenly spoken up. For some reason it made him feel as if he had firmer ground to stand on and even more reason not to take this hazing. Allen had Gail. Jason was elated that Leah had decided she would have him. He hadn't gone through all those years with Joe without learning something about the black male ego. He also had the satisfaction of knowing that Joe wouldn't like Allen any better than he did.

"Nobody works a beat anymore. I do the usual stuff. And I work with kids."

"Work with them?" Allen repeated skeptically. "I guess that's better than shooting them."

Jason's body stiffened for a moment, an old ghost moving silently past him. He narrowed his eyes against the cigarette smoke. "The idea is not to shoot anybody. People don't listen to you if you threaten them. Especially kids."

"I don't think I could be a cop," Allen announced, bored.

Jason nodded. "That's probably true. Always best to know your limitations."

Watching Allen and Jason in conversation, Leah wondered if Allen would be so bold as to mention their past relationship. She was glad, however, that Gail was being reasonably civil, and didn't seem inclined to join in as Allen and Jason circled like predators around one another.

Gail and Allen started talking to each other while basically ignoring Jason. Part of it was just rudeness, but Jason also realized that they really didn't have anything to say to him. There was no common ground, no common interest, beyond Leah. So Jason left them and followed Leah into the dining room, where she was placing napkins on the table. He took hold of her arms, turning her to face him.

"Don't work so hard," he teased affectionately. "This is only dinner."

"No, it isn't. I think it's setting the stage for an exhibition match," she muttered.

"I already know how your sister feels about me. Allen is just busting my chops because he thinks he has to. I think it has something to do with black pride."

Leah looked sad. "Why do we keep going through this?" she asked plaintively.

"Because Gail's your sister. She's family. You were the one who said you can't divorce your family. So don't. Go for a separation instead."

"I'm not always good at putting space between them and us."

Jason gathered her into a loose embrace. "That's easy enough. Just stay close to me."

Later that night it wasn't difficult for Jason to persuade Leah to come back home with him. As a matter of fact, he insisted on it. As emotionally drained as Leah felt after going twelve rounds with Allen and Gail, she much preferred the rest of the night with Jason to warding off sneak attacks from her sister.

Leah paid no attention to Jason's silence on the drive to his apartment and got only vague responses to her observations on the evening. She was glad it had been done because now she could be glad that it was over. For the first time since that embarrassing encounter at Christmas Leah began to feel free of the past. It had not occurred to her until that moment that Allen's rejection and betrayal, a double whammy, had so bent her ego out of shape. But now she had Jason. They had each other.

Leah stole a long, considering look at Jason's profile. She could see the muscles flexing in his jaw. There were slight crow's feet at the corner of his eyes, indicating weariness. His hair fanned over his ear and hugged the strong column of his neck. He needed a haircut.

Just then Jason reached out and took hold of her hand. His fingers closed tightly around hers, and Leah felt a thrill of possessiveness, a sense of belonging. A smile curved her mouth. She felt so hopeful. So happy.

At the apartment they were no sooner in the door than Jason roughly pulled her into his arms, kissing her with a demand and force that left her breathless. Rarely had they ever made love just as release of energy. Rarely had Leah felt as if Jason's attention was one-sided or routine. But he seemed angry and it changed the balance. Nonetheless, Leah melted against him and Jason slowly gentled his touch. His hands searched for the fastening to her dress, sliding the dress off her shoulders.

She lifted her hands to his face, but Jason moved his head aside impatiently. "What's Allen to you?" he asked bluntly.

Leah felt her stomach take a nose dive. She stepped back out of Jason's arms, and he let her go. She pulled the dress up again, looking at him doubtfully. But Leah knew she had nothing to hide.

"I used to date Allen. Long before I ever met you. We saw each other for more than two years. I told you it wasn't serious a long time ago."

Jason let his body lean against a wall. "Two years . . ." he repeated.

He looked at Leah, and he was unsure of himself. Jason suddenly realized that there had been another man before him. Black. Of course, black. Allen. The one who'd spent most of the evening trying to stomp all over his manhood, his color. Jason knew he'd been able to repel the hostility because he believed that he'd proven himself to Leah, showed her that he cared. Jason thought that that would have made them safe. They wouldn't have to fight the world anymore because he and Leah had each other. But now Jason considered that that wasn't a sure thing, either.

He continued to stare at Leah and saw also someone who was stronger than she thought she was. She was more than pretty; suddenly she was full and sensual and beautiful. She was talented and self-sufficient and probably didn't really need him at all. It hit him hard, like a blow to the gut, that he could lose her.

Leah turned away, her expression hurt and unsure. She walked toward the window. She didn't understand what Jason's question meant, or why he wanted to know about Allen.

"Did you love him?" Jason murmured.

"Why do you want to know?"

"Did you?" he persisted.

"That's unfair," Leah murmured.

"No, it's not. I told you about Lisa. You knew about the other women. None of them exist for me anymore." Jason walked halfway across the room toward her. "Did you love him?"

"No . . ." Leah finally answered, shaking her head, not looking directly at him. Couldn't Jason tell by the way she was with him that Allen didn't matter? Had never mattered as much? "Allen was someone I knew, like your Peggy, or one of the others. He was important to me for a while. But I didn't love him." Leah sat down in the chair by the window. "Allen wasn't in love with me, either."

Jason moved closer. He could feel the knot easing in his chest. "Leah . . ."

"I came home on Christmas Eve and found them together. Him and Gail."

"Leah . . ." He pulled her to her feet. He ran his hands across her shoulders and up the sides of her neck. He kissed her once. Twice. "Don't say any more. Please."

"Allen didn't want me—"

"It doesn't matter. It doesn't matter." Jason pulled her into his arms.

But in a way he couldn't understand yet, he knew it did matter.

Chapter Thirteen

Early in July Jason managed to get tickets for a concert and arranged to take about twenty young male
teens from his sports program. There were four other
off-duty officers as chaperons besides Jason, two of
them female. Leah had never met female officers from
Jason's precinct before, and it surprised her that she
still had nothing in common with them. Not that they
were unfriendly or kept themselves apart from her, it
was just that they, too, were totally focused on being
cops. And, Leah reasoned, they had not necessarily
volunteered expecting a fun evening. Like Jason, what
they were doing was extraordinary.

The music was not just loud, it was deafening. Leah
escaped halfway through to the ladies' room, where the
wall of music seemed to come right up to the door.
When she exited she was in no particular hurry to
return to her seat. At the concession stand she pur-
chased a soda and stood sipping as she idly watched
the crowds of young people, musing over the outrageous outfits, the messy hairstyles, the patterns of pairing off.

She finished her soda and turned to reenter the gate
leading to her seat. Near the men's room she spotted
Slack and two others from the group, standing in
closed ranks. Leah guessed immediately that they were
engaged in something Jason would not approve of. But

Leah could not actually see what they were up to, only the movements of their hands, their joking and sly attitudes. One boy handed a lightweight black jacket to Slack, who quickly rolled it down to a small bundle and stuffed it under his armpit. The third boy removed his beaked cap, which he'd been wearing backward. In a second it was being replaced. Something exchanged hands and was covertly pocketed.

A number ended and applause and screaming followed. Deciding not to linger any longer, Leah returned to her seat. Jason had been looking out for her. When he spotted her, he quickly stood and the frown lifted from his brow.

"I was beginning to wonder. Either there was a line or someone tried to hit on you." His hand on her waist guided Leah past him and into her seat.

"It was the first."

Jason put his arm across the back of her seat. "As long as you didn't try to use the men's room instead. I've heard of it happening."

Leah's smile faltered as she thought of the three boys outside the men's room, huddled in some sort of private negotiations. "There was a line there, too."

Slack and the other two boys returned, taking seats almost directly behind Leah and Jason. Their presence there made her nervous, but she had to admit they were unlikely to try anything. A quick glance at Jason showed him to be alert as always, but even he didn't have eyes in the back of his head.

"Aren't you concerned that one day some of these guys are just going to take a walk and not come back?"

Jason's crooked grin was indulgent. "And go where? Their circle of family and friends is pretty thin, and I know most of them. The choice is me or a public institute."

"You don't think you're too easy with them?"

Jason smiled and rubbed her shoulder. "I'm not as lenient as it looks sometimes. They don't get away with much."

For a moment Leah was tempted to ask Jason what would happen if one of the boys was caught stealing, but she held back, knowing that Jason would question her until the details spilled out. She didn't know for sure who'd taken her purse folder the night of the handball tournament. Leah simply recognized that given the opportunity, all the boys were suspect.

"What would you let them get away with?" she tried to ask over the noise.

"We catch them with beer or Champale sometimes. I can deal with that." Jason turned his head to regard her closely. He ran the back of his knuckles down her cheek. "Won't let them hurt anyone if I can help it. I won't let them fight. Too many of them keep grudges."

A drum solo started up from the set on stage, and Jason visibly winced.

"Not a great place for conversation. Do you like the music?"

Leah stuck a finger in one ear. "What music?"

Jason laughed.

When the concert was over, the chaperons and Jason ordered the boys to remain seated until most of their section had been emptied. Then they were all ushered out together. Leah was among the last to get up. Reaching for her purse, she saw the swatch of fabric wedged behind the seat one row up from where she'd sat. She pulled it free. It was a jacket.

It felt heavy and Leah could feel bulkiness in the two pockets. She stared at the coat, unwilling to investigate further. It was the jacket Slack had taken.

"Leah?"

She started and looked up as Jason called her name.

Then Slack pushed his way past Jason, headed for the seats.

"Almost forget my jacket, man." But he stopped when he saw the jacket in Leah's hands.

Jason hung back and stood with his hands poised on his hips. Leah watched them both.

"Is that your jacket?" Jason asked Slack smoothly.

Slack looked at Leah and his expression grew stony and cold. Leah held out the jacket to him. "It was on the floor under the seat," she said, feeling foolish. But she could see by Jason's expression, and by Slack's restlessness that he was about to be given up.

Slack looked at the extended coat. His head tilted in disgust. "Aw, man," he muttered, and cursed under his breath. He turned to glance once at Jason, who waited and watched. He tried to take the jacket from Leah casually, but he had no orientation as to how she was holding it, and when she let go, several small items fell from the pockets.

"Fuck," Slack exploded as the glycine packets lay at his feet. He glared at Leah.

Jason came to stand right next to Slack. He took hold of one of his arms. "Go ahead," Jason ordered, pointing at the floor. "Pick them up."

Slack shook his head. "They ain't mine, man."

"All right," Jason said as he grabbed Slack's arm and maneuvered back to the rest of the group. "Everybody gets shaken down."

There were protests, but Leah stood and watched as the five police officers acted in an organized way to efficiently and very carefully frisk each boy in turn.

"See that. She tell you some shit, and you believe her," Slack complained, jabbing a finger in the air at Leah. "Just like up in the Bronx. I *knew* you was trouble. Damn! Bitch is tryin' to toast me, just 'cause you doin' her . . ."

Jason stood in front of Slack. Leah was mesmerized by Slack's reasoning and how easily he could blame everyone else for his troubles. And she could detect Jason's disappointment and his regret at what he had to do now.

"It wasn't her jacket or her deal, Slack."

In the search nearly a dozen vials of crack were found, several sticks of marijuana, two knives, and assorted other homemade, pocketable weapons. And one small handgun. The boys were separated into two groups; the ones innocent were escorted back to group homes or shelters by three of the officers. The others, four teens and Slack, were held for backup and transport back to the precinct house. As Slack was being handcuffed, he jerked away from the arresting officers, only to be grabbed roughly by the arm and pulled into obedience. Leah stood perfectly still when Slack stared at her menacingly. She could guess that his opinion of her had not been helped by the night's episode.

"Bitch," he hissed suddenly. "You just wait. I'm gonna git your ass."

He spoke with such vehemence that for a moment everyone turned to stare at her. Jason casually stepped forward so that he stood between Slack and Leah.

"Shut up, Slack. Take him out in the corridor to wait," Jason ordered coolly.

Leah watched Jason deal with the concert hall house security, curious onlookers, and the remaining officers. They had no choice, given the number of recovered weapons, but to handcuff the boys detained.

And then Jason escorted her out of the stands.

"I'm sorry, I didn't realize—"

"It's not your fault," Jason reassured her.

"It's not yours, either. I know how hard you tried, Jason."

His mouth was grim. "Maybe too hard. Maybe Slack didn't try hard enough."

"He just didn't care."

"It's too bad he didn't. He's running out of chances."

"What's going to happen?"

"They've all violated the terms of their release. They'll get reprocessed and—"

Someone yelled out another threat to her. Leah watched the cold distancing in Jason's eyes and knew he felt to blame for that as well.

"Do you think he means it?" Leah asked in a small voice.

"What?"

"About . . . getting me. He thinks I ratted on him."

Jason's expression was guarded. He rubbed his hand across her shoulders. "It's just a threat, don't worry about it. He won't get a chance to do anything. And I can't help him this time."

Leah turned to him and gave him a brief hug. "Why don't I go on home? I'm in the way here and I'm starting to feel like . . ."

He nodded in agreement.

Leah swallowed and lowered her gaze so that he couldn't see her reaction. After a brief word to the others Jason led her down to the main entrance. There was no conversation as he searched the streets until spotting a yellow medallion and whistled to the driver to stop.

Leah got obligingly into the cab, but she didn't really want to go home. She didn't want to leave Jason right then. She was afraid to. She didn't want either of them to be alone. She had seen Jason work hard to gain the boys' trust, to direct them in making better choices for themselves. In her mind that made him special. But again she'd seen the part of his life that made her insecure and frightened. Jason lived too close to danger. Leah wasn't sure if he recognized it anymore as danger.

He slammed the back door of the cab shut and leaned on the lowered window ledge toward her. She didn't want to let him go yet, and she knew that she had to.

"Do you want me to wait for you?"

Jason thought about it but then shook his head wearily. "I don't know. I'm going to be awhile. I'm sorry about tonight."

Leah tried to smile as she briefly covered his hand. "I think you're more disappointed than I am. You had a lot invested in those guys. I was afraid of them."

"You never showed it," Jason said in some surprise.

Her smile got warmer. "I didn't want to disappoint you."

Jason looked at her steadily for a long time. It was as if he had suddenly gained a revelation from her admission. He turned his hand over to quickly grab and squeeze Leah's.

"I'll call as soon as I can," Jason said as the cab began to pull away.

Leah didn't turn around to wave at him, convinced that he would have already walked back to his responsibilities. And she was certain that if she turned and didn't see Jason, she would only start to cry. She was suddenly afraid she was going to lose him.

Leah wasn't sure if Jason really understood her fear of Slack. Maybe it was unreasonable, but she believed every threat the teen had hurled at her. She was glad when Jason finally called her, even though it was just after midnight. She waited for him to come. When he arrived, he got right into bed with her to hug closely and whisper in the dark. He was exhausted and Leah knew he was concerned about his failed efforts to avoid arraignment for the boys. They fell asleep in each other's arms, Leah particularly feeling vulnerable.

But Slack's venom grew to monster proportions, and he replaced the man in her dream. She was awakened by Jason just before dawn. He sat up alertly in bed and pulled her onto his lap and held her. Then he insisted on knowing why a dream held so much power over her.

So Leah told him everything.

Jason listened without interruption, studying her face, absently moving a strand of hair or touching her arm. When she was finished purging herself, when she'd said how she'd faked a bad head cold so as to call in sick and stay home in bed for a week afterward, he kissed her forehead and pressed her face close to his chest. He let her cry, and it gave him a moment in which to think. He didn't know what to say.

Jason was incredulous that Leah had never told anyone, not even her father or sister.

"Why?" he asked.

"I don't know. I thought . . . maybe it was my fault."

"For God's sake, Leah."

"I should have known better. I do. Jason, I'm not stupid. I know how to take care of myself. I know that . . . I know—"

"Okay, okay. Shhh. It's okay."

He rocked her, and knew it wasn't enough. And he was surprised at the amount of fear that now pumped through him. If something had really happened back then, he never would have met Leah. Or if he had, she never would have trusted him. And if anything happened to her now . . .

Jason knew better than anyone that only sheer coincidence had saved Leah from a tragedy. He knew that someone being a victim was often random. Sometimes nothing more than dumb luck determined whether someone lived or died on the streets of the city . . . or in deserted stairwells.

Except that Leah was not just anyone. Not to him. She was not anonymous, not just another constituent and part of his job. The truth was, there was no way he could keep her safe. It terrified him.

Leah could feel the pressure of Jason's arms tightening around her. "Jason? What?" she asked.

He was very slow in answering. "I was just thinking. I just wish that I—"

Leah put her fingers lightly to his lips to stop his words. "I'll be careful from now on. The dream will eventually go away." It felt good not to have it a secret anymore. It felt good that Jason understood. And then she had a revelation. "Does it . . . bother you?"

He'd never thought about it before. The people he was supposed to protect from being crime victims needed his empathy. It rarely was enough anyway, and it couldn't be sustained. What people mostly wanted from him was just his authority when it suited them, or his absence when it didn't. He realized he was seen as a necessary evil, the one person between an individual and injury, possibly even death.

Jason looked at Leah. It did something strange inside him to think of how close she'd come to being destroyed. For an instant he tried to remove himself from the imagined scenario of that happening. He'd get over it; after a war and Lisa and Michael and God only knew what else to come, he could get over anything. But then all the warmth drained from his body at the idea of Leah being hurt.

He nodded silently in answer to her question, and hoped that, for now, Leah wouldn't ask why.

She didn't. Instead she curled up into his arms. She heard him sigh as he stroked her hair. She smiled to herself.

It was better than anything else he might have said.

"Well, what do you think?" Jill asked.

Leah again read the inter-office memo that Jill had given her. It was a suggestion for an exhibition to be mounted in the lobby gallery of their office building. She was being asked to do a one-woman show of her artwork. It was Jill's idea.

Leah glanced at Jill. "Why me?"

"Because everyone thought it would be different to highlight someone's work that wasn't directly related to book design or promotion. You know. Sort of a showcase. Everyone loves your caricatures."

Leah nodded absently. Whenever she and Jill spoke these days, there was a sense of superficiality in the conversation. Not that it was strictly all business or unfriendly, but it wasn't as personal as it used to be between them. Leah had not forgotten Jill's opinion about her dating someone white. They had not spoken about it since.

"I know you've been working on your pictures. I'm sure there's more than enough to frame for a show. It could be fun. It's a great way for people to see how talented you are."

Leah pursed her mouth. "That's generous of you."

Jill shrugged. "It's good for the department to get some attention. How about it?"

Leah carefully folded the memo. "Okay. I'll do it."

"Great," Jill said, relief evident in her voice. "I guess I should let you know that I told the director there would be no problem. I told him you'd agree."

Leah got her purse from the drawer of her supply cabinet. "What would you have done if I'd said no?"

Jill laughed nervously. "Begged and pleaded. I know

that sometimes I put my foot in my mouth. Off to lunch?"

"Yes," Leah said, walking toward the door. "It's so nice outside I thought I'd get a salad or something and eat in one of the parks nearby."

"Mind if I join you?" Leah turned around to gaze silently at her. "I thought we could talk some more about the show."

"You did?" Leah asked. Not so much suspicious as curious.

Jill sighed. "Look, I miss not having lunch together. I miss not gossiping. We used to get along."

"We still get along," Leah said, turning to face her.

Jill shook her head. "It's polite. There's still a lot of distance between us. I know it's my fault. I shouldn't have said what I did about . . . that man you're dating."

Leah shrugged. "If that was how you felt . . ."

"But I never asked you what he was like. I never asked you how you met or how you were doing. I should have listened more instead of running my mouth."

Leah's smile was understanding. "Jason is a terrific man. And we're doing very well, thank you."

"I'm really sorry about what I said, Leah. It was just thoughtless."

"Don't worry about it. Where should we go?"

"By the U.N." They left the studio, heading for the elevators. "What's he like?" Jill asked eagerly. "What does he do?"

Leah couldn't help laughing, knowing the trouble that a three-word answer, he's a cop, could cause. "You'll meet him at this exhibition," she said.

She knew that Jason's presence and personality would speak louder than her words.

Leah sat next to Jason on the front steps to the brownstone and watched the sidewalk and street games of the neighborhood kids. It had become part of the summer routine when Jason brought her home after a day or evening out together. Mostly it was just fun to watch the adolescent antics. But every now and then something else was going on behind Jason's alert gray eyes and his quiet, thoughtful consideration of other people's children. It was getting dark now, and one by one the children were being called home. Jason finished his cigarette and leaned back with his elbows on the steps behind him.

Leah knew something was on his mind, and all evening she had waited for him to confide in her. She leaned back, too, and slipped her arm through his. "Okay. I think it's expensive, but I'm willing to offer a dollar."

Jason looked at her blankly, confirming Leah's opinion that he was preoccupied.

"What?"

She tapped his temple. "For your thoughts, Jay."

He arched a brow. "Thoughts used to be a lot cheaper than that."

"Inflation. And some thoughts are worth more from some people than from others."

"Thanks. But I think you're getting a poor bargain."

Leah grabbed his hand and held it. "If it's about me, I can take it," she said lightly, even though she was apprehensive that his thoughts were somehow connected to her.

Jason squeezed her hand. "It's about Slack."

Leah felt relief flow through her body. "What'd he do now?"

Jason shrugged. "I don't know. The trouble is, no one knows where he is."

"I thought he was in a minimum-security facility upstate."

"He was. Until a few days ago, that is. He apparently

took that long walk you used to ask me about. No one has seen him. If he's in the city he's being very smart about keeping a low profile."

Leah wasn't sure she believed that. Slack was out there somewhere. He was free. And she was still afraid of him.

"Are you still worried about him?"

Jason pursed his lips and slowly shook his head. "Not as much as I am about what he might do out there." He sighed deeply. "Slack is volatile. Unpredictable. I hate to admit it, but with him I probably bit off more than I could chew."

She stroked his arm. "You weren't wrong to want to help him, Jay. It's Slack's loss that he didn't take it."

Jason grinned at her and pulled his arm free to search for his cigarettes. "You're really good for my ego, Leah Downey."

She started to ask jokingly what else she was good for, but Jason's frown returned and he busied himself with lighting a cigarette.

"What else?" she quietly asked, but referring to other things that might be on his mind.

Jason's glance faltered and he half turned so that his back was against the banister. "I never used to be so easy to read," he murmured.

Leah looked right at him. "I'm presumptuous enough to think I might know you better than most people."

Jason nodded briefly. He stroked his free hand down her arm and covered her hand. "I agree." He looked at the burning cigarette and then out at the street where, just a half hour earlier, a dozen children's voices had been heard at play.

"I have to make a trip to Pennsylvania this weekend. It's about some property I own there."

Leah heard the two sentences and understood them perfectly. She also instantly realized what Jason was not telling her. The weekend also had to do with Michael. It had to do with his ex-wife. And he wasn't going to ask her to come along.

She, too, looked out over the empty street and saw that it was now as it had been almost a year earlier. She and Allen had arrived right below where she and Jason now sat. Allen and Jason had collided somehow, and a bottle of wine had broken. Leah had looked into the gray eyes of a man who, she was to learn, was honest, strong, and caring—and worth caring about. Someone worth loving. She didn't have to know Jason's reasons or his motives for going. She needed to know only that he had a strong enough reason to return.

"Is there anything I can do to help?" Leah asked.

Jason slowly extinguished his cigarette. He reached toward her and placed his hand around the back of her neck. He leaned even closer and captured Leah's mouth, kissing her sweetly and slowly, and with a great deal of lingering tenderness.

"Wait for me," Jason whispered against her mouth.

"I will," she answered.

It was the easiest promise Leah had ever made in her life. Especially since she already knew she was going to love Jason Horn forever.

When Jason had received the letter from Lisa's lawyer, he'd been immediately suspicious. He'd been pretty regular with child-support payments right up until Michael's death. And he'd maintained alimony until Lisa had finally gotten settled into her own career as a private-duty nurse five years ago. So the letter brought a surprise Jason had not considered before. Lisa was getting married again, to a doctor. And the house she'd lived in, had raised their son in, and which Jason had helped to finance, was to be sold and the proceeds split between them. His presence was needed to sign the transfer papers and other documents.

On the Friday afternoon that Jason left New York, it rained. A sticky, humid rain that made the city air smelly and thick and gave him an overall feeling of ill humor. He didn't want to make this trip. He wasn't ready for it because it had to do with much more than just the sale of a house. It had to do with finally ending a relationship that had produced one child, and a lot of acrimonious feelings. It had to do with repair and forgiveness and letting go. And, Jason hoped, it would finally give him the go-ahead signal for what he knew he wanted to do with the rest of his life.

The rain had stopped by the time he reached Kutztown. By five in the afternoon he was driving through the center of Pine Grove. It was small and charming and slow. It seemed a very different world here than New York, or even Harrisburg, where he and Lisa had both been raised. Jason felt a stranger in such a place. From the local pharmacy he called Lisa to let her know he'd arrived and to give the name of his hotel.

"You don't have to stay at a hotel," Lisa said expansively. "You can stay in the extra room. I don't mind."

Jason didn't particularly like that idea either, but it had nothing to do with not wanting to be around Lisa. He hesitated for so long that she made an impatient gesture.

"Look, it really doesn't matter to me, but you're going to have to come out tomorrow anyway. The appraiser from the bank is due, as well as a P.E."

"I don't want to get in the way, make you uncomfortable."

Lisa's laugh was amused. "David has a healthy ego, but he knows why you're here."

"I'm not concerned with David's ego. I'll be there in twenty minutes."

Jason hung up but didn't let go of the receiver. What was it Leah had said to him this morning? If he got homesick he could always call her to hear a friendly voice. He wanted to. But Jason decided against it. It was early yet. He decided to save Leah's offer, because before the weekend was over he probably was going to need it.

The modest cape was on an acre of land and set back from the road. Over the years Lisa had added gardening to her repertoire of domestic skills, and the property was beautifully landscaped. Jason pulled into the narrow driveway behind Lisa's car, although there was another parked along the side of the road out front. As he turned off the engine, he was stunned to see the log swing still attached to a lower branch of an old maple tree. He had put it up himself for Michael twelve years ago.

Jason sat staring at it until he heard the kitchen door open and Lisa step out under the entrance light. He turned his head at the sound, but couldn't make out her features. The light over the door shone brightly on her blond hair.

"Jason? Why are you just sitting there?"

He decided it was best not to try to answer. He stepped out of the car and got his nylon duffel from the backseat. He walked through the door behind Lisa, feeling very displaced and alien. He wished the weekend was already over. Lisa continued through the kitchen into the sitting room. The house was certainly bigger than his apartment, but to Jason it felt tiny and confined. He'd not spent time here for more than a dozen occasions in about as many years.

A man stood up from the sofa as he entered behind Lisa. She immediately crossed the room and stood next to him.

Jason watched the pairing with amused sarcasm and

knew that Lisa had arranged this on purpose. The other man wore aviator-type glasses, was slightly shorter than Jason and thin in an intellectual way.

"I'm David Flanders," he introduced himself.

Jason dropped his duffel and extended his hand. David's grip was firm and forthright, and Jason noticed how Lisa gazed up at him with loving attention.

"Nice to meet you," Jason responded politely.

"David is a prediatrician," Lisa volunteered proudly.

"And Lisa tells me you're a—a—"

"Cop," Jason said smoothly. He glanced sharply at his ex-wife. "Someone has to be."

"Nine-millimeter?" David asked, pointing at the gun belt Jason still had strapped on.

"Right."

"Jason, I've left something for you to eat. You can take the room in the back." Lisa retrieved her purse from the coffee table. "David and I had plans for the evening."

"I guess I won't have to worry about Lisa's safety with you around, right?" David joked.

" 'Night, Jason," Lisa said, heading for the front door before Jason could respond for himself.

He remained standing in the center of the room, listening to the sounds of the car disappear down the road. He slowly took off the gun belt, picked up his bag, and headed for the guest room. He walked straight past Michael's room, where the door was closed. On the outside hanging from the doorknob was a sign that read, "Don't come in unless you're carrying a payoff."

The guest room was stuffy and hot. Jason immediately opened all the windows to admit the cool night air and gentle breeze. He wandered silently around the house, again avoiding Michael's room but turning on the light to glance into Lisa's. He stood at the door and looked over the frilly orderliness, the rose and pink and lace of the curtains and comforter. There were framed photos of Michael and David on her bureau. Jason turned out the light and walked into the kitchen. He was tired and not particularly hungry.

He wasn't surprised that Lisa had no beer and apparently had not thought to get him any. Jason settled for a can of diet soda and went to stand outside the front door to smoke and listen to the peaceful night. He had no feelings one way or the other about Lisa marrying again. She was finally getting the kind of man she thought deserved her. Jason had no doubt that she and David would be happy together.

Jason finished the soda and two cigarettes, waiting until the stars were like specks of white paint against the black ceiling of the sky. Then he wearily made his way to the now cooled back room, where he stripped and lay naked on the bed, wide awake and staring at the walls.

After a while he heard the car return, and a giggly and gently amorous good night followed in the sitting room. The car finally left and Lisa could be heard entering her room and closing the door. It was a very long time before Jason could fall to sleep. He lay for a while, considering that after this weekend he might never see Lisa again. It didn't bother him. He only knew that the sooner their business was settled, the quicker he could get back home to Leah.

"That's a lot of money," Jason said.

"I thought you'd be surprised," Lisa said with a satisfied smile. "Of course, you could just buy me out and keep the house."

Jason shook his head. "It's too small."

"What difference does that matter? You're not married. You don't have kids."

Jason let the remark go and had the satisfaction of

watching Lisa blush. He turned to the lawyer. "Where do you want me to sign?"

"That's it? Don't you want to read that, or do you have any questions?"

"No," Jason said succinctly. He took the papers and, without looking them over, signed them. "I don't think Lisa is out to cheat me."

"Well, the house turned out to be a very smart investment. It appreciated almost a hundred and fifty percent."

Jason's smile was wry. He wondered if Lisa had learned that from David.

"What are you going to do with your money?" she asked as they left the lawyer's more than an hour later.

Jason walked her to her car. "I might buy some land and build my own house. I always wanted to do that."

Lisa shook her head. "Still daydreaming. It's too bad you don't have anyone to share the dreams with, Jason. You're not getting any younger, you know."

Jason watched her get settled in her seat and put on the safety belt. He stood back with his hands in the front pockets of his jeans. His smile was patient. "I never said there was no one to share my dreams with."

She shrugged, uninterested. "I'm meeting David for lunch. But we need to make some decisions about Michael's things," she said tightly.

"I know. I'll be back around five. I have something else to take care of first."

Lisa nodded and reversed out of her parking space.

Jason got back into his own car and found his way back to the road leading to the edge of the county. His hands were getting sweaty and his heart was starting to beat too fast. But Jason forced himself to keep driving, through a wrought iron entrance and along a path bordered by well-cared-for lawns. Up a hill and around a curving corner until he reached the assigned area of his son's grave. He got out of the car and approached the marker slowly, easily spotting the small gray stone that protruded from the ground. Impatiens had been neatly planted all around it. Jason stood for a long time staring at the spot unable to imagine his son dead and gone forever underneath. He fought against it, but finally gave it up, and let grief have its way. He rubbed briefly at his eyes, as his heart bled and poured out part of his soul.

Jason slowly opened the door, and the heat and musk assailed them both. Lisa coughed. Jason paid no attention to the stale air. His vision was filling with the room and things that had belonged to Michael. The bed was still unmade from that morning. That alone was nearly his undoing again. He turned to Lisa.

"Look, maybe you want me to go through everything first—"

Already she was shaking her head. "I don't want to look through anything. I—I couldn't bear it." She started to cry.

"What do you want to do with everything?"

"Give it away. I don't care where. I only want Michael's baby things, the silver set your mother gave him. And the photos."

Jason steered her out of the room. "You go get some boxes."

Lisa agreed and went off sniffling to do as she was told. And then Jason simply plowed in, because it wasn't going to get done otherwise, and the longer it took the more painful it would be. All the books went into a box marked for the local library. All the clothes into another marked for the shelter in town. It was well after nine when they finished and stacked all the boxes in the garage. Lisa was going to have someone pick them up on Monday morning.

She made a light dinner for the two of them, and she and Jason talked about Michael and their lives and what had gone wrong.

Jason shook his head. "I don't think anything went wrong. It was only meant to be for as long as it lasted. Now you'll go on with David, and I'll go on with my life."

"Alone?" Lisa asked, curious.

Jason smiled. "No, not alone, hopefully."

"I hope she's good for you, Jason. I hope she's what you need."

"She is," Jason said confidently, not unaware of the irony that his ex-wife was wishing him luck with a lover who was black, although she obviously didn't know that. But it had been his tolerance and her lack of it that had contributed to their breakup so many years before.

Jason helped her clean up, and it was also ironic that as they were about to go their separate ways forever, they were their most cooperative and understanding.

Lisa was on the phone with David when Jason left the guest room with his bag and several other items under his arm. Lisa glanced at him in surprise and covered the mouthpiece. "Where are you going?"

"I thought I'd get on the road back to New York."

"But it's after ten o'clock at night. Can't you leave in the morning?"

"No. I'm ready to go home," Jason said. "Good luck to you and David."

Lisa watched him with bewilderment and finally acceptance. She smiled sadly at him. "Good-bye, Jason. I hope you find some happiness."

He nodded briefly. "I will."

Chapter Fourteen

Jason got home, at about three in the morning, and he was exhausted. He was glad that he'd made the decision to drive back. He was glad to be in his own space, back in the insanity of New York, which made him feel alive. Back to Leah, who made him feel like a whole man.

Jason dropped the duffel just inside the door. He would deal with that later. But he took the time to carefully place Michael's well-used hockey stick and his helmet, along with several favorite children's books, on a wall unit. Other than photographs and his memories, this was all that Jason had left of his son. He'd have to deal with that later, too.

Having the few things in the car with him on the drive back had evoked more memories that had kept Jason company and, mercifully, entertained. For rather than being reminded of the loss of his son, Jason relived all the wonderful triumphant and funny moments when Michael's very existence had made Jason feel he'd accomplished at least one worthwhile thing in his life.

But for the first time that Jason could recall, as glad as he was to get back to his apartment, the quiet and stillness made him feel overwhelmingly lonely. His self-imposed isolation was no longer a protective measure which he deliberately perpetuated so that he could stay focused on his job. Now it just seemed pointless. Joe had Nora and often said he thanked God for her, Lisa now had David . . . he had Leah. Just the thought was enough to energize him for several moments of instant euphoria, until it quickly burned itself out in the more powerful stimulus of being bone weary and emotionally drained. He wanted to call Leah so badly. To let her know he was back. He picked up the phone, stared at it, put it down. It was the middle of the night. He could wait a few more hours.

Jason lay down on his bed. He thought of having one more cigarette, maybe even making a small drink. But he never made a decision because he fell to sleep fully clothed.

When Jason heard the lock turn on his apartment door, it startled him out of sleep. For a moment, he didn't know where he was as he also tried to remember where he'd put his gun, if this was an intruder. But the fog cleared quickly from his brain, and he rolled over as Leah stepped quietly into the room. He forced his eyes open and saw her silently regarding him with a beautiful smile on her face.

He'd never been so glad to see anyone in his life.

Leah put down her purse and keys. She kicked off her summer pumps and approached the bed. Already Jason was struggling up when she suddenly climbed onto the bed, straddling his waist and thighs to sit on his lap. He put his arms around her back and she looped her arms around his neck.

His eyes were tired but, his gaze was clear as he looked into Leah's eyes. Her mouth was bright with lip gloss. Jason kissed her lightly and shook his head, bemused.

"I thought you were someone coming to rob me."

She grinned. "I am."

"I'll make it easy for you. You can have everything."

She gave him a peck on his mouth. "How generous. I accept."

They slowly hugged.

"What are you doing here?" Jason pulled back to examine her outfit. "What are you dressed for? God, you look great." He nuzzled her neck. "Smell good, too."

"I just came from church. In case you don't know it's close to noon."

Jason shook his head. "Didn't know. Don't care."

She giggled, and scrutinized him more closely. It was obvious that he'd slept in his clothes. It looked like he hadn't shaved since leaving New York on the previous Friday. She touched his lips, his jaw. She smoothed his hair. "We were singing the offering hymn and I got this feeling that you were home. I wanted to be with you."

Jason smiled at her. "You read my mind correctly."

She tightened her arms around his neck, rubbing her cheek against his, unmindful of the scratchiness. "Well . . . here I am."

He removed her pert beribboned straw hat and sailed it across the room like a frisbee. Leah moved her hips forward against him and felt his full hard arousal under her buttocks and thighs.

"As long as you're here . . ." he murmured, before starting to kiss her with earnest, tender passion.

Some electric charge seemed to enliven them, heating their bodies and melding them together. They began pulling at each other's clothing, trying to get rid of the barriers as quickly as possible. Jason slid down on the bed with Leah on top of him. There was an erotic intensity to the way they wanted each other. Her body was ready when Jason finally sheathed himself deep inside. It was quick and explosive. They started the slow dance again, slower and longer and more deeply, trembling in each other's arms. She wrapped herself around Jason, never wanting to let go. When the throbbing tension was released in both of them, they lay quietly for a long time, Jason's head pillowed on her breasts. Her hand languidly stroked his hair.

Jason was almost asleep when Leah shook him, making him get up to take a shower. She joined him in the tub, but afterward stood watching him as he shaved. They eventually got dressed and went for something to eat, while Jason shared with Leah the details of his twenty-four hours in Pine Grove. Even when he talked about Michael he did so with more fondness than pain, and Leah knew that his healing had begun.

"Was it very hard?" Leah asked him.

Jason smiled thoughtfully, and reached for her hand across the table. He shook his head. "Some of it, I guess. But it was also a relief. I put a lot of stuff behind me. I also knew I had something to come back to."

"And I practically attack you before you've even unpacked," Leah laughed ruefully."

"Missed me?" Leah merely nodded. He laughed lightly. "See. I was right."

It was unbelievably hot. Leah felt like a limp rag. She wore her hair pulled back into a twisted knot these days to keep the thick mass from closing in around her face. A few weeks ago she'd given serious thought to cutting it short, but that had been in a moment of being irritated with the heat. Besides, Jason didn't want her to.

Leah wondered, as she climbed out of the underground inferno of the subway, why the commute had recently begun to seem so unbearable, why she dreaded the ride crushed against so many strangers. It was hard to breathe, and she'd felt particularly threatened underground. Trapped. Even now, up in the real air, there was a sensation of too many people, of someone being too close to her for comfort. Leah made her way to the corner store, deciding that an ice cream pop might revive her limp spirits.

The tall, skinny youth from the corner, her neighborhood nemesis, tried to stop her. In dark glasses he stood alone. Unsupported by his friends, he launched into his usual verbal romancing of Leah. It was like a game between them as he continued to test the waters of his manhood.

"Hey, sweet thang," he drawled.

"Don't you have someone your own age to play with?" Leah asked as she passed into the store.

"I like older women."

Leah emerged moments later, peeling the sticky paper from the cream pop. She rounded the corner heading for home.

"Hey, hey," the boy yelled after her. "You still seein' that white dude?"

The ice cream was wonderful. Soothing. For a moment she slowed her steps and glanced over her shoulder. The skinny youth had found another target, someone closer to his age. Someone easy to flatter. And there was no one else. She relaxed to enjoy the rest of the pop.

Her thoughts switched gears apprehensively to the exhibition coming up. She had been sorting through some of her caricatures, and Jill had helped to pick the ones with the most humor and which captured the personality of their subjects the best. Leah was glad that Jill had been able to work through her feelings and that they could be friends again. Leah also thought it interesting that, actually, Jill seemed a little envious of her relationship with Jason. Peter had not worked out after all.

After dinner, she sat on her bed contemplating the twenty or so art boards leaning against walls and furniture in her room. As she concentrated on picking the best samples of her work, she suddenly wasn't sure any of them were good. She was already discarding one picture when there was a knock on her door and Gail stuck her head in.

"Got a minute?"

"Sure. Come on in," Leah responded absently.

Her attention was still on a particular image when Gail sat quietly next to her, holding in her hands a black dress studded with rhinestones.

Gail waited out her sister's distraction, her patience an indicator that her visit might not necessarily be good news. But when Gail said nothing, Leah turned to her with a puzzled look.

"These are interesting," Gail hastened to say, pointing at one picture. "I sure hope they're supposed to be funny."

"That's the idea."

"Is there one of me?"

Leah hesitated. "I'm working on it."

"Oh-oh. That means I'm going to look evil," Gail muttered. Then she tempered her response with a wicked smile. "Where's the one of Jason?"

Leah tilted her head. "There isn't one."

Gail's gaze was steady, but her smile was amused. "Why not?"

She shrugged. "I haven't been able to do one that I like."

"How long have you been trying?"

"Just a few weeks."

Gail shook her head and chuckled.

"What's so funny?"

"I guess it hasn't occurred to you that maybe you're too close to the subject. Like, you're in love with the man and can't see straight?"

Leah stared straight ahead. Yes, that most certainly had occurred to her.

"I know what the problem is." Gail snapped her finger. "You can't decide whether to show him with a bunch of black kids, or dressed in that silly red cap, or with a smoking gun. Right?"

Still silent, Leah glared at her sister.

"Don't like those ideas, huh? Well, I think—"

"Did you want to say anything else to me?" Leah asked.

Gail grimaced good-naturedly. "Right. Shut up, Gail."

Leah looked at the black sparkling creation in her sister's lap. Gail fingered the cloth.

"I just thought you'd like to know Allen and I are getting married."

Leah stared. "You're serious."

"Dead on. Why would I kid you?"

Leah was stunned. "I . . . don't know."

"Does it bother you?"

"No. Why should it?"

"Well, given the way it all happened . . ."

"Let's not go into that again. It's done. I hope you and Allen will be happy."

"It'll be like playing house when we were kids," Gail said with uncharacteristic giddiness.

"Even then you did it poorly," Leah said dryly.

"Forget you . . ." Gail sucked through her teeth.

Leah changed her position on the bed so that the two women faced each other. "Have you set a date?"

"Probably in the next three months."

"Why so fast?"

"Well, for one thing Allen's getting a promotion and transfer. He's going to be a vice president."

"How nice. And what's the other reason? Oh, my God, you're not pregnant, are you?"

Gail grimaced. "Do I look stupid? It's just that we have a lot to do by the end of the year. Make arrangements, find a house—"

"House? Where?" Leah asked with sudden quiet.

"Atlanta." Gail looked at the dress in her hand and slowly, redraping the crêpe de chine folds, passed it carefully to Leah. "Here, this is for you. Remember that black number I designed that you liked so much? I know you think it's a bribe or something . . ."

"It's a bribe," Leah said, smoothing her hand over the textured ridges of the rhinestones.

"But I knew you wanted it."

Leah's smile was wry. "What's it for? Is this like the booby prize? You get Allen, and I get a designer dress?"

Gail got up from the bed, "Oh, lots of things. To say I'm sorry for the way things have been between us this year. I hope there's no hard feelings."

"Gail? Do you feel safe with Allen?"

Gail tilted her head. "Do I feel safe? You mean, am I afraid he's going to go off and try to hurt me one day? Umph! He'd be one sorry black man if he *ever* tried stuff like that. But he won't."

Leah smiled thinly. She began to fold the dress to put away. She had no idea where she'd ever wear it. "That's not what I mean, but never mind."

"Leah, we may have to do something about the house. You know. Like sell it. What do you think?"

Leah was bewildered again. "I don't know. I think I have to think about it. Everything is . . . happening so fast."

Gail reached out and took hold of her hand. Even in the feminine grip Leah knew her sister was the kind of person who wouldn't sweat the unimportant details like selling a house and picking up with her life elsewhere. Gail would quickly adjust . . . and always get exactly what she wanted.

Gail lightly squeezed her hand. "What about you? What do you want?"

Leah thought instantly of Jason. She flashed through an incredible sequence of events from the night they'd first made love all the way to the realization of how much she loved him. Her stomach tightened, but at that moment it was impossible for her to tell if it was from joy or fear. She finally smiled at her sister.

"I want what you have. I want my dreams to come true, too."

Leah was in bed, but she was wide awake. She was propped up against the pillows, her knees drawn up to create a tent out of the blankets. She was staring blankly at the black and rhinestone dress that hung from the back of her closet door.

It was after midnight.

The news of Allen's proposal to her sister had done something profound to Leah, although it wouldn't have surprised her if Gail had made the first move. It came to her slowly, gathering steam as the night grew later, that she was going to be alone. Gail and Allen were planning a future together, knew where they were headed . . . and she had no idea.

Leah felt a frightening sense of displacement, like everything that she'd always accepted as safe, routine, familiar, was about to change forever. And so would she.

She only knew one thing concretely: she didn't want to be alone. Jason hadn't called and that somehow made things worse. She realized that he'd probably had to work overtime. But not having any contact with Jason made her feel anxious and bottled up. She had a sense of being abandoned by Gail, and she wanted to be held and reassured. Jason did that well.

And then the phone rang.

The house was so quiet, the streets outside so empty of traffic, that the sound seemed shatteringly shrill. Leah jumped and reached for the phone before it could ring a second time.

"Jason?" she breathed into the receiver. She knew her voice seemed high and thin.

"You waited up," he answered in a tired drawl. "I thought you might be asleep. I'm sorry I'm so late."

Leah let out a soft, ragged sigh of relief, and her spine relaxed into the mattress. "It's all right. I knew you'd call. Is everything okay?"

"Yeah, fine. Just the usual. I had a late arrest and that means paperwork."

"You sound so tired," she commented solicitously.

"I am. I was going to come over, but . . ."

She giggled. "You'd get less rest than you really need."

His voice became playful and seductive. "Not a bad tradeoff."

Leah sighed again, winding her finger around the telephone cord. "I . . . miss you," she whispered sincerely. Did she sound desperate? She could sense his smile.

"I miss you, too."

There was a pause. Not much, but Leah knew that the silence was too long for Jason to ignore.

"Leah? What's wrong," he asked.

"I don't know. I think . . . maybe I'm nervous about the show."

"Don't give me that," he warned softly. "Something's got you upset and it's not that art show."

Leah took a deep breath, both grateful and nervous that he'd read into her anxiety. "Allen and Gail are getting married."

Jason was also propped up in bed. He was also feeling lonely, which is why he'd called Leah the moment he'd gotten home even though it was almost one-thirty. He'd just needed to hear her and know she was there on the other end of the line.

Jason blinked and looked across the room at the things that had belonged to his son, now displayed on his book unit. He felt so much in that moment the cutting off of his old life. So much of it he didn't want to think about, so much he couldn't recall. It simply didn't exist anymore. He'd have to create a new one.

He finished his cigarette and slowly crushed the butt flat in an ashtray. He suddenly felt extraordinarily peaceful and oddly light-headed. "So your sister's getting married. I wouldn't have bet on it, but you should be happy for her." He heard Leah sigh.

"I am."

"The only problem I can see is that Allen's going to have his hands full."

"Probably. But Allen's no fool. Sometimes Gail only thinks she's in charge."

Jason closed his eyes and ran a hand through his hair. He could easily picture Leah in his mind. He knew exactly what her facial expression was as she considered her sister leaving. He could see the soft, pensive shine of her eyes, and knew exactly how deep Leah's thoughts about her own future went, because he'd had the same thoughts recently.

"Sooner or later we may have to sell the house. I don't think I can manage it alone."

Jason had a better idea.

It had begun forming since the visit to Pine Grove. Now it was forced into full realization with precise details. It seemed so clear and simple that Jason suddenly felt buoyant and his mind raced with plans and solutions.

"Don't worry about the house for now. I think I know a way around having to sell it."

"You do?"

"I also think it's time you and I had a serious talk, Leah."

When he heard the pause again, he knew that he'd knocked any further concerns about Gail and Allen right out of her consideration.

"What about?" she asked very quietly.

"Us," he responded succinctly. "You and me."

"Jason . . ." Leah began. There was a thread of apprehension in her tone.

He sat forward on his bed, totally focused and knowing what had to be done.

"Leah, it's going to be okay. I promise. Everything will work out. What I have to say is very important, but I'm not going to go into it over the phone. I want us face to face. I want you right with me."

"Are you coming over?"

"No, not now. It's too late. I'll be over tomorrow after work. We'll sit down together, with no distractions, and I'll tell you what's on my mind."

Jason begun to feel excited because everything tumbling through his mind made so much sense. He chuckled to himself. It was so right, so simple.

"Can you wait until tomorrow? Is that all right?" He heard another deep sigh. It was resolved. Strong.

"I trust you. I can wait."

Leah thought the day would last forever. She worked mechanically because she knew what she was doing. The galley sheets from the type house were checked for errors and photostats ordered. She had a solitary lunch because she didn't feel like having company and was too distracted in any case. Her mind was on another plane, lost in dreams and possibilities.

She wanted to envision her and Jason together. In a world of so many other priorities, no one was going to care about the two of them. They could just become part of the mixed fabric of humanity; they could blend in and move along with everyone else. One of the first things Jill had told her that morning was that she'd met someone at the lobby art show. He was an insurance investigator, and they'd already had one date.

Maybe it was something in the air, Leah mused. Pollen or stardust that caused this sudden love among the mortals. New babies, and announcements of weddings . . . proposals and commitments. It was catching.

During the night of being alone, of having her anxiety reach nightmare proportions, of realizing that her fears were of her own making, Leah felt them all finally melt away. Suddenly the fear of ostracism from the rest of the world was not nearly as great a threat as the thought of losing Jason, of not having him to love. She would not become someone different because of his love or hers. She would not lose herself. There could never be less of her, only more. She had fought hard this last year, taking chances for what she wanted and had believed in. It had only made her stronger. She would *not* be annihilated by the intolerance of the rest of the world.

Leah left her office that afternoon feeling as if she'd just been set free. She was impatient with the trains, thinking she could have walked home faster. She counted the stops, one by one, not realizing that her trip home wasn't really any longer than usual, it only seemed to be.

Leah changed trains at Chambers Street, not conscious of the crowds of people around her. She moved around and through them to get to her next train, not feeling there was any need to look behind her. She had discarded all of her fears, and with them went all of her caution.

The dream had receded. It had slipped into a corner of her mind where she'd shut the door on it. With Jason's love had come less of the terror, fewer nightmares, and a healing of the memories. They were not altogether gone, but today, for the first time in months, she didn't look behind her as she exited the station in Brooklyn.

Slack tried to keep at least two people between Leah and himself as they proceeded through the station to the exit. It was humid today, and he could feel rivulets of sweat running down the center of his back and under his arms. Some of it was due to the jacket he wore on this sweltering day. Some was from pure tension and from being keyed up.

Once, after he'd gotten out of that shithole upstate and was hungry and tired from running and dodging people, he thought of giving up. He was going to find Jason and see if the man could get him another deal. Anything so he wouldn't have to go back to that place. But he'd hung out a block from the precinct house, and Jason was always with somebody else. That big dude, Joe, or other cops who would've cuffed him in a heartbeat. Or with that bitch Leah Downey.

Slack was sure Leah had told Jason lies about him, like he was no good and Jason shouldn't even bother. He hated her. Thought she was better than him. It was all her fault Jason let him go upstate. It she hadn't seen that jacket, if he hadn't forgotten about it . . .

In a group of eight or nine people, which included himself and Leah, Slack exited the station. The sunlight was blinding, but he adjusted the beak of his leather cap so it shaded his face. He had to keep his eyes on her in case she changed directions or turned around and he had to move quickly out of sight. In the jacket pocket his right hand was closed damply around a small handgun that looked remarkably like a child's toy.

She suddenly ran across the street, eluding him, as she just caught the changing of a light. A car horn blasted angrily at him as he made an attempt to follow and was forced back to the curb. He cursed at the driver and kicked at the rear fender of the passing car. Across the street ahead of him she had already started down the long block, walking faster than usual to get home. A space cleared in the traffic, and he jaywalked to the other side of the street. He trotted a little, unheard in his sneakers, until the distance was shortened between them. Now he quickly scanned the street and saw that almost no one was about. Up at the other corner a group of teenagers sat on brownstone steps but were half hidden by the row of cars and a tree in front of the house. They were laughing and joking and listening to music. Behind him there was a middle-aged couple just opening the front door of their building on the other side of the street.

Sweat ran down his back, into the waistband of his jeans, down his chest under his T-shirt. His heartbeat sped up as he realized this was it. He was going to do it.

Actually Slack hadn't decided what, exactly, he'd do once he got Leah Downey inside her house. He hadn't thought that far ahead. He just wanted to get to her and see her scared. He wanted to look into her face and see if she'd still look right through him, or laugh at him. Well, she better not laugh . . .

He walked a little faster, shortening the distance. He tested his hand to make sure he could easily free the gun from his pocket. He unzipped the front so he had better movement. Several trails of perspiration ran from his hairline down his brown cheek to his chin. He didn't notice. His most immediate thought now was that he was glad Jones had given him her ID with the address when he'd lifted her wallet.

Jason had been sitting for almost an hour at the wheel of his car. On the ground outside his car window were the results of his wait. Six cigarette butts. Even now, halfway through the seventh cigarette, his eyes were trained through his rearview mirror on the far corner nearest the subway as he waited for Leah. The muscles in his jaw worked convulsively between puffs, and only now as he realized he'd see Leah any minute did he suddenly feel nervous.

He'd gotten no sleep last night. Then he'd worked a full tour and several more hours in overtime. Even Joe must have sensed something because he had taken him out to lunch. Joe also had not asked any questions, for which Jason had been grateful. This act of understanding said more of Joe's feelings now about Leah than it did about him. Joe had apparently accepted that Leah was good for him. Having food in his stomach helped to settle down his adrenaline, which was now in overdrive. He looked at his watch. It was 6:23.

He closed his eyes and conjured up a picture of Leah walking down the block toward the house. When he opened his eyes again and looked through the window to the corner, Leah was really there.

She was still just a toy figure off in the distance, but there was no doubt that it was her. She wore a slim skirt with a front slit. She wore high-heeled sandals and a beige silk blouse. Her sunglasses were atop her loosened hair like a headband, the dark lens reflecting sunlight. She was walking briskly and with a purpose.

There was a black teenager just behind her who would probably pass her on the sidewalk at any mo-

ment. He was walking aggressively like all the young
blacks did, as though they owned the street and had
to get someplace quickly. Jason put his hand on the
car door and slowly began to open it.

His eyes followed Leah until she was almost to the
Chens' house. He could tell she'd spotted his car, and
when she smiled in recognition, it was all the signal
he needed. He got out of the car. He noticed that the
teenager was now right behind Leah, but as Jason's
head cleared the top of the car, the growing smile on
his face quickly faded and he stiffened alertly. Moving
surely but not too fast, he stood on the sidewalk just
as the boy closed the distance completely, grabbing
Leah abruptly by the hair and putting a gun to her
back. Jason went cold inside.

It was Slack.

She suddenly felt something catch her hair violently
from behind, and something else hard and sharp was
pushed into her back. It was cold through the silk
blouse. Her sunglasses were shaken loose, fell, and
were forgotten. Almost instantly Leah had flashes of a
stocky black man who had had a knife in his hand
and held her captive in a building stairwell. She was
momentarily paralyzed with the shock of remembering
and a sense of horror that it couldn't be happening
again. Her bag dropped to the ground.

Jason moved to the sidewalk in front of them and
extended his right hand to stop Slack, or to calm him.
His left hand was on his hip.

Slack looked panic-stricken for just a second. Jason
knew he hadn't expected him to be there.

"Shit! Back the fuck off, man," Slack gritted through
his teeth as Jason moved slowly forward.

"Slack . . . take it easy," Jason said.

Slack didn't want to show he was scared. But he

didn't have to be. *He* had the gun. He kept eye contact with Jason. The sweat dried on his skin and made him suddenly cold.

"Don't do anything stupid. Why don't you just put that down?" Jason advised.

Slack hated that Jason's voice was so calm, like he was in charge.

"We can straighten this out. Just let her go."

Slack watched Jason's left hand make a slow journey behind his back. He jerked Leah's hair. "I'll kill the bitch. Keep away from me."

"You're messing up, man. I can still help. Put the gun down."

For a second Slack thought about it. Maybe this was the only way out of this mess. But then he got angry, remembering why he was there. It was all the bitch's fault anyway. He tightened his fist in Leah's hair, and she emitted a grunt of pain.

With the hard tug on her hair Leah recovered from her stupor. She came back from a dark, narrow hallway into the light. She blinked rapidly and saw Jason just a few feet in front of her. The thing in her back was shoved hard under her shoulder blade, and the person behind her did not release the clutch on her hair. She began to struggle, twisting to swing around. Leah gasped when she caught a glimpse of Slack.

"Leah, don't move," she heard Jason order urgently, but she reached back instinctively to grab Slack's wrist.

Jason pulled his gun and cocked it. "Put the gun down, Slack. *Right now* . . ." he ordered loudly.

Leah tried to break free. The hold tightened, restricting any movement. Her scalp tingled. She saw that Jason had his gun drawn and was taking aim at Slack.

"Jason," Leah cried out. She reached behind, frantically grabbing at Slack.

"Leah, don't!"

Suddenly there were two sharp retorts. Leah watched as Jason cringed and fell to one knee. He made a short grunting sound. A dark circle of moisture created an ever-widening stain on his shirt.

"Jason!" she screamed.

She broke free from Slack with a final painful wrenching of her head. She ran toward Jason as he doubled over.

Jason's face tightened and grimaced in pain. He reached out and, with his arm, forcibly pushed her aside. "Get out of the way!"

He took aim at the slight figure fleeing erratically across the street. Another black kid from almost ten years ago flashed through Jason's head, and kids in 'Nam, and every kid who'd ever come through his office. Jason fought to keep his hand steady. There was a sudden searing pain in his upper chest that seemed to grip the entire right side of his body. He was mildly aware of the warm flow of blood seeping through his shirt and making the cloth stick to his skin. He could feel blood oozing from the wound, slowly pulsing from his body. But his mind was on Slack running with the gun still held tightly in his hand.

Leah staggered to within a few feet of Jason and stared at his pointing gun. "No . . . Jay, please . . ." she pleaded.

Maybe she wanted to save his soul . . . someone's life. But he thought of what that gun might have done to Leah, what it might still do to someone else. His hand began to shake. He took aim and fired.

Slack yelped, twisted, and dropped to the ground. His opportunity to escape was gone.

Jason gave way to the enveloping weakness and dizziness and fell the rest of the way to the ground. He started to cough and choke, feeling something bitter and warm running out of his mouth. Someone kept swaying in front of him, and it made him nauseous. He heard his name being cried plaintively, heard Leah's voice slurred in tears. She was trying to hold him, but he just wanted everything to stop moving. His head was spinning and his right side was absolutely numb. Gentle hands touched him, held and stroked him. But he couldn't respond, couldn't even keep his eyes open. His right side felt like hot lead had been poured along its length, and he struggled to get away from it, finally succeeding by slipping into quiet darkness.

It was 6:42.

Suddenly people were everywhere. In the gathering crowd stood a shocked Sarah Chen, and Biddy Rosen patted Leah's shoulder gently, trying to comfort her. There was the screeching of car brakes and car horns and shouts. Someone tried to pull Leah away from Jason's side, and she resisted forcefully, maintaining her grip on his limp body. Leah held the end of her skirt over the wound to still the flow of blood. Her hair fell in a frizzy mass around her face. When she impatiently tried to sweep it back, she ended up with Jason's blood smeared in her hair and on her face.

"Jason . . . Jason . . ." She kept whispering his name over and over so he wouldn't slip away from her. His mouth was working, but Leah couldn't tell if he was trying to speak or trying to breathe. His gun was on the ground at his side, and with his free hand he tried to touch the pain in his chest. Leah grabbed his hand and held it away from the wound.

The distant scream of sirens filled the air until it was deafening. Half a dozen cars and officers appeared at Jason's side, and Leah quickly gave his name and precinct. Two of the officers knew him. One recovered

Jason's gun, the other checked his vital signs and examined the wound.

"We're not going to wait. Let's get him in the car," he said with authority.

He slipped his hands under Jason's shoulder and began to lift him. Two other officers moved in to help. They transported him to the back of a squad car and shifted Jason into the backseat. Leah still had hold of his hand.

"Lady, get out of the way."

"I'm going with him," Leah said firmly, eyeing the officer defiantly.

"You can't come along. Who the hell are you, anyway?"

Leah was nearly hysterical. "I belong with him and I'm going. *I'm going . . .*"

"All right, all right . . ." Another officer tried to calm her. He looked at her closely. "You're Leah, aren't you?"

Leah tried to focus on him through her tears and hard breathing. It was Officer O'Neil. "Yes. Yes. Please help me . . ."

O'Neil turned and yelled, "Hey, Dave? Follow me in your car, and bring this lady with you."

Leah was quickly ushered into another squad car, and the sirens were turned on once again.

"I have your things, Leah. Don't worry," someone yelled to her. Maybe Biddy. She couldn't tell. It wasn't important just then.

Out the squad car window as they drove from the scene, Leah could see another half-dozen cops surrounding the wounded Slack. The officer driving called in the emergency, and the dispatch box in the front of the squad car hissed the call for a 1013: officer in distress. A trauma code was called ahead to the nearest hospital. It seemed like just a few seconds before the car was again screeching to a halt and a crew of five or six medical personnel from the hospital were preparing to lay Jason on a stretcher.

In the flurry of the emergency everyone forgot about Leah, but she followed closely behind. Someone, perhaps it was an intern, asked brusquely if she was hurt, seeing her covered with blood.

"No . . . no," she answered.

He turned and took off after the others.

The emergency room filled with shouted orders and intercom summonses for doctors. There must have been a dozen uniformed officers and plainclothes cops checking to see what had happened. In minutes some left to return to the scene, where the perpetrator was being taken by ambulance to another hospital for treatment of a gunshot wound to the upper leg. Other officers were checking to see if they had the right blood type for donation.

Leah tried to follow the stretcher into the treatment room, catching a mere glimpse of Jason's blood-soaked shirt being cut away from his chest, but she was stopped by a nurse.

"Sorry, hon. You can't go in there." She tried to steer Leah to another corner, out of view of the triage center.

The nurse looked at the distraught black woman, saw the dried blood, the disheveled clothes, the worn, worried eyes, and her voice softened. "Don't worry. He's getting the best."

She once again tried moving Leah, but Leah was centered on the people moving in and around the treatment room door, and she wouldn't move.

"Look, why don't we wash off some of the blood and get you something to drink? Then you can wait here until they're finished. Okay?"

Leah nodded wearily and gave in. The nurse escorted

her to a rest room and gently pushed her through the door. In a few minutes she was back with her face cleaned and her hair more or less smoothed into place. She'd tried to sponge her blouse, but now it just looked like a marbled pink design. the nurse could guess that the skirt and blouse didn't matter in the least. She pressed a cup of hot coffee into Leah's hands.

Leah was just holding the coffee when the treatment room door burst open and a gurney was wheeled out, Jason on it. He was hooked to an IV and tubes and portable machines. He was deathly pale and didn't respond when Leah called his name.

"Where are they taking him?" she asked the nurse anxiously.

"Up to surgery . . . no, no. You can't go," the nurse said. She grabbed Leah's arm when she tried to board the elevator with the gurney. The doors closed, leaving them standing there. The nurse again took pity on her.

"It's going to be a while before he comes out. Why don't you come with me and give some information? If we hear anything, believe me, you'll be in the right place to know."

Leah followed the nurse to the station. She looked at the clock, an then the phone, and back at the clock again. She looked down at her skirt and blouse, at the dried blood, now brown in color. Leah noticed now that the crystal on her watch was broken. Overwhelmed with the reality of what had happened in the space of just a few minutes, she stared blindly into space while tears silently rolled down her cheeks.

Joe had taken her home sometime after midnight, after Jason had come out of surgery. Leah was so numbed by the whole experience that when she got home she wasn't sure what day it was, what week. Even now, two days later, it seemed incredible that an angry youngster had pumped holes into Jason's body.

Leah couldn't remember the last time she'd actually slept, although she reasoned that she must have. She must have closed her eyes sometime during the two endless days and nights. She must have given herself up to a black abyss with no dreams at all. It was as if the incident with Slack had become one with the nightmare and canceled each other out.

Joe had come to the hospital just after Jason had been taken to surgery. Leah had finally permitted herself to collapse. She'd fallen into Joe's arms and wept. He'd comforted her awkwardly and sat her down to find out what had happened. Joe had seen that Leah's eyes were like saucers in a face grown tight and pinched with shock. He'd stayed with her at the hospital, had taken charge and phoned Nora and Gail.

When the surgery was over at eleven-thirty that night, it was Joe who grabbed the doctor and demanded answers.

"He's going to be fine. He came in in shock; that's because of the tremendous loss of blood. We had to clean out the chest cavity and reinflate his lung, but we got the bullet and did some other repairs. He's stabilized and resting easy now. You can see him tomorrow when he's out of recovery."

"Can't I see him now? For just a minute?" Leah pleaded.

"Brooklyn . . ." Joe began, shaking his head.

"I think it's best you don't," the doctor said. "For one thing, he won't know you're there. For another, you're not in such great shape, either. Let the officer take you home, get some rest yourself, and come back tomorrow." The doctor nodded to Joe and walked away.

She began to cry again, this time in sheer frustration.

"Come on, Brooklyn. Jace is a tough son of a bitch, and he'll survive. We'll deal with it tomorrow."

But tomorrow she still had not seen him. Only immediate family and what seemed to be hundreds of police officials had been allowed near him. A press conference had been called, and the daily papers carried the whole story. Even the mayor had made the standard visit to a wounded officer injured in the line of duty. Leah had to be content that at least Jason's sister and Joe were close at hand. If there had been anything to report, she would have heard through one of them.

Leah rubbed her throbbing temples. It was eight o'clock in the morning. It had been almost three days. She'd taken a shower and padded around listlessly in her robe. She was going to call in sick again. Food was the last thing on her mind, but she was aware of not having eaten a solid meal in over forty-eight hours. She got up slowly and made her way to the stereo and turned it on. She sat limply on the arm of the sofa and glanced out the window, where, just a few yards away, the shooting had taken place. She could almost hear the gunshots, hear herself screaming, see Jason falling.

The phone rang, scaring her silly. She stared at it, as if it was some odd, foreign presence. She finally picked it up on the fourth ring, holding the receiver as though it might burn her.

"Hello," she whispered.

"Hi. I'd like to speak with Leah Downey."

"Yes, I'm Leah."

"This is Nancy Collins. I'm Jason's sister."

"Yes, I know who you are."

"I got your number from Joe."

Leah was suddenly afraid to respond. Nancy Collins chuckled.

"Don't worry. This isn't bad news. Jason is fine and he's raising hell. He wants to see you."

"Yes, yes . . ." Leah said on a long sigh. "I'll be right over."

"No, you stay there. Joe's coming to get you. I'm looking forward to meeting you," she said with sincerity, and hung up.

Leah slowly replaced the receiver. She hastened to the radio and turned it off. With more energy and purpose than she thought she could ever command, she headed for the stairwell. She heard Gail start down and then saw her sister, smartly dressed and unscathed by what had been going on for two days. She had a suitcase in hand.

Leah knew that Allen was coming to pick her up and together they were flying down to Atlanta. She didn't mind. The night Jason had been shot, Gail had immediately canceled the flight that would have sent her and Allen on their way south. Leah had needed her and Gail had stayed.

Gail reached the foot of the stairs and frowned at her.

"Girl, you look awful," she said. "See what love does to you?"

Leah only smiled. She appreciated that in that moment she could smile.

"I'm sorry I have to leave you like this."

"It's okay. I'm going to see Jason. You and Allen have things to do."

"Are you sure you don't want to stay with someone rather than be here in this big old house alone?"

"Positive."

Leah made to pass Gail and head for her own room to get dressed.

"Leah . . . look, I know I've been real hard on you and Jason. I couldn't help myself. There's just too much stuff still goin' on out there. But I'm sorry this happened. I'm glad they got little punk that did it."

"It was a black little punk that did it," Leah responded.

"Figures . . ." Gail shrugged. "Tell Jason I wish him well. Now he'll get better just to get even with me. That ought to shock the hell out of him."

"Believe me, it will." Leah kissed Gail's cheek and hugged her. "I'm happy for you and Allen. I'm really glad there's someone out there who finds you lovable."

They both started to laugh. The doorbell rang.

"That's Allen," Gail said, breaking away.

"Bye. Have a good flight," Leah said as she watched her sister leave.

But before Gail had gotten into Allen's waiting car, Leah was already up the stairs and starting to change.

When Joe led Leah from the elevator, she had a moment's panic when she wondered what she and Jason would say to each other now, after what had happened to him. Leah stood rooted outside the elevator, staring down the hospital corridor. It was lined with cops and reporters. She couldn't help thinking that maybe she didn't belong here right now. Not yet.

But two women separated themselves from the group. One was Nora, who gave Leah a generous hug and told her not to look like *she* had been convicted and sentenced. The other woman was obviously Nancy Collins. She wasn't at all what Leah had thought Jason's sister would be like. She was petite and forthright but with an engaging smile. Her curiosity about Leah showed in her gray eyes as she shook Leah's hands, but there was also sincere empathy.

"Know what I think?" Nancy began with a broad smile.

"What?" Leah asked.

"I think you'll do Jace more good than any doctor."

Leah hoped that Nancy was right. She continued down the corridor, watching its occupants part before her. Her stomach tensed when she spotted Spano. It never occurred to her that he might be here. There was no love lost between him and Jason.

It made her wonder if the fraternity of being a cop was a stronger bond than she could ever understand. Spano glared at her and half turned away, continuing their Mexican stand-off. Leah didn't care. If anything like this happened to Spano, Jason would be there for him, too. That was the way the brotherhood worked.

With a sudden thought, she punched for a cup of coffee from a hall vending machine and held tightly onto the styrofoam cup. Finally she stood at the open door to Jason's room. He was seated on the side of his bed, his back to the door. He was wearing the red baseball cap. A nurse, who'd just finished drawing blood and taking his temperature, was talking cheerfully to him. When she noticed Leah in the doorway she smiled.

"You have another visitor. And she's a lot prettier than the crew in the hallway. Come on in. I'm finished here."

The nurse left, and slowly Jason tried to look over his shoulder. He winced painfully halfway through and elected to sit back instead against the pillows. Leah took a step into the room and stopped again. Visible through his open pajama top was a lumpy and awkward dressing over his chest wound. She grimaced with uncertainty.

"You look funny in pajamas."

Jason held out a hand. "Nora's idea. Close the door. I'll take them off."

Leah eagerly took hold of the offered hand, feeling her blood system begin to warm and flow normally again. Jason pulled her to the edge of the bed, and she handed him the coffee. "I hope it's okay for you to have this."

"It's the only thing that's safe to swallow around here."

He took a very small sip and put the cup down on his nightstand. He was still weak and exhausted, and his head fell back against the raised pillows. "Still saving my life, eh? You know the Chinese have a saying. When you save a person's life, it belongs to you."

"I'm not Chinese," Leah said quietly.

Jason squeezed her hand, pulled her closer. "Want to adopt me?"

Leah had to laugh. He seemed so irrepressible, so like himself. But the tension snapped within her, and the laughter quickly turned to threatened tears. Jason murmured something gentle and urged her against his shoulder. Leah hesitated, afraid to hurt him, but practically climbed onto the bed with him.

"It's okay. This is the good side."

They held each other as tightly as the pain permitted.

"This is all my fault," she mumbled.

"You know what? It could have been you he shot. That would have made me feel worse, Leah. I expect to get shot at. I'm better prepared for it."

"I'm sorry, but that doesn't make it okay."

"Well, we're both in agreement on that. Anyway, I was lucky. He missed the first shot altogether."

They hugged each other, just being able to touch working miracles.

"Jay, what will they do to him?"

Jason looked openly at her. His eyes, heavy-lidded, nonetheless read clearly her question. He was honest with her. "He'll be charged with attempted murder, aggravated assault. He shot a cop. That's not going to make it easy for him. We're becoming an endangered species."

Leah felt her heart constrict. Her eyes held poignant concern and sadness. "So are young black men."

He nodded. "I know. I've already asked Joe to keep on top of it. I can't say what will happen. We'll have to see."

She nodded. Her eyes filled with tears again. "It's so confusing. He could have killed you."

"The bullet broke a rib. The doctors took it out. I didn't need it anyway."

"Please don't joke about it—"

He put his hand over her mouth, and his eyes seemed to hold a bemused smile. She frowned at him.

"Stop talking for a minute."

She pulled the hand away. "Why?"

He grinned, putting the hand to the back of her head; he kissed her with a great deal of satisfaction. And he took his time. The kiss vanquished the rest of her guilt.

For the next half hour there was the joy of just the two of them together. The nurse poked her head into the door again, and quickly disappeared with a knowing smile. A doctor came by and did likewise, indicating that he'd return later. And mostly they just held each other and talked in peaceful whispers about how much they loved and needed each other. It was the best medicine for them both.

Feeling safe and settled at last, Leah kicked off her shoes and drew her legs up onto the bed. Lying next to Jason, she felt blissful and calm. "So what about this serious talk we were going to have?" she asked, threading their fingers together.

He tilted his head against hers. "I was thinking, why don't I buy out Gail's share in the house? Then you and

I can get married, too," he said smoothly, not missing a beat.

Leah looked sharply at him with a series of conflicting emotions—stunned surprise, a fleeting look of apprehension, and heartbreaking longing.

Nonetheless Jason smiled warmly at her. He squeezed her hand. "I bet you didn't think I could go the distance, but . . . I'm in love with you, Leah Downey. I think we belong together. I want to marry you."

Leah felt an overwhelming rush of relief burst through her chest. Jason had just confessed that he loved her. He'd just said he wanted to marry her. She'd wished for months that it was possible, and suddenly there it was. Spoken out loud.

Jason laughed softly at her expression and took advantage of her inability to speak by kissing her into further silence. The startled expression disappeared and her eyes shimmered with tears. Jason slowly put the good arm around her shoulder and gathered Leah as close as he could.

"Boy, am I going to look like a jerk if you don't feel the same."

Her shoulders shook, and she wrapped an arm around his neck. "I do, I do!" Leah sobbed.

"Good," Jason mumbled, his voice thick and ragged. "That's what I wanted to know."

"I didn't think you'd want to get married again."

"I never thought I'd want to, either. But that was before this past year. That was before I went away to Pine Grove and missed you before I'd even gotten past the city limits. I knew then what I wanted us to do. I *knew* that the thing I wanted most was to be with you."

She looked down at their joined fingers and the two colors intertwined so evenly. For a second it was almost a surprise. She almost never noticed that anymore. She examined his wrists, the veins and sinew in relief beneath his skin. Leah's fingers rubbed the fine layer of light brown hair.

"What about the police force? What about your family and friends?"

"I like my job and I'm good at it. But that's all the department gets out of me. My private life stays private. As for everyone else, forget them. I think we know by now who our friends are."

Leah felt her body begin to go soft, begin to loosen as the surprise finally settled in. She glanced at Jason with a poignant kind of sadness. "Just think," she whispered, once more on the verge of tears. "If we'd gotten together the other night, you could have saved yourself a bullet."

"I would have preferred skipping that part, too. So?"

She began to nod, to smile lovingly at him. "I accept."

His grin was boyish, almost foolish. "Do you want a ring?"

Leah shook her head. "This is so romantic. Just like a real old-fashioned proposal."

"I hope you don't mind if I don't ask your father for his approval. I'm getting too old to wait that long."

Leah put her head on his shoulder. "Jason Horn, I love you so much."

Jason was quiet for a moment, and chuckled softly. "That's the nicest thing anyone's ever told me."

He kissed her forehead, raised her chin so he could kiss her mouth again. The kisses held so many expectations.

"Then all is forgiven? I forgive you and you forgive me and we forgive the world?"

"No more apologies, please. We haven't done anything wrong, so let's just live in peace and try to be happy."

"Hey, we can do anything. Bend steel with our bare hands, leap tall buildings . . ."

She laughed, pulling the red baseball cap from his head. She eased herself from the bed against his protests but bent to kiss him once more.

"You're beginning to sound delirious. Maybe I should get the doctor—"

He grabbed her hand. "No, don't. Stay with me 'til I fall asleep."

"All right . . ."

His eyes drifted close, and his head sank back into the pillow. "Leah, we're going to be great together."

She stroked his cheek, but he was already almost asleep, still holding fast to her hand.

"I love you, Jay," she whispered.

She thought she saw him smile as he fell to sleep.